D0783189

SUMMER'S COVE

What Reviewers Say About Aurora Rey's Work

Crescent City Confidential

"*Crescent City Confidential* is a sweet romance with a hint of thriller thrown in for good measure."—*The Lesbian Review*

Built to Last

"Rey's frothy contemporary romance brings two women together to restore an ancient farmhouse in Ithaca, N.Y. Tension mounts as Olivia's colleagues and her snobbish family collide with Joss's down-home demeanor. But the women totally click in bed, as well as when they're poring over paint chips, and readers will enjoy finding out whether love conquers all."—*Publishers Weekly*

Winter's Harbor

"*Winter's Harbor* is a charming story. It is a sweet, gentle romance with just enough angst to keep you turning the pages. ...I adore Rey's characters and the picture she paints of Provincetown was lovely."—*The Lesbian Review*

Visit us at www.boldstrokesbooks.com

By the Author

Cape End Romances:

Winter's Harbor

Summer's Cove

Built to Last

Crescent City Confidential

SUMMER'S COVE

by

Aurora Rey

2017

ISBN 13: 978-1-62639-971-6

This Trade Paperback Original Is Published By
Bold Strokes Books, Inc.
P.O. Box 249
Valley Falls, NY 12185

First Edition: October 2017

CREDITS
EDITOR: ASHLEY TILLMAN
PRODUCTION DESIGN: SUSAN RAMUNDO
COVER DESIGN BY JEANINE HENNING

Acknowledgments

With each book I write, my appreciation for the Bold Strokes family increases. I treasure being part of such a smart, passionate, and professional group of individuals. Y'all have taught me the meaning of work hard, play hard, and I am forever grateful. Thank you to Ash, truly the best editor ever. Also, huge thanks to Nell and Tracy for being thoughtful, truthful, and good-natured beta readers.

While many of my stories include the search for family, it's never been more true than in *Summer's Cove*. So I especially want to thank my own family—many of my actual relatives, but even more the family I've found along the way. Your love and support and encouragement mean the world to me. Andie, you remain at the top of that list. Whatever the journey, whatever the adventure, I always want to come home to you.

Dedication

For families of choice everywhere.

CHAPTER ONE

Darcy took off her apron and tossed it into the bin in the corner of the kitchen. She hung her ball cap in her cubby and pulled out her bag, taking a final look around to make sure ovens were off and everything had been properly put away. Instead of heading out the back as she usually would, she walked through the swinging door to the front of The Flour Pot.

The usual cleanup was underway, with Jeff cleaning the espresso machine and Alex wiping down tables. Lia sat at a table by the window, staring intently at her computer screen. Darcy caught Alex's eye. "Are you ready for your last pre-wedding consultation with your caterer?"

Alex smiled and set down her towel and spray bottle. "Please tell me there are no more decisions to make."

Darcy returned the smile. "You're in the home stretch, I promise."

"If I'd known how complicated weddings were, I'd have suggested we elope."

Lia closed her computer and pulled out her wedding binder. She gave Alex a bland look. "There's still time."

"I'm kidding." Alex squeezed her thigh. "You're so organized, it feels like I'm hardly doing any work at all."

"Good answer." Lia gave Alex a quick kiss before flipping to one of the tabbed sections. "So, we pared down the ideas after our last meeting, but I think something might be missing. I know it's more than enough food, but it feels a little chintzy. Like it's not a full meal."

The seating would include tables on the patio, so Alex and Lia didn't want it to feel like a sit-down kind of thing. Darcy liked their plan of stations paired with passed hors d'oeuvres, but she knew what Lia meant. She drummed her fingers on the table. "What if we add something a little more substantial?"

Lia tipped her head to the side. "Like what?"

"Something warm, with protein. Like…" Darcy rolled her hands in front of her while she thought it out. "Mini beef Wellingtons."

Lia's eyes lit up. "You can do that?"

Darcy nodded. "Alex is already making puff pastry. All we need is beef tenderloin and some mushrooms."

Alex smiled. "I'll add it to this week's order."

They went through the photos and notes that Lia had compiled for everything else. In the end, Darcy felt good about the results. She was pretty sure Lia did, too. And with the two kitchen hands Alex hired on top of waitstaff, she'd have no trouble. "So, is everything else set?"

She admired the cake design again, along with the flowers. Alex excused herself so Lia could show off a picture of her dress, which Darcy hadn't yet seen. It was simpler than a traditional wedding gown, but lovely, not unlike the kind of dress Darcy would pick for herself. Assuming she ever got married, that is. She liked the idea of a partner, but finding one sat pretty low on her priority list. Liam was her focus. And while she didn't choose to be celibate, the bar to join her family was high.

When they wrapped up, Lia stood to give her a hug. "I love that you're the caterer, but I hate that you're not going to be able to enjoy the party."

"I'll enjoy it plenty, I promise."

"I hope we've kept it simple enough for that to be true."

"D. Belo Catering has everything under control. Who is your DJ?"

Lia grinned. "Karen. She does things at the Pied sometimes. She and Alex have been friends for years."

"Nice. What about the photography?"

"This artist friend of Alex's, Emerson Lange. She's mostly a painter, but does photography, too. I've met her a few times. She's nice. Cute, too."

Darcy raised a brow. "How cute?"

"In my book, full-on hot. Short, jet black hair. Maybe Asian, or at least part."

"Huh. I don't think I've ever met her." Darcy laughed. "But she sounds like my type."

"I can find out if she's single," Lia offered.

"No, no, no. I'm not looking. I just like to look."

"I hear you. How's Liam?"

Darcy smiled. "Eight going on eighty."

"That's my favorite thing about him." Lia's face softened, making Darcy wonder if she and Alex had started talking about kids.

"He's all about his science project and how often I take him to the library."

"How often do you take him to the library?"

"Once a week."

"Let me guess. That's not enough?"

"I'm not complaining. Trust me, I'd never complain about a kid whose favorite thing to do is learn stuff." Darcy loved Liam's bookish side. She just wanted to make sure he had a good balance.

"I know. I've got a good amount of science nerd in me. Maybe I can take library duty every now and then."

"Why do I get the feeling that would be as much fun for you as it would be for him?"

Lia shrugged. "Because it would."

"How about after the wedding? You're kind of busy right now."

"I have no idea what you mean. Everything is completely under control."

"What's under control?" Alex asked from across the room.

Lia and Darcy replied in unison. "Everything."

Lia turned back to Darcy. "I don't want to keep you. I know you need to get home."

"I should go. But if you have changes, you know where to find me."

"I do. Thank you for doing this. There is no one else I'd rather have in charge."

"It's going to be fun. And since I'll be behind the scenes, I don't have to worry about finding a date." Not that she couldn't find one. It just rarely turned out to be worth the effort.

Lia, who was more of an introvert than Darcy, nodded appreciatively. "I've so been there."

Darcy hugged Lia and gathered her things. "If you need anything, don't hesitate to ask, okay?"

"Thanks. I think we're good." Lia smiled, then took a deep breath. "Ask me again after my whole family gets here."

Darcy passed the school bus as she turned onto her street. Even though Liam rarely beat her home by more than a minute or two, she hated the idea of him coming home to an empty apartment. Even if he was the one who insisted it was no big deal in the first place, and that aftercare was for babies.

Inside, she found Liam with his head in the cupboard. He emerged with a granola bar, turned to her, and smiled. "Hi, Mom."

"Hi, honey. How was school today?"

He rolled his eyes. "We had library, which was awesome, but then Kevin and Bella got into an argument and we had to go back to class early."

Darcy had to suppress a smile. "I'm sorry your time got cut short."

"It's okay. I already had my three books and when we got back to the room, Ms. Shields let us read for a while. I just don't get why kids have to be so dumb."

Darcy snickered, doing her best to cover it up with a cough. "We don't call other people dumb."

Liam rolled his eyes again. "I know. But they were fighting about this book I read in like first grade. Or kindergarten."

He said the last word with such disdain. "I guess they can't all be voracious readers like you."

"Be what?" Liam had taken a bite of his granola bar, asking his question around a mouthful.

"Chew, then talk."

He made a show of chewing and swallowing, then repeated the question.

"Voracious. It means eager, like not being able to get enough of something."

"Voracious."

Having an intellectual child could be challenging, but she loved that she could almost always distract him by sliding a new word into a sentence. "People use it to talk about wanting lots of food in particular. He had a voracious appetite."

Liam nodded. "I have a voracious appetite for pizza."

She smiled. "Indeed you do. Maybe we can go out for pizza this weekend."

"Yes!" Liam jumped around like he'd just won the lottery.

"Tonight, however, is spaghetti. How about I get started on that while you do your homework?"

Liam finished his granola bar and walked past her to throw away the wrapper. "Okay. I have a pretty voracious appetite for that, too, especially if there are meatballs."

"I think that could be arranged. Do you want to do your homework at the table?"

Liam shrugged, as though her question was odd, but not unpalatable. "Sure."

He plopped his backpack on the table and took out a pencil and a folder of perfectly neat pieces of paper. Unlike her, who remained organized through discipline, the kid had a natural tendency to be tidy—one of the traits he got from his father. Along with his eyes and his propensity to snore like a freight train. "Let me know if you need any help."

"Thanks, Mom, but it's all pretty basic."

Darcy pulled out ingredients for their dinner, stealing glances at him while he worked. Other than their trip to the science museum and aquarium in Boston, she didn't think he was ever as happy as he was doing homework. When she brought their plates to the table, he'd finished everything and was reading one of his library books. She looked over his math problems and the worksheet of spelling words, along with his attempt to draw a cell and all its parts. She expected the first two to be flawless, but the quality of the drawing caught her off guard. "This is really good."

"Cells are so cool. We watched a video of them splitting and then we got to look at real ones under a microscope."

"I always thought biology was pretty cool, too." Maybe she shouldn't admit it, but she was more impressed with the artistic ability. "You didn't trace this?"

He slurped a string of spaghetti and shook his head. "I used the picture on the sheet as a guide."

They finished eating and Liam helped her with the dishes. He wasn't enthusiastic about chores, but he did them without complaint. Mostly. When they were done, he looked at her hopefully. "Do you want to play chess?"

"How about you take a bath, then we play one game before bed?"

"Okay." He dragged the word out for several seconds. Darcy smiled. Baths and bedtime reminded her that her kid was still a kid.

"Don't forget it's shampoo night."

Liam, who'd already started down the hall, groaned.

Darcy finished wiping the counters, pulled out the chess set, and sat at the table. When Liam emerged, his hair was wet and he wore a set of Spiderman pajamas. All the maturity, all the seriousness that so often made him seem older than he was, vanished. In that moment, he remained a little boy, her baby. Saying as much would lead to huffs and eye rolls, so she gave him a stern look. "You didn't just wet your hair, did you?"

That earned her an eye roll, but a playful one. "Mom."

Darcy shook her head and tsked. "I don't know. You better let me smell it."

He made a dramatic show of walking over to her, sticking his head under her nose. "I used gobs of shampoo."

True to his word, he smelled like superhero shampoo, which smelled more like oranges than superheroes in her opinion. Since the question was more about teasing him than not trusting him, she took advantage of the proximity to wrap her arms around his middle and tickle him. He giggled and squirmed, but didn't try to get away—a fact that melted her heart. "I guess it'll do."

"Sheesh," he said, extricating himself and taking the seat next to her at the table.

They set up the game and began. He was at the stage where she didn't put all her attention into beating him, but also didn't deliberately let him win. In that scenario, he won at least half the time, which she considered quite impressive. This time, she beat him and let him talk her into a rematch. When he took the second game fair and square, he pushed for a tie-breaker.

"Tomorrow. It's almost bedtime."

They read a chapter of *Harry Potter* together, then she left him with his library books for half an hour. She didn't expect it to last much longer, but more nights than not, he was already asleep when she returned to turn off his light.

Tonight was no exception. Darcy showered and pulled on a T-shirt and boxers, then stopped into Liam's room to turn off the light. She flipped on the night light that projected the Milky Way onto his ceiling, more out of habit than any need he still had for it, and quietly closed his door.

She curled up on the sofa in the living room and switched on her iPad. She had an email from Nick, confirming the dates of Liam's weekend visits for May and June, along with his two-week stay in July. She picked up her date book and wrote in all the details. She poked around Pinterest for a little while, adding recipes, a few outfits, activities for Liam, and some vintage photos of lesbians to her various boards. She had to laugh at the assortment, but they were a pretty accurate approximation of her interests, and her life. Maybe it felt sometimes like she was trying to be a dozen things at once, but she wouldn't change any of it.

Chapter Two

Although rain had been in the forecast much of the week, Emerson woke on the morning of Alex and Lia's wedding to sunshine. She checked her phone, thrilled to see that the rest of the day promised more of the same. She showered and dressed, choosing a lavender shirt with a gray tie for the day. She double checked her equipment, then headed out so she could stop by Wired Puppy on her way to Lia's hair and makeup appointment.

Emerson was not a wedding photographer, by trade or by choice. Still, she liked taking photos. And if the wedding in question was between two of her friends, she didn't mind pretending for an evening. She said as much to Alex and Lia when she found out they were engaged. Lia hesitated at first, saying she hated to impose. As soon as Emerson convinced her she'd enjoy it, they were in business. And since she'd successfully lobbied to have it be her gift to them, they got to save some money and she was spared having to go shopping. As far as Emerson was concerned, it was a win-win.

When she arrived at the salon, she found Lia and three other women sipping mimosas and giggling. While the scene might have felt cliché, Emerson couldn't be anything but happy for Lia. Alex, too. Even though they weren't the closest of friends, Emerson considered them one of her favorite couples.

Lia popped up to give her a hug, then insisted on pouring her a mimosa while making introductions—Lia's mother; Sally, her best friend from Louisiana; and Maggie, Alex's sister. The resemblance between Maggie and Alex was striking. She looked forward to capturing the two of them side by side.

She took some candid shots of the women together, then staged a few with Lia's mom. When it came to weddings, sentimentality reigned. That was followed by some silliness and a few photos of Lia getting her hair done. The upsweep wasn't unlike the way Lia often wore her hair, but the small pearls and perfectly placed curls made it a fancier and more formal look. Combined with the giddy glow, she was going to make a very beautiful bride.

When she left to meet Alex, Maggie joined her. The two of them walked down Commercial Street together. Maggie said, "I feel kind of ridiculous with my hair and makeup all done, wearing jeans and a flannel shirt."

"I'll rough up anyone who dares to point and laugh." Emerson lifted her fists and jabbed at the air a few times.

Maggie laughed. "Thanks. I think."

They arrived at Alex's and found Alex at the kitchen island, leg twitching. "I should have gone for hair and makeup just to have something to do," she said.

"Nonsense." Maggie squeezed her arm. "I'm here now and Dad will be any minute. We'll entertain you."

Alex smirked at her. Emerson recognized the deep affection behind the gesture and thought of her own sister. Alex folded her arms and said, "Please tell me y'all have a song and dance planned."

Maggie folded her arms in response. "Please tell me when you started using y'all."

Alex scowled, but without malice. "It's very catchy."

Before Maggie could retort, a bellowing voice came from the bottom of the stairs. "You girls up there?"

Alex stood. "Yeah, Dad. Come on up."

Patrick McKinnon bounded up the stairs to Alex's apartment and hugged both his daughters. Emerson realized the family resemblance extended to him as well. Emerson shook his hand, then did her best to fade into the background. She wanted to capture this family time, not become part of it. They took turns getting dressed, Maggie in a periwinkle dress and Alex in a cream-colored suit.

Emerson dragged them outside for photos. The three of them had the perfect blend of sweet and goofy; Emerson hardly had to coach them at all. Happy with the pictures she got, she left them to spend time together before the ceremony.

Emerson headed to the Unitarian Meeting House where Lia would be getting dressed. She found the bridal party in one of the rooms downstairs, along with a couple of Lia's sisters-in-law and her mother. Sally, wearing a dress identical to Maggie's, was telling a story from their childhood that had everyone in stitches.

Despite her efforts to blend in, Lia pulled her into the conversation and Emerson had to remind herself to stay focused on her job. Not a bad problem to have, really. She lingered until Lia got dressed, taking requisite shots of the dress itself, the shoes, and her mom zipping up the back. Emerson had her pose with her family and with Sally, although she planned to take more—in the church itself and outside. Lia's dress, while simple, made her look elegant and even more radiant than she had before.

Emerson excused herself to head upstairs to the main sanctuary. Other than some flowers, they'd done nothing to the church in terms of decoration. It didn't need it. The space felt bright and airy and had all the charm of an old New England church. Emerson scoped out a couple of locations, measuring light and figuring out the best vantage points. As guests started to arrive, she took the opportunity to capture some small groups and candids. With about fifty guests, she shouldn't have a hard time of making sure she got everyone in at least one or two, but she'd rather over-photograph than under.

When the prelude music began, the minister took her place at the front of the church, along with Alex and her sister. The music changed and all eyes shifted to the back of the sanctuary. Sally made her way up the aisle, followed by Lia. Although she'd only known Lia for the last year or so, Emerson felt a deep affection for her, something that bordered on sisterly. For the second time that day, Emerson thought of her own sister and wondered what she was doing at that moment. Emerson wasn't crazy about Will's current girlfriend and had allowed that fact to make her phone calls shorter and more sporadic than their usual communication. Kai and her drama notwithstanding, Emerson made a mental promise to call her sister the next day.

With everyone in place, the minister welcomed them and thanked everyone for being present to witness the joining of two special people. Emerson refocused her attention on the task at hand. The ceremony was brief—two short readings, the vows, and words of reflection and a blessing from the minister. Emerson still found herself choked up by the time it was over. She couldn't decide if it was because she considered Alex and Lia good friends or because she was getting older and perhaps more sentimental. Maybe it was because she knew Alex before Lia came along. They'd been bachelor buddies, going out for drinks and talking about women. Emerson didn't begrudge Alex her happily ever after. If anything, it stirred in her a longing for one of her own.

Emerson brushed the feeling aside with a chuckle. Weddings could have the funniest effects on people. Apparently, she was not immune.

The guests dispersed to make their way to the reception. Alex and Lia stayed back with their best women and immediate families. Emerson cycled through all the requisite permutations, again trying to capture a few quirky shots she thought Alex and Lia would enjoy. When she was done, she held Alex and Lia back so she could get a few of just the two of them. "I'll get plenty more at the reception," she said, "but you'll spend most of that time surrounded by people. This gives you two a minute to catch your breath before you go back to being the center of attention."

The last comment made Lia laugh. "Do I look like I need it?"

"You look nothing but radiant, but I know you're an introvert at heart."

Alex pulled Lia against her and planted a kiss on her cheek. "You're my introvert and I love you."

"I love you, too. I can't wait to spend the rest of my life with you."

"The feeling is entirely mutual."

Emerson captured the kiss, then shifted her camera. "Okay, I think we're good."

She ran ahead so she would be at the reception before they arrived. When she got to The Flour Pot, guests milled around with drinks. The café had been completely transformed. A white tent covered much of the patio and the front doors had been propped open to make the inside and outside feel as much like a single space as possible. Tables had been pushed to the perimeter and covered with white cloths, leaving a dance floor of sorts open in the middle. Candles and twinkle lights glowed, turning the normally casual vibe of the café into one that was elegant and inviting.

Alex and Lia arrived shortly after. The DJ, who Emerson recognized from events around town, introduced the wedding party. Then came toasts. Emerson had the perfect vantage point to capture the people who spoke as well as Alex and Lia's reactions. The background music resumed, mostly jazz, and food began to appear. In addition to stations set up around the room, waiters weaved around with trays of bite-sized things. Even though Alex didn't do the cooking, Emerson had no doubt the food fell under her direction. She made a point of sampling at least one of everything and wasn't disappointed.

Alex and Lia had their first dance, then Lia danced with her dad. Emerson smiled as she snapped photos. When Alex took the floor with her dad, they pretended to argue about who would lead, giving everyone a laugh. As they moved around the floor, Emerson wondered if Alex would have chosen to dance with her mom had she still been alive. Emerson sighed. That's what she would have done.

When the song ended, Emerson joined in the applause and shook off thoughts of her parents. The up-tempo song designed to kick off the dancing helped, as did the sight of a few little kids hamming it up for each other and the adults nearby. She started working the room, snapping candid photos of guests as well as some nice group shots.

Emerson took advantage of a lull in the reception to sneak into the kitchen. She imagined Alex and Lia would appreciate a few shots behind the scenes. If she happened to snag a couple of those bacon-wrapped scallops in the process, that wouldn't be so bad either.

The space was smaller than she expected, probably no more than two or three hundred square feet. As far as Emerson was concerned, it made the delicious things that emerged from it even more impressive. A waitress brushed past her with a tray of bite-sized croissants made into sandwiches. Another stood at the main work table, waiting for her tray to be filled by a skinny guy in a chef's coat that looked to be three sizes too big.

Two more women stood at the oven, also in chef's coats. "These look good." One of them pointed to a platter. "Go ahead and plate them up."

The other one pulled a large sheet pan from the oven and moved it to the table. She started moving small puff pastry pouches to a serving tray. The first woman slid something else into the oven and closed the door. When she turned around, Emerson's gaze locked on her. She was gorgeous—fair complexion and high cheekbones accentuated by cat-eye makeup and red lipstick. Even in the boxy chef coat, Emerson could tell she had curves. Really nice curves.

The woman looked at her with a raised brow. "Can I help you?"

Emerson hoped she hadn't been caught staring. "I was hoping to take some photos."

The woman narrowed her eyes and regarded Emerson with suspicion. "Like of the kitchen?"

Emerson offered a smile, hoping to win her over, in more ways than one. "For Alex and Lia. Since the reception is at the café, I thought they'd appreciate a few shots of things in the making."

"Oh." The woman nodded, then smiled. "That's a great idea."

"Thanks. I'll only be a few minutes and I'll try to stay out of your way."

"Take your time." The woman looked Emerson up and down. "Just don't touch anything."

"Promise. I'm Emerson, by the way." Emerson extended her hand.

The woman took it. "Darcy."

Emerson didn't want to be a nuisance, but she wanted to keep the woman talking. "Do you do catering full time?"

Darcy shook her head. "No, thank God. I work here."

Emerson cocked her head to one side. "I've never seen you. And I'm here a lot."

"I work in the kitchen." Darcy gestured to the space around them. "I'm the head cook."

"I thought Alex did the cooking."

"She does the baking. I'm in charge of the lunch menu—soups, salads, that sort of thing."

Darcy seemed mildly exasperated and Emerson realized she needed to switch tactics if she wanted to get on her good side. "Wait, does that mean you're responsible for the macaroni and cheese of the day?"

Darcy smiled. "It does."

"I think you're responsible for me gaining at least five pounds, then."

Darcy looked her up and down—for the second time since their meeting a few minutes prior. "You don't look any worse for wear."

The comment sounded like a compliment, but Emerson wasn't sure. "Well, since you must know both brides personally, I'm doubly glad I snuck in to take pictures."

"Right. I'll let you get to it."

"I'd love to get a couple of you, too, if you don't mind."

Darcy's smile turned into a playful smirk. "If you insist."

Emerson couldn't decide if Darcy had a playful personality or if she was flirting, but she spent the next couple of minutes posing and staging things for Emerson to photograph. Emerson hoped it was the latter. But when the timer for the oven went off, Darcy went back to all business. She didn't literally shoo Emerson away, but it came through loud and clear that she was done.

Emerson thanked her and returned to the reception. She resumed working the room, keeping one eye on the kitchen. Darcy emerged a couple of times, seemingly to make sure everything was under control and to chat with a few of the guests. Both times, Emerson tried to make her way across the room to talk with her. Both times, however, someone grabbed her attention and Darcy disappeared before she could extricate herself.

When Alex and Lia cut the cake an hour later, Darcy appeared again. Emerson captured the ceremonial first bite, the kiss that followed. She watched as Darcy moved the cake to a rolling cart, then followed her back into the kitchen.

"Back again?" Darcy asked with a playful smile.

"Couldn't resist. Did Alex make the cake?"

Darcy nodded. "It's beautiful, isn't it?"

Emerson considered a comment about it having nothing on the woman cutting it, but didn't. That would be cheesy, not to mention forward. But as she snapped photos of the cake being cut, she strategized ways she might ask Darcy out, or at least see her again. She reluctantly followed the wait staff out of the kitchen.

With the cake under control, Darcy turned her attention to filling the silver urns Alex had rented and set up on the main counter for coffee. She checked the supply of cups, along with the sugar and cream. With the bulk of her work now complete, she lingered for a moment and watched. Alex and Lia were in the middle of a slow dance, looking into each other's eyes with goofy grins on their faces.

In the six years she'd known Alex, Darcy had never seen her so happy. And although she'd only met Lia a little over a year ago, it was obvious that Lia was head over heels for Alex as well. Several other couples shared the small dance floor with them, including a few people she knew. Emerson stood on the perimeter, camera covering her face. When she pulled it away, she looked almost immediately in Darcy's direction.

They made eye contact and Emerson offered her a slow smile. Darcy held her gaze and returned the smile. She'd thought Emerson was flirting with her in the kitchen. Now she was sure. It was nice. She didn't have much occasion for flirting these days.

Of course, that didn't mean she couldn't enjoy sharing looks with an attractive woman. And Emerson was certainly nice to look at. Darcy had noticed that much the moment she turned around and found Emerson standing in the kitchen. Although Lia had described her as hot, her account hadn't captured Emerson's aesthetic—part androgynous, part butch, mixed with edgy artist. Hot was a total understatement. Even if that interaction was the end of it, knowing the spark was mutual gave her a little boost.

"Darcy?"

Hearing her name snapped Darcy out of her reverie. She turned to find Tamara, one of her sous chefs, standing next to her. "Yes?"

"We put out the truffles and caramels like you asked. Is there anything else you want us to do?"

"There's one last batch of coffee to add here. Do that and make sure there's still plenty of hot water for tea. Then we can start cleaning up."

Tamara nodded. "Sounds good."

Darcy indulged in one final look around the room. Everyone seemed to be having a good time and the party felt intimate, rather than cramped. Alex had worried the café might be on the small side, but Lia remained confident it would all work. Considering how significant the café was in both their lives, Darcy was happy it had.

She was about to head back into the kitchen when she stole one last look at Emerson, only to discover that Emerson was looking at her again. Or perhaps she'd never stopped. A surge of warmth radiated through Darcy. She held the stare for a moment before turning away.

Back in the kitchen, she started the process of cleanup. She didn't always like having to share her space with the interns and seasonal staff, but it had its perks. She set one of them up to scrub the pots and pans while she had the other begin cycling the rented dishes and glassware into racks for the dishwasher. That left her to focus her attention on packing away ingredients and supplies and wrapping up the leftover food for people to take home at the end of the night.

The next time she poked her head out of the kitchen, the crowd had thinned considerably. Alex and Lia stood near the door, talking with guests as they departed. A few enthusiastic souls remained on the dance floor. Emerson was nowhere in sight. She directed one of the waitstaff to collect abandoned dishes while she ensured there were enough sweets out for anyone in search of a final snack before calling it a night. She also checked in with Jeff, who'd taken on the role of bartender for the evening.

"I think we pulled it off," he said as she approached.

"I believe you're right."

"And we get two days off in a row. I might suggest we do weddings every weekend."

Darcy rolled her eyes. "Let's not get ahead of ourselves, shall we?"

"Fair enough. Can I pour you a drink?"

It was almost the end of the night. What the hell? "I'd love a drink. How about a glass of red?"

"You got it, gorgeous."

Darcy skirted around the edge of the temporary bar and leaned against it. She sipped her wine and watched as the DJ announced the last dance. Alex and Lia once again took the floor. She glanced at Jeff. "They're perfect together, aren't they?"

In her people watching, Darcy missed Emerson come up right next to her. "They are."

Darcy smiled at her. "Hello, again."

"Hi. You weren't talking to me, but I couldn't resist. It's fun to photograph people who are ridiculously in love. Even when they aren't trying, they look great."

Darcy was about to agree when Jeff spoke up. "Hey, Em. Are you in any of the pictures? You should be."

Emerson looked at Jeff and shook her head. "Why do you think I stay on this side of the camera?"

Jeff laughed, but put out his hand. "You have to be in at least one. Give me."

Emerson handed over her camera. "I know better than to challenge the guy who makes my coffee."

"Wise woman." He waved his hand between Emerson and Darcy. "You two get together. Act like you're having fun."

Emerson lifted a brow at Darcy. She responded with a playful shrug and a smile. Emerson moved in closer to her. She slid her arm behind Darcy, resting it lightly around her waist. The touch, although casual, sent a charge of electricity through Darcy and she shivered.

"You okay?" Emerson asked.

"Just a chill," Darcy lied and turned her attention to Jeff.

Jeff took a few pictures before handing the camera back to Emerson. Emerson, in turn, had Darcy and Jeff pose together. "I'm going to caption this one 'Intrepid Flour Pot staff pull off wedding of the year.'"

"I approve this message," Jeff said.

"Me, too. But for it to count, I've got to pull off the cleanup, too, so if you'll excuse me…" Darcy headed back to the kitchen, happy to discover how much progress had been made in her absence. When the final guests had gone, Alex and Lia poked their heads in to say thank you and insist that she go home. Darcy acquiesced, then hugged them both and offered her congratulations. She drove home, happy that Liam was with his grandparents for the night. She rarely felt the desire to sleep in, but she had a feeling tomorrow would be one of those times.

She showered off the kitchen smells and crawled into bed, running through the highlights of the day in her mind. And while seeing two of her favorite people start their married lives together was at the top of the list, Darcy couldn't keep her thoughts away from the sexy photographer who kept catching her eye. Not to mention the spark when Emerson's hand touched her. Such a simple thing, but it left her feeling attractive and feminine. Like getting a pedicure, only better. And free. She'd just have to make a point of flirting more often.

CHAPTER THREE

When Emerson walked into The Flour Pot a few days after the wedding, she half expected to see Darcy. She didn't, of course, just as she'd never seen her in five or six dozen other times she'd come in. The logic of that did little to quell the disappointment.

Lia, sitting at a table by the window, caught her eye and offered a wave. Emerson shook off the feeling and returned the greeting. Lia was who she was there to meet anyway. "I'm just going to grab a coffee."

Lia returned her attention to her computer and Emerson walked over to the register. Jeff stopped stacking cups next to the espresso machine and flashed her a grin. "Good morning, sunshine."

"Morning, Jeff."

"Flat white?"

"You know it, but for here, please. I'm meeting with Lia."

"You got it. Anything else?"

Emerson eyed the case. She didn't usually eat breakfast, but more because she had no food around than anything else. "A scone, I think. Maple pecan."

Jeff handed her a saucer, then finished her coffee. Emerson paid, then went over to join Lia. Alex emerged from the kitchen and looked their way. "Hey, Em. I thought I heard you."

Lia beamed at Alex in that way newlyweds do. "Emerson has the pictures from the wedding for us."

"Oh, nice. I'll be over in a minute."

Emerson pulled a flash drive from her bag and handed it to Lia. "I only deleted the blurry ones and closed eyes and weird faces and such. That left close to a thousand."

Lia chuckled. "Quite all right. I want them all."

"A wedding photographer would give you a finished set, with complete retouching. I adjusted lighting but not much else. If you want to pick a few dozen favorites, I can give them the full treatment."

"I'll let you know." Lia stuck the flash drive into her open laptop, but didn't immediately start clicking through them. Emerson admired her restraint. "If you got a few good ones of the ceremony and us with our families, I'm happy."

"The ones outside the church came out really well. I think you'll be pleased."

"I'm sure they're great. I'm beyond excited. Thank you again for taking them."

"My pleasure." Emerson smiled. It had been a pleasure.

"And you're sure you won't let us pay you?"

"I'm sure. I did it as a friend. And as a gift."

Lia shook her head. "I was afraid you were going to say that, so I took the liberty of setting up a tab for you. You won't be paying for your coffee for the next year."

"Lia, you didn't have to—"

"I wanted to. We wanted to."

"Well I'm not crazy enough to turn down free coffee."

"Good. It's settled."

Emerson sipped her flat white. It would be easy to turn her couple-times-a-week habit into a daily routine. And that might have more benefits than one. "So, how well do you know Darcy?"

Lia looked at her quizzically. "Alex's cook?"

"Yeah."

"Um, fairly well. She helped me plan the menu for the reception. We've hung out a few times. I've watched her son when her sitter fell through."

Lia's mention of a son stopped Emerson in her tracks. It never occurred to her that Darcy might have a child. Or be married. Or straight. "She has a kid?"

Lia smiled. "Liam. He's eight."

"Is she married?"

"No. I think she had him in college, or right after college. Alex would know. Why?"

Emerson sat back in her chair. "Well, I was thinking of asking her out, but it sounds like I might be barking up the wrong tree."

Lia shook her head. "Oh, no, she's definitely a lesbian."

"Who's a lesbian?" Alex pulled up a chair and joined them.

"Emerson was asking about Darcy."

"One hundred, well, ninety-nine percent lesbian," Alex said.

She'd not heard that phrase before. "Ninety-nine percent?"

"Lesbian who slept with her gay best friend once in college. That's how she ended up with Liam."

"Ah." She'd heard of such things happening, but didn't know anyone personally who'd had a child that way.

"Why do you ask?" Alex gave Emerson a look that implied she knew exactly why.

"She wanted to ask her out," Lia said.

Alex pondered for a moment. "You should. I don't know if she'd say yes, but you should."

"Not exactly a vote of confidence," Emerson said.

"Not like that. I mean she dates, just not a ton. And Liam's a hoot. If the kid thing doesn't bother you, then I say go for it."

She wasn't expecting it, but the kid thing didn't bother Emerson. Or, at least she didn't think it did. It really depended on whether Darcy was in search of a co-parent. That would not be up her alley. But hanging out with a kid could be fun. "It doesn't bother me."

"And assuming you aren't going to be weird about the fact that she's a single mother," Lia said.

Emerson scowled. "I wouldn't be weird."

Alex nodded. "Good. Darcy is great—as a mom and as a person. I don't think she gets enough adult time."

"Does she have full custody?" It occurred to Emerson that was a rather personal question, but she figured the more information she could gather ahead of time, the better.

"Liam's dad lives in Boston. I think Liam is with him one weekend a month and for a couple of weeks in the summer," Alex said.

"Huh." That might make dating difficult.

"Her parents are local, though." Lia tapped a finger on the table. "I know he spends time with them, too."

"Okay." Difficult, but not impossible. And she still had to find out if Darcy wanted to go out with her in the first place.

"You have to be cool, though," Alex said.

"What is that supposed to mean?"

"I think she means that Darcy is a good person. Neither of us want to see her get hurt."

Emerson understood what they were saying. She understood why, too. Still, she didn't like the implication that she would act like an ass. "I have no intention of hurting her."

Lia reached over and squeezed Emerson's hand. "Of course not."

"Yeah." Alex raised her hands. "I didn't mean it like that."

Emerson sighed. "I know. And I appreciate the context. Not like I was looking for a hookup, but knowing her situation will inform how I go about things. Thanks for telling me."

"So, you're going to do it?" Lia asked.

"I am."

Alex shook her head. "Not today."

"Alex." Lia's tone carried a hint of scolding.

"No, I mean you can't today. She's off."

"Oh." Lia and Emerson answered in unison.

"She'll be back tomorrow. And the rest of the week except for Sunday."

"Well, between that and the free coffee, I guess I'll be back tomorrow."

Lia smiled. "Thank you again for the photos. I can't wait to look at them."

"It was a lot of fun. Thanks for trusting me with such an important job." Emerson leaned in and kissed Lia on the cheek, then hugged Alex. "And congratulations again. You two might be my favorite married couple."

"We'll see you tomorrow." Alex raised an eyebrow suggestively. "I'll be here."

Emerson walked out of the café. Although the weather for the wedding had been perfect, a cold front had moved through. Between the chill in the air and the overcast sky, it hardly felt like spring. That wasn't all bad, since she felt less tempted to meander through town or go to the beach. She made her way back to her loft and prepared for an afternoon of work.

❖

Darcy used her day off to catch up on bills, email, and cleaning her apartment. And she was waiting for Liam when he got off the bus. "I thought we could go to the library, since we didn't get to this weekend."

"Awesome!"

The delight on his face put her in an even better mood. "Do you want a snack before we go?"

"Nah, I'm good."

"Bathroom."

"I can wait until we get there."

She might have pressed the matter, but the library was only a few minutes away. "Then I guess we're ready to go."

When they arrived, she let him wander on his own. The library was one of the places where she felt safe not keeping a constant eye on him. While he looked for books about turtles and planets and other topics of boyhood interest, she meandered to the fiction section. Since she started coming to the library with Liam a few years ago, she'd discovered a nice collection of lesbian fiction—romances and intrigue and even some fantasy. She'd gotten hooked on it, taking out a couple of books at a time for reading in bed.

After picking out a couple of titles she hadn't read yet, she tracked down Liam, who was holding at least ten books in his arms. "You know you can only check out six, right?"

He sighed dramatically. "I know. I have to prioritize."

Normally, she held fast to the rule. It was important he learned about rules and sharing and not getting everything he wanted. She was feeling sentimental, though, and maybe a little indulgent. "I'm only getting two. How about I get four of yours with my card?"

"Mom, you never let me do that!"

"I know. But if I do it this once, you have to promise not to beg every time we come."

Liam nodded. "Promise."

They took their respective piles to the circulation desk. She watched him hand over his library card, say thank you without being prompted. She never doubted he was a good kid, but there were moments when the fact of it overwhelmed her. Darcy swiped a tear from her eye and laughed at herself for being such a mush.

Books in hand, they made their way back to the car. "How about we pick up dinner on our way home?"

Liam's face lit up. "Pizza?"

"We had pizza two nights ago." Not that Darcy would have minded. She loved pizza, too. But she had guilt about indulging that love too often. Even in her sentimental state of mind, twice in three days pushed the envelope.

His shoulders slumped for only a moment before he perked up again. "Sushi?"

Darcy laughed, still amused that her eight-year-old loved raw fish, had loved it since he'd stolen a piece from her plate when he was four. "Excellent idea."

She called in an order to their usual place. When they got there, they went inside so Liam could look at the fish in the large aquarium just inside the door. They didn't have to wait long and were home, food in hand, less than half an hour later. Darcy divided everything up, making sure Liam got more of the California roll and she got all the spicy tuna. He devoured his share, along with more than half of the seaweed salad, before asking to try hers.

"It's spicy," she warned him.

"I know. I still want to taste it."

"If you insist." She picked up a piece with her chopsticks and moved it to his plate.

He picked it up and popped it in his mouth. "It's not that hot."

"It's because you didn't put any wasabi on it."

"I want one with wasabi."

"Yeah? Okay." She handed him another piece, one with a smear of green paste on top. "Don't say I didn't warn you."

It went in as quickly as the first and he chewed. In a matter of seconds, his mouth gaped open and tears welled up in his eyes. He blinked a few times and turned his head from side to side, but he didn't spit it out. He chewed some more, swallowed, then wiped his nose on the back of his hand. "Oh, my God."

"I told you." She handed him a napkin. "Blow your nose and have some water. The good news is it will go away in a second."

He did, then looked at her. "That was so good."

"You liked it?"

"It burned, but it was kind of cool."

"My boy likes wasabi."

Liam nodded with enthusiasm. "I love wasabi."

Darcy laughed. "I'll remember that for next time."

"Can there be a next time soon?"

"Sure. But in the meantime, go wash your hands so we can do homework."

Liam bounded out of his chair and went to the kitchen. Darcy cleaned up while he got started on his work. There wasn't much, so they had time for some TV before bed. She convinced him to save the snake documentary for when she wasn't watching and they settled on one about beavers. Despite only a casual interest in nature, she found it rather fascinating.

When it was over, Liam went about his bedtime routine without a single complaint or need for prodding. After kissing him good night, Darcy took her new books to bed. She huddled under the covers and lost herself in a world of lesbians who fought crime, made the world a safer place, and lived happily ever after.

CHAPTER FOUR

Emerson woke with a pain in her neck and no recollection of going to bed. She blinked a few times and looked around. Sunlight streamed through the window, confirming that it was morning. She rolled over and realized the pain in her neck had nothing on the one radiating down her arm.

The night before flashed into her mind and she bolted upright, looking over to where she left the painting, as though it might have disappeared during the night. It sat on the easel. Emerson dragged herself out of bed and walked over to it. Not only was it still there, it was stunning.

Emerson didn't consider herself a braggart, but she also had no use for false modesty. She'd been born with a degree of innate talent. She didn't pretend otherwise and she didn't take it for granted. She'd also spent years working on her craft. So, when she finished a painting, she didn't hesitate to be pleased with it. When doing so came in a massive burst of energy that kept her up half the night, the satisfaction was even more keen.

Emerson raked a hand through her hair as she moved back and forth, studying the painting from different angles. The woman, inspired by a snapshot she took of someone on the beach, lounged in the sand. Although the woman in her photo had been wearing a barely there bikini, Emerson had given the one in her painting a more vintage suit. The two pieces revealed only a fraction of her midriff; red and white polka dots made the look more playful than sexy.

But still. Something in the woman's posture, her face, radiated a kind of sensual confidence. Emerson picked up the photo she'd used as a guide. The woman in her photo was beautiful, but didn't have the essence Emerson had managed to convey. She glanced back at the painting. The image of Darcy popped into her mind and a slow smile spread across her face. That's where it had come from. The painting bore no physical resemblance to Darcy, but the mood reminded her of the way Darcy posed and flirted with her in the kitchen at the wedding.

Emerson stepped away from the painting and headed toward her bathroom. She rotated her shoulders and wrists, trying to loosen the muscles that ached. Her desire to ask Darcy on a date was joined by a desire to paint her. She turned on the water and stepped under the hot spray. Hopefully, she'd have the chance to do both.

After dressing, Emerson spent another few minutes admiring her work. Unless some stroke of brilliance hit, she'd likely use this as the centerpiece of her show in July. She had no doubt that it would sell, and give her a nice cushion going into fall.

Feeling upbeat and confident, Emerson jogged down the stairs of her building and walked along Commercial Street. She'd stop by The Flour Pot for some breakfast and see if she could catch Darcy on a break. Although the morning was sunny and promised a warm day, there were only a handful of people on the street. Weekends were getting busy, but the real onslaught of summer traffic wouldn't hit until late June.

It was nearly eleven when she strolled into the café. Most of the morning crowd had cleared and Alex sat at the register doing a crossword puzzle. Lia sat at her usual table, typing furiously—so much so that she didn't even glance up when Emerson waved. Alex did, however, and offered her a smile. "Morning, Em."

"Morning. How's business?"

"Picking up, enough that Lia has resorted to ear buds to get work done. She'll be abandoning me for the library before long. Coffee?"

"You know it." Emerson surveyed the case. "A muffin, too. Chocolate chip."

"Coming right up." Alex got her order and set it on the counter, then refused Emerson's money.

Emerson had a feeling it would become a ritual. She planned to let it go for a couple of months before insisting on paying again. "Is Darcy in today?"

Alex smirked and gave her a mischievous look. "She is."

"Might she be due for a break soon?"

"Due? No, but if she's at a good stopping point, you might be able to snag her attention for a few minutes. Do you want me to ask her?"

The last thing Emerson wanted when she asked Darcy out was an audience. Or to have Alex running interference like she needed a wingman to get a date. "Would you mind if I popped into the kitchen?"

Alex gestured to the swinging door. "Be my guest."

Emerson hesitated for a moment, then picked up her coffee and muffin. Even if it felt awkward, it was probably better than looking like she showed up solely to interrupt Darcy at work. She skirted around the counter and bakery case and pushed her way into the kitchen. Darcy stood at the stove with her back to the door. Not unlike the first time Emerson saw her, but now she wore an apron over a T-shirt and jeans instead of a chef's coat. Emerson felt that same stirring and wondered if Darcy had some crazy pheromone thing going on that affected her so immediately.

"I think this Buffalo chicken mac and cheese is going to be a hit."

Clearly, Emerson's mere presence didn't have the same kind of impact on Darcy. "It sounds good to me."

Darcy whirled around. "Sorry. I thought you were Alex."

"No need to apologize. And I meant what I said. It does sound good."

"It will be ready in about an hour if you want to try it. You're Emerson, right?"

Emerson smiled, glad that Darcy at least remembered meeting her, and her name. "I am. And you're Darcy."

Darcy smiled and the stirring intensified. "That's me. Are you looking for Alex? She's out front, I think."

"Actually, I was looking for you."

Darcy's face didn't give anything away. "Hoping for more samples?"

Saying she'd like to sample Darcy was probably too forward, at least at this point. "Not exactly. I really enjoyed talking with you the other night. I was hoping we could talk more when you're not otherwise occupied. Over dinner, perhaps."

Darcy considered, again giving nothing away. Emerson couldn't tell if she was formulating a clever reply, or looking for a way to let her down easy. Normally, she didn't mind being rejected. Well, didn't overly mind. Something about Darcy was different; the idea of not getting to know her was keenly disappointing.

"I think that could be arranged."

The answer interrupted Emerson's internal monologue and almost caught her off guard. "Great. My schedule is flexible. You name the day and time."

"I can let you know tonight or tomorrow. I'll need to arrange a sitter." Darcy tilted her head to the side, narrowed her eyes slightly. "Do you know I have a son?"

Emerson didn't want to reveal that she'd been snooping, but she also didn't want to lie or to make Darcy explain. "Alex mentioned it."

A good enough answer, because Darcy nodded. "Okay, well, how about I text you later? I need to get back to work."

"Right. Sorry. I didn't mean to pull you away from it." She glanced around, realized she was still holding her muffin and coffee. "I'll jot down my number and leave it at the front counter."

"Sounds good." Emerson turned to leave, but stopped when Darcy said her name. God, she loved the way Darcy said her name. "Yeah?"

"I meant what I said. The mac and cheese is going to be amazing."

Emerson flashed a smile. "It always is."

Darcy returned her attention to the stove and Emerson left the kitchen the way she'd come. Alex was helping a customer, but Lia's eyes were trained right on her. She wondered if Alex had gone over and given her an update while she was in the kitchen. Lia's look turned expectant and Emerson flashed a thumbs up. Lia proceeded to wave her over. Emerson joined her and took a long sip of her coffee. "Good morning."

"Good morning. So, you asked her? She said yes?"

"Yes and yes."

"Excellent. I think y'all will totally hit it off."

Emerson broke off a piece of her muffin and popped it in her mouth. "I agree, obviously, but I'm wondering what makes you think so."

Lia shrugged. "I don't know. Y'all are both creative types, good energy mixed with a sarcastic streak."

"High praise."

"Every time I turn around, you two have your heads together," Alex said as she joined them. "What are you plotting now?"

Lia beamed up at Alex. "Darcy said yes. They're going on a date."

"Nice. What are you going to do?"

"I'm not sure yet. She's going to line up a sitter and we'll go from there."

"Oh." Lia's eyes lit up. "I'll volunteer. I know she has a usual person, but I haven't seen Liam much lately."

Alex nodded. "Agreed. We can do it at her place or ours."

Lia stood just as Darcy came out with a large metal crock of soup. "Oh, hey. We were just talking about you."

Darcy set the crock into the warmer and turned. "That sounds dangerous."

"All good stuff, I promise. Alex and I want to hang out with Liam when you go out with Emerson."

"You really were talking about me."

"Sorry." Emerson tried not to worry about being caught. "I did consult with them before I asked you out, so I had to tell them you said yes."

Darcy lifted her hands. "I'm not mad. You look like a bunch of hens is all. I'm amused."

That was a relief. Emerson didn't want to get off on the wrong foot even before they got started.

"We're totally free this weekend," Lia said.

Darcy shook her head, but smiled. "I guess it's settled, then."

Emerson suddenly felt awkward about being part of the conversation. She couldn't decide if it was babysitting arrangements being made or because her friends were becoming so involved in the whole thing. "I should get to work. I'll leave you to sort out the specifics." She looked at Darcy. "Text me?"

"I'll get your number from Alex."

"Perfect."

Emerson picked up her coffee and the rest of her muffin and headed for the exit. She stood on the street for a moment, debating her next move. Since she'd just finished a painting, she didn't feel ready to start another. She usually took a couple days of downtime in between. But since she'd just said she needed to get to work, she felt guilty blowing off work altogether.

She meandered back toward her apartment, soaking up the spring sunshine. By the time she got there, she had a plan. She grabbed her camera and car keys, then made the short drive to Herring Cove Beach.

In the summer, she gravitated to Race Point. It was a buffet of inspiration—women and men, folks all along the gender spectrum, teenagers and little kids. Some came with nothing more than a towel; others arrived in packs, complete with coolers and colorful blankets and umbrellas. Unfortunately, Cape Cod remained a good month away from true beach weather. But since Herring Cove offered calm water and easier parking, it drew people year-round.

Today was no exception. An older couple strolled hand in hand, a young guy jogged along the water's edge. Emerson snapped photos, enjoying the way the late morning light reflected off the water. She made her way down the small incline, letting the camera rest on the strap around her neck. She closed her eyes for a moment and took a deep breath.

The ocean never failed to calm her mind, even when she didn't feel restless. It was one of the main reasons Emerson chose

Provincetown. That and its history as an artists' colony. The gay thing didn't hurt either. When she decided to make painting her living and not just a pastime, she wanted a place that would nurture that. And not let her become a hermit in the process. At the time, she hadn't known if it would be a permanent decision. And while she specifically refused to limit her possibilities, she couldn't imagine living anywhere else.

❖

When Darcy finished her shift, she went in search of Alex and Lia. Neither were anywhere to be found. With much of the seasonal staff already hired, Alex made a point of handing over the reins to her afternoon manager at a set time. Before Lia came along, Alex would often linger, saying there was always something to be done. Now, though, they had a routine. Lia would pack up her work and both of them would clear out by three.

Darcy commended her for it. Owning a business had a way of becoming all-consuming. Even though Liam consumed much of her non-working time, she felt like she had a good work/life balance. It was one of the main reasons she loved her job so much.

She contemplated knocking on their apartment door on her way out, but decided not to. Given they were in the honeymoon phase of being married, she didn't want to chance disturbing anything. She needed to get home to Liam anyway. She could confirm details later.

On the drive home, Darcy rolled down her window. With the sun out, and the temperature approaching eighty, she reveled in the approaching summer. Without a doubt, summer was her favorite time of year. Although the café got busier, the additional staff Alex brought on meant Darcy had a lot more flexibility with her schedule. Paired with Liam being out of school, it sort of felt like freedom. Even having to juggle how Liam would spend his time while she was at work didn't faze her. He'd have camp and time with his grandparents, a few days at the café. Any whining about getting dragged around with her would be made up for by the number of adventures they'd get to have. But they needed to get through the rest of the school year first. Just a few weeks to go.

And then there was her date with Emerson. Darcy smiled at the thought. She hadn't been on a date for a few months, and even then, the last few had been busts. She'd broken her rule about worlds colliding and had gone out with another single mom, a woman whose son was in Liam's karate class. Tina had been nice, if a little feminine for Darcy. Unfortunately, Tina and her ex—Noah's other mom—had only broken up a few months before and Tina was far from over it. Then there was the bartender. Darcy had known from the get-go that wouldn't amount to much. It had been fun, mostly. But since they worked opposite schedules, the stress of trying to make plans hadn't been worth it.

Emerson seemed different. In addition to her being gorgeous, Darcy felt drawn to her creative energy. Not that she would ever call herself an artist, but Darcy liked to think she had the soul of one. And while cooking satisfied that some, she missed the charge of art and her design-fueled college days. Maybe spending time with Emerson could feed that.

Darcy got home a few minutes before Liam. She took a quick shower and threw on leggings and a T-shirt for the evening, emerging from the bedroom just as Liam walked through the door. They chatted about his day and she slid the lasagna she'd made the day before into the oven. After throwing a quick salad together, she joined Liam at the table to check on his homework. After zipping through the math and vocabulary worksheets, talk turned to the upcoming science project.

"Mom, it's going to be epic. We got to pick an animal and we can do whatever we want. Like, whatever we want. I picked snapping turtles. And when we're done, they're going to hang them up around the school and the best ones are going to be displayed at the library." He lifted both hands in the air at the significance of this latest development. "The public library."

"So, what are you going to do?"

He sighed. "I have no idea. I mean, I'm going to do my report. Everyone has to do a report." He swept his hand in front of him. "I need something visual."

"Maybe you can draw a turtle. The drawing you did the other day of the cell was really good."

"Maybe. I think I need something bigger, something that will stand out. I want to win."

Other than chess, Darcy had begun to think Liam didn't have a competitive bone in his body. Not necessarily a bad thing, but she'd always thought a little healthy competition was good for character development—including the winning and the losing that came with it. Leave it to her son to get competitive about a science project. "We'll think of something."

They ate dinner and Liam dragged himself off to the horrors of the bath tub. Darcy put the kitchen back together and curled up on the sofa. She texted Lia to confirm that she and Alex really were free and wanted to watch Liam. The instant and emphatic response allayed her fears. She then texted Emerson to sort out the details.

Liam emerged in his pajamas, announcing he was all clean. Darcy called him over, slightly suspicious of how long he'd been gone. "Turn around."

He did so, slowly. "What?"

"If you're going to fake wash your hair, you're going to have to do a more convincing job of getting it wet."

He finished turning a circle and looked at the ground. "Sorry."

Of all the problems to have, having a kid who hated baths ranked pretty low. It didn't mean she wouldn't give him a hard time. "I should make you start over."

"Mom." He drew out the word, teetering on the edge of a full-on whine.

"And you're talking back?" She was sure to keep her tone light so he'd know she wasn't actually angry.

He straightened his shoulders and made a sheepish face, but still didn't make eye contact. "No. I'm not."

Because he wouldn't look at her, he didn't see her smile. "I didn't think so. No redos tonight. You'll just have to take another bath tomorrow and scrub extra hard."

He glanced up, eyes hopeful and with a lopsided grin. "Okay."

"Come here and give me a hug. We'll watch some TV before reading time." He piled onto the sofa and curled up against her. She kissed the top of his wet, unshampooed head and picked up the remote. "Let's see what's on."

They settled on a soccer match on ESPN. Darcy had no interest, but since it was the only sport he liked beyond karate, she didn't mind. Seeing she had a reply from Emerson, she picked up her phone and shot a quick text back.

Emerson's phone pinged again and she resisted the urge to roll her eyes, even though there was no one around to see her. The first text from Darcy had been to confirm that they were good to go on Friday night. The second informed Emerson that Liam would be at Alex and Lia's, so Darcy would just meet her in town. The third suggested they go to Tin Pan Alley, which Darcy had been wanting to try. Emerson didn't have a problem with any of that; it felt like typical date planning territory.

They were on text number eleven, though, and it was starting to feel less like a date and more like a high-stakes negotiation. They'd agreed to both a start time and an end time, the fact that they'd meet at the restaurant, and several other details that were making Emerson wonder if she'd misread Darcy. Not that she could have immediately known Darcy was a control freak, but still. Emerson tried to shake off the hesitation the exchange caused. It might be nothing. And if it turned out to be something, well, there didn't have to be a date number two.

She set down her phone and picked up her brush. The painting was nice, if nothing to write home about. This one included the lighthouse at Long Point and a sun-drenched beach. Emerson rarely found landscapes inspiring, but they sold well. They didn't require much thought at this point, either, and that meant they helped to pay the bills. She might be an artist, but she was practical, too. She'd rather supplement her income with beach scenes than a day job, or by making Ramen a staple of her diet.

She heard her phone again, but didn't pick it up. At this point, Darcy could wait. When she finished working an hour later, she took her time cleaning brushes and putting everything away. She picked up her phone with hesitation, half dreading what might be waiting for her.

Sounds great. Really looking forward to it. Have a good night.

Emerson did roll her eyes then, but at herself. Maybe she was being too hard on Darcy. It's not like she had a structured job and a child to juggle. She should cut Darcy a little slack. At least for now. She'd find out quickly enough if it was going to be more trouble than it was worth.

CHAPTER FIVE

Darcy glanced at her watch as she walked. Six o'clock on the dot. Since she was only a block away, she didn't think that classified as late. Even if it was late by her standards. The entrance to the restaurant came into view and she realized Emerson was standing just to the side of the door. Looking even sexier than she did the night of the wedding, if that was possible.

Dark jeans and a white oxford, untucked, hair artfully disheveled. Combined with the aviator sunglasses, she looked like some kind of hot dyke model. Whether she sensed being stared at or just happened to glance in Darcy's direction, Darcy couldn't be sure. But she turned her head and offered Darcy a slow, easy smile.

"Sorry if I kept you waiting," Darcy said.

"You haven't. I just got here."

Even though she couldn't see Emerson's eyes behind the dark lenses, Darcy got the impression Emerson was looking her up and down. The gaze made Darcy feel sexy. If nothing else came of the evening, she appreciated the chance to feel sexy. "Oh, good. I hate being late."

Emerson chuckled. "Why does that not surprise me? You look great, by the way."

Darcy soaked in the compliment. The dress, a black halter with cherries on it, had been a present to herself that she hadn't yet worn. "Thanks. You, too."

"Shall we?"

Darcy nodded. Emerson pulled open the door to the restaurant and motioned for Darcy to lead the way. The hostess smiled at them and greeted Emerson by name.

"Hey, Laurel. How's it going?"

"No complaints. You?"

"I am fabulous."

Laurel showed them to a table near the bar and left them with a pair of menus and a wine list. Darcy perused the selections, settling on an unoaked chardonnay before handing it Emerson. "Would you have a second glass if I ordered a bottle?" Emerson asked.

"Half glass, probably, since I'm driving."

"Close enough for me."

Emerson put in their drink order while Darcy looked at the dinner menu. "Do you share?"

"Excuse me?"

Darcy lowered her menu and made eye contact with Emerson. "I asked if you share. As in, order a few things and share them."

"Oh, um, yeah. Sure."

"First we have to see if our tastes are compatible."

Emerson shook her head, but smiled. "Why do I get the feeling this is a test?"

"That's ridiculous. I mean, if you don't like calamari, I'm leaving this restaurant right now and not looking back, but otherwise, totally ridiculous."

"Oh, well if that's all, I'm good."

Darcy laughed at Emerson's deadpan response. "That's a relief, because I've really been looking forward to dinner."

They settled on the calamari, along with a couple of other small plates and a salad. Darcy asked Emerson about her work, mostly subject matter and style. She'd taken art history classes to satisfy her fine arts requirement in school, so she knew enough to be curious. "I haven't wandered the galleries in a long time," she confessed. "I usually book it home to meet Liam when he gets off the bus."

"That's understandable. He's eight, right? That's a little young to be dragged along."

Darcy considered. "You know, I hadn't thought to bring him. He might be into it. We'll have to plan a field trip."

"Well, if I can ever play guide for you guys, you let me know."

Darcy nodded, unwilling to agree, but not wanting to dismiss Emerson out of hand. She probably didn't really mean it, and would forget anyway.

"So, did you grow up on the Cape?" Emerson asked.

"I did."

"Did you leave and come back or have you always lived here?"

"I went to college in Boston. I planned to live there, at least for a while, after I graduated."

"But?" Emerson's interest seemed genuine, not just requisite date banter.

"But I got pregnant my senior year. Logistically, it made sense to come home. After Liam was born, the idea of living in the city lost most of its appeal."

"I can imagine." Emerson nodded in that way that told Darcy she was dying to ask more questions, but wasn't sure if she should.

"Would you like the rest of the story?"

Emerson laughed. "Was I that obvious?"

"It's more that I'm used to it."

"Then, yes, but only if it's not too personal."

In Darcy's experience, "personal" was code for "unpleasant." Since it wasn't, she smiled. "Not at all. My gay best friend and I got drunk one night and decided that, if we were ever going to sleep with someone of the opposite sex, it should be with each other. Not being accustomed to the ways of the het world, it never occurred to us to use protection. Well, that and the fact we were shit-faced."

Emerson nodded. Technically, she knew some of that story from Alex, but it still struck her. "Wow."

Darcy laughed. "Yeah."

"Did you know right away that you wanted to keep the baby?" Darcy sighed and Emerson regretted not thinking about the question before she asked it. "Sorry. You don't have to answer that."

Darcy shook her head. "I don't mind. When I first found out, I totally freaked."

"Understandable. I know I would."

"Nick was completely cool. Short of offering to marry me, he supported whatever decision I made. I did a lot of soul searching, talked with my parents. They were great, especially given the fact that, with a lesbian daughter, this was the one thing they probably figured they'd never have to deal with."

Emerson thought about her own parents. She couldn't even fathom how they would have handled such news. Even as she chuckled at the thought, her chest tightened. Emerson shook it off. Since she hadn't even given thought to having kids, it was a silly thing to feel badly about. "I'm sure having that support meant a lot."

"It meant everything. I lived with them while I was pregnant, then for a whole year after Liam was born. They helped with money and taking care of him, and still play a huge role in his life."

"And Nick?" Again, Emerson realized after she'd spoken that she was asking deeply personal questions.

"We're still super close. He works in PR in Boston. Now that Liam is older and Nick is more settled down, Liam visits him one weekend a month and for a couple of weeks in the summer."

"That's really cool."

"It works. And Liam is happy and loved, which is what matters most. As much as I couldn't imagine being a mom at twenty-two, now I can't imagine life any other way."

Emerson knew a thing or two about life not turning out like you imagined. Probably not long after Darcy wrestled with the decision to become a mother, Emerson faced the reality of life without her parents. The loss made her rethink everything and ultimately change the course of her future. And as dramatic as the change had been— medical school to semi-starving artist—she couldn't imagine her life had she not made that decision. Rather than putting all that out there, she settled for, "I know what you mean. So how did you end up working for Alex?"

Darcy shrugged. "Not a lot of demand for graphic designers out here. I thought about starting my own business, but I wanted something more stable than that. I worked kitchen prep in high school, so it wasn't completely out of left field. My friend told me about the opening. The hours were perfect and Alex decided to give me a chance."

"That's quite a story."

"It's funny. I picked graphic design as a major because I liked the idea of being creative, but can't draw or paint to save my life. Cooking is different, but it satisfies that need. Between that and being a mom, I never have the chance to get bored."

Emerson appreciated the analogy. She also admired Darcy. Really, she'd admire any woman—or man, for that matter—who braved parenting primarily on their own. But Darcy was more than that. She'd built a life for herself as much as for her son. Emerson knew plenty of people with much easier circumstances who'd not managed to do that.

"What about you? How did you end up here?"

Emerson considered how much to share. "When I decided to pursue art full-time, Provincetown is the only place I seriously considered."

Darcy nodded. "It is a place like no other. Where did you grow up?"

"Maryland, just outside of D.C."

"Did you visit P-town as a kid?"

Emerson laughed. "Sadly, no. I discovered it in college. One of my girlfriends was from Boston and brought me for Memorial Day weekend. I'd never been surrounded by so many queer people. I thought I'd died and gone to heaven."

Emerson talked a little more about herself before steering the conversation back to Darcy. She asked about Liam. Apparently, he was an earnest kid, nerdy even. In a lot of ways, he sounded like Emerson as a kid. Will had been the free spirit while Emerson took everything seriously.

Darcy's eyes sparkled as she spoke about him and Emerson found herself overcome by an unfamiliar longing to meet him, to spend time with the two of them. Maybe she could make that happen. Darcy would probably appreciate not having to get a babysitter every time they went out. Assuming they went out again, which Emerson hoped they did.

As they exited the restaurant, Emerson realized that the Darcy she'd just spent the last two hours with was the Darcy she'd sensed when they first met. Maybe the borderline anal Darcy only came out in texts. Or when ironing out the specifics of plans. Whatever it was, the unease of wondering what she'd gotten herself into was gone. In its place, a salient desire for more. More time, more conversation. Then there was the physical desire. That was an entity unto itself. "Could I talk you into coffee and dessert?"

Darcy glanced at her watch. "I told Lia and Alex I'd pick Liam up in about half an hour."

"How about ice cream, then?" Relief shone on Darcy's face and Emerson wondered if she'd been expecting more pushback.

"Sold." They bought cones and meandered toward The Flour Pot. When they arrived, Darcy stopped and turned to face Emerson. "Thanks for dinner. I had a really nice time."

"Thanks for saying yes. I had a great time, too."

"I'll see you around the café?"

Although Darcy didn't say as much, she was clearly ending their date. Not wanting to jeopardize her chances of getting a second, Emerson followed her lead. "Absolutely. I didn't get any of that Buffalo mac and cheese, and I've been craving it ever since."

"I'm planning to do it on Tuesday. You're welcome to visit the kitchen again if you'd like."

The invitation eased any worry that Darcy hadn't enjoyed herself. Emerson decided not to press her luck with anything else. "I'll be there."

Emerson expected Darcy to turn and walk away, but instead she paused. "Hug?"

Emerson was tempted to laugh, but resisted. She had a feeling that the Darcy from the text messages was making an appearance. Maybe it was because they were in such close proximity to her son. That at least made sense. "Yeah."

Darcy closed the distance between them and they exchanged a hug—not a lingering one, but more than what you'd give a family member you didn't really like. Darcy's hair smelled faintly of jasmine. Emerson tried to commit the fragrance to memory, along with the feel of Darcy's body pressed against her.

"So, I'll see you Tuesday."

"Tuesday."

Darcy waved, then turned and walked down the side street that led to the back of the café and the entrance to Alex and Lia's apartment. She smiled to herself. That was fun. At the door, she rang the bell and waited. A moment later, she heard footsteps on the stairs and the door opened. Lia stood on the other side. "You're here early."

"I said nine o'clock. It's eight fifty."

"I didn't think you really meant nine o'clock." Lia's eyes darted left and right. "Where's Emerson?"

"On her way home, I imagine. We said good-bye on the street."

Lia narrowed her eyes. "You know she could have come with you, right?"

Darcy smiled. "I know. It wasn't you I was avoiding."

Lia cocked her head to one side. "Huh?"

"I like to keep Liam separate from the people I'm dating. It's neater that way."

"Ah." Lia turned and headed back up the stairs. "I guess I already think of Emerson as part of the fold."

Darcy followed. "Yeah, I felt a little awkward not having her come up with me, since she's your friend, but that's how I always do it. It seemed weird to do something different."

Liam sat at the table with Alex, a game of Sorry spread out in front of them. "Hi, Mom," he said with enthusiasm.

"Hi, honey. Did you have a good time?"

"Do we have to leave already? I'm winning."

It would be well past his bedtime by the time they got home, but they had nowhere to be in the morning. "Well, if Lia and Alex don't mind."

"I haven't given up the ship, yet," Alex said. "Lia, it's your turn."

Lia hustled back to the table and rolled the dice. The roll got one of her pieces home, but she had two barely starting out. Darcy sat in the open chair and watched as the game continued. Liam took his turn, getting his third guy home, then looked back to her. "Did you have fun on your date?" he asked.

"I did. We had dinner together, and then got ice cream."

"You had ice cream without me?" Liam's tone reflected both disbelief and disapproval.

"Hey, we had cookies." Alex gestured with both hands.

"Sorry." Liam looked at Alex sheepishly.

Alex punched him gently in the arm. "It's okay, buddy. I was only teasing. Ice cream is serious business."

"I'll make it up to you tomorrow. Promise."

"Two scoops?"

Darcy laughed. "Two scoops."

Liam won the game. Alex and Lia insisted he did so fair and square. Given how quickly his chess skills were developing, she believed them. She helped him gather up his things and they said good night to Lia and Alex.

On the drive home, Liam told her all about his evening, which in addition to Sorry, included grilled cheese sandwiches, a display of his karate moves, and a brief dance party. Darcy was going to have to tell her usual sitter, Sara, to up her game. When they pulled into the small lot of their building, Liam freed himself from his seat belt and climbed out of the car. "I think you should go on more dates," he declared.

Darcy couldn't help but chuckle. "Is that so?"

"You had fun, didn't you?"

"I did."

"Me, too. It's good for us to mix things up, Mom."

"Mix things up?"

"Yeah. You know, do something different."

"Where did you learn that phrase?"

"Sensei Le used it at karate last week. She said that having a ritual is important, but it's also important to mix things up so you don't get bored or lazy. Then we did class all out of order."

Darcy wondered why she was only hearing about this now, then remembered that their after-class conversation had been dominated by the fact that he was officially working toward his orange belt. "She is a wise woman."

"So, you'll go on more dates?"

She knew his underlying motivation was to spend more time with Alex and Lia, but Liam's words of encouragement rooted in her mind. There was no getting around the fact that she was majorly attracted to Emerson. And if she wasn't reading things wrong, the feeling was mutual. It would be good for her to get out more, especially if Liam was getting to the point where he truly liked spending time away from home, and from her. "I'll see what I can do."

"Excellent."

"Since it's already past your bedtime and tomorrow is Saturday, how about no bath tonight?"

Liam pumped his fists in the air. "Double excellent."

Darcy unlocked the door and Liam charged into the living room, running in a circle with his arms over his head. "Pajamas and teeth brushing, please."

"Yes, ma'am."

He might be a serious kid, but he was still a little boy. And Darcy wouldn't have him any other way.

CHAPTER SIX

Darcy looked up from chopping onions to find Alex standing in the doorway holding two cups of coffee. Darcy set down her knife and wiped her hands, then accepted one of the cups. "Thanks."

"How's it going?"

Darcy studied Alex over the rim of the cup. "Good." Alex lingered. She didn't say anything, but she didn't have to. Darcy knew what the question meant. That didn't mean she had to make it easy for her. "And how are you?"

Alex sipped her coffee and smiled. "Good."

"Did you need something?"

Alex tipped her head to one side. "Well, you can tell me how your date went or you can hold out for Lia. For what it's worth, I'm a lot less nosy."

Darcy laughed. "It was good. Nice. Really nice, actually."

"That's less than you said in front of Liam. You know if I convey that to Lia, she's going to give me a pitying look, then come for the rest of the story herself."

Darcy shrugged. "What do you want to know?"

"Did you like her? What did you talk about? Are you going to go out again?"

Darcy gave Alex a hard time, but she didn't mind the questions. Aside from her parents and a couple of other moms she knew, Alex and Lia were two of the people she considered herself closest to.

She appreciated that they cared enough to ask and, even more, they cared about the answer. "Yes, all sorts of things, and we'll see."

"We'll see?"

"We'll see if the feeling is mutual. We talked about Liam quite a bit. That might have scared her off. If it didn't, then maybe. Yeah. I'd go out with her again."

Alex grinned. "I don't think you have to worry about that."

"What do you mean?"

"She already texted me and said she was trying to wait at least twelve hours before she asks you out again so she doesn't seem like a stalker."

Darcy rolled her eyes. "Maybe tell her to pass me a note asking if I like her. I'll be sure to circle yes."

Alex snickered. "You know her heart is in the right place."

She did, or, at least she had a strong inclination that was the case. And even if it felt a little bit high school, there was something to be said about dating someone sort of already in her circle. Even without knowing Emerson well, the fact that she was Alex's friend made it much less likely she'd turn out to be crazy pants. "I do. It's sweet, actually."

"Should I tell her she can text you?"

"I'll do one better." Darcy pulled her phone out of her back pocket. She pulled up their previous exchange and dashed off a new message.

I hear you like me.

"What did you say?" Alex asked.

Darcy flashed her screen at Alex, causing her to chuckle. "Two can play that game, right?"

"Something like that. Let me know what she says."

"Okay, boss."

"Now, get back to work, will you?" As Alex turned to leave, Darcy launched a pot holder at her head. It caught her on the shoulder and she looked back. "I suppose I deserved that."

"You most certainly did." Despite her show of defiance, Darcy retrieved the pot holder and got back to work. The clam chowder wasn't going to make itself.

❖

Emerson woke to the ping of her phone. She blinked a few times and rolled over. It was just after nine. Who in the world was texting her at nine in the morning? She picked up her phone and read the brief message from Darcy. If she was at all annoyed with Alex for outing her, the result made up for it. She flopped onto her back and thought for a moment before typing a reply.

Maybe. Is your source reliable?

When an answer didn't come immediately, Emerson decided to haul herself out of bed. She made her way to the shower and wondered if Darcy was a morning person or if it was a requirement of her work schedule. Not that it mattered one way or the other. Some of her best friends were morning people. She didn't judge. Mostly.

She emerged from the bathroom a few minutes later wearing a clean T-shirt and boxers. She picked up her phone and found Darcy's response—assurance that she had a good source and an invitation to do dinner on Thursday. Emerson readily accepted, then sent a message to Alex.

I don't know what you said, but it worked. Thanks for sticking your nose in. (No, really.)

Deciding it might be awkward to stop by the café now, she started a pot of coffee and checked the weather, wondering how she should spend her day. While she was pouring her first cup, Emerson's phone pinged again. She picked it up, wondering if it was Alex giving her a hard time or Darcy laying out all the specifics of their second date. What she found was a message from her sister.

Wondering how you might feel about some company…

Emerson smiled. After Alex and Lia's wedding, she'd made a point of calling Will. At the time, Will sounded distracted and in a rush. They'd texted on and off since, but Emerson couldn't help but feel like something was up. She thought maybe Will was mad at her about something, although she couldn't put her finger on anything specific.

Always.

How about this weekend?

Sure it was short notice, but Emerson didn't have anything planned. Other than spending time with Darcy and fitting in enough work, she didn't even have anything on the horizon. And she missed Will. On top of that, Will coming to P-town meant she wouldn't have to see Kai, which made it even better.

Perfect. Send me your ETA and I'll be waiting.

Emerson had a moment of worry about the apparent spontaneity of the whole thing, but she brushed it aside. Will worked at a mom-and-pop hardware store. It was probably easier to get a random long weekend than plan something too far in advance. And nothing in her messages hinted that something was wrong.

She glanced around her apartment and frowned. Even if Will didn't count as real company, she should probably clean a little. And she hadn't washed the spare sheets from changing the bed last week, so that meant a trip to the laundromat. And groceries. Even by her Spartan standards, there wasn't much in the house. Looked like she had her day figured out after all.

CHAPTER SEVEN

Darcy finished applying her lipstick and glanced up to find Liam's reflection watching her. He stood in the doorway of the bathroom, studying her. She offered him a smile. "What's up, buttercup?"

"Nothing. I just wanted to tell you I think you look pretty."

Darcy narrowed her eyes. Even though Liam was a sweet kid, compliments were not his usual style. Unless he was angling for something. "Why, thank you."

"Are you going out with your friends tonight or do you have a date?"

"I have a date." Just because she went out of her way to keep her worlds from colliding, she didn't keep the fact that she dated a secret from him. Not only did she want to be honest with him, she wanted to model for him that dating—as much as settling down and getting married—could be a normal part of adult life.

"Is she pretty, too?"

Darcy smiled. He used to want to know where she was going to eat and when she'd be home. "I think she's good-looking, handsome more than pretty."

Liam scowled. "Can girls be handsome?"

"They can. And boys can be pretty."

"Hmm." He nodded slowly, acclimating to the idea.

"Just like how sometimes boys like to put on dresses and girls like to have short hair and wear jeans."

"I guess that makes sense."

"Gender is about how you feel and what you wear and what words you like to use to describe yourself."

"And gender can change."

"Exactly. Sometimes it changes from one to the other."

"Like Kyle."

One of Liam's friends had a parent who'd transitioned from Kim to Kyle the year before. "Yes, and sometimes more of a mix. Some people feel like they don't want to choose one. They like being fluid."

She watched him process this. "There's a kid in my class who paints his fingernails. Some of the other boys make fun of him."

"I hope you would never do that."

"I wouldn't. Those kids are mean, and dumb, too. I think it looks cool."

"We could paint yours too, if you wanted."

Liam's eyes lit up. "Yeah?"

"Yeah. I'm sorry I never thought to offer."

"That's okay." His shrug told her it wasn't something that had been weighing on him.

"You know who paints their nails all the time?"

"Who?"

Darcy pointed at him. "Guys who play catcher in baseball."

"You're right! Bright yellow so the pitcher can see their signals."

"Exactly." Darcy realized she should go out of her way to talk about stuff like that with him, even if he didn't initiate it. "So, you should never feel like there's something you can't do because it's something for girls."

Liam nodded, his expression serious. "Thanks, Mom."

"Is there something you're thinking about in particular?"

Liam looked down at his feet, shuffled back and forth. "Nah."

"Are you sure?" She sensed he was hiding something, but she couldn't figure out what.

He looked up and nodded. "I'm sure."

"Okay, then. I never want you to feel like there's anything you can't tell me."

"Okay, Mom."

He turned to go, but Darcy sensed there was still something on his mind. "Anything else you wanted to talk about?"

"Can I stay up until you come home tonight?" He looked at her with big brown eyes.

"It's going to be pretty late, honey. Why do you want to stay up?"

"Because I'll miss you."

Darcy studied her son. It wasn't like him to be clingy. "Would you rather I stayed home tonight?"

"No, you should go out."

The speed of his reply assuaged her concerns, but made her suspicious. "What's going on?"

Liam sighed as though admitting defeat. "There's a show on about the solar system. It starts at eight, but isn't over until ten."

A show about the solar system. Darcy resisted the urge to laugh. "I think that sounds like a pretty good reason to stay up past bedtime."

"Really?" His excitement seemed laced with incredulousness and Darcy wondered if she'd been saying no more than yes lately. She'd need to pay closer attention to that.

"Really. I'll let Sara know when she gets here."

"Yes!" Liam put his fists in the air and ran from the room. She was going to miss the days when something so small filled him with glee.

She finished getting ready, then went to the kitchen. She'd just finished putting her purse in order when Sara knocked on the door. Darcy greeted her, then watched as Sara gave Liam a high five. In addition to being a great babysitter, she played lacrosse. Although Liam had yet to express interest in the sport, he adored her so much Darcy thought he might.

"There's a pizza in the freezer and salad in the fridge," she told Sara. "Salad is required," she added, looking at Liam.

"And I get to stay up late," Liam said.

"There's something on TV about the solar system. I'm guessing PBS. I told Liam he could stay up to watch it."

"Cool." Sara punctuated the comment with another high five.

"I'll be home by ten, so you don't need to worry about bedtime routine."

"Sounds good."

"Text me if you need anything."

"We will. But we're cool, right L-man?"

Liam stood a little taller at the use of a nickname. "We're cool."

"Not too cool for a kiss, I hope." Liam made a face, but didn't hesitate to give her both a hug and a kiss. "You guys have fun. I'll see you soon."

"You have fun, Mom." He put extra emphasis on the "you," making Darcy laugh.

"Bye, Ms. Belo."

"Bye, Sara. Thanks again. Bye, L-man. You be good."

"Bye." Liam took off for the living room and the television remote. Apparently, her using the nickname wasn't nearly as cool.

Darcy made her way to her car, then to P-town. It was still early enough in the season that she found parking on a side street right off Commercial. After checking her makeup in the rearview mirror, she headed to Ciro and Sal's.

Emerson waited on the sidewalk, black pants replaced the dark jeans of their first date, paired with a striped shirt with the sleeves rolled up. Even in the subdued clothing, she managed to look like an artist. Maybe it was the hair—longer on top and just the right amount of messy—or the kind of facial features that made it difficult to pinpoint her ethnicity. Darcy smiled, thinking about Lia's initial description of her: full-on hot.

Darcy approached and Emerson greeted her with a kiss on the cheek. "Hi. You look fabulous."

Darcy smirked. "You don't have to say that every time."

"But what if it's true every time?"

"Then by all means." Darcy tipped her head toward the white gravel path. "Shall we?"

"Absolutely. I haven't been here since they opened the new wine bar upstairs. Have you?"

Darcy shook her head. "Liam is adventurous with food, but he likes his Italian pretty American."

Emerson laughed. "I'm glad we get to try it out together."

They were seated at a small table near a window. Even with the sun setting, the space offered far more natural light than the dim and cozy main dining room downstairs. They ordered wine, then Darcy encouraged Emerson to pick a variety of dishes at random. Emerson ran them past her before putting in the order and Darcy nodded her approval, enjoying that they had similar tastes and could sample more things.

The wine came, then a slow progression of antipasti, mussels, and pasta. Darcy savored each bite, thinking how unfortunate it was that she only seemed to go out for nice meals when she had a date. Not that she had any issue with her dates thus far with Emerson. She enjoyed the adult conversation, not to mention the chemistry between them. The way it simmered just below the surface felt exciting—more exciting than her last three or four dates for sure—but not in the giddy, nervous way of her youth.

Plus, there was the whole getting to know each other. In talking with Emerson, who seemed so interested in her life and her stories, Darcy realized how superficial many of her first and second date conversations were. She'd convinced herself that kind of connection was her preference, but it felt bland, boring even, compared to this. With their main courses in front of them, she said, "I feel like I've told you my story, but you haven't told me yours."

Emerson shrugged. "That's because yours is more interesting than mine."

"I doubt that's true. Do you have any siblings?"

"A sister."

Darcy smiled. "See? I'm an only child. Already more interesting. Is she older or younger?"

"Older."

"So, you're the baby. Does that mean you were spoiled?"

Emerson chuckled. "Hardly. If anything, Will was the free spirit—outgoing, popular, willing to try anything."

"Fascinating."

"I was more of a nerd, and an introvert. Very serious." Emerson's face grew serious to match her description.

"You sound like Liam."

"Based on what you've told me, I definitely think that's the case."

"And what about your parents?"

"They died in a car accident six years ago."

Darcy's hand reached across the table and took Emerson's. "I'm so sorry."

Emerson nodded. "Thanks."

"How old were you?"

"Twenty-two. Not a child by any means, but that didn't make it feel any less devastating."

Darcy's heart ached at the thought. "I'm sure. I can't imagine not having my parents around."

"They were just about to retire. They'd spent years planning and saving. They were going to see the world." Emerson shook her head. She missed them, but it was the timing that still got to her. All that working and waiting for a life they never got to enjoy. "That's what drove me to paint full-time. Live in the moment, you know?"

"It's a hard way to learn that lesson."

"Yeah. I spent about six months feeling like I needed to make them proud and another six feeling guilty about doing what I wanted."

Darcy set her elbow on the table and propped her chin on her hand. "So, what was your turning point?"

Emerson smiled, remembering the countless conversations she'd had with Will about it. Will had been so worried about her that she drove ten hours to visit her in the tiny room she was renting in the West End. "My sister, actually. She came to see me and we stayed up all night talking. I showed her some of the paintings I'd been doing, then we went for a walk on the beach as the sun came up."

"And she convinced you this is what would make you happy?"

The conversation had turned into an argument. They stood alone on the beach at Race Point, yelling at one another over the sound of the waves and gulls screeching overhead. By the end, they sat on the sand, sobbing and holding onto each other like they hadn't since they were kids. The memory remained vivid; it choked her up still. "She convinced me that being happy, and living life on my own terms, is what would make our parents proud."

"Wow."

The look of rapt attention on Darcy's face made Emerson smile. She didn't tell that story often. And while she never forgot it, she sometimes lost track of how much impact it had. It made her appreciate even more the fact that Will was coming for a visit. "Yeah."

Darcy nodded slowly. "I'm glad. It would be so hard to live your dream, but constantly second guess yourself while you did it."

"Exactly. And I owe it all to my sister." Emerson paused for a moment, then added, "She's actually coming to town in a couple of days."

Darcy sat up and smiled. "That's fun. Does she visit often?"

Emerson frowned. "Not very."

Darcy noticed the shift in Emerson's demeanor. She tried to decipher whether the seeming disappointment was tied to the visit itself or to the fact that visits were infrequent. "Do you not get along now?"

"No, we…It's more that…It's complicated."

Darcy tried to offer a reassuring smile. "Family often is. Do you want to talk about it?"

"It's not bad or anything. We've always been super close."

"But?"

Emerson smiled. "But I get the sense that something is up with her and she's not telling me. I don't know if that's true or if we've lost that ability to sense one another. I'm worried about her."

"What are you worried about?"

"She said something about needing to get away, wanting to regroup. That's so not like her."

"What do you mean?" Darcy was curious, but she also wanted Emerson to feel like she could open up.

"Will has always been indomitable. She bounces back. I'm not sure if something bad happened that she hasn't told me about or what."

Having been an only child, Darcy knew about that connection siblings often professed to have, but she'd never experienced it herself. She had it for Liam, though, so maybe it had something to do with the womb. "Are you going to ask her about it when she's here?"

Emerson nodded, as though coming to a resolution in her mind. "I am. I hope to God she's not engaged. I can't stand her girlfriend."

"Well, I hope it's not that, or anything really bad."

"Thanks."

Because Darcy felt like she had more time, she let herself be talked into dessert. Emerson offered to share, but she was feeling indulgent, so they ordered both a lemon cake and a cannoli. A full moon was just beginning to rise when Emerson walked Darcy to her car. "Thank you for dinner."

"My pleasure. I hope we can do it again soon."

Darcy smiled. "I think that could be arranged."

"Maybe you'll let me pick you up next time, take you somewhere nice."

"This was plenty nice," Darcy insisted.

"You know what I mean."

Darcy gave her a playful look. "Do I?"

"You most certainly do. Real date. A whole evening, or afternoon. You pick the day and time and I'll take care of the rest."

Emerson had a way of making Darcy feel like she was being courted. And while old-fashioned would be the last word Darcy used to describe herself, something about it made her feel fluttery. It was appealing in a way that caught her off guard. "Okay. I'll set something up with my babysitter and let you know."

"Good. I hope," Emerson gave her a suggestive look, "you won't make me wait that long for a first kiss."

"I wouldn't dream of it."

"And I hope you don't have personal objections to public displays of affection."

Darcy realized just how much she'd been looking forward to kissing Emerson. The fact that it was about to happen gave her a feeling of giddiness. "None."

"Excellent."

Emerson leaned in. Darcy closed her eyes in anticipation. She'd never admit it, but on more than one occasion, she found herself making a grocery list or thinking about a bubble bath while kissing a woman. She knew this wouldn't be that kind of kiss.

Emerson's lips brushed lightly against hers. Darcy leaned in and the kiss grew firmer. Emerson's lips covered hers in a way that both teased and promised more. When Emerson's tongue slid into her mouth, Darcy felt a jolt of electricity course through her. Emerson's hand fisted lightly in her hair.

She'd expected Emerson to be a good kisser. But even with that expectation, Darcy was caught off guard by the skill and sensuality of Emerson's mouth. She took her time, changing the angle and the intensity in a way that was hot, but unhurried. It satisfied, but left Darcy wanting.

Emerson made her stomach do flips; Emerson gave her goose bumps.

The breeze kicked up, cooling Darcy's skin as the rest of her heated, creating a delicious juxtaposition of sensations. She moaned, equal parts pleasure and frustration. The rest of her body wanted in on the action.

When Emerson broke the kiss, Darcy opened her eyes to Emerson's intense gaze. She felt both relief and regret that they weren't somewhere more private because it was the only thing that stopped her from taking things farther.

"I'll call you." Darcy's voice was breathless, giving away how much the kiss had affected her.

"I'll look forward to it."

Emerson seemed to have more control of her faculties, but the look in her eyes was hungry. It filled Darcy with a yearning to give in, to let go and see where it might take her. But they were standing in the street. And even though it was a quiet side lane with no traffic and even though they were in perhaps the most gay-friendly place in the country, she resisted. Not because she was afraid to go there with Emerson, but because she was expected at home. And if—no, when—she gave herself over, it wouldn't be for some quickie before her self-imposed curfew.

Because of that, and because she wanted to fist her hands in Emerson's shirt and pull her close, Darcy busied her hands with digging out her keys and unlocking the car. Emerson took a step back, but didn't go anywhere. She just stood there looking relaxed. Well, except her eyes. They still had a look that said she'd happily drag Darcy into the back seat of her car. Darcy wouldn't go there, but maybe one more kiss. What was the harm in that?

Darcy took the lead this time, pulling Emerson's bottom lip into her mouth, teasing it with her tongue. One of Emerson's hands returned to her hair, the other slid around her waist, pressing their bodies together. Darcy put her hands on Emerson's narrow hips. She moved back slightly, letting her back push against the side of her car. Emerson followed, giving Darcy a hint of what it would be like to have Emerson on top of her.

Maybe the backseat wasn't such a bad idea after all. Realizing how close she was to suggesting it, Darcy pulled back and shook her head, trying to clear her mind. Holy crap. "Uh, good night."

Emerson trailed a finger along Darcy's jaw to her chin, tipping it up slightly. Her eyes now had a sparkle of humor in them. No, not humor. Satisfaction. And just a hint of challenge. Darcy swallowed. Emerson leaned in and gave her a quick, almost chaste, kiss. "Night."

CHAPTER EIGHT

Emerson scooped noodles from the wok into two large bowls. She tucked a pair of chopsticks into each and brought them to the futon where Will sat waiting. She handed Will one of the bowls. "Bon appétit."

"Thanks." Will sampled her food. "Your cooking has improved."

Emerson smiled. "It's amazing what having free time can do for one's skills in the kitchen."

"Touché."

They ate in silence for a few moments. Emerson figured now was as good a time as any to broach the subject of Will's arrival. "So, is everything okay? You know I love you visiting, but this trip feels out of the blue, even for you."

Will glanced up at Emerson, then back down at her bowl. "I'm in between jobs and I wanted to get away for a while."

"Is that it?"

She continued to look down. "I got fired."

Emerson studied her sister. In a lot of ways, they couldn't be more different. Will never suffered from the ambitious, over-achiever streak that dominated the first twenty or so years of Emerson's life. She never finished college, she hopped from job to job. But even then, Will didn't typically cross the line into irresponsible. That included getting fired. "Are you going to tell me what happened?"

"I just did. I. Got. Fired."

Emerson worked to keep her patience. "You don't owe me an explanation. You never have to explain yourself to be welcome here. I'm asking because I care."

Will rubbed her eye like she might be wiping away a tear. "I know."

Emerson reached over and squeezed her arm. "Talk to me."

Will sighed, confirming there was more to the story than she'd initially disclosed. "Kai and I had been fighting a lot. I walked out on one of those fights to go to work and she followed me to the store."

"And caused a scene." She'd only met Kai a couple of times, but everything about her set off alarm bells in Emerson's brain. She was arrogant, short-tempered, and Emerson was sure she drank too much. Saying as much to Will set her off, so Emerson had let it go.

"Yeah. The first time, my boss cut me some slack."

Emerson felt her spidey sense tingle. "The first time?"

"It happened again when she came to meet me for lunch and thought I was flirting with a customer."

"Are you serious?" Emerson fought to keep her voice calm. As far as she was concerned, only two types of people behaved that way—those with the maturity of a fourteen-year-old and those who were abusive. The idea of her sister involved with someone who was either filled her with rage.

Will looked almost sheepish. "I know. Things between us had gotten pretty bad."

Emerson narrowed her eyes. "How bad?"

Will looked away. "At first we just fought. You know, the usual kind of stuff. One of us forgot to pay a bill on time or didn't stop at the grocery store."

Emerson let out a disgusted snort. Those were the things of mild irritation, not fights. Emerson wondered if the 'one of us' was always Will. "And then?"

"Then it was her accusing me of hiding things, seeing other people."

"And were you?"

"Of course not. I mean, I meet a lot of people at the store. Being friendly is part of my job."

Emerson's jaw tightened. "And she had a problem with that?"

"Only that one time. Usually, she'd freak out when one of my regulars saw me when we were out and said hi. She was convinced something more was going on."

"I'm sorry, Will, but that kind of jealous and possessive thing is bullshit."

Will looked so defeated, Emerson's heart broke. "I know. She always apologized, though, convinced me it was because I was so attractive, that she didn't think she deserved me and was convinced she was going to lose me."

Emerson didn't want to ask the question burning in her mind, but knew she needed to. "Did she ever hit you?"

Will sat for a long time before she answered, looking at her bowl. "Only once."

Emerson pushed down the bile that threatened to rise in her throat. Being outraged wouldn't help anyone at this point. If anything, it might make Will clam up entirely. "What happened?"

"She'd been drinking. We both had. I made a joke about something, I don't even remember what now. It set her off. She started yelling, then I did. She was in my face and I pushed her, not hard, but enough to make her step back. She backhanded me. It wasn't a punch; it didn't even leave a mark."

"Will." Emerson's voice was louder than she wanted it to be.

"I know, I'm making excuses. I'm sorry."

Emerson took a deep breath. She couldn't let her anger make Will think any of this was her fault. "You don't need to apologize. You didn't do anything wrong."

"I did plenty wrong, but I know what you mean."

"Is that what made you decide to leave?"

"In retrospect, I wish it had. Kai was horrified, though, and begged me to forgive her. She spent the next week showering me with gifts and attention. I told myself it was the heat of the moment, you know?"

Emerson couldn't imagine ever wanting to speak to a person again after something like that, but didn't say so. "So, what made you leave?"

Will shook her head. "The second time she caused a scene in the store, it was last week. My boss called me into his office and said he had to let me go. He couldn't tolerate that sort of thing."

Emerson was pretty sure that was illegal, but now wasn't the time to go there. "I'm sorry, Will. I bet that was really hard."

Will chuckled. "It definitely sucked. The worst part was how apologetic he was about it, like it wasn't my fault."

"It wasn't your fault."

"It was, in the fact I let her get away with it. Anyway, he seemed to feel sorry for me. That's what did it. Kind of a dumb thing to bring me to my senses, isn't it?"

As much as Emerson wanted more of the details, as much as she wanted to get Kai's number and track her down and beat the living shit out of her, that's not what Will needed. Will needed to know she'd made the right decision in the end, and that she was going to be okay. "It doesn't matter what did it, only that it did. We all have to get to those places in our own way."

Will nodded, then took a big, intentional bite of her food. "Right. And my focus now is on the future."

"That sounds like a plan, but cut yourself some slack. Give yourself time to regroup. You know you're welcome here as long as you want."

"About that."

"Yeah?" Emerson got a sinking feeling in the pit of her stomach that Will planned to take off as quickly as she'd arrived.

"I was thinking I might try to get a job in town."

As close as they were, Will had always been very adamant about living her own life—independent and apart from Emerson. "Really?"

"I might need to stay with you a little longer than we initially talked about, but I promise I won't be a total mooch."

The worry in her stomach became a hopeful swelling in her chest, laced with excitement. "I'd love for you to stay in town. You're welcome here as long as you need."

"I'll chip in for rent and stuff. I'm not completely broke."

"Don't worry about that for now."

Will nodded. "Thanks, Em."

"Of course. Thanks for telling me everything that's been going on. I'm sure it's not easy to talk about." It was hard for Emerson to admit that Will would hesitate to confide in her, that her avoidance of Kai might have made it even harder for Will to talk about it. But they were talking now and she wasn't going to let that kind of stuff come between them again.

They finished eating and Emerson washed the dishes while Will took a shower. By the time Will emerged, hair wet and wearing a tank top and boxers, Emerson had opened up the futon and was making it with her spare set of sheets. Will walked over and they finished it together. "This is perfect. Thank you for letting me crash here."

"I meant what I said. You are always welcome."

Will glanced across the room to Emerson's bed. "It kind of feels like old times."

Emerson chuckled. "Something like that. Can I get you anything?"

"I'm good."

"I don't have cable, but we could Netflix a movie if you wanted."

Will smiled. "I'd love that, but not tonight I think. I'm beat. If you want to watch something, I don't mind. I can sleep through anything."

"Don't I know it. I'll just read for a bit." Emerson started to walk toward her bed, then paused. "I'm really glad you're here."

Will, who'd started pulling back the covers to climb into bed, stopped and walked over to where Emerson stood. "Me, too."

She threw her arms around Emerson and squeezed. Emerson returned the hug and they stood like that for a long moment. As much as they'd had their differences, and as differently as they'd handled their parents' death, they were sisters. Emerson knew better than to think that the distance between them would magically disappear, but she allowed herself to be hopeful.

Will broke the hug. "Night, Em."

Emerson smiled. "Night, Will."

Will settled into the futon and Emerson switched off the main light. She climbed into her own bed and picked up her book. She barely read a page before the snores started on the other side of the room. Will had made a joke about old times, but Emerson truly couldn't begin to count the number of nights this exact scene had played out during their teenage years. Will, home late after yet another basketball game or soccer match, would tumble into bed and fall asleep almost instantly. Emerson would lie awake, studying or reading or sketching.

At the time, Emerson resented Will's athleticism, her outgoing personality, her popularity. She'd also resented Will's ease with boys, a fact that exacerbated Emerson's fumbling attempts at coming to terms with her sexuality. It wasn't until Will went away to college that Emerson learned the flirting and dating and making out had been Will's way of covering up her own attraction to girls.

Emerson had a flashback to the week before she left for college—she and Will sat their parents down and came out together. Despite the anticipation and anxiety, the whole thing had gone surprisingly well. The days that followed were some of Emerson's favorite memories, not because anything special happened, but because there were few other times she remembered feeling such a sense of family harmony.

She let the memory, and the bittersweet pang that came with it, wash over her before turning her attention to her book. She'd never been a reader of romance, but Lia had lent it to her, insisting she give it a try. Between the fact that it was set in Provincetown and it featured a doctor and a cop, Emerson relented. And she'd be damned if she wasn't completely into it. She read a few chapters, until her eyes grew heavy, then turned off the light and fell asleep to the reassuring sound of her sister sleeping nearby.

CHAPTER NINE

Darcy looked at her phone. Sara had a sore throat and a fever. She sent a text back, assuring Sara that she should stay home and get better. Darcy went to the kitchen, where Liam was having a bowl of cereal and reading a book. "Sara's sick."

Liam looked up at her and frowned. "That sucks."

"Hopefully, she'll feel better soon. But it means she isn't coming today, so you've got two options."

Liam closed his book. The seriousness with which he took decisions like this made her smile. "You can go to Nana and Pop's or you can come to work with me."

He nodded slowly, weighing his options. He loved his grandparents, but it wasn't very often that he got to go to the café. In addition to seeing Lia and Alex, he'd eat really well. "I'll go with you."

"Okay. Can you get dressed and then put together your backpack with things to do?"

"Yep." He finished his cereal, then tore off down the hall.

Normally, she'd make him come back to put his bowl in the sink, but since he was following other instructions, she didn't want to nitpick. She tidied the kitchen, then went to her room to finish getting ready for work and text Alex. Ten minutes later, Liam was back in the kitchen stuffing things into his bag. "I've got two library books, math homework, and my science project."

Darcy smiled. "Do you want the iPad?"

His eyes lit up. "Yeah! I can use it for research."

She grabbed it from the coffee table and handed it to him. "Are you ready?"

He zipped up the bag and slung it over his shoulder. "Ready."

On the drive into P-town, they reviewed the ground rules of a day at the café. Mostly, it entailed not going outside alone and not asking too many questions of Alex and Jeff while they worked. "If Lia is there, that goes for her, too."

Liam nodded. "Got it, Mom. Don't worry, I can occupy myself."

Darcy might be tempted to laugh at such an assertion, but it was true. "I know you can. And you can always come into the kitchen if you need something."

"Like mac and cheese."

"Like mac and cheese."

When they got to the café, Alex was pulling bread from the oven. "Morning, Darcy."

"Morning, Alex. I don't know if you got my message, but I've got Liam with me today. I hope that's okay."

Alex slid the pan onto the cooling rack and turned. "Of course. Morning, Liam."

Liam grinned. "Morning, Alex."

"I'm just going to set him up at a table. He'll keep himself busy."

"I have no doubt. Lia's already out there. I'm sure she'd love company at her table."

Darcy smiled, relieved. She didn't expect Alex to give her a hard time. Alex had always been flexible when it came to Liam and, in return, Darcy had done her best through the years not to take advantage. But it still amazed her that Alex never hesitated, never even implied that it was an inconvenience. Alex might not think of it as a big deal, but Darcy knew better. "You're the best."

Alex smiled. "You're the best. And I have a vested interest in keeping you happy."

"Trust me, I am." Because she was on the verge of getting sentimental, she focused her attention on Liam. "Let's go say hi to Lia."

As promised, Lia sat at one of the tables near the window, laptop open. She glanced up and smiled. "Hey, you two."

"I'm working with you today," Liam announced.

"Are you? That sounds like fun."

Darcy smiled. "Do you mind if he joins you? He has plenty to keep him occupied."

"I'd love it. Come on over, sir, and pull up a chair."

Liam raced over and took the seat opposite Lia, hefting his backpack onto the table with a thump. Darcy shook her head, amused by his enthusiasm. "I know you had cereal, but do you want anything to eat?"

"Well…" Liam lifted a shoulder and looked at her hopefully. "A muffin would be nice."

He was such a good sport about it all, Darcy didn't hesitate. "Chocolate chip?"

Liam nodded eagerly. "Yes, please."

"Lia, can I get you anything?"

Lia glanced into her coffee cup, which looked almost full. "You know, I think I'll have a muffin, too."

Jeff, who'd been helping a customer, turned his attention to them. "Two chocolate chip muffins, coming up. Milk?"

"Yes, please."

Darcy brought the muffins and a paper cup of milk over to the table. "Okay, I'll come and check on you. You know where the bathrooms are. If you need anything, I'll be in the kitchen."

"Okay," Liam said through a mouthful of muffin.

"We'll be fine," Lia said. "I love having company."

Jeff nodded. "Agreed. And if he gets too wild, we'll put him to work."

"If he gets too wild, please come and get me."

"Yes, ma'am." Jeff offered a salute.

Darcy returned to the kitchen, wondering when exactly the staff of The Flour Pot had become her extended family. It went way beyond flexibility, she realized. She could count on these people just as readily as she could her parents. In danger of getting sentimental for the second time that morning, she shook her head at herself and turned her attention to work.

Emerson walked into the café, thinking about Darcy and trying to come up with a reason to poke her head into the kitchen to say hi. Even for a Saturday, the morning crowd had mostly cleared out and she found Jeff standing next to one of the tables, talking to Lia and a kid she didn't recognize. Jeff saw her first and waved. Lia followed suit and the kid looked up at her and smiled.

"Good morning," she said to Jeff as he headed back to the register.

"Good morning. Long time no see."

"I was here two days ago."

Jeff shrugged. "Exactly. We missed you yesterday. Coffee?"

"You know it."

Jeff started her coffee and Emerson headed over to where Lia and the little boy sat. "Hey, Emerson. Have you met Liam yet?"

"I have not." Even without the name, she would have picked up on the resemblance. He had his mother's eyes. She stuck out her hand. "I'm Emerson."

He took her hand and shook it, all business. "I'm Liam. It's nice to meet you."

Knowing it was Darcy's son, Emerson would have tried to be friendly no matter what. Something about his earnest expression, though, combined with the pile of books in front of him, won her over. "What are you working on?"

The way his eyes lit up, Emerson would have thought he'd just been told he was going to Disneyland. "It's a science project for school. We had to pick a species of animal that lives on Cape Cod or in the water around it."

Lia angled her head. "I didn't know that's what you were working on."

Liam shrugged. "Mom said I wasn't supposed to disturb you."

Lia chuckled, so Emerson figured it was safe to do so as well. "So, what did you pick?"

"Snapping turtles."

Emerson guessed sharks, whales, and seals got most of the attention. She wondered why he would pick something with a rather boring reputation. "Why them?"

"Turtles are so cool. I think sea turtles are the best, but I already know a lot about them, so I picked one that's more land-based."

Emerson couldn't figure out which part of his explanation was the most charming. Probably that he picked something specifically because it wasn't the easiest, or most obvious. "Well, I don't know too much about turtles, but I did major in biology in college. I'd love to see what you have so far."

"Me, too," Lia said.

"You would?"

Jeff walked over with her coffee. Emerson set it on the table and pulled out one of the empty chairs. "Definitely. I love to learn new stuff."

Lia nodded "Agreed."

Liam launched into a laundry list of turtle facts, including habitat, diet, breeding habits, and more. She figured he must be in third or fourth grade and, based on that, he'd done an impressive amount of research. "You've done a lot of work."

He shrugged. "I want a few more things for my report, but I'm not sure what. And then I have to figure out what my display is going to be."

"Hmm." He'd covered most of the bases she could think of. "What about taxonomy?"

His eyes narrowed. "What's taxonomy?"

Emerson grinned. "Taxonomy is how we classify and organize all living things."

She enjoyed watching his eyes get big. "Really?"

"Yep. You know the scientific name of your turtle, right?"

He flipped through a notebook. "*Chelydra serpentina.*"

"Every plant, animal, and so on has a unique scientific name."

"I knew that."

Of course he did. "Well, that scientific name is made up to two parts—the genus and the species. The genus is the fact that it's a turtle, and the species is the kind."

Liam nodded. "I get it."

"But it's a reptile, too. And an animal." Emerson glanced at Lia, who had a look of amusement on her face.

"Right."

"Taxonomy is each category. There are seven of them. Each category gets smaller and smaller and the things in them have more and more things in common. Animal is at the top. It's one of the kingdoms. Then there's phylum, class, order, and family. Last are genus and species."

"Wow."

"Cool, right? So, we can look up all the classifications of your," she peered at the notebook, "*Chelydra serpentina*."

Liam frowned. "I didn't find that in any of my books. I think we'll have to look it up online."

Emerson took out her phone and pulled up a browser. "No problem."

❖

Darcy glanced at her watch, a little surprised that Liam hadn't come in to bug her about lunch yet. She decided to take advantage of a lull in the flow of orders to go out and check on him. She walked out of the kitchen and her heart stopped. Or, at least that's what it felt like. Liam was not where she'd left him—sitting at a table with Lia and working on his science project. He'd moved to a different table, spread out all his things. He also appeared to be engrossed in a conversation with Emerson.

Not wanting to come across as angry, or make Liam think he'd done something wrong, she plastered a smile on her face and walked over. "Hey, guys. What's up?"

Liam looked up at her, beaming. "Mom, this is Emerson. She's Lia and Alex's friend."

"Is that right?" Darcy shot Emerson a look and was met with a casual smile.

"Yeah, and she is so cool. Is she your friend, too?"

At least Emerson had the decency to let Darcy decide how much to share. "We are friends, but we've only known each other for a little while."

"Did you know Emerson went to medical school? She took gross anatomy and got to dissect a whole person."

Darcy returned her gaze to Emerson. "I did not know that."

"I was only there for a year. I didn't finish."

"She went to college and was a biology major, for four years. I didn't know you could pick one thing to study all the time. I want to go to college."

Darcy pinched the bridge of her nose and tried to process the plethora of information that had just been dumped on her. Combined with the shock of seeing Liam and Emerson chumming it up, she was struggling. "It's a ways off, but I'm glad to hear it."

"Emerson was telling me all about how King Phillip came over for…"

He trailed off and Emerson chimed in, "good soup."

Darcy looked at Liam with suspicion. "I thought you were working on your science project."

"I am!" His reply was equal parts excitement and exasperation.

"It's a trick for remembering the way all living things are categorized. Kingdom, phylum, class—"

"Order, family, genus, and species." Liam finished the sentence, referring to a list he'd written in his notebook.

"Ah."

"He was telling me about his report on snapping turtles and I asked if he planned to include all the classifications."

"And I wasn't going to, because I didn't even know about them, but I am now."

As was so often the case with Liam, Darcy found herself so caught up in his enthusiasm, she'd forgotten she started the conversation angry. Mostly forgotten. "That's really cool. I'm glad she gave you that idea."

"I hope that's okay," Emerson said.

"Of course. Actually, can I talk to you for a minute? In the kitchen?"

"Sure." Emerson stood. Despite Darcy's upbeat tone, Emerson got the distinct impression that it wasn't okay. What she couldn't figure out was why.

"Thanks for your help," Liam said.

"Anytime. I hope I get to see it when it's finished."

"If it's good enough, it's going to be put on display at the library."

Emerson stood. "Well, you better work hard, then."

"I will. Maybe if mine gets picked, you can come and see it."

"I would love to."

"Cool."

Emerson turned her attention to Darcy, who seemed to be glaring at her. When Emerson made eye contact, Darcy turned on her heel and stalked back to the kitchen. Emerson followed, bracing herself for whatever bee had flown into Darcy's bonnet.

In the kitchen, Alex had a large pastry bag and was frosting cupcakes. Emerson thought for a second that Darcy might ask her to leave, but instead she said, "Let's go out back."

Emerson followed her through another door and found herself behind the café. She realized it was the same door she used the few times she'd been to Alex and Lia's apartment. "Is something wrong?"

"We didn't discuss you meeting my son."

Emerson didn't appreciate the accusing tone in Darcy's voice. "It just happened. It's not like I was going behind your back."

"I didn't say you did, but it's also not something I'm blasé about."

Confused more than irritated, Emerson wanted to give her the benefit of the doubt. "What exactly are you saying?"

Darcy took a deep breath and Emerson wondered if she was going to regret asking. "I keep my son and my dating life separate."

That wasn't an unreasonable thing. Even without children of her own, Emerson could appreciate that there were some things kids didn't need to know. "I didn't tell him we're dating, if that's what you're worried about."

Darcy closed her eyes. "It's more complicated than that."

"Does he not know you're a lesbian?"

"No. I mean, no, it's not that. He knows."

"What is it, then? I'm not challenging you, I'm trying to understand."

"Liam gets attached very easily."

"Attached?" Even if she understood the general sentiment, Emerson didn't understand what it had to do with her half-hour interaction with Liam.

"Yes. He's an introvert, but he connects with people, becomes invested in them. When he really likes someone, and that someone disappears, he takes it really hard."

If Emerson thought Darcy was overreacting, she knew better than to say so. "It was a casual, chance meeting. Until you came out, he didn't even know that you and I knew each other."

"Yes, but then you said you'd go to see his project."

"I would. His project is cool. And he's so excited about it."

"I don't want to set him up for disappointment."

Emerson had a flash of planning Darcy, the Darcy of a dozen texts. "Aren't you getting a little ahead of yourself?"

Darcy rolled her eyes. "That's easy for you to say."

"What does that mean?"

"It means we've been on exactly two dates. We haven't even slept together. You saying that implies that we're going to be together, that you're sticking around."

Emerson didn't know which bothered her more—the fact that Darcy seemed convinced they wouldn't be together or the implication that, if they weren't, Emerson couldn't be bothered to do something nice for Liam. "I'm not sure all that has to be negotiated now."

"As far as Liam is concerned, it does. I refuse to let my relationship choices spill over onto him."

As much as it bristled, Emerson could see where Darcy was coming from. She could hardly begrudge her being protective. She took a deep breath. "Let me start over."

Darcy narrowed her eyes, but said slowly, "Okay."

"I came into the café today and met Liam by accident. I hope you can believe I didn't—or wouldn't—try to do that behind your back or against your wishes."

Darcy's features softened. "I do."

"That said, I'm glad I did. He reminds me of me at that age. Nerd bird, as my sister would say." When Darcy made a face, Emerson added, "That's what she called me, I mean. I loved learning, especially science. Liam seems the same."

Darcy smiled then. "Fair enough."

"I'd like to spend more time with him, completely separate from my desire to spend more time with you."

"What exactly are you saying?"

"I'm saying I want to respect your boundaries, but I don't think that means he and I should never cross paths. Can't I just be his friend and your friend, too?"

Darcy took a deep breath. She didn't have that many points of reference, but she'd never dated a woman who specifically tried to negotiate spending time with Liam. She'd certainly never dated anyone who wanted to get to know Liam in his own right. She couldn't decide what to make of it. "Are you super into kids? Is that it?"

Emerson chuckled. "I wouldn't use the term 'super.' I do like kids, though, and I don't have much opportunity to hang out with them. I'm not trying to swoop in and play family or anything. But Liam's great, and if we do things all together, I'll probably get to see more of you."

Shelly had said something similar when she and Darcy began dating. Well, minus the part about liking kids. She'd realized that offering to spend time with Liam meant spending more time with Darcy. Which went fine until she decided she didn't actually like kids at all. The breakup was abrupt and came without warning. And as hurt as she'd been by the whole thing, her disappointment had nothing on Liam's. He'd only been four, but he felt the sudden absence and was convinced he'd done something to make Shelly not like him anymore.

That had been Darcy's line in the sand. She hadn't stopped dating, but she went out of her way to keep that part of her life separate from the family side. It had been surprisingly easy. No one she dated really pressed the matter, and none of those relationships ever got serious enough for it to be an issue. Until now.

Her first instinct was to deflect. At the very least, that might put Emerson off long enough to see if it was worth the risk to go there. Darcy hesitated, though. Emerson seemed completely at ease with Liam. That wasn't the sort of thing a person could fake. Like Shelly, who always seemed a little detached. And Liam certainly seemed taken with her. Not knowing she and Emerson were dating might be enough.

"Darcy?" Emerson's voice snapped her back to the moment.

"Sorry, my mind wandered for a minute."

"Should I ask where it went?"

The playful tone cut through the fog of Darcy's worry about what ifs. It couldn't hurt, especially if she went in with her eyes open and some very clear boundaries. "Just a brief detour. To answer your question, yes, I think it would be fun to do something together."

"Good. I happen to be both a responsible adult and a science nerd. I'm right up Liam's alley."

Darcy looked Emerson up and down. She wore paint-splattered clothes and her hair stood out at odd angles. "A responsible adult, huh?"

Emerson laughed, but folded her arms. "I can tell you one thing. You don't get into medical school by being irresponsible."

Darcy angled her head. "Right. I think I need to hear more about that."

"What? You don't think I have it in me?"

"I think you've got all sorts of things in you that I'm just starting to discover."

Emerson took a step toward her. "Does that mean you want to?"

What a loaded question. Darcy didn't give herself the chance to think out her response, or the implications. "You know, I think it does."

"Glad to hear it. And you won't flip out if I check in with Liam on how his science project is going?"

"I didn't flip out."

Emerson raised a brow. "You kind of did."

"Maybe a little. Either way, I won't flip out. You're friends. I can handle that. Although I'd probably feel more comfortable if you didn't become best friends."

"I can work with that."

"Good. Now let's go back inside before Lia starts to worry we've run away."

They did and Darcy looked on as Emerson asked Liam questions, offered a couple of suggestions. They discussed the merits of pyramid diagrams versus flow charts to display taxonomy. She got lulled into their back and forth, only half paying attention to the specifics that seemed to excite them both.

"Hey, Mom?"

Now what? "Yes?"

"Is it lunch time yet?"

Darcy laughed. "It is. Mac and cheese?" He nodded excitedly. "Emerson, can I get you something?"

Emerson offered her a wink. "I'll have what he's having."

CHAPTER TEN

Darcy had to give Emerson one thing at least, she didn't waste time. She hadn't waited twenty-four hours before reaching out. Her text had come at one in the morning, inviting Darcy and Liam to the Salt Pond Nature Center that afternoon after school. Darcy broached the subject with Liam over breakfast. His response was instant and enthusiastic. And so here they were, getting ready to go out as a threesome—an idea Darcy would have shunned just a couple of weeks ago.

She'd just have to find a way to maintain boundaries and manage expectations. A tedious task, but not an impossible one. Of course, the alternative was to stop seeing Emerson romantically. Part of her anxiety came from just how much she didn't want to do that. So, boundaries would be the name of the game.

"Are you almost ready?" Liam had gone to his room after getting home.

"I'm ready." He came into the kitchen wearing his backpack.

"What's in the bag?"

"My camera, a notebook, pencils, and a draft of my science report in case I need to make any annotations."

Darcy bit her lip to keep from laughing. "Right. Sounds like you're ready, then."

They went downstairs to wait just as Emerson pulled into the parking lot. Emerson got out of her car to greet them. No paint on her clothes this time, but she was dressed more casually than she had been for their dates. Even in jeans and a T-shirt, she looked good.

"Hi." Emerson smiled at Darcy, but nothing more. She had every intention of playing by Darcy's rules. Giving in to the urge to kiss her was not going to help her cause. "Hey, Liam. It's good to see you again."

"You, too. When Mom said you invited us to go to Salt Pond, I was so excited. Wasn't I, Mom?"

Liam looked up at Darcy, who nodded. "I believe there was some jumping around."

"When I heard you said yes, I jumped around a little myself." That earned her a smile from Darcy and a giggle from Liam. "So, are we ready to go?"

"Ready."

Emerson opened the back door and Liam climbed in. She then opened the passenger door for Darcy. When everyone was buckled in, Emerson backed out of the space and made the short drive to the visitor center.

When they arrived, Emerson let Liam take the lead. Instead of running around and touching everything like so many kids would, he methodically walked them from station to station, reading each sign and description aloud. Except for a few scientific words, he read smoothly and confidently—more so than she would have expected for someone his age. Both Darcy and Emerson asked questions. Liam answered a few himself, but noted they should ask an expert while they were there.

At the display about indigenous turtles, Liam took a small notebook out of his bag and started taking notes. Emerson thought she might fall over with the sheer cuteness of it, but she did her best to remain serious. One of her more vivid childhood memories was the frustration she felt when adults dismissed her or treated her like a little kid, especially if it was a subject she knew more about than they did.

They stood there for quite a while, discussing diet and reproductive cycles, habitat and predators. Liam compared the information to his own research on snapping turtles, pointing his finger back and forth as he talked about similarities and differences between the different species. Emerson nodded, throwing in a question here and there.

She kept her primary focus on Liam, but she stole glances at Darcy, who regarded them with what appeared to be a slightly bewildered amusement. Emerson might confess later that she'd done some homework before the outing so she could seem smart and, hopefully, get herself into Liam's good graces. Now, though, it seemed to be working and that's what mattered. Liam bubbled with excitement and talked to her like they were the oldest and dearest of friends.

They finished the circuit of displays and Emerson was able to snag the attention of the center's guide. She joined the three of them and Liam displayed a level of awe little boys usually reserved for superheroes and professional athletes. Emerson learned some new things and it was clear that Liam did, too. His head bobbed up and down and he furiously scribbled in his notebook.

A group of about a dozen people walked in and the guide excused herself. Liam thanked her for her time, again overwhelming Emerson with how adorable he was. "Do you have enough to finish your project?" Darcy asked.

"More than enough. I wish I was going to summer school."

Emerson glanced at Darcy, who shook her head. "Only my son would long for summer school."

Emerson smiled. "I know the feeling. I hated summer. Not only was there no school, I was expected to play sports."

Liam lifted his hands in exasperation. "Right?"

Darcy put her hands on her hips. "Hey, sports aren't all bad."

Liam sighed. "I know. I just wish I could go to science camp instead of soccer. Or chess."

Emerson raised a brow. "You play chess?"

"I love chess. Do you?"

"I do. I'm pretty good, too."

Liam's eyes got big. "Do you want to come over and play?" He turned and looked at Darcy. "Mom, can Emerson come over?"

"She's certainly welcome, but she might have other plans."

Emerson shook her head. "No plans."

Liam pumped his fists in the air. "Yes!"

They piled into Emerson's car and headed back to Darcy and Liam's. Their apartment was small, but homey. Bold, modern art adorned the walls, and every shelf in the bookcase was crammed with a mixture of books and framed photos of Liam at every age. An old cedar chest doubled as a coffee table in front of a nicely broken in red sofa. Emerson didn't see any toys scattered about, but the stack of library books on the coffee table was definitely Liam's. She could imagine him sitting on the sofa like a little grown-up, reading about insects and the solar system.

Liam pulled out his chess set and began arranging the pieces. Emerson looked at Darcy and tried to read the expression on her face. "You okay?"

Darcy nodded. "Yes. Sorry. In a bit of a daze."

"I hope it's okay that I accepted the invitation," Emerson said quietly.

Darcy nodded again, this time with more emphasis. "Absolutely. I'm good. We're good."

"Good. Because I really do love chess." Darcy seemed to relax. Emerson decided against making a joke about this not being the way she'd expected to see the inside of Darcy's place. Emerson took a seat opposite Liam. Liam had given her white, so she made the first move. And they were off and running.

Darcy looked on with a mixture of awe and worry. Liam and Emerson hit it off like nobody's business. In addition to turtles, they talked about biology, ecology, and even a little astronomy. Liam went on and on about the documentary he'd watched on the solar system. And while many adults would have succumbed to boredom, Emerson never missed a beat. To Darcy's amusement, it didn't even look like she was trying. She seemed in her element and as engaged in the conversation as Liam did.

As the game progressed, it appeared they were evenly matched. Darcy wondered if Emerson was tailoring her skill level to Liam's. She'd have to talk to Emerson the next time they were alone to make sure she knew Liam didn't need to always win. When Liam won, Emerson asked for an opportunity to redeem herself. And before

Darcy could intervene, the pieces were arranged and a new game started.

About halfway through the second game, Darcy glanced at the clock and realized it was after six. The afternoon had flown by. "You guys seem to have this under control. I'm going to start dinner."

Liam glanced up, then turned to Emerson. "Would you like to stay for dinner?"

"I would, but we should ask your mom first. She might not have been expecting company."

They both looked at Darcy and she was struck by how much Emerson was playing the role of Liam's friend, not the woman who'd taken Darcy to dinner and kissed her senseless. It reassured her, but at the same time, made her wonder what other switches she could flip on and off at the drop of a hat. "We'd love you to stay, but only if you don't have other plans. We've already taken up most of your day."

Emerson grinned. "I'm having so much fun. I'd love to stay for dinner. Can I help?"

"You guys keep playing. I'm going to make burgers. Is that okay?"

Emerson said, "Sounds great," just as Liam said, "Yum."

Darcy got to work making kale chips—the sure-fire way to get Liam to eat leafy greens—and cheeseburgers. She puttered around the kitchen, stealing glances at Liam and Emerson, who went right back to their game. She couldn't help but think of Shelly and the times the three of them spent together in this very same way. No, not quite the same. Shelly would have been at the table with Liam. But while he colored or drew, she'd be on her computer, answering email or surfing the web.

It probably wasn't fair to compare the two. Liam had only been four at the time and not nearly as able to maintain a prolonged conversation. It hadn't stopped Liam from worshiping her. And although Darcy thought they'd gotten along well at the time, it had never been like this. Watching the two of them convinced her that Emerson would happily be friends with Liam whether they were dating or not.

When Darcy announced dinner would be ready in five minutes, Emerson helped Liam clean up and set the table. Darcy pulled out rolls and condiments and piled everything on the table, along with a plate full of burgers and a bowl of kale chips.

Darcy watched Liam watch Emerson make her burger. Although he was a ketchup purist, he followed Emerson's lead in adding a squirt of mustard to his bun. Darcy didn't comment on the departure from his usual routine. They ate quietly at first, the kind of comfortable silence that comes from spending the day with people and then settling into a meal.

Emerson studied a piece of kale before putting it in her mouth. "Why have I never eaten kale chips?"

Liam helped himself to another serving from the bowl. "They're so good, right?"

Emerson grinned. "So good. And I never eat enough vegetables."

Darcy wasn't surprised. "Salt, pepper, olive oil. That's it. Bake them for about twenty minutes."

Liam crunched another one. "Sometimes, after Mom cuts it up, I mix everything together."

"Yeah? Do you like to cook?"

Liam shrugged. "It's okay. I like baking more. Like Alex."

Darcy laughed. "That's only because you like eating dessert more than dinner."

Emerson leaned over so she could elbow Liam lightly. "It's hard to find fault with that logic. So, do you have much left to do on your science project?"

"I still need a visual." He told her about wanting to do something cooler than a poster for his display, and not being allowed to bring in a live turtle.

To Darcy's relief, Emerson nodded her agreement. "That's probably for the best. What about a painting?"

"A painting?"

Emerson glanced at Darcy, her eyes offering an unspoken question. Darcy shrugged. Emerson smiled. "Yeah. I paint pictures. That's my job, so I'm pretty good at it. If that's what you wanted to do, I could help you."

Darcy watched him mull over this option. "Could it be a big painting?"

"Depends on what you mean by big." He stretched out his arms and Emerson nodded. "Definitely."

Liam turned his attention to Darcy. "Mom, how cool would that be?"

"That's a very generous offer. Emerson, are you sure you have the time to do that?"

"Sure. When's it due?"

"In two weeks," Liam replied.

"Definitely. We could do it Saturday if your mom is okay with it."

"Can we, Mom?"

Darcy nodded. "Let us know what supplies to get."

Emerson grinned. "I've got everything we need."

"You don't have to share your supplies on top of your time."

"I really have everything, though. And I don't mind. We're going to have a blast."

Liam lifted both hands in the air and offered his signature, "Yes!"

So much for boundaries. Darcy might not be crazy about the idea, but she thought back to the drawing Liam did for his science homework not that long ago. If he had a penchant for art, she wanted to encourage it. Besides, her other option would probably be helping him construct some massively messy diorama. Maybe this would turn out well for everyone. "Thank you. I—we—appreciate it."

Emerson waved a hand. "It's my pleasure."

When they'd finished eating, Emerson insisted on helping Liam with the dishes. Emerson got ready to go and, without being prompted, Liam thanked her for spending the day with them. Darcy echoed the sentiment.

Emerson walked to the door. "Thanks for dinner. And for showing me a tolerable way to eat kale."

Liam giggled. Darcy chuckled, then said, "You're welcome."

Emerson left and Darcy nudged Liam toward the bathroom for a shower. She let him pick out a movie and they curled up on the sofa together. Since it was one she'd already seen four times, she picked up her phone. She spent a few minutes looking at email and Facebook, then gave into the urge to text Emerson.

You were great with Liam today. Thank you.

A moment later, her phone pinged. *I meant what I said. I had a great time. Confession: I love science projects.*

The fact that Darcy believed her made it even funnier. *Your secret is safe with me.*

Thank you for blurring your lines for me.

Blurring the lines. That was one way of putting it. Emerson was probably teasing her, but at least she got it. On top of that, Emerson seemed to take her role as Liam's friend—and hers—to heart. It didn't feel like she was just playing along. *If you're not careful, Liam will decide you're best friends. You don't want the first time you stay over to be in a sleeping bag on his floor.*

I wouldn't mind the sleeping bag or the floor, but it would be hard with you right next door.

And just like that, they switched from talking about Liam to flirtation. Fortunately, the movie ended and Liam decided to read in bed. Darcy took her phone into her room and settled under the covers. Emerson made it all seem so easy. Darcy shook her head. She needed to keep her guard up because, if she'd learned anything, easy usually led to trouble.

Chapter Eleven

The week flew by. Emerson had a meeting with the owner of the gallery where her show was going to be and two commissions to finish. She put in late hours, which made for late mornings. On Wednesday, she managed to stop by the café, but Jeff was out sick and Darcy had been too busy for more than a passing conversation. It had been a delightfully flirtatious conversation, but still. At least she had plans to get together with Liam to do his painting.

When her alarm went off at eight, Emerson rolled over and groaned. Knowing she had to get up so early, she should have gone to bed earlier. But she didn't. She'd been working and, as it so often did, time got away from her and the next thing she knew, it was two in the morning. Will had been sound asleep for hours—neither the light nor Emerson's movement around the apartment had stirred her.

A glance at the futon revealed Will was not only up, but long gone. Emerson thought she'd heard the door close, but she didn't know what time. And even though she'd insisted Will didn't need to clear out, Will was adamant she had things to do with her day. Apparently, for morning people, things to do started before eight a.m.

Emerson stumbled out of bed and started a pot of coffee before getting in the shower. Between setting the water temperature to cold and downing her first cup, she felt semi-human. She poured a second and got to work preparing for her day with Liam.

Emerson set up the second easel next to hers. She placed matching pads of watercolor paper on them, then checked that paints and brushes were ready to go. Her plan was to paint one step ahead of him so he could watch and then mimic the way she layered the colors and textures. If it went well, he could use the painting in the final presentation for his science project. If it didn't, hopefully they'd have fun in the meantime. She'd never attempted to teach anyone painting before, but that was okay. She hoped.

When Darcy and Liam arrived, Emerson tried to hide the fact that she'd gotten herself nervous with anticipation. Darcy was already dressed for work. Liam wore shorts and a tank top, a testament to how warm the last few days had been. She ushered them in, enjoying Liam's fascination with the fact that everything—work space, kitchen, living room, bedroom—was in one big room.

"The bathroom is separate," she assured him.

"Oh." He seemed genuinely disappointed, a fact that made Emerson smile.

"Are you sure you can handle this?" Darcy asked for probably the tenth time since agreeing to it a few days ago.

"We're fine. Right, Liam?"

"Uh huh." He'd gone over to look at the setup and his distracted reply seemed to reassure Darcy.

"We're coming to the café for lunch. We'll only be by ourselves for like three hours. Maybe four."

"That's longer that you might think."

"Are you worried that I can't handle him, or that he can't handle me?"

"Both." Darcy rolled her eyes. "Neither. I know you'll be fine."

"We have a project to keep us busy and a built-in expectation of a mess."

Darcy smiled. "When you put it that way."

"Exactly. Now go to work so there are delicious things for us to eat when we come down."

"You're right." She took a deep breath and squared her shoulders. "Liam, I'll see you guys soon. Listen to Emerson, okay?"

"Okay, Mom."

Darcy smiled again, but didn't initiate any physical contact with Emerson before turning to leave. That was okay. They weren't there yet. Emerson returned the smile and tried to convey reassurance. "We'll call if we need anything. And if you need anything, you can call us, too."

That seemed to break any remaining tension. Darcy laughed. "I'll be fine. Bye, you two."

Darcy left and Emerson turned her attention to Liam, who'd given in to the desire to touch things and picked up a couple of brushes. "You ready to paint?"

He nodded with enthusiasm.

"Do you need something to drink first? Or to eat?" Not that she had any breakfast food, but she could improvise if she needed to.

"No, I'm good."

"Let's get started, then."

She figured he wore clothes he could get paint on, but she had him wear one of her T-shirts anyway. It hung down to his knees, but he didn't seem to mind. She explained blocking off the paper with a pencil, then drew a series of faint matching lines on each. She drew the same lines on the image she'd printed out to use as a guide. "Then you can sketch your primary shapes and make sure the proportions are right."

"Cool."

"We'll use a light color as the background so we don't lose our lines." She dipped her brush in water, then mixed brown and yellow together to make a sandy color, then handed him a brush. "The big thing to remember with paint is that less is more."

He nodded. "Okay."

She dipped her brush into the paint, then dabbed the excess off. Liam followed suit. "Big strokes back and forth. Like this." She demonstrated and he mimicked her movements.

"Uh-oh." His motion was good, but he had a sizable dribble left where he'd started.

"It's all good. The cool thing about painting with watercolor is that, even if you mess up, you can fix it." She flicked her brush a few times across his paper until the color was smoothed out and it looked like hers. "See?"

Liam nodded slowly. "Uh-huh."

"The other big thing to remember is that we do everything in layers. We start with our outline, then keep adding details, one on top of the other." He looked at her intensely, like he understood what she was saying, but didn't quite get how it worked. "Just trust me."

"Okay."

He proved himself an eager student and a quick study. She tried to break everything down into basic steps, modeling each stroke for him so he could replicate it. His hands weren't as steady as hers, but he had a feel for it. Once they got the shape of the turtle down, she instructed him to fill it in with a medium green they'd use as the base. She focused on her own piece for a few minutes before looking over to check his progress. When she did, she couldn't help but smile at the look of fierce determination on Liam's face. He dabbed at the paint on their shared palette, then the paper. "Hey, that's really good."

He beamed at her. "Thanks."

They worked for about an hour, making slow but steady progress. Liam seemed to be getting a little impatient and Emerson felt the same. It wasn't time for lunch yet, but she figured they could both use a stretch. And maybe a snack. "How about we take a break?"

Liam looked relieved. "Sure."

Emerson grabbed two bananas and handed him one. "Now we get to sit and watch the paint dry." That earned her a laugh.

"Liam is spending the morning with Emerson. They're painting a picture of a turtle for his science project."

Alex chuckled. "That sounds like fun."

"That's what I keep telling myself."

"Emerson is great. I'm sure Liam will have a good time."

"Yeah, that's sort of what I'm worried about."

Alex turned from the oven, tray of loaf pans in hand, and gave her a quizzical look. "What does that mean?"

Darcy sighed. "It means I think he's getting attached to her."

"And that's bad?"

"It is if she gets bored with him, or if she and I stop seeing each other, and he ends up disappointed."

"Even if you guys don't end up together, I don't see Emerson as the disappearing type. She's not that callous."

"She pretty much said the same thing."

Alex slid the tray onto a rack to cool. "See?"

Darcy set down her knife. How could she explain in a way that didn't make her seem over-protective? "But it's one thing to say and another to do."

"I get that."

"Especially for someone who's all about living in the moment." Darcy thought about Emerson saying as much—right after telling her she'd lost her parents.

Alex folded her arms. "Yeah, but for her I don't think that means always running off to the next new exciting thing."

"I know. She seems to genuinely like Liam, spending time with him. And I think Liam has some potential as an artist. If Emerson can help him tap into that, it would be awesome. It doesn't mean I can't freak out a little."

Alex crossed the room and slung an arm around Darcy's shoulder. "You're a great mom. And being a great mom doesn't mean you keep your child in a bubble. No matter what happens, this is good for him. You, too."

"Thanks. I hope you're right."

"I have a good feeling about this." Alex picked up a tray of rolls. "I'm going to go cover the front. Holler if you need me."

Darcy nodded, feeling better. "I will. Thanks, Alex."

Alex gave her a squeeze before letting go. "Anytime."

Darcy returned her attention to chicken chili, then mac and cheese with ham. Time dragged by. When she checked the wall clock for the tenth time in as many minutes, she berated herself for being uptight. She followed that up with a pep talk and the decision to keep herself extra busy with making some homemade stock for the freezer.

The additional work did the trick. When Alex stuck her head in to say Emerson and Liam had arrived, she realized with surprise it was after noon. She poured the stock into a shallow pan to cool before heading out to the dining room to see how the morning had gone. She found them already at a table with matching bowls of chili and hunks of cornbread. "Hey, guys. How was painting?"

Emerson offered a "hi" and Liam launched into a blow-by-blow of their morning. He even threw out a few technical terms she didn't know, which she took as a good sign. "I'm impressed you got all that done. And you don't even look dirty."

"Oh, Emerson lent me a shirt."

Darcy turned to Emerson. "You didn't have to do that."

"It's okay. I have plenty. And that way we didn't have to worry about getting messy."

"And I take it you got messy."

Emerson smiled. "We used watercolor, so it cleaned up easy enough."

"So, when do I get to see the finished product?"

"We aren't done yet." Liam looked at her like that was the most obvious thing in the world. "It has to dry before we can do the finishing touches."

"If you don't mind, we'll go back to my place after lunch."

Darcy frowned. "I don't mind, but I don't want to take up your whole day."

"It's fun. We're each doing one. I've never done marine life before."

Darcy had an image of the two of them standing side by side, each wielding a paintbrush. It gave her a flutter in her stomach that felt like anxiety and excitement at the same time. She tamped it down and focused on the matter at hand. "How long do you think you'll need?"

"Probably an hour or two. Do you want to come to my place when you're done with work?"

"That would be great."

Liam grinned. "And we'll see if you can figure out who did which one."

Even if Liam proved to be a painting prodigy, she didn't think that would be difficult, but she appreciated his confidence. "I'll see you guys around three." Darcy turned to leave, but stopped and looked squarely at Liam. "How come you're not eating mac and cheese?"

Liam shrugged. "Emerson said the chili sounded good. I thought so, too."

"It's more than good," Emerson added.

"Thanks. Okay. I'll see you later. Good luck." Darcy went back to the kitchen, mulling over Liam's comment. He was an adventurous eater, but he never—never—turned down mac and cheese. Maybe he was beginning to outgrow that tendency, which would be good. Or he was straying into Emerson worship. Darcy shook her head. Since there wasn't anything she could do about it now, she turned her attention back to her work.

With two staff members filling lunch orders, that meant planning her menu for the week after next and making her order list. She finished that and still had time to organize the tiny supply closet before her shift ended. She left instructions for the afternoon staff, did a final check of the soup station, then clocked out.

She left the café via the front entrance, turning left to walk back down to the East End. Now that Memorial Day had come and gone, the crowds were picking up. Between that and the sunshine, it felt like summer was upon them. She got to Emerson's building and climbed the narrow staircase to her studio. She hesitated for a moment before deciding to knock. Even though she was expected, she wasn't ready for the intimacy implied by simply walking in.

"Come in." Emerson's muffled voice came through the door. Darcy did, expecting to find her and Liam up to their elbows in paint. Instead, she found Emerson, Liam, and someone she assumed was Emerson's sister sitting in a circle on the floor with cards in their hands and spread out in front of them.

"Hi, Mom."

"Hi." Darcy smiled, realizing there were also several piles of jelly beans on the floor. "What's going on here?"

Liam beamed at her. "I'm learning how to play poker."

Darcy arched a brow. "Are you?"

Emerson looked at her sheepishly. "We finished our paintings and Will came home, so we decided to play a game."

"And Go Fish is so boring," Liam said so matter-of-factly she had to smile.

"I see."

Emerson stood. "I hope you don't mind. We aren't playing for money or anything."

So, that's what the jelly beans were for. "Not at all. I was the queen of nickel poker in college."

Liam's eyes lit up. "Do you want to play with us?"

Darcy glanced at Emerson, who quirked a brow. "Pull up a patch of rug and we'll deal you in."

Emerson returned to her spot and Will and Liam scooted back to accommodate another person in their circle. Darcy took a moment to study Emerson's sister. They looked nothing alike. While Emerson's features were darker and hinted at her Asian roots, Will had a mess of light brown curls and blue eyes—the kind of blue you noticed from across the room. "Hi, Will. I'm Darcy."

"Sorry." Emerson shook her head. "Will, this is Darcy. Darcy, Will."

If Emerson's vibe was edgy, Will's was soft and smooth. Even in faded jeans and a T-shirt, she looked sweet, wholesome even. Darcy sat next to her and stuck out her hand. "It's really nice to meet you."

"Likewise." Will took her hand and smiled. It was one hell of a smile. "I've heard a lot about you."

Darcy raised a brow at Emerson. "That sounds dangerous."

"All good, I promise," Will said.

Emerson nodded. "Yeah. All good."

Emerson dumped a handful of jelly beans in front of her. Meanwhile, Liam pointed to a bowl. "Those are for eating."

"Got it."

They finished the hand in progress, then Darcy anted up two jelly beans to join in. "What are we playing?"

"Texas Hold'em," Will said.

"Excellent." It only took a couple of hands to see how quickly Liam had picked up the rules. His poker face, on the other hand, needed work. Still, it was exciting to see his enthusiasm and Emerson and Will were exceedingly patient with him. No one seemed in any hurry to do anything else, but Darcy remained cognizant of the time and the fact that Emerson had essentially given up her entire day to entertain her son. After Will took a pot with a full house, Darcy decided to move them along. "So, when do I get to see these paintings?"

"How could I forget?" Liam waved his arms in the air. "They came out so good."

Liam jumped up and everyone followed suit, walking over to where the easels stood. Emerson flipped on a light and Darcy felt a lump rise in her throat. The precision and sophistication of Emerson's work made it immediately clear which one was hers, but the one beside it was beautiful in its own right. She'd never have thought Liam—with his virtually non-existent experience or training—capable of producing something at that level. "Wow."

"Do you like it, Mom? Emerson showed me what to do and helped me, but I did most of it myself."

"It's really, really good. I'm so proud of you." Darcy glanced over at Emerson and found Emerson's eyes on her. "Thank you."

Emerson smiled. "He's right. I only helped a little. He's got quite the natural talent."

"Do you think I'll get picked for the library?"

Darcy put her arm around his shoulder and gave it a squeeze. "I don't know. But I know you have a project you can be proud of. That's what matters most."

"It needs a couple more hours to completely dry," Emerson said. "I can bring it by your place tomorrow if that works for you."

"I don't want to put you out."

"Will you stop with that? I wouldn't offer if I didn't want to."

Darcy nodded. "Right. Sorry. That would be great." Darcy tucked her hair behind her ear. "But for now, we're going to clear out so Emerson and Will can get on with their evening."

4

Will laughed. "You say that like we have plans."

"Right?" Emerson shrugged. "We won't keep you, but trust me when I say you aren't interfering with anything."

Darcy smiled at that. She assumed people her age without kids still had wild Saturday night plans. Whether she was genuinely wrong or Emerson and Will were trying to make her feel better, she didn't know. Either way, it was nice to be told she wasn't dragging them down. "Ready, Liam?"

"Yep."

"Have you thanked Emerson for spending the day with you? And for helping you make such an awesome painting?"

"He absolutely—"

Emerson didn't get the chance to finish her sentence before Liam launched himself into her arms. "Thank you, thank you, thank you."

Emerson squeezed him back. "You can be my painting buddy anytime."

Darcy cleared her throat to mask the emotion in her voice. "Be careful. He might try to hold you to that."

Emerson looked directly at Darcy. "I meant it."

Darcy nodded. "All right. One thing at a time. Thank you for everything. We'll see you tomorrow."

"Sounds good."

"We'll be home all day. You're welcome anytime. Just text me."

"Will do." Emerson looked on as Darcy ushered Liam to the door. When they'd gone, she turned to find Will staring at her. "What?"

"You're falling for them."

Emerson scowled. "What are you talking about?"

"Liam and Darcy. You're falling for them."

Emerson shook her head. She wasn't against the idea, but they were light years away from that territory. Light years. "Liam's a hoot. He's so much like I was at that age. It's fun to watch. Darcy and I haven't even slept together."

Will shook her head. "If you say so."

"I like them." Emerson was more emphatic this time. "I like new people—spending time with them, getting to know them. It's how I live my life. It doesn't mean I'm falling for them."

"Okay. Don't get your boxers in a bunch. I didn't mean to start something."

Emerson scowled. "My boxers aren't in a bunch."

Will put both hands in the air. "I stand corrected. Let's change the subject. What's for dinner?"

"You tell me. It's your turn to cook."

Will shrugged. "Sounds like pizza, then. Unless you're in the mood for Chinese."

Emerson made a face. If she could find one fault with P-town, it might be the utter lack of legit Chinese food. "Pizza it is."

Chapter Twelve

Emerson sat with Will on the sofa, half-watching a movie. When her screen lit up, Emerson looked down at her phone and smiled.

"You're doing it again."

She looked over at Will. "What?"

"Smiling at your crotch."

Emerson rolled her eyes. "You're a jerk."

"You're the one with the goofy look on your face. I can't help it if you look like an idiot."

In high school, Will had teased her mercilessly over her unattainable crushes. She'd hated it at the time. Now, with the prospect of seeing Darcy—just Darcy—taking shape, she didn't even care. "You're just jealous."

Will poked her. "Maybe. I think it comes with my recent history of crash-and-burn in the relationship department."

Emerson set down her phone. "I'm sorry, Will. I didn't mean to—"

"Stop. I'm kidding. I'm embracing my celibacy for a little while. It's good for me. Like a cleanse."

"Still. I didn't mean to rub salt in it."

"You didn't. Promise. I'm enjoying the distraction of giving you a hard time."

"It's always been one of your favorite pastimes."

"So, what's up?"

"Darcy asked if I wanted to get together this weekend." She'd dropped off Liam's painting a couple of days before, but they hadn't discussed getting together again, with or without Liam.

"Kid time or grownup time?"

"Grownup time, I think." Emerson picked up her phone and typed a response.

What did you have in mind?

Will pretended to peek at her screen. "Are you finally going to get laid?"

"God, you have a one-track mind."

Will shrugged. "Maybe, but at least it's on my mind. Have you even kissed?"

Emerson glowered. "Yes, we've kissed." A mind-blowing, earth-quaking, still on her mind kiss. "She has a kid. That complicates things."

"I'm not judging. I just thought maybe you'd decided to stick with play dates instead of," she looked at Emerson suggestively, "play dates."

Emerson's screen flashed and she glanced down at it.

Drinks, dinner, walk on the beach, dessert...

She might be giving Will a hard time, but there was some truth in her words. Her last three interactions with Darcy had been dominated by Liam. Not that she minded. But she didn't want the prospect of dating Darcy to get lost in the shuffle. "I think we might be planning the latter."

"Totally kid free?"

Emerson nodded. "One thing I learned quickly is that Darcy doesn't mix her romantic life and her son. So, if she's asking me on a date, it's a date date."

"Fascinating. Does it feel like you're spending time with two completely different people?"

Did it? No. "It's more like what I imagine inter-office dating to be like. When you're at work, no funny business. Not even flirting."

"Huh."

"And she's much more laid back when Liam's not there. That's not surprising, I guess, but it's maybe more extreme than I thought."

"How so?"

"She's not just laid back. She's flirtatious, brazen. I think I find it weird that she turns it on and off."

Will tipped her head to the side and looked at the ceiling. "I wonder if that's a parent thing."

"I don't remember Mom and Dad being like that. Do you?"

"No, but they were married. It was expected that they'd be affectionate with one another. But I have no memories of them getting frisky in front of us. Not even a PG version."

"I guess you're right." Emerson didn't make a habit about thinking about her parents as a romantic, sexual couple. Not that she thought parents shouldn't have that, she'd just never thought about it. And since she'd never dated a parent before, she'd not thought about it on that level either.

"Well, I'm glad one of us is getting lucky."

Emerson studied her. "Are you getting restless already?"

Will lifted a shoulder. "Not really. I have moments of missing a warm body next to me, but I know that's not what I need right now."

"Good." Emerson nodded. She didn't want to tell Will what to do, but she'd been thinking the same thing. It was a relief to know Will was on the same page.

"Are you really going to have sex?"

"I'm trying not to think about it or plan it too much."

"But…"

"But I hope so. Jeez, do we have to talk about this?"

Will lifted both her hands. "Nope."

"Okay, good."

Will rested her hands in her lap and started to twiddle her thumbs.

"What?"

"This is me not talking about whether or not you're going to have sex this weekend."

"Cut it out." Emerson leaned over and shoved her.

"You just let me know if you need me to clear out for the night."

Emerson couldn't help but snicker. They'd never lived together after moving out of the room they shared for most of their childhood.

The thought of negotiating this aspect of being roommates was beyond weird. "I won't do that, but thanks for offering."

Will shrugged. "Just saying. I support you getting some."

"And now we're officially done talking about this. I'm going to read before bed." Emerson stood and pointed to her bed on the other side of the room. "I'll be over there."

"Hey, Em?"

Emerson turned back. "Yeah?"

"When you go on your date, might I suggest not smiling at your crotch? It tends to freak girls out."

Emerson responded by throwing a pillow at Will's head. But then she laughed and walked back across the room to retrieve it, since it was her favorite pillow. "Good night, Will."

"Good night, Casanova."

Emerson climbed into her bed and opened her book. She read a page, then realized she had no idea what she'd just read. Whether it was the text exchange with Darcy or the conversation with Will, her mind was now fully consumed. She didn't want to assume or think too much about the prospect of having sex. It felt like those awkward pseudo relationships in college when she had no idea what she was doing, but thought about sex far too much of the time. She laughed at herself, then flipped the page back to start over. Her date with Darcy was still four days away. If she spent that entire time anticipating what might or might not happen, she'd drive herself absolutely nuts.

Darcy slid the pan of macaroni and cheese into the oven. She set the timer and wiped her hands on a towel just as Alex popped her head into the kitchen. "You have a visitor."

She disappeared without giving Darcy the chance to ask her who it was. Not that she needed to. Emerson was the only person who came to see her at work. Darcy stripped off her gloves and washed her hands, pausing in front of the oven to check her reflection. It might not be her best look, but at least she could make sure her hair was tucked up neatly and she didn't have flour smeared across her face.

When she stepped out to the register area, she saw Emerson and Will chatting with Lia. She skirted around the counter and walked over to join them. "I'm glad you're here so I can tell you in person. Liam's painting got picked for display at the library."

Emerson beamed. "That's awesome. Tell him I said congrats."

"He's over the moon, and gives you all the credit."

Emerson stuck her hands in her pockets. "He did the work. I just coached him."

"He wants me to invite you to the opening night. You don't have to say yes, but I promised I'd invite you."

"That's adorable," Will said.

Lia nodded. "Completely adorable."

"I'll be there," Emerson said.

Darcy had expected Emerson to say nice things, but the level of her enthusiasm surprised her. "They're doing a little reception. It should be cute."

"Wouldn't miss it. Let me know the details."

"I'll text you. He'll be so excited."

Alex, who'd been at the register, walked over to join them. "What are we talking about?"

Lia slid her arm around Alex's waist. "Liam's painting. It's going to be displayed at the library."

"That's so cool," Alex said.

"What are you two up to today?" Lia asked.

"Delivering a painting to Hyannis," Emerson said.

"And I'm going along for the ride."

Darcy smiled. "Sounds like fun."

"We just wanted to stop in and say hi."

"And get coffee." Will took a sip from her cup. "It's really good coffee."

"Agreed."

"Thanks," Alex said. "We do our best."

Emerson turned to Darcy. "I'll see you Friday night, right?"

Since there were three extra pairs of eyes on her, Darcy swallowed the suggestive reply on the tip of her tongue. "Yep."

Coffees and pastries in hand, Emerson and Will left. There was a brief lull in the flow of customers in and out of the café, so Darcy and Alex lingered at the table with Lia. Darcy thought of Emerson's worry about her sister. Will looked to be doing okay, which was good.

"So, are you two a thing?" Lia asked.

Darcy pulled her attention back to the moment. "A thing? I'm not sure we're at that level yet."

"Do you want to be?"

"I guess it depends on your definition of thing."

Alex folded her arms. "What's yours?"

For all that she'd thought about it, Darcy didn't have a clear answer to that question. "I like her a lot. And she's really good with Liam."

Lia lifted a brow. "But?"

Darcy sighed. "But those two things are very separate for me."

"What does that mean for you?" Lia asked.

"I don't want the lines to blur. Dating Emerson is one thing. Emerson being friends with Liam is another."

Alex nodded slowly. "Right. Are those things in conflict?"

Darcy shook her head. "No, but if you add them together, it looks a lot like playing family."

"Oh." Lia and Alex said in unison.

"It's not bad, but I'm not sure if I'm doing a good job with the boundaries. Liam doesn't know that Emerson and I are seeing each other."

"Oh." Again, Lia and Alex answered together. This time, the "oh" elongated. Not helpful, but at least they got it.

"Exactly. I'm not sure if I should tell Liam. He's not still scarred about Shelly or anything, but I don't want to go down that road if I don't have to."

"That makes sense." Alex glanced at the door as a customer walked in. "Sorry, I need to take care of that."

She moved away and Darcy knew she needed to get back to the kitchen. Before she did, she leaned down slightly and whispered to Lia, "We haven't even slept together yet."

Lia smiled. "Do you want to?"

"Oh, yeah." That was one thing she was absolutely sure of.

"Are you going to?"

She hadn't told Emerson about arranging for Liam to spend the night at his grandparents, but she had no uncertainty about her motivation. "That's my plan."

Lia grinned. "Excellent. You deserve it. And even if you aren't looking to play family, Emerson is great. And hot."

That pretty much summed it up. "You're right. And thanks."

"Don't forget you have a pair of babysitters who don't mind sleepovers."

"Thanks for that, too. Are you…" Darcy paused, searching for the right word. "Practicing?"

Lia blushed. "Not officially."

"But…"

"But we're talking about it."

"'Might be nice one day' talking about it or 'where are we going to get the sperm' talking about it?"

"Somewhere in the middle, I think."

Darcy nodded. "Nice. Well, I'm here for you—friendly ear, advice, doctor's appointments, whatever."

"Thanks."

Lia seemed alarmed by the mention of doctor's appointments, so Darcy took that as her cue to leave. "I'm going to get back to work."

"Okay. Good luck."

Darcy smiled at her. "You, too."

CHAPTER THIRTEEN

It might be cliché to enjoy walks on the beach, but Emerson didn't mind. She believed firmly in the magical and romantic powers of the ocean. With a brilliant orange and purple sunset and virtually no one else around, she figured few things could rival it.

"Do we have a curfew tonight?"

Darcy offered her a slow smile. "Nope."

Emerson raised a brow. "None at all?"

"Liam is spending the night with his grandparents."

Emerson didn't want to assume that meant what she wanted it to mean, but she couldn't stop her mind from going there. She cleared her throat. "I see."

"He does sleepovers once a month or so. My parents would have him once a week if I'd agree to it."

"He seems to have that effect on people."

Darcy smiled. "That's a sweet thing to say."

"It's entirely true. I'm sure he has bad days, but he's a riot."

"That's one way of putting it. So, yes, I'm officially free for the next twelve hours."

Something in Darcy's inflection made it clear that what Emerson had hoped a moment ago was, in fact, the case. Her mind instantly produced an image of Darcy naked in her bed, her creamy skin against the dark sheets. Remembering that Will was and would be at her apartment hit Emerson like a bucket of cold water. And even though Will had offered—either as a joke or in earnest—to clear out, Emerson would never ask her to. "Nice. There's only one slight problem."

"What's that?"

"My sister is staying with me."

"Ah. Well," Darcy shrugged, "if you don't mind a short drive, we can go to my place."

Emerson had the feeling Darcy didn't readily invite the women she dated into her home. If she was putting that out there, Emerson wasn't about to pass it up. "That sounds perfect."

They headed to Emerson's car, pausing so Darcy could slip her shoes back on. Emerson opened the passenger door and Darcy slid in. Emerson watched her sit and pull one high heeled foot, then the other, into the car. The practiced grace of the move, the femininity of it, turned Emerson on. She walked around to her side, stretching her neck and trying to work out some of the nervous energy suddenly coursing through her.

On the drive, Darcy asked Emerson what she was working on. Emerson talked about her upcoming show, the paintings she planned to include. "How do you decide what to paint?" Darcy asked.

"I take a lot of photos. Whatever I find striking. It's not about doing exact replicas. I'm mostly looking for a feeling, the composition of things."

Darcy nodded. "I forget that's how we initially met. You were taking pictures of Alex and Lia's wedding."

Emerson smiled at the memory. "Right. I kept trying to get you to talk to me."

"I talked to you."

Emerson glanced over at her. It felt like more than a few weeks had passed since that night. "You were all business. And I was clearly in your way."

Darcy laughed. "That's not how it happened."

"No?"

"I mean, sure, you swaggered into my kitchen with your camera like a hot dyke on a mission. But I was very accommodating."

Emerson stole another glance at Darcy, who was looking at her with a nonchalant smile. "Dyke on a mission. I can't tell if that's an insult or a compliment."

"Compliment. Definitely a compliment. You'll notice I said hot dyke."

"Oh, well as long as that's the case."

"And would you say I wasn't accommodating?" Darcy used an innocent tone that had Emerson thinking all sorts of not innocent things.

"You most definitely were. Even if you resisted flirting back with me."

"I flirted back. I made you work for it."

"Ah. I see." Emerson pulled into the parking lot of Darcy's apartment building. She followed Darcy up the stairs, resisted touching her as she opened the door.

Inside, Darcy set down her keys and purse. "Can I get you something to drink?"

The question pulled Emerson back to the moment. "Sure. Whatever you're having."

Darcy walked into her kitchen and returned a moment later with two glasses of wine. "It's a Pinot Noir."

"Perfect." It was only a week ago that Emerson had been there, playing chess with Liam and discovering kale chips. The space seemed quiet without him there. She wondered if Darcy felt the same, or thought about how different tonight was from that night. Then she wondered if Darcy brought women home often.

"What are you thinking about?" Darcy took a seat on the sofa.

Emerson hesitated for a moment. "The last time I was here."

She smiled. "Yeah. It's a little weird."

Emerson was at once relieved and bothered by how readily Darcy admitted it. "Sorry if I'm making it so."

Darcy shook her head. "No, it's not you. I know I've said as much, but I really don't mix the two."

Emerson sat down next to her. "I'm glad you made an exception for me. Well, sort of an exception."

"I'm glad you understand why I want to keep things separate."

Emerson smiled. "It sounds like we're toasting compromise."

Darcy lifted her glass. "To compromise."

Emerson tapped her glass against Darcy's. They sat for a while, sipping wine and talking about movies and books and college misadventures. "You still haven't told me about medical school," Darcy said.

"What do you want to know?"

"Was it something you always wanted?"

Emerson appreciated that the first question wasn't why she quit. She'd told the story probably a thousand times. It felt like a fable at this point, handed down to her from some sage of self-discovery. "I thought I did. I think when you're good at math and science, it just becomes part of the narrative."

Darcy laughed. "I wouldn't know. I sucked at both math and science."

"I loved them, especially biology and chemistry. My parents were thrilled with the idea. I was thrilled with the idea of pleasing them. I minored in art instead of majoring in it. I got the grades, the MCAT score."

"What happened?"

"A week into my first semester, I knew it wasn't what I wanted. But I didn't see any way of escaping. Walking away wasn't an option."

"But you did."

"I went back for my second year, completely dreading it. Less than a month later, my parents died."

"Oh, Emerson." Darcy put a hand on her leg. "I'm so sorry. That must have been devastating."

Emerson took a deep breath. "It was. But it also opened my eyes. It sounds cliché, but I realized in that moment that life doesn't come with any guarantees. I took a leave for the semester, then decided to live the life I wanted."

Darcy shook her head. "When you mentioned moving here after they died, I didn't realize what a dramatic life change that was."

"Yeah." Emerson nodded. "Sorry. I didn't mean to be so heavy. I hope I didn't ruin the mood."

Darcy smiled. "Not at all. I asked. Thank you for opening up."

"Thanks for asking."

"Would you like more wine?"

Emerson smiled at the attentiveness. "I think I'm good."

"Okay. Are you still…I mean after talking about…"

Emerson silenced Darcy's partially formulated questions with a kiss. "Mood unbroken."

"In that case…" Darcy set her glass aside.

Emerson did the same, glad Darcy gave such clear signals. She leaned in, pausing a few inches from Darcy's face. Darcy's lips parted in anticipation. It had to be an unconscious gesture and it drove Emerson absolutely nuts. Emerson closed the remaining distance.

The taste of Darcy's mouth permeated her senses. Emerson had thought, perhaps, that the electricity of their first kiss stemmed from the newness, from the fact she'd not been with anyone—kissed anyone, even—in months. But this kiss seemed even more powerful, if that was possible. It stirred something in her. Arousal, yes, but also something more. It filled her chest, pressing against her lungs and making it hard to breathe. It made her tingle. It made her want more.

Darcy shifted so that she hovered over Emerson, then crawled into her lap. Having Darcy straddle her took Emerson's desire to a new level, one that made her lose track of time and place. The next thing she knew, Darcy stood and took Emerson's hand. She smiled a knowing smile. Emerson allowed herself to be led, following Darcy down the short hallway to her bedroom.

Darcy let go of her hand long enough to turn on a small lamp near the bed. Emerson's eyes adjusted to the soft light as she took in her surroundings. If the apartment as a whole felt homey, Darcy's room was all woman. A vintage dressing table stood in the corner, complete with more jewelry and makeup than Emerson would know what to do with. The duvet on the bed had a bold black, white, and red floral pattern that matched the red shade of the lamp.

For the first time in as long as she could remember, Emerson was nervous. Not about the sex specifically, but something. She brushed it aside. Now was not the time for analysis. She leaned in and kissed Darcy, softly at first. She pulled back to look into Darcy's eyes. In them, she saw desire, encouragement. Her lips formed into a slow smile. "Are we good?" Emerson asked.

"We are. And I think we're about to be a whole lot better." Darcy brought her mouth back to Emerson's. She sank into the kiss. Or, maybe more accurately, allowed herself to be carried away by it. Emerson was an expert leader and Darcy was more than happy to follow. It was subtle, but sure. Confident. It made Darcy weak in the knees.

Emerson abandoned Darcy's mouth to trail kisses down her neck. From there, she kissed along one of Darcy's collarbones, then the other. She returned to Darcy's throat, then ran her tongue down Darcy's sternum to the deep vee of her dress's neckline. Darcy shivered.

Emerson pull away far enough to make eye contact. "You okay?"

Darcy licked her lips and nodded. "More than."

"Oh, good. Because I'd like to do more of that."

"Yes, please."

Without breaking eye contact, Emerson reached around and unzipped Darcy's dress. She spread the fabric apart, her fingers lightly brushing Darcy's skin. Another shiver. "You're sure?"

By way of answer, Darcy slid her arms from the sleeves, then shimmied until the dress pooled at her feet. Emerson's gaze traveled down her body slowly, then back up. "Okay, then."

Darcy took that as her cue to dispose of some of Emerson's clothing. She started with her shirt, undoing the buttons of her sleeves. She kept her movements slow, methodical. After the sleeves, she went to work on the other buttons. She gave each one her full attention, pausing in between to lock eyes with Emerson. Underneath, Emerson wore a tight undershirt instead of a bra. So. Fucking. Hot.

Darcy pulled it free from the waistband of Emerson's pants, then over Emerson's head. Emerson's breasts were small. Dark nipples stood erect from her tawny skin. The plane of her stomach was smooth and flat. The waistband of her boxers peeked out from the top of her pants. Darcy ran her hands along the bottom of Emerson's ribcage and over her breasts, grazing her nipples with her thumbs, then her palms. She loved the way Emerson pressed into her, the warm smoothness of her skin.

Darcy moved her hands up to Emerson's collar bones, around her neck. Emerson reached around and unhooked Darcy's bra, sliding it down her arms and tossing it onto the floor with their other discarded clothing. With that barrier now gone, Emerson closed the short distance between them, pressing their torsos together.

It had been just under a year since Darcy had slept with a woman. Most of the time, she stayed busy enough and tired enough not to mind. When she found herself wanting, she took care of matters herself. She realized just how much that contentment depended on her options. The feel of Emerson's hands on her changed things. It was like being plugged in. She was illuminated, electrified.

As this revelation played out in her mind, Darcy guided them slowly toward the bed. When the backs of her knees bumped the edge, she sat. The move brought her eye level to Emerson's breasts. She enjoyed the view while she unbuttoned Emerson's pants, slid down the zipper. Emerson wore plaid cotton boxers—so old school it made her smile.

"What?" Emerson asked.

"Just admiring." Darcy slid her hands into Emerson's pants, pushing both the pants and boxers down. Emerson stepped back just far enough to kick them free.

Darcy leaned back on her elbows and Emerson returned to her. She hooked her fingers through the thin strips of lace at Darcy's hips and slid her panties off. Then she crawled onto the bed, placing one knee between Darcy's legs and straddling her thigh. Darcy rose to meet her.

Emerson planted a hand on either side of Darcy's head. She dipped her head, traced Darcy's lips with her tongue. Darcy sighed and Emerson used the opportunity to slip into Darcy's mouth. Her lazy exploration belied any sense of urgency. Darcy, on the other hand, felt nothing but urgent. She wanted Emerson to touch her, be inside her, release the familiar yearning that had taken on an unfamiliar edge.

Darcy resisted the urge to ask for what she wanted. Part of the pleasure in being with someone was not knowing what they would do next, or how. She scraped her nails up the back of Emerson's neck and into her hair. When Emerson pulled away, breaking the kiss, Darcy made a sound of displeasure.

"Patience." Emerson whispered the word against her ear before kissing her way down Darcy's neck, along her jaw. When Emerson's mouth got to Darcy's breasts, the kisses became gentle bites interspersed with slow circles and rapid flicks of tongue.

Darcy's hands remained restless, moving up and down Emerson's back. She wanted to yank Emerson close, feel the full length of her body. But she didn't want to restrict Emerson's access to touch her anywhere, everywhere. Emerson continued to bask attention on Darcy's breasts. Meanwhile, her fingers danced along Darcy's thigh, teasing and taunting. Darcy shifted, trying to convey her readiness, her need. Finally, Emerson slid a finger over her, into her. Darcy arched into the touch, hungry for more. One finger became two and Darcy clamped around her. "More."

Emerson obliged, adding a third finger and making Darcy feel perfectly, exquisitely full. Darcy rode her hand, reveling not only in having Emerson inside her, but also in the way Emerson's fingers curved and stroked. It was as though Emerson knew her secrets, all the hidden places that gave her pleasure, and how to play each and every one of them. The pressure built quickly. It started as a tension in her lower belly, but spread. It radiated out in waves, an eruption that pulsed through her—fingertips, toes, the top of her head. The orgasm reached each hair follicle, each pore.

When the roaring in her ears finally stopped, Darcy blinked her eyes open. Emerson stared at her, smiling. Darcy swallowed, returned the smile. "Damn."

Emerson's smile widened into a full grin. "I was just thinking the same thing. Are you always so gorgeous when you come?"

Darcy shook her head slowly. "You got me into bed. There's no need for that kind of flattery."

Emerson's face became serious. "I mean it. Watching it play out on your face was incredible."

The sex she'd just had was in a league all its own, in a good way, but the intensity of Emerson's words made her uneasy. She made sure to keep her tone playful. "Stop."

Emerson lifted a shoulder. "I'm just saying."

Darcy propped herself up. "I guess I'm going to have to find a way to distract you."

Emerson flopped onto her back, lifted one arm over her head. "By all means."

She'd been teasing, but Darcy wanted to reciprocate. No, more than that. She wanted to touch and to taste, to feel Emerson unravel beneath her. That was the other thing she missed when going solo.

Darcy knelt next to Emerson, appreciating the lines and angles of her body. She leaned in, pulling a taut nipple into her mouth. Emerson groaned. Her hand, that had been resting lightly on Darcy's thigh, gripped it. Darcy smiled around the breast in her mouth. She moved her hand down Emerson's abdomen and into the patch of dark curls. Without hesitating, she thrust two fingers into Emerson and had the pleasure of hearing her gasp in surprise and pleasure.

She worked Emerson, pumping her fingers and pressing the pad of her thumb against her hard center. Emerson matched her pace, thrusting back, lifting her hips to meet her each time. Darcy switched to her other breast, flicking and sucking in time with her movement of her hand. She felt Emerson's body bear down, a little longer and a little harder with each thrust. She resisted the urge to speed up, wanting to draw out the moment, hold Emerson on the edge of release as long as possible.

Even with that intention, she could feel Emerson's body begin to quiver. She brought her free hand to Emerson's other breast, pinching and tugging it. Emerson's grip on her tightened, her arms and legs went stiff. Darcy reveled as her body began to quake, a trembling that seemed to emanate from her core and down her limbs. She held her hand in place and felt the orgasm pulse around her fingers. The sound Emerson made turned her on all over again, made her clench and long to have Emerson inside her.

Emerson went lax, inside and out. Darcy swallowed and eased her hand away. She collapsed beside her, placed a hand between Emerson's breasts. Emerson's skin was slightly damp and her heart thudded so hard that Darcy could feel it under her hand. When Emerson's ragged breaths began to even out, Darcy picked up her head. Emerson's eyes were open and she appeared to be staring at the ceiling. For some reason, Darcy hadn't expected her to be so affected.

They lay like that for a little while, in the quiet and with the soft glow of the lamp casting shadows on the walls. Emerson rolled her head to the side and locked eyes with Darcy. "Do you need me to go?"

Darcy picked up her head. "No. Do you want to go?"

"Not at all. I just didn't know…" Emerson trailed off.

"When I said all night, I meant it."

Emerson rolled over. "All night?"

"I meant stay all night, not, you know."

"Ah. So, does that mean you're done with me?"

Darcy looked Emerson up and down. This was fun; she'd forgotten just how much. "I didn't say that."

"Oh, good." Emerson leaned in and kissed her. "Because I was just getting started."

CHAPTER FOURTEEN

Emerson woke to the aroma of coffee. She had no idea what time it was, except that it was far too early. Coffee meant that Darcy was awake, though, so she resisted the urge to burrow deeper under the covers and go back to sleep. She opened her eyes to find Darcy setting a mug down on the bedside table. "Thanks."

"It's the least I can do before dragging you out of bed."

Emerson sat up and reached for the mug. "Where are you dragging me?"

"Only to the door, I'm afraid. It's a little after eight and Liam will be home at nine."

Emerson sipped her coffee while her still-fuzzy mind processed Darcy's words. Liam. Right. Darcy's rules of engagement surely didn't include the option of Liam coming home to find a stranger in his mom's bed. Or a friend, for that matter. "Right. I'll go."

Darcy put a hand on her shoulder. "Enjoy your coffee. That's why I woke you up now, so you wouldn't have to rush out."

"You've got a whole system, don't you?"

Darcy shrugged. "It makes life easier."

Emerson couldn't fault her for that. Even if the idea of there being a system left her a little deflated. "If I haven't said as much, I'm impressed by how together you are."

Darcy smiled. "Thanks. I'm lucky. I have a lot of help."

"But still, you're doing the bulk of it on your own. You're the one who keeps it going. And you still manage to make time for yourself. So many moms get sucked into being the martyr."

Darcy laughed. "I still have moments of guilt."

"You shouldn't. I'm sure Liam is more self-sufficient and more confident because of it. And you're setting a good example on maintaining that balance."

Darcy's face softened and she took a deep breath. "That might be the nicest compliment I've ever gotten."

"A good note to leave on, then." Emerson climbed out of bed and pulled on her clothes from the night before.

"I had a great time last night."

Emerson smiled. "Me, too. Does this mean we get to do it again?"

"I'd like that."

"Look, I don't mean to be weird or anything..."

Darcy slipped on her robe and wondered where Emerson was going. Nothing good ever followed that line. "But?"

"But I just want you to know that I'm game to hang out with you just about any time. With or without Liam. I mean, at the moment, I'm feeling partial to the non-Liam time, but I'll take either happily."

"Oh." Totally not what she was expecting.

Emerson sipped her coffee, looking casual and relaxed. "I guess I wanted to say it out loud. I know you're a one or the other kind of woman, but I'm hoping when it comes to us, we can do both/and."

Darcy nodded, letting Emerson's words sink in. Emerson wasn't asking for things between them to change. Maybe she could relax a little. Liam knew she was dating and seemed completely fine with it. He certainly loved Emerson, and by all accounts the feeling was mutual. Between Liam's show at the library and his birthday coming up, it might be nice to have Emerson there as her girlfriend.

"Why do I get the feeling I said exactly the wrong thing?"

Darcy shook her head. "No, not at all. Quite the opposite, actually."

Emerson gave her a quizzical look. "Opposite of what?"

Darcy ran a hand through her hair. "I was thinking the both/and thing has its merits."

"Oh. I was worried there for a second."

Darcy picked up her coffee, which she'd set on the dresser when she came in. "If anyone is going to worry in this scenario, it's going to be me."

Emerson crossed the room and kissed her. A quick kiss—sweet, innocent almost. "How about neither of us worry?"

Could it be as easy as that? Say the word and no more worry? No, but she could appreciate the sentiment. And Emerson wasn't flip; she didn't say things because she was supposed to. "I'm not sure I can do that, but I'll try to worry less."

"I'll take it."

"Do you want a quick breakfast before you go?"

Emerson waved a hand. "No, no. I'm going to get out of your hair so you have a few minutes to yourself before Liam gets home."

Darcy wasn't the kind of woman who looked for signs. For the most part, she went out of her way not to read meaning into coincidences or passing comments. But she couldn't ignore that Emerson said and did all the right things—not the perfect, movie script sort of things, but the things that mattered to her. "Thanks. I'll see you later this week, at Liam's show?"

"Wouldn't miss it."

Darcy took their coffee cups to the kitchen, then walked Emerson to the door. When Emerson reached for the knob to open it, Darcy stopped her. She leaned in and kissed Emerson in a way that was anything but innocent. "I'll let you know when Liam's next sleepover is."

Emerson's smile was slow and sexy. "Please do. I wouldn't want to miss that, either."

❖

Emerson arrived home to find Will already up and gone. She'd left a note, not with her whereabouts, but a hope that Emerson's night had been worth the wait. She even included a winky face. Emerson shook her head. It was probably for the best that she and Will hadn't gone to college together, but these little glimpses of what it might have been like made her happy.

She contemplated a shower, but decided she'd earned going back to bed for a little while. She stripped down to her underwear and flopped on the mattress, pulling the covers up and falling asleep almost instantly. When she woke, it was nearly noon. A far more civilized hour.

Still no sign of Will. Emerson showered and got dressed. After checking the weather—mid seventies and sunny—she gathered up a large pad, easel, and portable kit of watercolors and brushes. Photos for inspiration worked fine, but there was no substitute for the real thing. She wrote Will a reply note and headed to the beach.

Since she knew she wouldn't see Darcy at the café, Emerson made a quick stop at Cumbie's for an iced coffee and a sandwich before making the short drive to Race Point. The lot already held a few dozen cars. High season wouldn't kick in until July, but weekends were busy already, especially when the weather was good.

She slung her bag over her shoulder and tucked her pad and easel under her arm, then took the sandy path that led to the beach. Umbrellas dotted the sand, along with brightly colored blankets and towels. No one appeared to be swimming, but quite a few people walked along the water's edge or waded in to their knees. Emerson set up to the left of the lifeguard stand, giving herself a view of the water as well as several of the families and couples enjoying the day.

She scanned the crowd, setting her sights on an older man who was alone. He wore a yellow Speedo and had a tan that belied the long months of winter. He lay on a towel, face up and angled toward the sun. Emerson smiled. She'd made peace ages ago that her paintings of men sold better than those of women. Even though she preferred women, she didn't mind. And this guy was perfect.

She took some photos in case he up and left, then worked for a couple of hours, doing a light sketch before pulling out her paints. When the man left, she took a break to eat her sandwich. The beach continued to fill and she was glad she'd arrived early enough to get a good spot. When her hand began to cramp and the need to pee took on a level of urgency, she decided to call it a day. She packed up and went to her car, making a pit stop at the park restrooms.

As she climbed the stairs to her apartment, Emerson wondered what Will had been up to for the day. It likely wasn't grocery shopping, and there wasn't much in the house. Maybe they could go out to dinner. But when she opened the door, the air smelled of garlic. Emerson sniffed a few times. Yep, definitely garlic.

The absolute last word Emerson would use to describe her sister was domestic. So the sight of Will standing at the stove, wooden spoon in hand, took her by surprise. Clearly, something was up. "What are we celebrating?"

Will turned and flashed a grin. "I got a job."

"That's awesome. I want to hear all about it, but first things first. What are you making?"

"Carbonara."

"Where did you learn that?"

"YouTube."

Emerson laughed. Of course she learned it on YouTube. Will would try just about anything. Seeing a video online might as well be a full course on a subject. "It smells fantastic. Can you talk and cook at the same time?"

Will glared, but in a playful, sisterly way. "Yeah, although walking and chewing gum still trips me up sometimes."

Emerson gave her an exasperated look. "That's not what I meant."

"Make it up to me by opening the wine I picked up. It's in the fridge."

"Fancy."

"We're celebrating. Besides, you can't drink beer with carbonara."

"Right." Emerson pulled out the bottle of Sauvignon Blanc, opened it, and poured two glasses. She handed one to Will, then lifted hers in a toast. "To new starts."

"And sisters who are generous with their sofas."

After clinking glasses, Emerson perched herself on one of the stools at the tiny breakfast bar. "Tell me everything."

"It's on a whale watching boat."

Emerson, who'd taken a sip of wine, choked. When she caught her breath, she looked at Will. "I'm sorry?"

"My job. It's on a whale watching boat."

"I heard you. I'm just not sure I understand. You don't know anything about boats."

"Well, I'm not going to be driving it. Or steering it. Or whatever it is you do to a boat."

"Yeah, but—"

"It's like customer service. I take tickets and chat up the passengers, run the little canteen. Plus, I used to be a lifeguard. I hopefully won't need to use those skills, but it helped that I have them."

The way Will described it made it seem less absurd. And it's not like whale watch boats were fishing vessels. She wouldn't be hauling nets or chumming the water or anything like that. "What made you decide that's what you wanted to do?"

Will plated up the pasta, going so far as to sprinkle chopped parsley over the top. She set the plates on the bar and sat on the stool next to Emerson. "I wanted something different."

Different. That was a massive understatement. "Have you ever even been on a whale watching boat?"

Will furrowed her brow. "Before today you mean?"

"Yes, before today."

"I don't think so. I've been on other boats, though. I can't imagine it's all that different."

Emerson still couldn't figure out why Will would choose something completely new over something like bartending or working retail, which she both knew and could make good money at, especially in a place like Provincetown. Then again, Emerson had never been thrilled when Will did work in bars. Not in a judgmental way or anything, but the hours were shit. On top of that, Will got hit on. A lot. Even without Kai around to be obnoxious and stir up trouble, Will struggled to be friendly but firm when it came to unwanted attention.

Maybe this new gig wasn't all that different from retail. Only on a boat. Either way, it was yet another example of how Will would try just about anything. Since they were kids, it was a trait Emerson both admired and envied. "That's one way of looking at it. I'm proud of you."

"And I can get discount tickets. You should come out sometime."

Emerson immediately thought about Darcy and Liam. She wondered if Liam had ever been on a whale watch before. "I am definitely going to take you up on that."

They finished eating and Will insisted on doing the dishes, even though the rule of their childhood had been that whoever did the cooking was exempt from cleaning up. It probably had to do with Will feeling guilty about crashing at her place. While unnecessary, it was a nice gesture. It was also nice to see the lightness in Will's demeanor. She'd been so down when she arrived. And while things had been slowly improving, today was the first time she seemed like her usual, indomitable self.

Will curled up on the futon with her computer to learn as much as she could about the whales of New England and Emerson wandered over to her studio space. She needed to finish the piece she started earlier, but it would keep. She flipped through some of her recent photographs, stopping at one she took of a mother and toddler on the beach, building a sandcastle. Kids weren't Emerson's usual style, but she liked this one. Maybe she just had kids on the brain.

She sent it to her printer and set up a canvas. Charcoal in hand, she did a rough sketch of the figures, blocking in little more than the shapes and positions of their bodies. As much as Emerson appreciated the cash flow of commissioned pieces, she preferred using real people as no more than basic inspiration.

"I'm still amazed that you can do that."

Emerson dropped her charcoal and nearly fell off her stool. She had not only lost track of time, she'd lost track of the fact that her sister was in the room. She hopped down to retrieve the errant charcoal. "Doing it for a living has definitely honed my skills."

Will shook her head. "Maybe you've sharpened your technical skills some, but you always had the eye, the feel. If anything, you've gotten faster."

Emerson smiled. "That is definitely true."

"As impressive as it was that you got into medical school, I'm glad you're doing this instead."

Emerson felt the same way, even though it was still hard at times to reconcile the joy of that decision with what triggered it. "Thanks."

"Mom and Dad would be proud, you know."

When Will and Emerson were younger, that fact—their parents' pride as well as Emerson's driving need for their approval—created no small amount of friction between them. It had also been the reason Emerson applied to medical school. While they never dismissed Emerson's talent or passion for art, it clearly couldn't hold a candle to the financial security and prestige of becoming a doctor. "I'm not sure that's true, but I'm okay with it."

Will put a hand on Emerson's shoulder. "I'm proud of you, too."

Emerson wrapped an arm around her sister and squeezed. "Now that's saying something."

"I mean it. I was always proud of you. I just couldn't tell you when you were younger. You would have been insufferable."

Emerson chuckled. "I don't know. It might have made me slightly less jealous of you."

Will leaned back and punched her in the arm. "Stop."

"No, really. Well, maybe more envious than jealous, but still. You managed to be smart, athletic, and popular. The high school trifecta."

"It's funny how that works." Will shook her head. "We can't help but think the grass is greener on the other side."

"Truth. You're not going to be in a hurry to move out, are you? You know you're welcome to stay as long as you want."

Will smiled. "I'm not moving out tomorrow, I promise. I do want my own place, though. An extended slumber party probably isn't the best thing for our relationship."

"That's fair. I'm kind of liking it for now, though."

"Thanks for saying that. I'm going to hit the hay. My first shift starts tomorrow at eight."

"Ugh. What an ungodly hour."

Will shook her head. "It's later than I used to have to be at the store. You know, now that you're an adult, you might want to try keeping normal hours."

Emerson lifted her charcoal in defiance. "Never."

Will went to get ready for bed and Emerson continued her sketch. She worked for a while longer, happy that she'd be ready to start painting the next day. By the time she flipped off the light, Will had been snoring for a good half hour. The sound remained nostalgic, but Will was right. She'd likely not feel that way in a couple of months. Even still, it was worth having Will in town. And as far away from Kai as humanly possible.

CHAPTER FIFTEEN

Emerson woke to the sounds of Will getting ready for work. She propped herself up on her elbow to wish Will good luck on her first day. Will thanked her, then said, "Dinner tonight?"

Emerson shook her head. "Liam's science project is being displayed at the public library in Wellfleet. I'm going to the little reception they're having for all the kids who got chosen."

"Right. So cute. I'll see you later then. Have a good one."

"You, too." Emerson offered a wave, then flopped back in bed and pulled the covers over her head.

She woke for the second time a couple of hours later. She decided to clean and make a run to the laundromat before settling in to work. Chores complete, she ate the leftover pasta right out of the container, washing it down with a glass of seltzer. She did up the few dishes, then turned her attention to the canvas she'd sketched the night before.

Emerson clipped her inspiration photo to the top of her easel, then squeezed several blobs of paint onto her palette. She picked up a brush, but set it down. Mood music. She scrolled through her playlists and Pandora stations, settling on Yacht Rock. Will might tease her about her old-school tastes, but as far as she was concerned, the seventies were timeless. For music, at least.

As usual, she lost track of time. She stopped once to go to the bathroom and once to make coffee. She decided to make the toddler a little girl, and gave her a tiny red bucket and shovel. One of her favorite things about the photo was the late morning light, so she continued glancing back at it as she added the various shades and shadows, the reflection of the light across the water. The painting was coming together quickly and she didn't want to stop while she had such a good flow.

She gulped her now-cold coffee, added more paint to begin layering in the details. At one point, she realized her music had cut out. She reloaded the app, switching over to classical, since singing along wasn't always the best thing for her concentration.

The sound of the door opening broke Emerson's concentration. She spun around, raising her brush in the air like she might a wield a weapon against an intruder. Will stood on the other side, several grocery bags in hand. "Hey. Need a hand with those?"

"I'm good." Will walked the rest of the way in. "Aren't you supposed to be somewhere?"

Emerson looked at the clock, then spent a second processing what day it was. Liam's show. "Shit."

"How late are you?"

She cringed. "An hour."

"Better get moving then."

"Yeah." Emerson grabbed her phone. She'd missed several texts from Darcy. She dashed off a reply and tried not to think about how mad Darcy would be. She ran around the apartment, changing her shirt, then grabbing her keys. "How was your first day?"

"Fine. Good. I'll tell you all about it later. Go do your thing."

"Right. I'm going." Emerson wrapped her brushes in plastic. She'd deal with cleanup later. She passed Will, still standing in the middle of the room holding her bags. "I'll see you later."

"Bye."

Emerson jogged to her car and hit the road. Everything was fine until she hit Truro. Something slowed traffic to a crawl. She drummed her fingers on the steering wheel, trying not to lose her patience. Getting all worked up wouldn't get her there any faster.

❖

Darcy glanced at her watch for the tenth time in the last five minutes. She watched Liam look toward the door yet again and it took all the restraint she could muster to keep her temper in check. "Do you want to go get some punch? Or a cookie?"

Liam shook his head. "I don't want to miss Emerson when she gets here."

"You won't. I promise."

He looked at her before sulking off, clearly not interested. She pulled out her phone and sent Emerson another text. Was she running late or not coming at all? She didn't want to be a nag, but she really wanted to know how much of a disappointment Liam would be in for.

A couple of minutes later, Liam returned, accompanied by his friend Carlos and Carlos's mom, Maria. They exchanged greetings and Darcy asked Carlos if his project was at the library as well. He nodded. "I did piping plovers."

"Nice. We'll have to come over and check out your display."

Carlos grinned. "I made eggs out of clay and then built a nest for them."

Darcy had seen signs about the birds and roped off areas at the beach, but didn't know much beyond that. "Cool. Hey, Liam, why don't we take a walk around and look at all the other projects?"

He glanced at the door as a new batch of people came in. None of them were Emerson. "Okay."

They meandered around. Darcy recognized several of Liam's friends from school and their parents. In an effort to keep Liam distracted, she asked him to introduce her to people and to explain some of the projects. There were dioramas and collages, a couple of sculptures, and Carlos's nest. The nest, it turned out, was nothing more than a hollow in the rocky sand, which explained why they needed protection.

She enjoyed the creativity and the sophistication of the different displays, wondering how much help some of the parents had given. Either way, she was certain she wouldn't have done anything nearly as impressive at that age, even with her parents' help. And while some of the projects were more innovative than Liam's, none had the level of artistic ability, at least not in her opinion. It was a shame that her pride was marred by her annoyance at the person who helped him create it.

They made their way back to Liam's painting and Darcy looked at her phone once more. Finally, Emerson had replied, declaring she was on her way. The relief was short-lived, however. The text had come only a minute before and, assuming she sent it as she was leaving P-town, she wouldn't make it before the library closed. She debated for a moment whether to tell Liam. Ultimately, even if Emerson missed the show, at least she was coming. "Emerson just texted. She's on her way."

"Yeah!" Liam pumped his fist, a mixture of joy and relief on his face.

Darcy hated being the wet blanket, but she didn't want Liam to get his hopes up too much. "She's on her way, but still a ways away."

"She'll make it." Liam's tone was insistent.

Minutes ticked by and the crowd started to thin. Liam, his spirits renewed, milled around and talked to his friends. His teacher came around to say that the library would be closing in a few minutes. Darcy nodded and thanked her, contemplating a plea for a few additional minutes. By the time Liam returned, only a couple of people remained. His joy had given way again to worry. "Are they going to kick us out, Mom?"

"Let me go ask." Darcy tracked down the librarian, who was at the circulation desk shutting down computers. Darcy explained the situation and asked for a few more minutes. The woman, while sympathetic, refused. Her husband was away and her own children were home waiting for a late dinner. Darcy delivered the news and Liam nodded his understanding. She hadn't seen him so deflated in a long time.

They gathered their things and headed for the exit, officially the last to leave. The doors locked behind them. They stood for a moment, Darcy wondering if she should send Emerson a message telling her not to bother. She'd just started to type as Emerson's car turned into the lot.

Emerson pulled into a spot and jumped out. "Did I miss it?"

"Yeah." Liam's voice radiated disappointment. Darcy sighed.

"Dude, I'm so sorry. I was working on something and I completely lost track of time. I can't believe I missed it."

Darcy didn't say anything. Emerson certainly looked disheveled. Her hair was messy—even for her—and she wore a dress shirt over paint-splattered jeans. Liam offered a weak shrug. "It's okay."

"I bet it looked great. Were there a lot of people there?"

Another shrug. "I guess."

Under normal circumstances, Darcy wouldn't tolerate such dismissive behavior. But these weren't normal circumstances. Considering she had half a mind to yell or knock Emerson upside the head, she figured dismissive was acceptable. That said, she might prefer it if Liam got angry. Anger wouldn't tear at her heart the way his disappointment did.

Emerson didn't give up. "Can we check it out tomorrow, maybe?"

"Sure."

Emerson glanced at Darcy. "I really am sorry. I have no idea what happened to the time. I was in a complete work trance."

"I tried texting you."

"I know. I didn't even hear it. Will got home and asked me if there wasn't somewhere I was supposed to be."

Darcy understood what it was like to lose track of time. If it was just the two of them, she might even be able to let it go. But it wasn't just the two of them. And she'd given Emerson the rundown of why she didn't let just anyone waltz into Liam's life. At the end of the day, it hadn't made a lick of difference. "It's getting late. We should head home."

Emerson squared her shoulders. "Have you eaten yet? Can I take you to dinner?"

It was after eight. Darcy resisted the urge to roll her eyes. "We ate before we came."

"Right. I don't want to keep you." Emerson returned her attention to Liam, who was shuffling his feet and looking at the ground. "I'm really sorry, Liam. I'll make it up to you, okay?"

He nodded, but didn't say anything. Emerson stayed where she was, clearly not wanting to be the first to leave. Darcy, exhausted suddenly, wanted nothing more than to be home. "Okay. Come on, Liam, let's go."

They got in the car and pulled away. In the rearview mirror, Darcy watched Emerson stuff her hands into her pockets before walking back to her car. They got home and she let Liam get right into his pajamas. She changed her clothes before going to his room for their nightly reading session. She found him sitting in the middle of his bed, still looking dejected. The desire to lash out at Emerson returned full force. "Are you mad that Emerson missed your show?"

Shrug.

"Or sad, maybe?"

"I guess it wasn't all that important."

Darcy sighed. The last thing in the world she wanted to do was come to Emerson's defense. But that's what Liam needed, so that's exactly what she had to do. "Of course it was important. Being on display at the library is a big deal. Emerson didn't mean to miss it."

"But she did."

"I know. And I'm pretty sure she feels terrible about it." She'd better.

"Yeah."

"Doesn't that happen to you sometimes? You're working on something or watching a movie or reading a book and you completely lose track of how much time has passed?"

"Yeah."

"I think painting is the same way for her."

He nodded, considering her words. "That makes sense."

"I'm not saying it's okay. Friends shouldn't let you down. But it doesn't mean you aren't important, or that Emerson hurt your feelings on purpose." Darcy couldn't believe how convincing she was. If only it worked on herself.

Liam nodded again, but with more feeling. "Thanks, Mom."

They read together, then she left him on his own. She found another text from Emerson waiting for her, reiterating the apology. Without saying it was no big deal, or that she wasn't upset, Darcy assured her they were fine. And really, she wasn't all that angry. If anything, she was annoyed with herself for being so blasé about letting Liam get attached so quickly. She'd just have to keep a better handle on things moving forward.

She went to her own bed and picked up her book. She only got through a couple of pages before setting it down again. Her mind kept circling back to Emerson. Emerson's apology and Liam's disappointment. Emerson's carelessness and Liam's seeming forgiveness. One of the hardest things about being a parent was mediating the mistakes and hurt feelings, helping Liam develop a healthy sense of self that balanced compassion with good boundaries, flexibility and resilience. Usually, Liam was working through something with a friend or classmate, maybe a teacher.

In those cases, she only had to grapple with Liam's feelings. This time, she had her own and Emerson's as well. She didn't want to consider Emerson, but that didn't stop her. Darcy didn't like the added complication, but she'd created the situation. She'd allowed their friendship to develop and so now it was her job to navigate it. She'd have to see how Liam felt in the morning, and if Emerson made any attempt to make things right.

As for her feelings, they might be the least of her worries. She turned off the light and tried unsuccessfully to hold onto that sentiment. She'd not been able to push Emerson completely from her thoughts since the night they spent together. Unfortunately, that was especially true in bed.

CHAPTER SIXTEEN

By the time Emerson made it home, she'd given herself a headache. She walked into her apartment and found Will sitting on the futon with her computer in her lap. Will looked up and gave her a funny look. "You're home early."

Emerson flopped next to her. "I missed it."

"It wasn't tonight you mean?"

She shook her head. If only. "It was tonight and I was late and I missed it."

"Oh. How mad were they?"

"Hard to say."

Will closed her laptop and angled herself toward Emerson. "How so?"

Emerson sighed. "Liam was definitely upset, more dejected than mad."

"And Darcy?"

"Eerily calm."

Will shook her head. "That's worse than yelling sometimes."

"Tell me about it. I can't believe I forgot." Emerson looked at her phone to see if there were any new messages from Darcy. There weren't.

"It happens to the best of us. Did you apologize?"

Emerson nodded. She had, but she wasn't sure how much good it did. "And I promised to make it up to Liam."

"How are you going to do that?"

"His birthday party is this weekend, so I don't think I can do much before that. Thanks to you, at least I got him a really great present." She'd been pleased with the idea to get him whale watch tickets. So pleased, she'd imagined herself going along. With any luck, that wouldn't be off the table.

"Hopefully that will earn you some points. You should show up extra early for his party, offer to help out."

"Yeah." It was a start, at least.

"What?"

"I'm pretty sure that will work for Liam. His mom is a tougher nut."

"Mama bear?"

Emerson could still see the cool dismissal in Darcy's eyes. "Something like that."

"How are you going to make it up to her? Grand gesture?"

It was tempting, but she had a feeling anything flashy would backfire. "I think this is more of a tortoise situation than a hare."

"Slow and steady."

"Yeah, reestablish myself as reliable."

Will laughed. "You appreciate the irony of this, right?"

"What do you mean?"

"You are the responsible one. You've always been the responsible one." She reached over and squeezed Emerson's leg.

Emerson cracked a smile. "Compared to you."

Will put a hand on her chest. "You wound me."

"You'd argue otherwise?" It wasn't an insult. Will not only embraced her free spirit, she took pride in it. Emerson was always the square-pants.

"Well, no."

"Exactly. Anyway, what are you up to? How was your first day?"

Will took a deep breath. "Good. I spent the morning in the shop learning the ticketing system and the afternoon on one of the boats."

"Nice. Was being on the boat cool?"

Will nodded. "It was. I need to work on my sea legs, but it's beautiful out on the water. I think I'm going to like the Dolphin Fleet."

"I'm glad. Like, really glad."

"And to add to the irony of the evening, I'm being responsible."

Emerson raised a brow. "How so?"

"I'm looking for an apartment."

"I thought you weren't going to rush into that."

"I know. But I don't want to wear out my welcome. Besides, I know I'm cramping your style."

"You really aren't."

"We're sharing sleeping quarters, Em. I know you aren't going to bring your girlfriend back here as long as I'm crashing with you."

Emerson rolled her eyes. "If only that was the only reason."

"I don't want to be any part of the reason."

"Have you found anything? Rentals around here can be so overpriced."

Will nodded. "Anything solo is totally out of my range, so I'm looking for a roommate situation. And before you say anything, yes, you would be my first choice. But I want my own room."

Will had a point. As much as Emerson wanted to be welcoming and supportive, sharing a studio wasn't a viable long-term solution. Besides, if Will got her own place, she'd be more likely to stick around than if she felt like an extended house guest. "I totally get it. Any luck so far?"

"A couple with potential. I'm going to go see one tomorrow."

"Nice." Emerson, happy for Will, but otherwise annoyed and restless, heaved herself off the couch. She walked over to the refrigerator. "Want a beer?"

"Sure."

She grabbed two bottles, opened them, handed one to Will. She raised hers in Will's direction. "Here's to being responsible."

Will laughed. She lifted her bottle and clinked it against Emerson's. "To being responsible."

Will returned to apartment hunting on her computer. Emerson wandered over to her painting area and picked up the notebook she used for sketches and lists and such. She'd already planned the thirteen pieces she wanted to include in her show. Nine were done and number ten was in progress. Even with a couple of commissioned pieces, she should have no trouble getting everything done on time. Still, she couldn't shake the feeling that something was missing. She hadn't planned a focal piece—a painting that tied the others together or was striking in its subject matter or size. Maybe that was a mistake.

Even more annoyed than she'd been a minute ago, she set the notebook down. She studied the painting she'd been working on earlier. She'd not intended it, but it reminded her of Darcy and Liam. Even though she'd chosen to paint a little girl, the posture was all Liam. She smiled over just how much the two of them had permeated her subconscious. Maybe this could be her focal point.

She realized she'd dumped her palette and brushes when she left. The upside of being home so quickly was that the paint had only begun to dry. She dunked the brushes into a cup of paint thinner, then wiped down her palette. Once she'd cleaned up the mess, she looked around. It was still only about nine. And there was enough nervous energy pumping through her, it would be hours before she'd be able to sleep. Might as well get some work done.

She dried her brushes, squeezed out some fresh paint. She got three strokes in before noticing the tap-tapping of Will's fingers on the keyboard. She snagged her headphones and plugged them in. Then she realized she was still wearing a dress shirt. At least she'd managed not to muck it up. She stripped it off, leaving her in an undershirt and jeans. She cranked the music and slid her phone into her pocket. She picked up her brush for the third time, rolled her shoulders, and dove in.

By the time she came up for air, it was nearly three in the morning. The painting was done, Will was fast asleep, and for the second time in one day, Emerson had completely lost track of time. She pulled off the headphones and tipped her head back and forth, trying to work out some of the tightness in her neck. It might have gotten her in trouble, but it was a damn good painting.

Part of her wanted to snap a photo and send it to Darcy with another apology. But sending texts in the middle of the night was probably not the best way to win Darcy over. Or to prove that Emerson was a reliable, responsible adult. Tomorrow perhaps, after she'd returned to the library and seen Liam's work on display. She nodded to herself. Tomorrow.

❖

Darcy opened the door and found her mom standing on the other side, holding two cups of coffee and what appeared to be a bag of malasadas. "Good morning."

Darcy smiled. "Hi. You didn't have to come bearing breakfast."

Gloria handed her a cup and shrugged. "You seemed upset."

They'd had a three-minute phone conversation, but it didn't surprise her. Her mom had always been able to read her moods. "I appreciate that your answer to that is sugar and caffeine."

"The answer is talking, but the sugar and caffeine don't hurt."

Gloria stepped inside and Darcy closed the door. "I can't disagree with you there."

"Liam's gone already?"

"Yeah, his bus came about ten minutes ago. I can't believe it's his last day of school."

"Summer seemed to sneak up on us this year, even after the brutal winter."

"It always sneaks up on me, although I think it's Liam's birthday as much as anything else."

Darcy grabbed a pair of saucers from the cupboard and they sat at the table. Gloria removed the lid from her coffee and took a sip. "I can't believe he's going to be nine."

"You?" Darcy shook her head. She opened the bag and took out a pastry for each of them. "I've taken to pressing the top of his head and telling him to stop getting taller."

Gloria laughed. "He's going to take after his father in that department, I think."

Liam's dad was six-four, so it was likely he'd end up taller than her, but she'd expected that not to happen until he was in his teens. "Yeah. Although I think there are still a few girls in his class taller than him for now, so I shouldn't complain."

"Agreed. Height aside, is Liam's birthday what's bothering you? The fact that he's growing up too fast?"

Darcy sighed. "No."

"Do you want to talk about what is?"

"Yeah." She'd told her mom about Emerson's friendship with Liam. She'd not told her that Emerson was the woman she was seeing. She relayed the details—dating, keeping everything separate, thinking maybe she didn't need to keep everything separate. She ended with the previous night, including Emerson not showing up and Liam's disappointment.

Gloria made a sympathetic sound. "That's complicated."

Darcy took a bite of her pastry and sighed. "I'd figured that much out already."

"But complicated isn't always bad."

"Are you sure? It feels kind of bad."

Gloria put a hand on hers. "Complicated is usually a mix of good and bad. That's what makes it complicated."

"That's deep, Mom. It doesn't help me, but it's deep."

"You know, you've always been one for compartmentalizing everything."

It wasn't the first time her mother had pointed this out. As a child, she didn't like her food touching. She kept her dolls and stuffed animals in separate groupings on her bed. When she'd gotten pregnant, the only thing that kept her sane was making lists of what she needed to do by category and order of importance. She liked to think she hadn't imposed too much rigidity on Liam, but had a feeling that's where her mother was going. "And you think that's bad."

"Not bad. Limiting."

"Safe." And it worked. Mostly.

"Yes and no."

"You're going to give me the whole 'nothing risked, nothing gained' speech, aren't you?"

"Do you need it?"

Did she? She knew it by heart. It wasn't that she didn't get it, she just hadn't come around to believing it completely. When life came with so much uncertainty, the price of feeling like a few things were under control seemed worth it. She wasn't ready to give that up. "No."

"Then I guess my question for you is the kind of example you want to set for Liam." Gloria folded her hands and set them on the table.

"I want him to feel like he can count on the people in his life. I don't want him to worry, or be afraid." Surely her mother could relate to that.

"And you think protecting him from hurt is the way to do that."

"Isn't it?"

"Is that what your father and I did for you?" Gloria asked.

For a moment, Darcy thought it was a trick question. She nodded slowly. "Yes. I never felt unsafe or unloved."

"But you were disappointed from time to time."

"But nothing huge."

Gloria's face softened and she smiled. "I'm glad you feel that way, but it's not true."

Darcy crossed her arms. "What do you mean?"

"We tried to keep you out of harm's way, sure, but we didn't try to keep you from failing. We tried to help you learn from those failures."

"It didn't feel that way." She'd failed from time to time, but never anything major. Nothing she looked back on as traumatic or scarring.

"Life will have its share of failures and disappointments no matter what. I think being a parent isn't about preventing that. It's about helping children become resilient in the face of it."

"Is this where I tell you you clearly did a good job?"

Gloria smiled. "I'm not fishing for a compliment, but I'll take it."

Darcy thought back to the night Emerson stayed over. The next morning, before Gloria brought Liam home from his sleepover, she'd been toying with the idea of signs and whether she believed in them. What happened at the library certainly wasn't the kind of sign she was hoping for. Her mom was right about one thing—she'd gotten herself into a complicated situation. Now she had to figure out what to do about it.

"Is Emerson coming to Liam's birthday party?"

The question snapped Darcy back to the conversation. "I don't know. I haven't uninvited her."

"Maybe you should see if she shows up."

Darcy sighed. That didn't sound too difficult. "That makes sense."

"Look, I haven't met her. I don't know if she's worth the effort or not. But from what you've told me, she seems pretty invested—in you and Liam."

"You're right."

"I'm looking forward to meeting her."

For probably the millionth time in her life since Liam was born, Darcy found herself feeling deeply grateful for the decision to come home. Not only were her parents supportive and helpful grandparents, they'd turned out to be her biggest allies as well. Had she stayed in Boston, she knew for a fact that her mom would not be on the list of her five closest friends. "Thanks, Mom."

"Now, speaking of party. Do you need any help?"

And just like that, the pep talk was done. Darcy appreciated that as much as the pep talk itself. "Just setting up at the park on Saturday."

"Excellent." Gloria stood. "We'll see you there."

CHAPTER SEVENTEEN

Emerson finished getting ready and got on the road to Wellfleet a good half hour before she needed to. She took Will's advice about arriving early to heart. Maybe she'd even be able to help with setup. When she got to the park, she found Darcy and Liam already there, along with an older couple she assumed were Darcy's parents. Dark green plastic tablecloths and a few bunches of balloons announced there was a party. Liam ran around while the adults arranged things on the picnic tables. It reminded Emerson of her birthday parties growing up. While many of her friends had parties that involved laser tag or bowling, her parents had insisted on keeping things simple. Although she'd been annoyed by the lack of coolness at the time, she appreciated it now.

"How's my favorite nine-year-old?" she asked by way of a greeting.

Liam looked up and flashed her a grin. "Actually, I won't be nine until eleven forty-two tonight."

"Fair enough. How's the birthday boy, then? The man of the hour, the prince of the park."

"Incorrigible, if you keep that up." A smile accompanied Darcy's reply.

Emerson didn't want to admit that she felt relief, but she did. Having Darcy be slightly standoffish for the last few days had taken a toll. "Liam's far too good natured for that. Hi."

"Hi." Darcy turned from the table and gestured at her parents. "Mom, Dad, this is Emerson. Emerson, my parents, James and Gloria."

Emerson walked over to shake their hands. "Pleasure to meet you." They returned the greeting, then Emerson asked, "What can I do to help?"

Darcy looked around, as though confirming everything was exactly as it should be. "Nothing, really. I think we're good to go."

James made a face. "We forgot to get ice."

Darcy frowned. "Do we really need it?"

"I'm on it," Emerson said. And before Darcy could argue, she started backing away. "Two bags? Three?"

Darcy's face softened. "Two would be great. Thanks."

Emerson jogged to her car, then drove to the closest gas station. By the time she returned, several other children and their families had arrived, as well as Alex and Lia. She helped dump the ice into a bowl, arrange the drink table—trying to be helpful, but not part-of-the-family helpful. She met some of Liam's friends and chatted with other parents. She introduced herself as a friend because she wasn't sure if she could call herself more than that. A few people knew her as the one who helped Liam with his turtle painting.

When pizza arrived, she stood in a circle with the adults, talking about the arrival of summer and the masses of people that came with it. As a year-round resident, she identified with the mixture of anticipation and dread that the high season brought. After pizza, there were a few games, which Darcy ran with absolute efficiency, then presents. Everyone gathered around Liam, who despite being shy on occasion, seemed perfectly happy to be the center of attention.

Emerson took advantage of the focus on Liam to study Darcy. Emerson had the feeling she was back in Liam's good graces. Darcy remained more reticent. She seemed, not angry, but detached. Emerson wanted to press it, but hesitated. She'd rather her actions speak for themselves anyway.

Telling herself that didn't mitigate the tightness in her chest as she studied Darcy's face. There was something especially beautiful about her when she smiled in that open, carefree way. She'd smiled at

Emerson that way when they spent the night together, as well as the next morning. Emerson hadn't been on the receiving end of it since. She wondered if that was a temporary situation, or a permanent one. She refused to accept that a single instance of running late would cost her so dearly. Emerson shook her head, pulling her attention back to the moment and to Liam, who'd just started to tear into his first gift.

Darcy stole a quick glance at Emerson, who seemed to be looking at her, but not. Through her, maybe. Given her coolness toward Emerson, Darcy was a little surprised that she showed up. Not that Darcy was testing her, but it counted for something that she came, that she seemed to take her promise to make things up to Liam seriously. She also appreciated that Emerson's attention was focused on Liam and not her, since that's who she'd really let down. Maybe it wasn't a lost cause after all.

Liam opened each of his presents, reading the cards aloud and exclaiming his excitement about each one. Darcy smiled as she looked at the pile of things he'd already unwrapped—books, a terrarium, and a couple of Lego sets. Not a single action figure in the mix. His friends, or at least their parents, seemed to know him well.

He got to the small box Emerson had brought. Darcy thought maybe Emerson would go with art supplies. Maybe it was a gift certificate to the art store, which would be nice even if a little impersonal for a kid's gift. Liam opened the lid and squinted at the contents, clearly reading something. His eyes got big and he looked up, right at Emerson. "A whale watch?"

Emerson nodded. "On the Dolphin Fleet."

"Awesome!" Liam jumped up and down, literally. "Thank you!"

Darcy swallowed, stealing another glance at Emerson. Those tours weren't cheap, and she figured Emerson must have purchased at least two tickets. And, even more than art supplies, it was a gift so quintessentially Liam. Add to that, Emerson wasn't even looking her way to see if it had made an impression. How was she supposed to keep Emerson at arm's length when she went and did something like that?

For the rest of the time Liam opened presents, Darcy felt her mind divided between the happenings of the party and thinking about Emerson. Fortunately, cake came next and required her full attention. Of course, it didn't help that Alex had tried out her new edible image printer to put a replica of Liam's painting on his cake. Emerson, it seemed, had worked her way into much more of their lives than Darcy had bargained for.

Not ready to think about what that might mean, Darcy focused on lighting the candles and singing, then doling out slices of cake to everyone. The party wound down and guests dispersed. Alex and Lia hung back to box up the leftover cake and offer help packing the car. Emerson lingered, too, picking up trash and chatting up Darcy's mom about her job as an emergency dispatcher. When Alex and Lia said their good-byes, Darcy realized Emerson was the only non-family member remaining. She made her way over to her and said, "I think we're good."

Emerson's smile was easy and warm. "Good. I know you had help loading. Would you like a hand unloading back at your place?"

"You don't have to do that."

"I'm happy to. I just don't want to interfere with anything."

Darcy interpreted her words as code for not wanting to go where she wasn't wanted. She sighed. "That would be really nice."

"Excellent. I'll follow you there."

She and Liam carried the last load of things to her car and they made the short drive home. Liam was unusually quiet. Clearly, he'd reached his maximum threshold of fun. When she pulled into her usual spot in front of the building, she realized he'd fallen asleep. She sat for a moment looking at his face, enjoying the reminder that, even with another birthday under his belt, he remained her little boy.

Emerson pulled in next to her and got out of her car. She peered into the back seat and smiled. "Big day, huh?"

"Apparently. I imagine he'll stir as we come and go."

They carried gifts and leftover party supplies up the stairs to her apartment. After four trips, the car was empty except for Liam. "Do you want me to carry him?" Emerson offered.

"He's a little big for that," Darcy said. She shook his arm and he half woke, just enough to get out of the car and be led upstairs. She let him flop into bed still dressed, pulling off his shoes and pulling the covers over him. When she emerged, she found Emerson standing in the kitchen, looking unsure of what to do with herself.

"Is there anything else I can do?" Her tone was hopeful and Darcy got the feeling she was talking about more than helping her pick up from the party.

"I think you've done plenty. That was an incredibly generous gift you gave Liam."

Emerson smiled, but shrugged. "Will works there now. I got the friends and family discount."

"Still."

"Besides, I'm hoping I get to go, too."

"You got him three passes?"

"One for him, one for you, and one for a guest of his choosing."

Darcy shook her head. Emerson had played her cards well. Assuming, that is, her plan was to make Liam completely forget about her missing his show. In a subtle, not overbearing way, of course. "That's really thoughtful. We've never done a whale watch before."

Emerson grinned. "Me either. Truth be told, if Liam wants to invite one of his friends, and you wouldn't mind having me along, I'd happily get another ticket."

"I have a feeling you won't have to do that." Although her tone was teasing, Darcy knew it was true. Liam didn't hold a grudge.

Emerson made a face Darcy couldn't decipher. "I hope you don't think I'm trying to buy his affections. I'd bought his gift before the other night."

Did she think that? Did it matter? Either way, Emerson had gone out of her way to show Liam that she cared about him. She crossed the room and put a hand on Emerson's arm. "I hope you know he'd forgive you without fancy gifts."

Emerson nodded and Darcy thought for a second she might be a little choked up. "Thanks."

Wanting to lighten the mood, Darcy gave her arm a squeeze. "So, what's on your agenda for the evening?"

Emerson chuckled. "Nothing."

"Come on. Saturday night, gorgeous weather. Things will be bumping in town."

"I guess I've never been one for nightlife."

"Really?" Darcy had pegged Emerson, not as a wild child necessarily, but as someone who enjoyed going out, meeting people. Hooking up.

"Really. I was the awkward, shy one when I was younger. I'm mostly over that, but I'm still an introvert at heart. The idea of a bar or club full of people is not my idea of fun."

Darcy smirked. "Even if it's a bar full of beautiful women?"

Emerson looked almost offended. "Not my scene. At all."

Great. Now she felt bad. "I didn't mean to imply anything by that."

Emerson smiled, the same easy, genuine smile that had piqued Darcy's interest in the first place. "No offense taken. I just think it's funny you'd think I'm into that. Have we ever gone to a club?"

She'd stuck her foot in it now. "I figured that had to do with having an eight-year-old in tow more than half the time we spent together."

It was Emerson's turn to smirk. "Nine."

"Nine. God, how did that happen?"

"I hear that's a common sentiment in parenting. Honestly, though. The time you and I spend together, and the time I spend with you and Liam, is what I love. New experiences and little adventures, relaxing and playing games. I'd take that stuff any day of the week."

Darcy had assumed, not that Emerson was faking it when they spent time together, but that she did so because it was part of the deal. She almost laughed. Not only had she been selling Emerson short, she'd inflated her own importance in the relationship. "Fair enough. I'm sorry I assumed otherwise."

Emerson waved a hand. "It's all good."

"Would you like a drink?"

Emerson studied Darcy, searching her face for meaning. She didn't want to read too much into the invitation, but it was hard not to see it as an olive branch. And she wasn't about to pass it up. "Definitely."

Darcy turned to the fridge. "I have a few beers, I think, and a bottle of chardonnay."

"A beer would be great."

Darcy busied herself opening the beer for Emerson, then pouring a glass of wine for herself. They stood in the kitchen for a moment. "Shall we sit?"

Emerson chuckled. This felt a million times more awkward than their first date. She couldn't decide if it had to do with them making up or Liam sleeping a room away. "Do you and Liam have big summer plans?"

"Liam has a couple of camps. He'll spend extra time with his grandparents, too. I have more flexibility at the café with all the summer help, but I still need to get in my hours."

"I'm happy to chip in here and there. I have work, too, but tend to do a lot of it at night."

"Thanks."

Darcy didn't sound negative, but noncommittal. That was okay. Emerson had established herself as good with Liam, but not as someone Darcy could count on. They'd get there. "And you told me Liam spends a couple of weeks with his dad, right?"

Darcy nodded. "Yes. That will be in July."

Emerson couldn't help but wonder what Darcy would be like with Liam gone for two whole weeks. Would she be a worrier, always checking in? Or would she embrace the time to herself, be carefree? Emerson hoped she'd get the chance to know. "And he likes going?"

"Absolutely. I think he enjoys being around men. It's weird to say, especially since they're gay and Liam hasn't shown any leanings in that direction, but it speaks to a different part of him."

"That makes sense."

"Or maybe it's because there are no rules."

Emerson laughed. She liked that Darcy didn't seem too bothered by the lack of structure. It made her feel better about her own presence in Liam's life. "I can see the appeal there."

"I won't say they completely spoil him, but it's close. Fortunately, he's good natured enough that he doesn't come home acting like a total monster."

Emerson tried to imagine Liam having a tantrum. She couldn't. At least not the kind of behavior she thought of as a tantrum—screaming and kicking and throwing things. Of course, that had never been her nature either. She'd been more of a silent, mopey type when things didn't go her way. "That's good."

"Yeah."

They sat on opposite ends of the sofa. Awkwardness hung between them. "So, do we need to talk about what happened?"

Darcy took a deep breath. "No."

"Are you sure? I feel like it's still hanging out there."

"It was. I'd be lying if I said otherwise. But today was a good day. Clearly, Liam is over it. That's what matters."

If only it could be that easy. "Liam definitely matters, but you do, too. I get the feeling you're tougher than he is."

"That's how it should be, right? I have to be."

The weight of her words settled into Emerson's stomach. Romantic connection aside, Darcy's opinion of her mattered. More importantly, being that person—the good, reliable person—mattered. Emerson wanted to be that for both of them. She didn't know what that meant, now or for the future, but she needed Darcy to believe it. "I don't want you to have to be."

Darcy shook her head. "It's not a bad thing. Protecting your children, looking out for them even when they aren't looking out for themselves, is part of being a parent."

"That's just it. I want to be one of the people who looks out for Liam, and for you."

Darcy raised a brow. "I don't need protecting."

Everything had been going well. How was she making such a mess of it now? "That's not what I meant."

"Look, I'm not upset with you anymore. Can't we just drop it?"

It was so tempting to take the easy out. There was no reason to drag this out. "I'm not trying to start an argument. I just…I know you don't think of me as someone you can count on."

Darcy closed her eyes. "It's not you."

"It is, at least in part. And I know that's at least partially my fault."

Darcy opened her eyes and looked at Emerson. "You don't owe us anything."

That stung. It surprised her just how much. "I like being part of your life, and Liam's. I want that feeling to be mutual."

Darcy seemed to relent, at least some. "We like you, too."

"But you're determined to keep me," Emerson pointed back and forth between them, "us, in a box."

"That's not fair. Boundaries are not the same thing as a box."

Emerson didn't want to start a fight, but she needed to get her point across, explain herself. "Call them whatever you want. But I'm telling you, with whatever credibility I have with you, that I'm not going anywhere."

"It's not that I don't believe—"

Emerson lifted a hand. "You don't need to believe me right now. I just want to know you'll give me the chance to stick around."

Darcy sat silently for a long moment. Emerson thought she might ask her to leave. Eventually, she nodded. "Okay."

"Okay?"

"Okay, I'm not going to drive you away with a stick. And I'm not going to ask you to prove anything. I'm going to be open-minded."

Emerson grinned. "See? That wasn't so hard, was it?"

Another raised brow. "Piece of cake. But I'm still not ready to tell Liam that you and I are an item."

"I completely understand. I hope that means you and I are still an item."

Darcy smiled. "Item might be a strong word."

"Thing?"

"That's even worse."

"Possibility? Experiment? Dalliance?"

"Oh, I like dalliance."

Emerson raised a brow. "So, you'll continue to dally with me?"

"I suppose. At the moment, however, it's my bedtime."

"Is that an invitation?"

"No."

She didn't expect Darcy to say yes, but the banter was good. Banter meant they were in a good place. "Can't blame a girl for trying."

"I'll walk you out, at least." Darcy stood and Emerson followed. Darcy took the empty beer bottle and placed it in the sink with her wineglass. She opened the door and Emerson stepped across the threshold to the outside. Darcy fiddled with the lock for a moment, then stepped out to join her. "I wouldn't say no to a kiss."

Emerson smiled. Apart from Liam's excitement when he opened his gift, that was the best thing she'd heard all day. "In that case, may I give you a kiss?"

Instead of answering, Darcy stepped toward her. She slid a hand between Emerson's arm and her side, right above her waist. Emerson bent her head slightly, closing the remaining distance between them. She brushed her lips lightly over Darcy's, soaking in the familiar taste of Darcy's mouth and the fragrance of her hair.

Emerson planned to keep the kiss brief, show that she had restraint. She didn't want to press her luck. But Darcy's tongue slid across her bottom lip, inviting more. Emerson eased a hand into Darcy's hair, tilted her head slightly to give herself better access to Darcy's mouth. Darcy opened for her and Emerson slipped her tongue inside. Darcy sucked it gently. Emerson heard a groan, then realized she'd been the one to make it. Darcy pulled away and offered a seductive smile and the most alluring bedroom eyes Emerson had ever seen. "That's so not fair."

Darcy lifted a shoulder and blinked with a facade of innocence.

"When can I see you again?"

"Liam has a birthday sleepover Friday."

Emerson resisted the urge to groan again, this time in frustration. Six days. She wouldn't get to see Darcy, or put her hands on her, for six excruciating days. "Does that mean I might get a sleepover, too?"

"I think that could be arranged."

Emerson could have stood there all night, flirting and kissing and torturing herself about how badly she wanted to drag Darcy to bed. Darcy had an early morning, though, and she wanted to be respectful of that. After all, that was the responsible thing to do. "I'll look forward to it. In the meantime, I shouldn't keep you."

If Darcy was surprised that Emerson was excusing herself, she didn't let on. "I'll text you."

"I'll look forward to that, too." Emerson leaned in and gave Darcy the light kiss she'd initially had in mind. "Good night."

Darcy smiled. "Night."

Darcy opened the door and went inside. Emerson walked toward the stairs, but turned before starting down them. Darcy hovered in the doorway, watching her. Emerson offered a wave and another smile. The smile stayed the entire drive home.

CHAPTER EIGHTEEN

When Darcy offered to make dinner, Emerson didn't hesitate for a moment. The idea of spending an entire night in with her was beyond appealing. But since Darcy probably did the cooking a lot of the time, she offered to bring groceries and make it a joint effort. She also stopped by the bakery and picked up one of Alex's flourless chocolate tortes. She'd sleep with a woman who showed up bearing chocolate, so she figured it couldn't hurt her prospects with Darcy.

Not that she was worried. Liam's birthday had smoothed over any hard feelings. And there was that kiss in the doorway of Darcy's apartment. No, Emerson had every reason to believe that tonight would deliver all the things that kiss had promised and more.

It felt strange to pack an overnight bag, but Darcy had encouraged it. Emerson liked the prospect of having both a toothbrush and a clean pair of boxers for the morning. And there was the strap-on. Darcy had requested that specifically. Yeah, there was definitely something to be said for being prepared.

She pulled into the lot of Darcy's apartment building, slinging her duffel bag over one shoulder. She grabbed the bags of groceries with one hand and balanced the bakery box in the other. She made her way up the stairs, then managed an awkward knock with the hand holding the bags. When Liam opened the door, Emerson bobbled the torte and almost dropped it.

"Emerson!" Liam's tone was equal parts surprise and delight.

"Hi, buddy."

Darcy appeared behind him. "Hi. Did you not get my text?"

Crap. She should have known to check her phone before heading over. "No?"

"Liam's friend has strep throat."

"Oh."

"I sent you a text an hour ago."

Liam looked back and forth between them. "Mom, you didn't tell me Emerson was coming over."

"It was kind of a surprise." Emerson kept a smile plastered on her face. "I knew she was going to be by herself, so I thought she might want to hang out."

"Now we can all hang out. This is way cooler than spending the night with a bunch of kids from school. I'm glad Carlos is sick."

"Liam." Darcy's tone was stern.

"Sorry."

"Emerson, come in. I'm sorry to leave you there holding all that stuff."

"No worries." Emerson handed over the bakery box and followed Darcy into the kitchen. She never minded seeing Liam, but there was a keen disappointment over the loss of the night she had planned.

Liam followed them, oblivious and chipper. "Did you bring dinner?"

"I brought stuff to make dinner. Chinese dumplings."

Liam's eyes got big. "You can make those?"

Emerson nodded, her disappointment fading in the glow of his enthusiasm. "I sure can. My mom taught me."

"Is she Chinese?"

"Liam." Darcy pinched the bridge of her nose. She hated quashing his curiosity, but the stream of questions frayed her nerves.

"It's okay," Emerson interjected. "My mom was Chinese. Well, Chinese-American at least. Her parents moved here before she was born."

"Cool!"

"I didn't know that." Emerson looked like she had Asian heritage, but Darcy had never asked.

Emerson smiled. "And my dad was Jewish. Quite the pair they were. They used to joke about whose parents were more upset by the marriage."

Despite the lighthearted tone, Darcy couldn't help but hone in on Emerson's use of the past tense. Emerson had shared that her parents were killed in a car accident, but that detail had slipped to the back of Darcy's mind. She wondered if Liam picked up on it.

"Have you ever been to China?" Liam asked. Apparently, he didn't. Darcy breathed a small sigh of relief. Not that she didn't want him to know or understand, but tonight had enough twists and turns for her already.

"I haven't. I grew up in Maryland. It was very boring and ordinary, I'm afraid."

"Probably not all that different from growing up on Cape Cod, I imagine," Darcy said.

"Probably not. But I bet you didn't celebrate both Hanukkah and Chinese New Year."

Darcy smiled. "Got me, there."

Emerson placed her hands on her hips like a woman on a mission. "So, we're going to cook?"

"Yes!" Liam nodded eagerly.

"Go put on shorts and an old T-shirt," Darcy said to Liam. It didn't really matter if he changed, but Darcy wanted ten seconds alone with Emerson.

"On it." Liam ran to his room.

Darcy turned to Emerson. "I'm so sorry about tonight."

Emerson smiled. "It's okay. I'm sorry I missed your message."

"You really don't have to stay. I know this isn't what you had in mind."

"Not at all. I mean, I'd be lying if I said I wasn't disappointed." Emerson tipped her head and gave her a flirtatious look. "I was very much looking forward to all the things I was going to do to you."

Darcy's shoulders slumped. She'd been looking forward to them, too. "I know."

"Which isn't to say I'm not going to have a great time anyway."

"You don't have to say that."

"I mean it. Besides, it won't be long before he's gone for two weeks. I'm hoping to get some quality time with you then."

She'd intended to make Emerson feel better and Emerson had gone and turned it all around. "Definitely."

"In the meantime, I'm going to go put my bag back in my car."

Darcy glanced at the bag in the corner. "You don't have—" Emerson didn't say anything. She merely lifted a brow. Realization dawned. "Oh, right. That's probably a good idea."

Emerson grabbed the bag and left. The door closed just as Liam emerged from his room. "Where did Emerson go?"

The look of worry on his face was a wakeup call. He might be quick to forgive, but his heart remained squarely on his sleeve. "Just to put something in her car. She'll be right back."

And just as quickly as the alarm came, it went. "Oh. Okay."

Emerson returned and gave Liam the once over. "Nice shirt."

He glanced down at it. A hand-me-down from a cousin, the shirt was faded and beginning to fray. It had Chewbacca on it, though, so it remained one of his favorites. "Thanks."

"Who's ready to make dumplings?"

"I am!"

Darcy laughed. Liam wasn't disinterested in cooking, but he never showed that much enthusiasm for learning, or helping. Except maybe chocolate chip cookies. Clearly, Emerson had the magic touch. "Me, too."

They took turns washing hands, then set up shop at the kitchen table, Darcy chopping scallions and garlic and Emerson explaining the different spices to Liam. Once she'd added everything to the ground pork filling, she passed the bowl to Liam and told him to go to town. He did, plunging his hands in and squishing all the ingredients together.

"It's so gross."

"Why do you think I made you do it?" Emerson asked.

Liam giggled. Such a carefree, little boy sound, it allowed Darcy to forget for a moment how quickly he was growing up. Emerson showed them how to stuff the wonton wrappers, then fold and seal them. Darcy arranged them in the makeshift steamer

Emerson rigged up and washed the few dishes. Emerson poured soy sauce and a bunch of other stuff for the sauce into a little bowl and had Liam stir it.

"We won't make it hot," Emerson said.

Liam looked indignant. "I like it hot."

Emerson glanced at Darcy. She smiled. "Not crazy hot. But his tolerance rivals mine. Dude just discovered wasabi and is in love with it."

Emerson lifted her hand and Liam obliged her with a high five. The dumplings took only a few minutes to cook, even less time to devour. When they were done eating, they lingered at the table, discussing favorite foods and places they'd like to travel. Darcy was grateful that dumplings turned out to be easy, since she had a feeling they'd be requested again and again. Liam loaded the dishwasher with Emerson and Darcy wiped the table and counter.

"Now what?" Liam asked.

Emerson shrugged. "Seems like a game night to me."

"Yes!"

Liam got something called Code Master for his birthday, so they decided to give it a go. Darcy unpacked the pieces while Liam read the directions aloud. Emerson helped put everything in place. Liam won the first round. Darcy didn't let him, but wondered if Emerson had. Emerson took the second round, though, so she decided not to press it. Once everything was back in the box, Darcy looked over at Liam. "Shower time."

Liam scowled. "But it's not even my night."

"Yes, but you cooked, so you're dirty."

"Am not."

"Are too."

"Am not."

Darcy sensed that the switch had been flipped. Playful griping teetered on the edge of a full whine fest. "Liam, I don't want to argue with you tonight."

"But you're being unfair."

"I'm being the mom. We had a fun night. Please don't ruin it."

"I'm not ruining it. You're ruining it."

"That's enough. Shower, now."

Liam glanced at Emerson, hoping perhaps for an intervention. "Sorry, buddy. I'm with your mom on this one."

Without a word, he stomped down the hall and into the bathroom, slamming the door for good measure. Darcy didn't hear the water turn on. She rolled her eyes. "Sorry."

"Should I go?"

"You can. You can also stick around for the apology Liam owes you."

Emerson smiled. "I don't need an apology."

"Maybe not, but Liam still owes you one."

"Then I'll stick around for it."

The water turned on and Darcy put a finger to her lips. Emerson gave her a quizzical look but didn't say anything. When she heard the irregular sound of the water indicating Liam had gotten in, she nodded. "Just had to make sure he's not sitting on the toilet seat pouting with the water running."

Emerson laughed. "Wow, you're good."

"Eh, I just know his tricks."

"I hope you don't figure out all my tricks."

Darcy closed the space between them. "I look forward to learning them. Slowly. One at a time."

Darcy kissed her and enjoyed the way Emerson's expression went from amused, to surprised, to aroused. Emerson leaned in and kissed her again, reminding Darcy of exactly how they'd planned to spend their evening. "You're something, you know that?"

"Thank you." The water turned off and Darcy snapped back to reality. "Let me grab him some pajamas so he doesn't go streaking to his room."

She went to Liam's room and grabbed a set of PJs. She knocked before going into the bathroom. Emerson stood in the living room, listening to the murmur of their conversation. When the door opened a moment later, both Liam and Darcy emerged. Liam walked over to Emerson and stared at his feet. "I'm sorry I was rude to you."

Emerson resisted the urge to tell him it was no big deal. Obviously, Darcy considered it a big deal. And Liam should get credit for apologizing. She got down on one knee to be at his eye level. "Apology accepted."

He looked at her then and offered a lopsided smile. "Thanks."

"We all say stuff we wish we hadn't sometimes. It's okay."

He nodded, face serious. "Yeah?"

"I still had a really fun time tonight. I'm sorry your party got canceled."

Liam shrugged. "I'd rather hang out with you anyway."

Emerson swallowed. The meaning of Liam's words sank in. She'd never considered herself a kid person. It still caught her off guard that Liam not only liked her, but wanted to spend time with her. The significance of that hit her. And while it didn't make her panic, it changed things. Darcy's rules and reservations suddenly made sense. "Well, it's important to have friends your age, but I like hanging out with you, too."

Liam launched himself at her, wrapping his arms around her neck and squeezing. Emerson returned the hug and stole a glance at Darcy. As she expected, Darcy was watching them, but she couldn't tell what Darcy was thinking. When Liam let go, Emerson stood. "Do you have to go?" Liam asked.

"I think it's almost your bedtime, so yes."

"We should have a sleepover."

Darcy stepped forward. "Maybe some time, but not tonight."

Liam, perhaps still under the influence of his bathroom conversation with Darcy, nodded. "Okay."

Emerson would have given anything to know if Darcy's answer had to do with the maintenance of boundaries or the way she and Emerson had planned to spend their evening. Because as much as Emerson might like Darcy to relax some of those boundaries, she wasn't sure she could stay the night and keep it G-rated. Still, just leaving felt strange. "You haven't gone on your whale watch yet, have you?"

"Not yet." His eyes lit up. "Are you coming with us?"

"I gave you an extra ticket to invite a friend. It can be anyone you want."

The look of exasperation made Emerson chuckle. "Of course I'm inviting you. Jeez."

"In that case, I happily accept your invitation." She looked up at Darcy. "My sister says the mid-week trips are the least crowded."

"Let me see what day I can get off."

"We can go before I go to Boston?" Liam asked.

"I don't see why not."

Liam threw both fists in the air. "Yes!"

Liam's instant and unbridled enthusiasm was one of Emerson's favorite things about him. "I'm flexible. Text me."

Darcy nodded. "You got it."

"All right. I'll see you both next week."

Darcy gave Emerson a decidedly platonic hug. "Text me when you get home."

"Will do." Emerson opened the door. "Have a good night, you two."

Darcy and Liam's good-byes followed Emerson down the stairs. She drove home, singing along to seventies music that reminded her of road trips with her parents when she was a kid. So maybe things hadn't gone like she expected, or even wanted. Still, she'd had fun. She had as much of a soft spot for Liam as she did for his mom. She wondered if Darcy might relax eventually, let Emerson be both her girlfriend and Liam's friend simultaneously.

When she got home, she sent Darcy a text. Will was out with a friend she'd made at work, so Emerson climbed into bed with a book. She checked her phone to see if Darcy had replied and was greeted with a photo. It was Darcy, in a red and black negligee that revealed nothing, but promised everything.

I wanted to at least show you some of what I had in mind for tonight.

Emerson shifted in her bed, imagining the way the silky fabric would feel in her hand. *I can't decide if that's nice of you or infinitely cruel.*

While she waited for a reply, Emerson pulled up the photo again. Darcy's skin looked like porcelain against the dark fabric. But if Emerson was there, and could touch her, it would flush pink.

Are you alone?

Emerson squinted at the message. She thought for a second before typing her rely. *Yes. You coming over?*

No, but Liam's in bed and so am I. I could call you.

Whether Darcy meant to chat or something more, Emerson couldn't tell. Either way, she wasn't about to say no. *I'd like that.*

Her phone rang less than thirty seconds later. She swiped her finger across the screen and smiled. "Hi."

"Hi." Darcy's voice was low. Not a whisper, but soft. Seductive, too.

"Miss me already?" Emerson asked. Darcy laughed, making Emerson shift again. It was kind of ridiculous that she was this turned on.

"Something like that. I meant what I said earlier, about being sorry our original plans got waylaid."

"I'm sorry, too. Especially now that I can see the outfit you had planned."

"I'm wearing it now, in bed, all alone."

Okay, so maybe they were doing this. "Is it as soft against your skin as it looks?"

"It is."

"But it couldn't possibly be as soft as your skin." Emerson imagined running her hand from skin to fabric and back to skin.

"I guess it depends on what skin you're talking about."

"I'm partial to the underside of your breasts and the insides of your thighs."

"Mmm."

"Are you touching yourself in those spots right now?"

"Yes."

At Darcy's whispered response, Emerson slid her own hand into her boxer shorts. "Fuck."

Darcy snickered. "I wish that's what you were doing to me right now."

"God, I'm not even in the same room as you and you're driving me crazy. Do you have any idea how turned on I am right now?"

"Tell me."

Emerson did tell her. She told her how wet she was, and how hard. How ever since Darcy had asked her if she had a strap-on, all she could think about was what it would feel like to slide into her.

Darcy took over, then, describing in exquisite detail what she wanted, how she wanted it. Her whispered fantasies were interspersed with ragged breaths. The sound, the image of Darcy touching herself, drove Emerson crazy. She closed her eyes, stroking herself harder and faster.

Darcy came quietly, but it pushed Emerson over the edge. Her body quaked and she didn't worry about being quiet. She almost dropped the phone. Darcy laughed again, her breathing still uneven.

Emerson chuckled as well. "Did you have that in mind when you texted me?"

"Maybe."

"I like the way you think."

"Thanks."

"So, we're going to get to do that for real soon, right?" Please, God, let it be soon.

"Soon."

"Good. Because that was nice, but did nothing to satisfy how badly I want you."

"Same."

Emerson nodded, even though Darcy couldn't see her. "I'm glad we're in agreement."

"I should go."

"Yeah. Will should be home soon. Thanks for calling."

"Have sweet dreams."

"Oh, I'm sure I will. You, too. Good night."

"Night."

Emerson ended the call and stared at her phone. When was the last time she had phone sex? She couldn't even remember. College, probably, when she and her girlfriend at the time were home on break, a thousand miles apart. That relationship had brought with it a whole host of firsts for Emerson. She smiled. Even though it hadn't lasted, she'd learned a lot and had plenty of fond memories. And as far as Emerson was concerned, that's what relationships were all about.

CHAPTER NINETEEN

Based on Will's suggestion of when it would be the least busy, they decided to do the whale watch early afternoon in the middle of the week. Because it was summer, Darcy had no trouble switching her day off to accommodate that plan. From the moment he woke up a little before seven, Liam talked nonstop about what it might be like and what he hoped to see.

After an early lunch, they piled into the car and headed to Provincetown. They parked at MacMillan Pier and made their way to the giant anchor where they'd agreed to meet Emerson. She was already there, waiting for them. Liam ran ahead, launching himself at her with an even more enthusiastic hug than usual. When he finally let go, Emerson leaned in to give Darcy a quick hug and kiss on the cheek.

"Who's ready to see some whales?" Emerson asked.

"I am! I am!" Liam waved his arm in the air.

"I just need to pop in and get our tickets." Emerson gestured to the Dolphin Fleet storefront.

Emerson went in while Darcy and Liam waited on the pier. Liam literally bounced with excitement. "Do you think we'll see any whales, Mom?"

"I'm sure we'll see some." Since Darcy didn't know what to expect, she didn't want to get his hopes too high. "I'm just not sure how close we'll be able to get."

"What if one swims right under the boat? What if it knocks the boat over?"

For a kid who'd yet to see *Jaws*, he had a robust imagination. He seemed more enthralled by the prospect than frightened. "It's a pretty big boat."

Emerson returned, three tickets in hand. "We're just in time for the one-thirty. The ticket lady said it wasn't too crowded, either."

"Yes!" Liam jumped in the air and pumped his fist.

The gesture made Darcy smile. And while she'd been slow to admit it, he'd been doing it a lot more since Emerson came into their lives. It still made her nervous, but at least the adoration didn't seem entirely one-sided. "We'd better hustle then. Liam, don't run too far ahead."

Rather than running ahead at all, he fell into step between them and held their hands. "Do you think we'll see a lot of whales, Em?"

Emerson smiled at him. "I sure hope so."

They made their way down the pier to the Dolphin VII. There was no line to board, only a teenager taking tickets. "Is your sister working this one?"

Emerson shook her head. "She's got the nine and one. Since she's still in training, I didn't want to make her nervous. If she sticks with it, we'll have to go out again on one of hers."

Darcy glanced down at Liam. "I don't think it will take much convincing."

Emerson smiled. "Let's make sure he actually likes it first."

They handed over their tickets and boarded the boat. Darcy was happy to see it was only about half full. "Should we go up to the top deck?"

"I have on good authority that we should start up there so we can see the lecture at the beginning, but that the lower deck is best for viewing. We might miss a few, but it's worth it to be closer to the water."

They climbed the stairs to the top deck, taking a seat front and center. Not long after, the boat cast off and began puttering out of the marina. Once they'd cleared the breakwater, the captain picked up speed. Darcy grabbed Liam's hat and stuffed it into her bag.

Liam sat in rapt attention as the naturalist explained the feeding and migration habits of humpback whales, along with minke and finback whales and some of the sea birds they were likely to see. When the lecture was over, Emerson led them down the stairs and along the side of the boat. The main section of seats on that level was enclosed, but a narrow bench ran the length of the outside. They took a seat near the front so they could see around to the other side, too.

The wind whipped through their hair, heightening the sense of adventure. Before long, they began seeing sprays in the distance. Darcy recognized them from sightings at the beach, only these were more numerous and frequent. Once or twice they slowed and the naturalist pointed out pairs and trios of whales not too far from the boat. Their humps glided smoothly in and out of the water; every so often, a tail would emerge. Liam pointed and exclaimed each time, completely in awe.

They didn't linger in one place for long. The tour that had gone out ahead of theirs had found a large group of mothers and calves, so that's where they were headed. When they slowed again, Darcy noticed three other boats within a few hundred yards. Everyone on their level crowded to the front to have the widest view, but the three of them remained where they were, standing right on the rail.

Liam spotted the pair approaching even before the guide. "Mom," he said, almost yelling, "did you see them?"

A moment later, a voice came over the speaker, announcing the sighting on their side of the boat. "I did. They're so close."

Darcy glanced over at Emerson, who had her camera up and was snapping photos. The whales surfaced again and Liam grabbed her shirt. "They're coming closer!"

According to the guide, it was a mother and calf, probably a yearling. The next time they appeared, their massive bodies couldn't be more than a hundred feet from the boat. Sprays of water were followed by the curve of their black backs rising gracefully above the waterline. Darcy was torn between watching them and watching Liam. She'd never seen such delighted wonder on his face before and felt torn between sharing his delight and a pang of guilt for never having given him this experience before. Darcy stole a glance at Emerson, who continued to take photos, a huge smile on her face.

A flash of white caught Darcy's attention. She looked to see the mama whale roll onto her side, lifting a huge flipper from the water and showing part of her belly. Almost immediately after, the calf launched himself into the air. At least three quarters of his body rose from the water. He rotated in the air, then landed back in the water with a huge splash. Darcy heard gasps and shouts around her and the guide kept saying "full breach" over and over in an excited voice. Darcy looked down at Liam and found him staring, mouth open, at the place where the whale had been only seconds before. Emerson's mouth hung open as well. She'd lowered the camera and looked right at Darcy.

"Did you see that?" Liam hollered, his voice pitched high with excitement.

Emerson directed her attention to Liam. "Not only did I see it, I got pictures of it."

"Mom, did you see it?"

Darcy laughed, in part at her own sense of wonder. "I did."

"That was incredible!"

Emerson pointed. The mother and calf had moved a little farther away, but continued to glide above the surface, tails gracefully lifting and falling. The boat remained in that spot for a little while longer. They saw more whales, but nothing as spectacular as the full breach. Since the tour had already overstayed their allotted time, the captain headed back to shore at a brisk pace.

Liam chattered away, rehashing every moment of the sighting, until the boat docked at the marina. They made their way down the gangplank and onto the pier. Liam ran ahead a little ways so he could turn and reenact what they'd seen.

"I can't thank you enough." Darcy put a hand on Emerson's arm. "This was not only an incredible gift, it was a once in a lifetime experience."

Emerson smiled, offered a slight shrug. "I had no idea it would be this cool. I'm pretty sure our experience was above and beyond the usual."

"Even better."

"I hope you had a good time, too," Emerson said, almost shyly.

"I did. I'm not nearly the nature buff Liam is, but it would be pretty hard not to be awed by what we saw."

"Would it be cool if I framed a couple of the photos for Liam for his room?"

"He would love that." Darcy swallowed the lump that had formed in her throat. "I would, too."

Emerson walked Darcy and Liam toward their car, enjoying Liam's blow-by-blow retelling of the events of the day. She'd known he would like it, but she realized now he would talk of little else for at least the next few days. She gave Darcy's hand a squeeze. "You okay?"

Darcy smiled. "I am. Tired, but in a happy sort of way."

"Good."

When they should have turned left into the parking lot, Darcy paused. "Are you hungry?"

Emerson couldn't tell if she was talking to Liam or to her. Liam either didn't notice or didn't care; not surprising since he was always hungry. "I am."

Darcy looked to Emerson. "You?"

It was possible that Darcy, in her fatigue from the day, merely didn't want to think about making dinner. Emerson hoped, though, that it was something more. Like Darcy wasn't quite ready for the day to end. Maybe it was wishful thinking on her part. "Starved."

"Can we have pizza?" It hadn't taken long for Emerson to learn that, when there was a question about dinner, Liam's answer was invariably pizza.

"We could grab one from Twisted and sit outside," Emerson offered.

Darcy's smile looked like a combination of gratitude and relief. "That would be great."

They walked the short distance to Commercial Street and turned left. "I'll go order and you guys scout out a table."

"Yes!" Liam did his usual fist pump.

"You're the best." Darcy reached for her wallet. "We usually get half pepperoni, half mushroom, but I'm flexible."

Emerson waved her away. "I got it. And half pepperoni, half mushroom works for me."

"Thanks." Darcy shifted her focus to Liam. "Shall we go find a place to sit?"

They parted ways and Emerson went into the restaurant to order the pizza. She grabbed some bottles of water while she waited and, before long, left with a bag in one hand and a pizza box in the other. She walked down the gravel alley and found Darcy and Liam at an umbrella-covered table. As she predicted, Liam spent every moment not chewing talking about the whales they saw. More than once, he did the chewing and talking simultaneously and Darcy had to remind him of his manners. It all felt so casual and relaxed, Emerson was sorry to see it end.

At the car, Emerson exchanged hugs with Liam, then Darcy. As she walked home, a feeling of melancholy fell over her. She tried to shake it off—the inevitable crash after the rush of adrenaline. But it was more than that and she knew it. She didn't want to be walking back to her place alone. She wanted to be going home with Darcy and Liam.

Emerson let the reality of that settle. She hadn't written off the idea of building a family, but she hadn't planned on it, either. She specifically didn't try to orchestrate her future. That had made it easy for people to flow in and out of her life. Her experiences thus far had been mostly good, occasionally terrible. Even with her best relationships, though, she'd not had a burning desire to keep people around or hold onto anything. Until now.

She wondered if the sudden change had to do with Liam. Seeing how much he'd grown in the few months she'd known him made Emerson long to remain in his life. She wanted to see what he would be like at ten, at thirteen, at twenty. The permanence that implied should have made her anxious. In reality, it was the idea of not having the permanence that filled her with a nagging unease.

Rather than dissect or try to dissuade herself from her feelings, Emerson's mind turned to Darcy. The flash of attraction, the date that followed, spending the night together—none of that was out of the ordinary. But somewhere along the way, her feelings for Darcy had transformed into something more. Emerson didn't want to label it, but it was intense. It had its own legs, too, apart from her growing attachment to Liam.

And now Liam was leaving for two weeks. He wasn't even gone yet and already she missed him. That said, she had no intention of wasting her time with Darcy. Initially, Emerson had focused on the nights they could spend together without worrying about babysitters or sleepovers. She still looked forward to the sex, but Emerson was anticipating the rest of it, too. Dinners and long conversations about nothing and everything. She'd started thinking of Darcy as a girlfriend and it would be nice to have time to explore being a couple. Then, when Liam got home, they could figure out the rest.

CHAPTER TWENTY

Instead of texting or calling Darcy, Emerson showed up at the café. Darcy would be more inclined to say yes if Emerson presented her idea in person. When she got there, Lia was at her usual table, the one she'd abandoned more days than not lately to free up space for customers. Emerson walked over. "How's my favorite newlywed?"

Lia smiled and blushed. It never failed to amuse Emerson that she seemed to both enjoy attention and be embarrassed by it. "I'm good. We're good."

"That's good. Since you're my role model for true love, I'm invested in you being blissfully happy."

Lia's face grew stern. "Stop."

"You're right. That's not fair. It's a lot of pressure. But still, I'm happy you're so happy."

"What about you?" Lia angled her head and studied Emerson. "How are you in the happy department?"

Emerson nodded slowly. "Better than I've been in a long time, actually."

"Things with Darcy going well?"

"They are. Not what I expected, but in a good way." Not that Emerson had clear expectations to begin with, but being with Darcy—and Liam—was uncharted territory for her. And she liked it. "And I love that Will has decided to stick around for a while."

"That's great."

"She loves working for the Dolphin Fleet. She's made friends."
Friends that weren't Kai. "She's even found a place."

"That's awesome."

"Right? Anyway, I don't want to keep you from your work. It's always good to bump into you."

Lia smiled. "You should do it more often."

"I will. Promise." Emerson glanced over at the register. Behind it stood a twenty-something she'd never seen before. She looked back at Lia. "Is it okay if I go on back?"

"Of course."

Emerson skirted the counter and went to the swinging door that led to the kitchen. She opened it slowly, always afraid of colliding with someone coming from the other side. She found Alex pulling a tray of something out of the oven and Darcy chopping vegetables at the work table. She'd never been one for still lifes, but the rainbow of colored peppers and purple onions struck her. And not only because Darcy's capable hands were masterfully arranging them. "I hope I'm not popping in at a bad time."

Both Alex and Darcy looked her way and smiled. "Not at all," Alex said. "Although I'm guessing you're not here to see me."

"It is always nice to see you," Emerson said.

Darcy set down her knife. "Is everything okay?"

"Completely. And I don't want to interrupt your work. May I hover and chat with you for a minute?"

"Sure." Darcy smiled, but looked wary.

"I'm going to take these out front." Alex picked up a tray of muffins.

"You don't have to—" Emerson stopped because Alex was already gone. She returned her attention to Darcy.

"What's up?"

"I don't want to step on any toes, but I was wondering if you might like company for the drive this weekend?"

"To Boston?"

"Yeah. I love the ride along Route 6. And I don't make it to Boston nearly as often as I'd like to."

"That would be nice." Darcy wondered if there was a motivation behind Emerson's offer. Not if there was a motivation, really, but what it was. Did she want to spend even more time with them? Was she curious about Liam's dad?

"How would you feel about a night or two in Boston after we drop Liam off?"

Oh. That wasn't what she expected. Darcy blinked at her. "You mean together?"

Emerson laughed. "Well, I don't mean apart."

Darcy gave her a look of faux exasperation. "You know what I meant."

"Is it the Boston part that's giving you pause, or the together part?"

That was a good question. She loved Boston. And the idea of spending a couple of days with Emerson certainly had its appeal. It was the idea of a weekend away that made her hesitate. Going away together implied things. She wanted to be clear about what Emerson meant—or didn't mean. "Neither."

"So, is that a yes?"

"It's a definite maybe." As much as she might be tempted to agree to anything Emerson had in mind, she couldn't. Or didn't want to. At least not without understanding the parameters.

Emerson looked at her. "Anything I can do to turn that into a yes?"

"Describe what you have in mind." Darcy realized how much she wanted to be talked into it. She tilted her head slightly and narrowed her eyes. "And why."

"Fancy dinner, nice hotel, maybe some sightseeing. P-town is great, but when you live in it, it's not really a vacation. I haven't gotten away in like two years and this is a good excuse."

Darcy nodded. It sounded perfect. "And do you ascribe meaning to going away with someone?"

Emerson laughed, but quickly stopped. She folded her arms and regarded Darcy seriously. "Sorry. I know you didn't mean that in a humorous way."

"It's okay. It was very process-y of me."

"But a fair question."

"So?" As much as she didn't want to be the lesbian who processed everything, she wanted Emerson's answer.

"So, it means I'm really into you and I'd love the chance to spend a couple of days with you."

"Okay."

"What does it mean to you?"

Another good question. "The same, I think. I was just checking."

"Do you want it to mean something more?"

Darcy shook her head. "No. I think, if anything, I wanted to make sure it didn't."

Emerson looked at Darcy. She didn't mind that Darcy liked to talk through everything before they did it. Or while they were doing it. It felt honest, earnest even. Emerson wasn't looking for commitment or big, showy gestures, but she liked where things with Darcy were going. Unfortunately, some of Darcy's road signs felt more like speed bumps. Darcy seemed to do it as a means of keeping her at arm's length, a fact she found discouraging. "Well, as long as we're in agreement."

"And we split the cost of everything."

Emerson shook her head. "Sorry. That's where I draw the line."

"Seriously?"

"It's my idea. And I want to be a little indulgent. I'd be all weird and self-conscious if you were on the hook for half."

It was Darcy's turn to fold her arms. "You're being ridiculous."

"Stubborn. It's different." Emerson had a feeling she didn't want to, but Darcy cracked a smile. "How about I arrange our digs and you can buy dinner?"

Darcy shook her head, but chuckled. "Deal."

Darcy eyed Liam in the rearview mirror. Only last summer, he still needed a booster seat in the car. He'd been excited to finally grow out of it and she, in true mom fashion, had cried. Only a little, though. Now, he sat on his own with a book in his lap, chatting away with Emerson.

"So, what's your favorite thing to do in Boston?" Emerson asked him.

"The aquarium."

Emerson nodded. "And what's your favorite animal?"

Liam thought for a moment. "The rays are really cool. The sharks, too. But Myrtle is my favorite."

"Myrtle?"

"The sea turtle," Darcy said.

"She's eighty years old." Liam set the book aside. "Maybe eighty-one now."

Emerson nodded. "Wow. I might need to meet this grand dame."

"She's so cool. She's, like, this big." Liam spread his arms.

"And what else will you do?"

Liam rolled his eyes. "We'll go to a baseball game. Julien loves the Red Sox."

Darcy couldn't suppress a grin. Liam loved Nick's husband, but not his obsession with baseball. Emerson turned around in her seat and looked at Liam accusingly. "You don't like baseball?"

Liam shrugged. "It's kind of boring."

"Boring?" Emerson's tone radiated dismay. "Dude, there is so much science in baseball."

"Science? What kind of science?"

Darcy bit her lip. Emerson knew every button to push to get Liam's attention. Almost more than the time they spent together, that meant something to Darcy. It told her Emerson made the effort to get to know Liam, not just play along when he was around.

"Physics, statistics, psychology. You name it."

"Really?" Liam was hooked.

"Ask Julien about the different kinds of pitches. Then when you get home, I'll show you how they work and why."

"You mean I could throw them myself?"

"Absolutely. And if you like it, we can practice until you're so good you'll want to play for real."

"Huh."

Darcy glanced at Liam again and found him nodding thoughtfully. He'd never shown the slightest interest in playing baseball. Except for karate, he'd shown little interest in any sport. And while she had no interest in raising a jock, she did want him to be well-rounded. Not only did that make for a more fun childhood, it made for an easier one. "There's a standing offer to sign up for Little League if you're interested."

"Let's not get ahead of ourselves, Mom."

Darcy laughed, as did Emerson. The phrase was one Darcy used when Liam's enthusiasm—never about sports—got a little out of hand. "Fair enough."

Because it was a Friday afternoon in the summer, traffic wasn't bad heading into Boston. Everyone seemed to be leaving instead of arriving. Darcy made her way up I-93 into the city, giving Emerson a primer on the two men she was about to meet. "Nick and I went to school together, which you know. He works for an ad agency. Julien is from Senegal and is a professor of African Studies at Harvard."

"Impressive."

"You'd never know it by talking to them, though. I mean, their house is to die for, but they're both easy-going, down to earth."

Emerson nodded. "I'm sure they're great. I'm looking forward to meeting them."

Darcy wound her way to the Back Bay neighborhood where Nick and Julien had a townhouse. As usual, they had invited her—them—to stay for dinner. Even though Darcy hesitated to include Emerson in the family-esque ritual, she hated to give up the opportunity to see Nick and catch up. So instead of pulling up for a quick drop-off, she began the hunt for a parking space.

In a stroke of pure luck, she found one only a block away from their place. With the three of them each taking a bag, they easily carried all of Liam's things. Before she could knock, the door flew open. Nick stood on the other side with open arms. "Family. I'm so glad you're here."

Liam got squeezed first, then Darcy. "Hi, Nick."

"Hi, Dad."

When Nick's gaze fell upon Emerson, he offered an appreciative smile. "And you must be Emerson. I've been dying to meet you."

Darcy poked him in the side. "Don't be dramatic."

"I'm never dramatic," he said.

"Well, we all know that's a lie." Julien stood slightly behind Nick in the foyer. "Darcy, it's always lovely to see you."

"Hey, Julien." Liam offered him a hug.

Julien returned the embrace. "Liam, you're going to be taller than me any minute. You must stop growing so fast."

"You wish."

He sighed. "Actually, I wish I could start growing again. Then we could be six feet tall together."

Darcy shook her head. "Could we not rush things, please?"

They brought Liam's things to his room, then went out to the back deck. The table was already set for five and a bottle of wine sat in a bottle chiller on the table. For the briefest moment, Darcy felt a pang for how grown-up and sophisticated it was. She didn't regret a single meal she shared with Liam at their little kitchen table, but she realized how much her life was split between that and dinners out on a date. This felt adult, but also homey. She shook off the feeling and turned her attention to Emerson, who appeared to be sharing state secrets with Julien.

"What are you two whispering about?"

"We aren't whispering at all," Emerson said, but with a wink that told Darcy otherwise.

Nick opened the wine and poured four glasses, then went to the kitchen for a glass of milk for Liam. Dinner followed and they sat down to eat like old friends. No, that wasn't quite it. They felt like the family Nick alluded to when they arrived. The reality of that struck Darcy with a mixture of wonder and alarm.

"Are you okay?" Emerson placed a hand on her leg under the table.

"Yeah. Sorry. My mind wandered for a moment."

Emerson smiled. "No need to apologize. I was just checking. You looked like you were a million miles away."

Darcy gave Emerson's hand a squeeze. "Right here." Then, allowing herself a moment of indulgence, she added, "Nowhere I'd rather be."

"The feeling is mutual."

They finished dinner, but lingered at the table. Darcy gave Nick a few details of note since their last visit, including Liam's new fascination with painting. "Maybe we'll have to check out a museum or two while you're here," Nick said. Liam nodded eagerly.

After hugs and good-byes and promises to be good, Emerson and Darcy made the short walk back to Darcy's car. Emerson studied her. She didn't seem upset, but she'd gotten very quiet. "Is it hard to leave him?"

Darcy let out a small chuckle. "It is. It's good for him, not just to see his dad but to have time away from me. It's good for me, too."

"But it doesn't mean it's easy."

"The drive home is usually hard. I'm glad to have a distraction this time."

Emerson smiled. "I'm glad we're not getting right back on the road. And I promise to do my best to distract. Would you like me to drive since I know where we're going?"

Darcy handed over her keys. "I'd love it."

"Excellent. It's not too far from here." Emerson pulled up directions on her phone and handed it to Darcy. "We shouldn't need this, but hold onto it just in case."

"Where are we staying?"

"It's a hotel that used to be a prison."

Darcy raised a brow.

"In a cool way, not a creepy one."

When they arrived, Emerson pulled up to the front door and gave the keys to the valet. She handed Darcy her overnight bag from the trunk, grabbed her own. As promised in the pictures, the lobby of the hotel was a huge vaulted space in the center of the building. Dark wood and heavy light fixtures maintained the aura of a prison in spite of the plush chairs, sleek reception area, and concierge desk.

Emerson handled the check in, stealing glances at Darcy while the guy behind the counter sorted out the reservation and keys. It didn't seem to matter what the surroundings were. Darcy always looked at ease. And beautiful. Even after spending the entire day with her, Emerson found her striking. After getting their key cards, Emerson led them to the elevator and up to the fourth floor. Once in the room, Darcy set down her bag and turned a slow circle. "This is way too nice."

"One, there is no such thing. Two, with school out and the Sox on the road, I got a great deal. I promise."

Darcy raised a shoulder. "I'm not in the mood to argue. I'd much rather focus on enjoying it."

They spent a few minutes unpacking and settling in. Emerson came out of the bathroom and found Darcy sitting on a corner of the bed with a blank look on her face. "Are you okay?"

Darcy looked up, seemingly startled by Emerson's presence. "Yeah."

Emerson eyed her with suspicion. It didn't sound like it. "Are you sure? Do you want to go out for a drink?"

Darcy's smile reassured Emerson more than her words had. "I hate to seem old and boring, but I'm exhausted."

Thank God. Emerson was, too, but hadn't wanted to admit it. "Same. What if we veg tonight and make up for it tomorrow?"

Darcy bit her lip. It was a rare display of indecision that Emerson found charming. "You really don't mind?"

"I'm beat, too. I'd rather sleep now and have twice as good a time tomorrow."

"And by good time, you mean—"

"Sightseeing, of course."

Darcy nodded slowly. "Right."

Emerson lifted a brow. Given what Darcy had asked her to pack, she had every intention of spending as much time in the luxurious and mammoth bed as she did looking around the city. "And some other things that maybe don't involve leaving the room."

Darcy smiled. "I like the way you think."

CHAPTER TWENTY-ONE

Darcy woke with a start. It took her a moment to realize where she was, whose arm was slung across her. Emerson lay on her stomach, her face half obscured by the pillow. Darcy rolled onto her side; Emerson didn't stir.

She'd talked herself into believing that having Emerson along for the drive, spending a couple of nights in Boston, didn't mean anything. But as she lay there in a posh hotel room with nothing on her schedule for the next twenty-four hours except spending time with Emerson, it suddenly felt like a big deal. Weekends away were what couples did.

Darcy drummed her fingers on her thigh. Then, afraid her fidgeting would wake Emerson, she slipped out from under the duvet and got out of bed. She put on one of the plush hotel robes and went to the window. Angry droplets of rain splattered against the window, slapped into the glass by irregular gusts of wind. There went a day of wandering the sights.

She glanced around the room, contemplated making coffee in the miniature, four-cup pot that sat on the dresser next to the television. Emerson might be one of those people who could sleep all day. Coffee, at least, was a kind, civilized sort of way to wake a person.

She filled the tiny carafe in the bathroom sink and set the pot to brew. While she waited, she curled up in one of the chairs with her phone. After checking her email, she started looking for rainy day activities in Boston. It didn't take long for the aroma to waft from the coffee pot. As predicted, Emerson shifted in the bed. She made a noise that sounded like a cross between a groan and a sigh. It was cute. And sexy as hell. Darcy poured two cups and brought them to the bedside table.

After a moment of hesitation, she took off the robe and slipped back into the bed. Like a moth to a flame, Emerson moved toward her. Without speaking, Emerson pulled Darcy close, nuzzled her breasts. Darcy loved the instinctive sensuality of the move and the fact that, even in sleep, Emerson was drawn to her. "I was going to suggest a museum, but maybe we should just stay in bed all day."

That got Emerson's attention. "What? Bed? All day?"

Darcy laughed. "It's raining."

Emerson picked her head up, but didn't let go of Darcy's midsection. "It is?"

"Yeah, I just looked out the window. And then I checked the forecast. It's going to rain all day."

Emerson made a face, loosened her grip. "I guess we should have looked ahead of time."

"Probably, but it's all good. There are plenty of indoor things we could do."

"Like stay in bed all day."

"Or go to a museum. Or a movie. Or the aquarium."

Emerson pouted. "You'd pick the aquarium over bed?"

Darcy raised a shoulder. "Not over. In addition to. As anticipation for."

"What?"

"As tempting as it is to stay in bed all day, I'd rather go out and do something, knowing the whole time I have tonight to look forward to."

Emerson narrowed her eyes. "You are a very interesting woman."

"Why do I get the feeling that isn't a compliment?"

"Total compliment. I promise. I love being with a woman whose outlook on the world is so different from mine."

"Okay, now you're being dramatic."

Emerson nipped her shoulder, then bounded out of bed. "I'm not. I swear. I've given a lot of thought to world views. And I think one of the best things about being in a relationship is getting to experience one that's different."

Great. Now they were in a relationship. The unease Darcy felt after waking returned and multiplied. Time to change the subject. "So, you'll go to a museum with me?"

Emerson stood, completely naked, at the foot of the bed. She planted her hands on her hips, looking like some kind of dyke superhero. "Yes. Yes, I will."

Without another word, Emerson disappeared into the bathroom. Darcy remained in bed, wondering what the hell had just happened. Thinking about it would likely make her more anxious than less, so she decided to join Emerson in the shower.

The bathroom was already steamy when she walked in. She opened the large glass door and stepped into the large enclosure. "I'm joining you."

Emerson turned, wiping water from her eyes. "Hi."

"Hi."

Emerson's arms wound around her. The warmth of the shower and the slickness of her skin made Darcy instantly and intensely aroused. Emerson leaned in and kissed her, slid her hand down to grab Darcy's ass.

Shower sex had its merits. In fact, Darcy had a real fondness for shower sex. But that wasn't the point. Her entire speech to Emerson hinged on the premise of delayed gratification. She wanted to save herself, store up all her energy and desire so their night together would be a culmination of built up sexual energy. She wanted the same for Emerson. She wiggled her way free. "Ah, ah. Right now, we shower. I promise I'll make it up to you later."

Emerson threw her head back and groaned. "That's just cruel. You're the one who joined me."

"I guess I'll have extra making up to do."

Emerson grabbed the soap and began rubbing it over her skin. Darcy watched the bar slick over her breasts, her abdomen, the patch of dark hair at the top of her thighs. She felt her resolve waver and wondered if Emerson was taunting her. She shook her head, as if that would dispel the ache that had taken root between her legs.

It was okay. The more she wanted it now, the better it would be later. She swiped the soap from Emerson and started lathering her own body. She made a show of it, too, working the soap over her torso and between her legs. She allowed her head to roll back, imagining Emerson's hands on her.

When she felt Emerson's hands on her head, she opened her eyes. Emerson was staring right at her as she worked shampoo into her hair. The pressure of Emerson's fingertips on her scalp sent pulses of pleasure through her. It hit her so quick, she had to clench her thighs together. Emerson leaned in, creating a brush of nipples and another ripple of arousal. She came close to Darcy's ear and whispered, "Two can play at that game."

A quick nip of her earlobe and then Emerson was gone. Hands, body, mouth—all of it. Darcy had to brace a hand on the shower wall to steady herself. She opened her eyes to find Emerson rinsing herself, then shifting out of the spray. She opened the shower door and was gone. Darcy stood, hot water coursing over her shoulders and down her body. For the first time in as long as she could remember, she'd been given a taste of her own medicine.

They spent the day wandering the MFA and the Isabella Stewart Gardner Museum, with a casual lunch at Legal Seafood in between. Darcy loved looking at art with Emerson. In addition to having an artist's eye, she had this infectious enthusiasm for different styles and techniques. Darcy asked lots of questions, feeling a bit like she was back in school.

"I do mostly oil paintings, but watercolors are so much easier at the beach or, really, anywhere that isn't my studio."

"But watercolor is what you used with Liam, right?"

"Yes. It's an easier medium to learn with. Less messy. Less expensive, too."

Darcy smiled. Liam had already requested painting supplies of his own. "I appreciate you considering that."

The questions weren't one way, either. Emerson asked about her graphic design studies in college. Darcy didn't spend much time thinking about that part of her life, or her brain, these days. Talking about it made her miss getting her hands on a new project, plotting the perfect mixture of creativity and structure. On a whim, she asked Emerson if she had a website, then offered to help her spruce it up. The idea of dabbling excited her, made her wonder about the website for The Flour Pot.

She went with Emerson to an art store, following her around the aisles and making mental lists of what it might take to open a small design business on the side. It would never take the place of her job at the café, but it might be fun. And if it brought in a little extra income, even better. Before she knew it, Emerson had picked out a starter kit of paints and a large pad of art paper for Liam, and insisted on paying for them herself. It melted her heart more than she wanted to admit.

They returned to the hotel to change for dinner. Darcy successfully rebuffed Emerson's attempts to lure her into bed. The anticipation was enough to consume her and she loved every minute of it. They took a cab to the restaurant Emerson had picked for them—Eastern Standard—and had a perfectly indulgent conclusion to a perfect, if soggy, day in Boston. By the time they climbed out of the taxi and strolled into the hotel lobby, Darcy's mind had taken on a singular focus. Emerson took her hand. "Would you like a nightcap? The bar downstairs is called Clink."

Darcy laughed. "Cute. I'm good. I'd like to head up and not leave the room until brunch time tomorrow."

Emerson smiled. "I like the way you think."

They made their way to the elevator, then the room. "You'll like the way I packed even better."

Emerson offered her a quizzical look. "I thought I was the one who was supposed to do the packing."

Darcy unzipped her bag and riffled through it. "Well, let me pop into the bathroom for a minute, then we can do show and tell."

"Only if I get to touch, too."

Darcy sashayed by Emerson on her way to the bathroom, stopping for a slow, teasing kiss. "If you play your cards right."

"I'll play whatever cards it takes to get more of that."

In the beautiful, ultra-modern bathroom, Darcy changed into the sheer black baby doll that had been a present to herself the previous Valentine's Day. In addition to the lace and ribbon detail over her breasts, it had ribbon lacing up the back reminiscent of a corset. She slid it over her head, happy with the way it clung and fell in all the right places. She dabbed a small amount of perfume behind her ears and between her breasts.

She emerged from the bathroom, and found Emerson lounging casually on the bed. She was naked, save the tight black briefs that held the cock in place. Even though it wasn't their first time together, Darcy's breath hitched in anticipation. Maybe it was the hotel room or the freedom of having the next two weeks ahead of them. It might be the strap-on itself. Something about this moment carried a heady combination of intimacy and abandon.

"You look absolutely stunning."

Darcy basked in the heat of Emerson's stare. "Thank you. You look pretty fucking amazing yourself."

Emerson beckoned her with a single crook of her finger. Darcy took her time walking over, enjoying the way Emerson's eyes devoured her. Emerson sat up and scooted to the edge of the massive bed, her tawny skin and dark underwear a sharp contrast to the crisp white sheets. She spread her legs and Darcy stepped into the vee of her thighs. "This is quite an outfit."

"I told you I'd packed something special."

Emerson swallowed. "Yeah, I think you win this one."

"Now, now. It's not a competition." Darcy reached down and wrapped her hand lightly around the dildo. "What you brought is far more...practical."

Emerson slid a hand up the back of Darcy's thigh, resting it on her bare ass cheek. "Practical. That's one way of putting it."

"Utilitarian."

"Better. I think. No bother. We're not here to discuss semantics."

"Thank goodness." Darcy grazed her fingers over Emerson's chest, enjoying the way Emerson's eyes closed when she brushed over the nipple.

"Did you have something in mind?"

Darcy pinched the nipple, eliciting a small moan. "Something."

Emerson's free hand slid up to Darcy's other exposed cheek. "Care to be more specific?"

"Actually…" Darcy stepped back and walked over to her bag. She pulled out the blindfold and the length of satin rope she'd tucked into her things just in case.

Emerson watched Darcy with anticipation. When her brain registered what Darcy held in her hands, she tried to keep the surprise from her face. She wasn't opposed to being tied up. She just never had. She liked being adventurous. On top of that, she trusted Darcy. "You want to tie me up?"

Darcy crossed the room again and resumed her position between Emerson's legs. She maintained eye contact as a slow smile spread across her face. "Not exactly."

"No?" Emerson's mind scrambled for a clever comeback. And then realization dawned. With it, a sharp stab of desire. "Oh. You want me to do it to you."

The seductive smile was replaced with a playful grin and an arched brow. "No pressure. If you're not into it, it's not a big deal."

"No, I…" What? She wasn't not into it. And Darcy wanting the opposite of what she expected upped the intrigue. "I'm into it. I mean, I could be. I'm just…"

Rather than being turned off by Emerson's floundering, Darcy seemed amused. "Surprised?"

Emerson nodded slowly. "A little. Maybe. Only that you don't want to do the tying."

"Because I'm a control freak."

That was one way of putting it. "I wouldn't use the word freak."

Darcy trailed a finger down Emerson's chest. "Don't you know it's the women who have to keep everything under control who most want to have it taken away?"

The question, combined with the sultry look in Darcy's eyes, did more to turn Emerson on than the negligee or the blindfold or the rope. "I confess I've never thought about it that way."

"The moment has to be right." Darcy licked her lip. "And the person."

Darcy trusted her. The significance of that was not lost on Emerson. "Then there's nothing I'd like more."

"For the record, if that's something you wanted, I wouldn't be opposed to being on the other end of the rope."

Emerson fought to keep her tone light and even. If Darcy was on the other end of the rope, she might be into it after all. "I'll keep that in mind."

Darcy placed the rope and the blindfold in Emerson's open palm. "Then these are for you."

Emerson swallowed. "Will you tell me what you like? What you want?"

Darcy smiled. "I like not knowing what you're going to do next. Tell me what to do. I want to be completely in your hands."

"And is there anything you don't want?"

"I like directive, not demeaning. Does that make sense?"

That was a relief. Emerson didn't take issue with that kind of play, but it didn't do it for her. "It makes perfect sense."

Darcy nodded. "Good."

"Okay. Take a step back." Darcy immediately complied. Emerson stood and dropped the rope onto the bed. "Close your eyes."

Emerson slid the blindfold into place, then looked around the room. The headboard didn't offer anything she could loop the rope to, but she wasn't about to let that stop her. She placed her hands on Darcy's shoulders and guided her to the bed. Emerson had her lie down across the middle, then lifted her hands over her head. She wrapped the cord around each of Darcy's wrists a couple of times, trying to make it snug without cutting off circulation. "Is this okay?"

"Mmm hmm."

Emerson reached over to the table in the seating area by the window. She dragged it closer to the bed, pleasantly surprised by how heavy it was. She looped the rope around the pedestal base and, without pulling it too tight, made it so that Darcy would be unable to go very far. "Give that a tug and tell me if it's too tight."

Emerson watched the rope go taut and the look of surprise come over Darcy. Clearly, she hadn't anticipated being attached to anything. The smile that followed proved infinitely satisfying. "It's good."

"Good." Emerson took her time walking to the other side of the bed. Standing at Darcy's feet, she ran her fingers from Darcy's ankle to her knee, up her thigh and back again. She repeated with her other hand on Darcy's other leg. Then both legs at once, stopping just short of Darcy's hips and teasing the triangle of soft hair. She was rewarded with a sound somewhere between a sigh and a moan.

Emerson straightened and took a moment to soak in the image in front of her. Darcy lay still for a little while, but soon started rubbing her legs together and twisting her torso gently. She didn't say anything, though, and Emerson realized that taking her time would only heighten the anticipation. The extent to which Emerson held all the power struck her, leaving her aroused and… Something in addition to power, but Emerson couldn't put her finger on it.

She crawled onto the bed and knelt beside Darcy. Even with the blindfold, Darcy's face turned toward her. Emerson leaned forward and kissed her. Darcy parted her lips and Emerson slipped inside. As it always did, the taste of her mouth sent swells of desire through her. The way Darcy sighed made Emerson's stomach tighten.

Go slow.

Emerson moved from Darcy's mouth to her neck, from her neck to her breast. Darcy's nipples strained against the lace. Emerson sucked them lightly, enjoying the texture against her tongue.

Darcy arched against Emerson, absorbing the sensations of Emerson's skin and mouth on her. In addition to the element of surprise that came with being blindfolded, she was convinced that having one of her senses taken away heightened all the others. The sound of Emerson's breath, the sheets rustling as they moved, filled her ears along with her own sighs.

Emerson pulled back and Darcy felt the absence of her body keenly. Part of her longed to feel Emerson's face, to run her fingers through her hair. But being restrained brought its own pleasure. She was at Emerson's mercy. It had been so long since she'd given that power to someone else. She'd missed it.

With gentle pressure, Emerson eased her legs apart. Darcy complied, lifting her knees slightly as Emerson ran her hands along the backs of her thighs, around her hips to her abdomen. Fingers brushed through the tuft of hair, making her shiver. Emerson's mouth replaced her hands, pressing kisses across her belly and the insides of her thighs. Darcy squirmed, anxious to have Emerson's mouth on her.

"Patience." The single word between kisses calmed Darcy's restless movement, but not the churning need. That continued to build until Darcy thought she might have to beg. But then Emerson's tongue slid over her. The intensity of it made her cry out. Rather than easing back, Emerson urged her higher, bringing her close to release before teasing away. This continued for what felt like an eternity and Darcy realized that Emerson had no intention of letting her come like this. Knowing that made Darcy want it even more. She began to squirm in earnest, hoping Emerson might lose her patience. Or take mercy. Either would be fine.

The kisses stopped and Darcy could feel Emerson's weight shift on the mattress. Soon. Emerson would be inside her soon.

"You're ready for me, aren't you?"

Darcy nodded. "Mmm."

She expected to feel Emerson kneeling between her thighs, spread her apart. But nothing. "Is that any way to answer when you want something?"

Oh. They were going there. Darcy's pussy clenched in anticipation. "Yes."

"Yes, what?"

"Yes, please. I'm ready."

Emerson's breath was warm on her ear. "What are you ready for? Tell me."

Darcy swallowed. "I'm ready for you to fuck me."

She sensed Emerson move away again. The gentle tease of Emerson's fingers on her thighs resumed. "And how would you like me to fuck you?"

Darcy barely stopped herself from saying "hard" or "fast." She smiled slowly. "Slow, at least at first. I want you to make me want it."

Emerson didn't respond.

"Please."

Darcy felt Emerson settle between her thighs. Emerson slicked two fingers along her slit. Darcy gasped. "I guess we don't need lube."

Darcy let out a ragged laugh. "No."

Emerson placed her hands on Darcy, opening her. She moved closer. The silicone pressed into her, warm from the extended foreplay. Emerson pushed the head in, then stopped. Darcy adjusted to the sensation, wanted more. She arched her hips. In response, Emerson eased deeper. But slowly. Like, ridiculously fucking slowly. Darcy wondered if she was going to regret what she asked for.

Eventually, Emerson eased all the way in. The fullness paired with the pressure of Emerson's pelvis against hers. No, that was definitely worth waiting for.

Just as slowly, Emerson pulled out. Then in again. Each stroke was a languid journey. Darcy felt each ridge of the cock, the split second of anxiety each time she thought Emerson might pull out entirely. They continued like that for a while. Because the pace wouldn't make her come, Darcy concentrated on each sensation. In addition to the cock, she could feel Emerson's hands gripping her thighs. Each thrust created tension in the rope, making it dig ever so slightly into her wrists. The smell of Emerson's cologne laced with the scent of sex. And even though she couldn't see, Darcy imagined Emerson's face, intensely focused on the movement of the cock in and out.

Emerson increased the intensity before the speed. What started out as an even glide became marked thrusts, punctuated with just the right amount of force. Each one coaxed a small noise from her. When

Emerson picked up speed, Darcy's noises alternated with a chorus of "yes" and "please." Emerson nudged her knees up, supporting their weight and increasing the angle of their bodies. The shift added just the right friction against her clit and did her in.

Darcy came and the orgasm went on and on. She clenched around Emerson. Having something to hold onto grounded her in the pleasure, gave it an anchor as the vibrations moved through her. She called out Emerson's name, hoped vaguely that there was no one in the adjoining rooms that might hear her.

Emerson continued to hold her legs, steadying her as she came down. When she finally stopped trembling, Emerson eased out of her—both a relief and a disappointment. Emerson moved and Darcy wished she could see her. Emerson hadn't come and she planned to do something about it.

Breaking contact allowed Emerson to regain a small semblance of control. She brushed her fingers through Darcy's hair and removed the blindfold. Darcy blinked at her, her dilated pupils adjusting to the light. "You okay?"

Darcy nodded. "You didn't…I want…"

Emerson smiled. It was the first time she'd seen Darcy at a loss for words. "Don't worry, I'm not done with you yet."

Darcy licked her lips. "I want you to come as hard as you made me. Tell me what you want."

Emerson loosened the knots of the rope, then leaned in to whisper in Darcy's ear. "I want you on your hand and knees. Can you do that for me?"

Darcy nodded. Emerson eased back so Darcy could comply. Emerson knelt between her ankles. She ran her hands over Darcy's ass and into the deep curve of her lower back. Darcy leaned back slightly, seeking.

"Would you like me to fuck you again?"

"Yes." The response was ragged, breathy.

"Yes?"

"Yes, please." Emerson positioned herself so that she could take Darcy again. When the head of the cock pressed against her, Darcy said again, "Please."

Emerson braced her hands on Darcy's hips and eased into her. The pressure against Emerson's clit was exquisite. She eased out, then pressed in again. Darcy moaned. "Do you want me to take you fast or slow?"

Darcy's back arched. "Fast."

Emerson smiled. "Fast?"

"Fast, please."

"That's better. I will, but I'm going to enjoy myself first. Don't try to speed up or I'm going to have to stop. Do you understand?"

"Yes."

Emerson punctuated Darcy's reply with a long, forceful thrust. She'd swear she could feel Darcy tighten around her, pull her deeper. Emerson placed a hand on each of Darcy's hips, guiding her forward as she pulled out, then, when she was on the verge of breaking contact, she dragged Darcy back. Each time, Darcy made the most beautiful noise—not quite a moan and not quite a whimper. The fully kneeling position gave her exceptional leverage. Even with Darcy no longer tied, she was completely and utterly in control.

She maintained the long, slow thrusts as long as she could take it, enjoying the visual as much as the physical sensation. But her vision was beginning to blur. She tightened her grip, digging her fingers into Darcy's flesh and holding her still. No longer concerned with the length of each stroke, she pounded into her again and again. Darcy's noises became more frequent, more frantic. The thrumming in Emerson's low belly gave way to a tremor that shook her entire body.

Darcy cried out. Over the rush of blood in her ears, the sound of Darcy coming again undid her. She clutched Darcy to her, vibrating with a pleasure so fierce her legs began to buckle. Darcy collapsed under her and Emerson fell to the side, weak and panting.

"Holy fucking fuck."

Emerson cracked a satisfied smile. "Yeah."

They lay like that for a while. Eventually, Emerson summoned the energy to lift her head. Darcy remained splayed on her stomach and the cock bobbed enthusiastically between Emerson's thighs. She laughed at the sight—the erect silicone unaffected by what had just transpired.

"What?" Having her face pressed against the mattress slurred Darcy's speech.

"Just admiring the stamina of my friend here."

Darcy lifted her head and glanced toward Emerson's crotch. "Are you not done? Because if you're not done, I am here for you."

Emerson chuckled. "You don't look like you could move."

"I could move."

Emerson leaned over and brushed the hair from her face. "That's sweet. But there's no need. I'm beyond satisfied. For now at least."

Darcy returned her face to the mattress. "Thank God."

Emerson slid the harness down her legs. Since Darcy was already lying across the bed, she grabbed a pair of pillows and joined her, yanking the duvet over them both. Darcy rolled onto her side and Emerson curled around her. She put an arm around Darcy's waist and kissed the back of her head. "Good night."

"Night."

CHAPTER TWENTY-TWO

Darcy opened her eyes and stretched, again feeling the weight of Emerson's arm slung over her. Apparently, if they were going to continue sleeping together, this was something she'd have to get used to. Not that it was a bad thing. A sliver of sunlight shone through the blackout curtains, making it impossible for her to determine the time. She glanced at the clock on the bedside table and discovered it was after ten. "Holy crap."

"Huh? What?" Emerson lifted her head and squinted at her. "What's wrong?"

"Sorry, sorry. Nothing's wrong. I just can't believe how late it is."

Emerson blinked a few times, looking around the room. "What time is it?"

"Almost ten-thirty."

Emerson rolled onto her back. "I thought you were going to say two in the afternoon."

Darcy laughed. "You really aren't a morning person, are you?"

"I thought we'd already established that."

"Yes, but you're much worse than I thought."

"One is not better than the other." Emerson tickled Darcy's ribs until she squirmed.

"Okay, okay. Let me rephrase. As a morning person, I can't believe how late we slept."

"Well, we were up pretty late."

That was putting it mildly. After the initial sex, they'd dozed for a little while. But the light had remained on and Emerson's roaming hands led to a second round. After Emerson made her come for the fourth time, Darcy stopped counting. And she had no idea what time they finally fell asleep for good. "True. It was way past my bedtime."

Emerson rolled again, this time until she lay on top of Darcy. "Would you like to file a complaint?"

Darcy shook her head. "I couldn't possibly find a single thing wrong with last night."

"Good. I'll buy you a huge breakfast, too. Brunch, technically."

Darcy couldn't remember the last time she'd gone out to brunch. "With a Bloody Mary?"

Emerson leaned down and kissed her. "With a Bloody Mary."

The kiss, more of a peck than anything sexual, stirred something in Darcy. While she wouldn't have thought it possible to be turned on after everything they'd done every which way, it seemed she'd become insatiable. She hooked a leg around Emerson's thigh and pulled her closer. "Not that we need to be in any rush."

Emerson rotated her hips, pressing even further against Darcy. "All the time in the world."

By the time they walked out of the hotel lobby, it was after noon. "Will anyone still be serving brunch?" Darcy asked.

"I know just the spot. And it's only a short walk away."

Darcy turned her face into the sunshine and allowed Emerson to take her hand. They had the entire day in front of them. Really, they had the next two weeks ahead of them. She had to work, but with Liam not home, Darcy would have a huge amount of free time. The thought of being a little reckless—of spending most of it with Emerson—sent a wave of excitement through her. She hadn't been irresponsible in so long, probably since college. The idea of it made her giddy.

Emerson delivered on her promise of brunch, complete with Bloody Mary. After, they walked off a few of the calories along the Charles, soaking up the sunshine they'd been denied the day before. Without waiting for Emerson to take the lead, Darcy asked her, "When we get home tonight, will you stay over?"

"On one condition."

The sternness in her voice made Darcy curious. She considered asking what it was, but decided she'd be unlikely to refuse anything Emerson requested. And she'd decided to be reckless. "Okay."

Emerson smiled. "You didn't even ask what it was."

Darcy lifted a shoulder. "I have a feeling I'll be on board."

"Tomorrow, spend the night at my place."

"What about Will?"

"She's officially gotten her own place. Well, not all on her own. She's moving into an apartment with a couple of other people."

"That's great." Darcy studied Emerson's face. "It is great, right?"

Emerson nodded. "Definitely. It's good for her and I think it makes it more likely she'll stick around."

Given what she'd learned about Will's recent past, Darcy knew that was a good thing. "I'm glad."

"It also means I get my apartment back. Not that it hasn't been fun having her there, but..."

Darcy grinned. "She's been cramping your style?"

"Fortunately, I have a very understanding girlfriend."

"Is that what I am?"

"Understanding? Absolutely."

"No. Your girlfriend."

Emerson stopped walking and looked at Darcy. She was the last one to obsess over labels, but she couldn't think of another way to define them "Aren't you?"

Darcy put a hand on her arm. "I'm not denying it, we've just never discussed it."

Something in Darcy's tone felt forced, like she was trying to keep it light. "I think of you that way."

Darcy angled her head and narrowed her eyes, as though it was a test. "I guess I do, too."

"And, for the record, I'm not seeing anyone else. I don't want to see anyone else."

Darcy nodded slowly. "Same here."

"I guess it's settled then."

They started walking again, but Darcy continued her slow nod. Emerson wanted nothing more than to know what she was really thinking. Eventually, Darcy made eye contact and asked, "Is this a big deal?"

Emerson picked her words carefully. She wanted to be honest, but not scare Darcy off. Of course, she didn't even know which extreme would scare her off at this point. "Sort of, but it doesn't have to be."

Darcy laughed and hooked her arm through Emerson's. "A perfect answer."

What did it mean that Darcy was completely satisfied with such a non-answer? Did it matter? It didn't today. For now, she was going to enjoy having Darcy all to herself.

They meandered back to the hotel. Since they'd checked out before leaving, Emerson got their car from the valet and they were on their way. The sun really seemed to be making up for lost time and the drive down and along the Cape was bright and beautiful. They got back to Darcy's apartment early evening. They climbed the stairs and went inside. For all the times she'd been there, only once had it been when Liam wasn't home. It felt oddly quiet without him. "Can I be excited to stay over and also miss Liam?"

Darcy's smile told Emerson it was the right thing to say. "I know what you mean."

"Oh, good. So, what time do you have to be at work tomorrow?"

"Nine."

"God, that's early."

"You know Alex is in by five, right?"

If she'd thought about it, Emerson would have known that. But she never had. "I appreciate the profound sacrifice you both make so we can have coffee and pastries and macaroni and cheese."

Darcy shook her head. "Thanks."

"I promise I won't keep you up as late tonight."

Darcy stepped closer, ran a finger along the neckline of her V-neck tee. "Don't be making promises you might not be able to keep."

Emerson put her hands on Darcy's hips. "I'm figuring if I drag you to bed now, we'll get to sleep at a reasonable hour."

Darcy bit her lip. "I see."

"I mean, unless you're hungry. We could eat first."

"Food is so overrated sometimes."

"And we did eat a huge brunch."

Darcy took one of Emerson's hands. "Exactly."

Emerson allowed herself to be led to Darcy's bedroom. "I'm so glad we agree."

Chapter Twenty-three

Darcy walked into work, fifteen minutes late and out of breath. "Sorry," she said to Alex as she hastily put her things away and pulled on her cap.

"No need to apologize." Alex looked at her with what appeared to be worry. "Are you okay?"

"Yes. Good." Darcy's mind flashed to what she'd been doing half an hour before. She could feel the smile spread across her face. "Great."

Alex narrowed her eyes. "Were you at Emerson's?"

Darcy flashed a coy grin. "Maybe."

"Have you been there every night this week?"

"No." Darcy arched a brow. "A couple of nights, we were at my place."

Alex laughed. "Getting serious, huh?"

"More like on vacation, I'd say."

"Vacation?"

"Yeah. With Liam at his dad's, I sort of feel like I'm on vacation. I figure I might as well live it up while I can."

Alex frowned. "Does Emerson know that?"

"What do you mean?"

"I mean, I'm not sure that's how I'd interpret things. Have you said as much to Emerson?"

"Well, not in so many words, but she knows." Didn't she?

"Okay."

"Did she say something to you?"

"No."

Darcy folded her arms. "Then what aren't you saying?"

Alex sighed. "Nothing."

"Come on, Alex. Don't start something, then backpedal."

Alex turned away from the oven and gave Darcy her full attention. "When Lia and I started seeing each other, we had this mutual understanding that it would be casual."

Darcy chuckled at the memory. Casual had quickly morphed into something more, but neither Alex nor Lia wanted to admit it. At least at first. "This is different, I think."

"Maybe. I'm just saying that Emerson might have more feelings than she's letting on. You should talk to her."

"Are you implying I'm taking advantage of her?"

"Not at all. Like I said, I don't know what her feelings are. But me not being completely open with Lia almost cost me our relationship."

"I thought her crazy ex almost cost you your relationship."

"If I'd been more honest, her crazy ex wouldn't have mattered. My point is that you should both know where you stand. No matter where that is, it's better for everyone."

Darcy nodded. As much as she hated being put on the spot, Alex had a point. And since Alex was friends with Emerson, too, Darcy couldn't blame her for trying to look out for both of them. "Thanks. I'll keep that in mind."

Alex nodded, too, looking relieved. She started to leave, but turned back. "Being on vacation. Is that really how you feel?"

Darcy squared her shoulders. "I don't see how I could feel any different."

"Okay."

Alex left, leaving Darcy standing alone in the kitchen with her thoughts. Emerson had given her no indication she wanted something more than what they had. After all, Emerson seemed to be all about living in the moment. Surely, serious relationships and settling down were not part of that plan. Nor were they what Darcy wanted. Yes, it was nice to have a couple of weeks that were all about her own enjoyment and pleasure. But that's not what her life was about, or even what she wanted. Being selfish and self-indulgent was fine when Liam was away, but he'd be home soon. And she wanted him home. No matter how nice the last week had been, she wouldn't choose that over her actual life.

She was pretty sure Emerson got that, with or without a discussion.

Darcy tried to shake off the uneasy feeling that had crept into her stomach and got to work. She'd do a check in at some point before Liam got home. To make sure they were on the same page. Having a plan made her feel better. She nodded, even though there was no one in the kitchen to see. Then she shook her head and chuckled at herself. She went to the fridge and started pulling out ingredients for the day's specials. The kitchen help would be in soon and she wanted to have clear task lists to keep everyone busy and the lunch menu on track.

Emerson waited until about two to stop by the café. The worst of the lunch rush would be done and, with all the extra staff, Darcy should be able to take a break. When she poked her head in the kitchen, three people milled around assembling salads and sandwiches and dishing up macaroni and cheese. None of them was Darcy. She looked again and realized that Darcy was standing in a corner with a clipboard, lost in thought.

"Darcy."

Darcy looked up, clearly startled. She glanced in Emerson's direction and her face relaxed into a smile. "Hi."

"Do you have time for a short break?"

"I'll do you one better. Have you eaten?"

"Not yet."

"Requests?"

A few minutes with Darcy and lunch. Lucky her. "Surprise me."

"Grab something to drink from the case and meet me out back."

Emerson offered a small salute and returned to the main part of the café. She picked up a couple of flavored seltzers, letting Jeff know she'd pay him when things settled down. Instead of weaving her way through the kitchen staff, she went out the front door and walked along the side of the building. She found Darcy already sitting in one of Alex and Lia's Adirondack chairs, holding two bowls of salad. "No mac and cheese?"

Darcy smiled. "Given how we've been eating since Boston, I thought we could both use some leafy greens."

"Fair enough." Emerson sat, placing the seltzers on the arms of their chairs and taking one of the bowls. She studied the contents—spinach with cranberries and bleu cheese and what appeared to be candied walnuts. "This looks delicious. Thank you."

They ate for a moment, then Darcy said, "So, did you miss me or were you hungry?"

Emerson laughed. "I don't see why it has to be an either/or."

Darcy tipped her head and gave Emerson's phrase back to her. "Fair enough."

"I did want to talk to you, though."

"About?"

"About you spending the day with me tomorrow. You're off, right?"

"I am." Darcy answered slowly, as though it might be a trick question.

"Well, I'd love you to spend it with me, and I sort of already made us plans."

Darcy raised a brow. "Do tell."

"I rented a boat and I'm hoping you'll go out with me."

"You rented a boat?" Darcy's expression was incredulous.

"I wanted to do something special for your day off. It's not that hard to find one that you can take out for a day."

"But still. Can you drive a boat?"

Emerson raised a shoulder and smiled, beginning to second guess herself. "I learned to sail in high school. My best friend's family spent practically every weekend on the water."

"It's a sailboat?" Darcy's voiced pitched higher.

"I can cancel it if you don't want to go. I thought you'd enjoy it. I should have asked first."

Darcy shook her head and waved her hands. "It's not that. I'd love to go. I'm just surprised."

As far as Emerson was concerned, living this close to the ocean and not spending time on the water was far more surprising. She didn't say as much, suddenly cognizant of how privileged that sounded. "So, you do like boats?"

Darcy nodded. "I just haven't had much occasion. I love the water. The whale watch was amazing. I guess I've always been more of a beach person."

"Well, I promise I won't put you to work."

It was Darcy's turn to shrug. "It sounds fun. I'd like to learn."

"Great. We can pick it up at nine. Our reservation is until four. We don't have to stay out that long, but we can if we're feeling it."

"How about I pack us a lunch?"

"That sounds perfect."

"I'll bring the sunscreen, too. I keep so much around for Liam, I should just buy stock in the company at this point."

Emerson laughed, feeling much better about everything. "Deal."

CHAPTER TWENTY-FOUR

Darcy chose a sundress to put over her bathing suit and a floppy hat, deciding that if she was going to spend a day on a boat, she might as well go all out. She finished putting together the picnic, then headed into P-town. She met Emerson at the marina, unloaded her car, then pulled around to the parking lot. Emerson escorted her to a little rowboat and loaded the cooler and picnic basket into it. "A little smaller than I imagined."

Emerson gave her an exasperated look. "This is just to get us to our boat."

"Ah." She'd been kind of kidding and kind of not. She'd always wondered how people got to the boats moored in the harbor.

"You sit here." Emerson pointed to a short bench seat.

Darcy did as instructed. Emerson took off her shoes and pushed the boat into the water. When she hopped in—far more deftly than Darcy could have managed—Darcy shook her head and smiled. "I can help row."

Emerson grinned at her. "I got it. We aren't going far."

In a few minutes, they pulled up alongside a perfect little sailboat. Well, perfect in Darcy's mind. Even though she'd never been on one, she thought it looked fine. Polished wood trim and shiny chrome fittings stood out against pristine white paint. "She's very pretty."

"I wouldn't promise you a sailboat and deliver a dinghy." Emerson attached a rope to the mooring ball, then another to the side of the boat. "Let me get our stuff settled, then I'll help you board."

Darcy stayed put, having no desire to fall head first into the water. "You can relax. You've officially over-delivered."

Emerson hefted herself into the sailboat, then leaned over to get their things. Darcy handed her the basket, then the cooler, and finally the small tote bag where she'd tucked sunscreen and a couple of towels. "Okay, when you stand up, keep your feet apart. You want to keep your center of gravity as low and wide as possible."

Darcy laughed at the instructions, but did as she was told. "Got it."

"Take my hand. You can try to step in, but it's easier sometimes to sit and swing your legs around."

Darcy liked the sound of that. With minimal effort, she managed to switch boats and found herself seated on one of two narrow benches that ran along the inside of the boat. The hull. She'd done some research so she wouldn't look like a complete idiot. "That was easy. Thank you."

"You're very graceful. Now, you just sit there and look pretty while I get us ready to go."

Even if she wanted to protest, she didn't know enough to be helpful, so she leaned back and struck a pose. "Happily."

Emerson leaned in and kissed her. "And you do look exceptionally pretty. My apologies for not saying so earlier."

Darcy studied Emerson—black board shorts and a tank top over what appeared to be a sports bra-style bikini top, sunglasses, perfectly tousled hair. "You look pretty fine yourself."

"Thank you." Emerson kissed her again, then turned her attention to the boat. Darcy watched as she untied the rope that connected the sailboat to the rowboat, as well as the one that held the sailboat to the mooring ball. She powered up a small motor at the back of the boat and slowly guided them through the other boats and around the breakwater. When they were clear of both, she cut the motor and started fidgeting with the sail.

"Can I help?"

Emerson clearly had everything under control, but she walked Darcy through the process of hoisting the sail, securing the battens.

It was complicated, but not difficult and Darcy enjoyed the lesson. Whether she would ever use it didn't matter. With the sail up, they moved through the water at an impressive clip. Emerson showed her how to use the tiller to steer them into open water. "My suggestion would be to skirt the shoreline. That'll keep us clear of any bigger boats or whales."

"Right. Whales. Good plan." They made their way around Long Point and Wood End. "So, we're in Herring Cove?"

"We are. That's one of the nice things about the Cape. You have a lot of options that don't involve open ocean."

Darcy thought about how choppy the water could be at Race Point, not to mention places like Marconi and Nauset. "Agreed."

Emerson let Darcy steer for a while. Darcy soaked in the sunshine and the breeze. She could see people beginning to fill in the beach and realized how nice the privacy of a boat could be. A little before noon, Emerson took over and angled the boat out of the wind. "Are you okay to drift while we eat or would you like me to anchor?"

Darcy looked around. There was nothing to run into. "Drifting is fine."

Emerson pulled drinks from the cooler and Darcy took out sandwiches. She'd pilfered some croissants from the bakery and made what she believed to be Emerson's favorite—smoked turkey and Swiss. She handed one to Emerson, then opened bags of chips, baby carrots, and cherry tomatoes. "This is perfect. Thank you." Emerson took a bite. Then, with her mouth full, she added, "More than perfect."

After finishing lunch, they continued to drift. Darcy took off her dress. Even coated in sunscreen, she loved the feeling of basking in sunshine.

"Would you let me sketch you?"

Darcy turned her head toward Emerson and peered over her sunglasses. "Sketch me?"

"I've wanted to since the day we met."

"Stop."

"It's true. I want to photograph you, too."

Darcy let that sink in. "Okay."

"Really? Right now?"

Why the hell not? "Yes."

Emerson reached for the bag she'd brought on board and pulled out a large pad and a couple of charcoal pencils. "You're actually sitting perfectly right now. Is that okay? You don't need to be completely still."

Darcy arched her back slightly and draped an arm on the side of the boat. She tipped her face to the sun. "I am utterly content to sit here as long as you require."

Without another word, Emerson opened the pad. Darcy could hear the scratching of her pencil against paper. She glanced sideways to sneak a peek at Emerson. The look of intense concentration reminded Darcy of when they made love. Just the thought sent a wave of warmth through her; it gathered in her center. She resisted the urge to move against it, into it, something. No matter how many times they were together, she'd come to live in a state of near constant arousal.

Emerson continued to draw and Darcy tried to shift her attention elsewhere. "I don't think I could ever grow tired of looking at the sea."

"I agree. Although, in this moment, I'm more inclined to say I don't think I'll ever grow tired of looking at you."

Darcy turned, slid her sunglasses down her nose, and peered over the lenses at Emerson. "You've already gotten me into bed. There's no need to lay it on quite so thick."

Emerson laughed at being called out so blatantly. "But it's true. You are infinitely captivating."

"Flattery will get you everywhere."

"Is that so?" Emerson shifted her weight so she could lean toward Darcy. "In that case, you are the most beautiful creature I've ever seen. Stunning. I can't look at you without wanting you."

Darcy slid her sunglasses the rest of the way off. "Keep talking."

"I'd like to have my way with you right here."

"What's stopping you?"

Emerson glanced around. She'd never been an exhibitionist, but the idea of taking Darcy, in broad daylight, as they floated in the cove, stirred something inside her. And it wasn't like they had an audience. Even as boats came and went from the marina, none came within a hundred feet of them. "Not one single thing."

Emerson leaned in the rest of the way, removing her own sunglasses before pressing her lips to Darcy's. She could feel Darcy smile against her mouth. Emerson took advantage of the opening, sliding her tongue inside. Darcy opened further, her own tongue darting out to glide over Emerson's. Emerson sucked it lightly, relishing the taste and texture.

Emerson released her hold on the side of the boat so she could pull out the clip holding Darcy's hair. The wind immediately took it, inviting Emerson to grasp fistfuls with both hands. Darcy kept one hand braced on the narrow bench seat, but Emerson felt the other on the side of her ribs. What had been playful arousal only moments before became something more potent, pressing.

Figuring the shallow hull was both the most spacious and private place in the small skiff, Emerson released Darcy's hair long enough to guide her hips from the bench to the boat floor. She sat up just enough for Darcy to reposition herself without rapping her head on the wood, then reached for the blanket so Darcy could have a makeshift pillow. The sudden shift in weight caused the boat to lurch. Darcy squealed, then giggled. Emerson braced herself until the rocking slowed. "Sorry."

Darcy hooked a finger in the waistband of Emerson's shorts. "Don't be sorry. Just get down here."

With the gentle lull restored, Emerson lowered herself so that she was braced half over Darcy and half to one side. She kissed Darcy again, then ran a line of kisses along her jaw. She continued the trail, zigzagging her way down Darcy's neck, down her collarbone, and across her breast. Even through the fabric of Darcy's bathing suit, Emerson could feel her nipple grow hard. Emerson bit at it gently through the material, eliciting a small gasp.

Emerson reached behind Darcy's neck, working at the knot of her halter top. It took a moment to accomplish with one hand, but when she finally loosened the tie and peeled the fabric back, she was rewarded with the sight of Darcy's breasts, full and pale against her tanned arms. Her areolae were pink and puckered, topped by perfectly erect nipples.

Emerson sucked one, then the other. They tightened further, becoming hard as pebbles against her tongue. She ran her hand up and down Darcy's torso and leg, fingers grazing the smooth lycra and soft skin of her thigh. She watched Darcy's face as her head lolled gently from side to side, her mouth slightly open.

Emerson eased her hand between Darcy's legs. She slipped the fabric aside and found Darcy hot and slick with arousal. She traced the silky contours, entranced by how easily her fingers slid up and down. Although her intention was to go slow, Darcy moaned and arched against her. Unable to resist, she eased two fingers into Darcy. She was even softer inside, but Darcy clamped around her with surprising strength.

With each stroke, Darcy's hips rose to meet her. Emerson kept her pace even, wanting to draw out the moment as much as possible. She tried to commit each detail to memory—Darcy's wind-tossed hair, the sunlight slanting over them, the gentle sway of the boat. More than anything, she tried to imprint Darcy's face in her mind. Her eyes were closed, but she had a look of fierce concentration. Between each noise she made, she bit her lower lip. It was a look so perfect, Emerson would never try to capture it in a painting.

Darcy's breaths grew shallow. The small sounds of pleasure became more urgent. Emerson shifted her hand slightly, increasing not her speed, but the force of each thrust. She positioned her thumb over Darcy's swollen center. Feeling Darcy's pulse on her clit drove Emerson crazy. She fought to maintain some semblance of control.

It didn't take long to push Darcy to climax. She felt Darcy clench around her fingers; her entire body stiffened. Emerson counted four breaths before Darcy went lax with a shuddering sigh. She waited another moment before withdrawing her hand.

Emerson was still basking in her own version of an afterglow when she felt Darcy shift beneath her. Without a word, Darcy eased her hand into Emerson's shorts. Emerson repositioned herself so that she was almost kneeling, straddling Darcy's thigh. Darcy took advantage of the access, easing into her.

"Fuck."

Darcy laughed, a low and sexy sound that drove Emerson nuts. "That's my plan."

Darcy curved her fingers, causing Emerson to buck involuntarily. Emerson eased herself forward and back. "Fuck, yes."

Darcy held her hand steady and Emerson rode her. The pressure began to build and Emerson did all she could to hold the orgasm at bay. Just one more minute, one more thrust. If she could hold on a little bit longer, she'd be able to etch this moment—Darcy's look of concentration, the smell of the ocean, the heat of the sun on her back—into her memory forever.

When the pressure between her legs began to spread, Emerson was powerless to stop it. It moved from her center, through her belly, and up her spine. It made her limbs tremble and stole her breath. When the shudders finally ended, she collapsed to the side of Darcy. "Fuck."

Darcy moved her fingers. "I can do it again if you want."

Emerson grasped her wrist. "Only if you're trying to kill me."

Darcy gently pulled her hand away. "I wouldn't want to do that." She chuckled. "I don't know how to get this thing back to shore."

Emerson let out a ragged laugh. "It's good to know what your priorities are."

Darcy shrugged, but lifted her head and placed a noisy kiss on Emerson's mouth. "As impressive as it sounds, I promise I don't want to fuck you to death. At least not literally."

"That's a relief."

"I am, however, beginning to worry about awkward sunburn."

Emerson had almost, at least sort of, forgotten they were in a boat. "Right."

Darcy glanced at the sun, which remained high in the mid-afternoon sky. "We should probably head in."

"The thought of a cool shower with you is awfully appealing."

"I've got grilled chicken and veggies at my place. And clean sheets on the bed."

"Say no more." By the time they got to Darcy's, the heat and exertion—not to mention the orgasm—were starting to catch up with her. She peeled Darcy's clothes off for the second time that day, adding them to the pile Darcy had already made of Emerson's tank top and shorts.

"Shower with me?" Instead of answering, Darcy took her hand and pulled her to the bathroom. She fiddled with the knob for a moment, adjusting the temperature, then pulled back the curtain. Emerson stepped in behind her, enjoying the cool spray on her skin. Darcy tipped her head under the water, then began lathering shampoo into it. "Let me."

Darcy dropped her hands to her sides and Emerson took over, massaging her scalp. Darcy's moan of pleasure made Emerson smile. It made her hot, too, and she wondered whether Darcy would balk at being wanted again so quickly. She slid her hands down to Darcy's breasts to test the waters. When Darcy moaned again and leaned into her, Emerson took it as all the invitation she needed.

She squirted body wash into her hands, then slicked them over Darcy's skin. The scent, floral and fruity, was so quintessentially Darcy. Emerson breathed it in as she ran her hands up and down. When Darcy started to squirm, she rinsed her hand and slid her fingers into Darcy. It was like being surrounded by her in every possible way. As Darcy moved against her, opened herself even further for Emerson's touch, Emerson fought to keep her concentration, to remain in control of the situation.

Darcy came with a noise that was high pitched, but quiet. Surrender. It was unlike any sound Emerson had ever heard and she wanted nothing more than to capture it, hold onto it. But before she could sort out the mix of emotions it stirred up, Darcy was turning around, sliding her arms around Emerson and kissing her. Emerson sank into the kiss, feeling at once weak and incredibly strong. When Darcy eased away, Emerson groaned in protest. But then Darcy's hands went to Emerson's hips and she bent down, dropping to a kneeling position. Just the sight of Darcy—naked, wet, looking up at her—sent a flood of liquid heat to Emerson's core.

Darcy smiled a knowing smiled and dipped her head. Without warning or any of the teasing Emerson might have expected, Darcy plunged her tongue into her. Emerson gasped; her knees almost buckled. Darcy held on, her arms around Emerson's thighs while her mouth did exquisite and excruciating things to her. Emerson had been wrong. This was the feeling she wanted to capture, fix in her mind somehow so that she could revisit it over and over again.

The orgasm hit her, not with the punch of force she expected, but like a waterfall. It poured over her, sending pleasure into every curve and crease of her body. Emerson shuddered with it, struggled to keep her footing.

Darcy stood and held her. Emerson let herself be wrapped up in the embrace and the unspoken assurances it seemed to offer. After a long moment, Darcy moved one hand and turned off the water. She slowly let go and eased away. Emerson looked into her eyes, searching but unable to decipher what Darcy was thinking.

Before Emerson could study her further, or ask questions, Darcy pushed open the shower curtain. And the spell was broken. Darcy smiled, leaving Emerson to think the feeling had been hers alone. Darcy reached for the towel hung on the back of the door. "Stay there. I'll grab you a fresh towel."

She disappeared, giving Emerson a moment to collect herself. When she came back a few seconds later, Emerson accepted the towel and returned the smile. "Thanks."

"You have some T-shirts and boxers in the laundry basket in my room. I threw them in with my wash."

Emerson nodded. "Thanks for that, too."

"Ready for dinner?"

"Starved."

Darcy disappeared again and Emerson dried off. She went to Darcy's room and put on the clothes that now smelled like Darcy's place. She found Darcy in the kitchen making plates of cold chicken and vegetables. Darcy flashed her a smile and Emerson returned it. They'd just had an incredible day. There was nothing in the world to be disappointed about.

CHAPTER TWENTY-FIVE

Whatever saturnine feelings had threatened to creep in the day before dissipated. Emerson woke with Darcy's naked body pressed against her and she felt nothing but sated and happy. Darcy, already awake and alert, looked at her and smiled. "Good morning."

Emerson returned the smile. "Morning."

"You don't need to get up, but I have to get ready for work."

"I'm awake. And I should get some work done today, too." They'd also come to Darcy's in one car and Emerson felt weird about being stranded at her apartment all day. "Want to stay at my place tonight?"

Darcy considered, or at least pretended to consider, for a moment. "I suppose that could be arranged."

"I'll even make you dinner."

"Then I'm definitely in." Darcy climbed out of bed. "I'm going to take a quick shower."

"I'll resist joining you and make some coffee."

Darcy turned back and kissed her. "You're the best."

Less than an hour later, they pulled into Darcy's parking spot behind the café. "I'll see you around four, yeah? Any requests for dinner?"

"Probably 4:30. Nothing fancy. I'm not really coming for the dinner."

"I'll keep that in mind."

They parted ways and Emerson walked to the little market she passed on the way home. She wandered the short aisles, settling on angel hair pasta with pesto. She picked up some shrimp to make it more special and the ingredients for a basic salad.

At home, she put away the groceries then spent a few minutes tidying up. Satisfied everything looked sufficiently put together, she grabbed her bag from the day before and went to her work area. She pulled out the sketch pad and flipped through it. She'd only managed two rough drawings before she'd given herself over to more pleasurable pursuits. Still, there was more than enough to inspire a painting.

Emerson set down the notebook and looked at the canvas she'd only started working on. What she'd really love to have were photographs. Even a dozen images would give her inspiration for months, if not more. Would Darcy agree to a photo shoot? The idea, and how to broach it with Darcy, percolated as she got to work. Instead of distracting her, it fueled her. Emerson channeled the energy into the painting she had in progress. This piece, a woman standing on the pier and looking at the ocean, would be a good one to show Darcy. Inspired by a photo she took, it would have the essence of the woman without looking exactly like her. Hopefully, that would nudge Darcy in the direction of agreeing to model for her.

Emerson continued to work, stopping once for the bathroom and an apple. The painting continued to come together—the texture of the sand and the light on the water in the background, the shadows along the woman's back and the wispy curls falling from her pinned up hair. When a knock came from the door, she jumped. She set down her brush and glanced at the clock. Where the hell had the day gone?

Emerson hurried to the door and opened it to find Darcy on the other side. She eyed Emerson with suspicion. "Why do you seem so surprised to see me?"

Emerson laughed and stepped back so Darcy could come in. "I'm not. I just lost track of time."

Darcy shook her head and smiled. "That seems to happen to you a lot. Is it an artist thing or a bachelor thing?"

"I'm going to go with artist. Seems more palatable." Emerson closed the door. "Can I get you something to drink?"

"Definitely. Do you mind if I shower first?"

"Help yourself."

Darcy headed to the bathroom with her overnight bag. Emerson cleaned up her painting area and turned her attention to the kitchen. She opened the Malvasia she'd bought to go with dinner and poured two glasses, then filed a small plate with olives, marinated artichoke hearts, and bocconcini. Darcy returned a few minutes later, hair wet and wearing a red and white striped sun dress. "Feel better?" Emerson asked.

"Much."

They sat on the sofa, drinking wine and sampling the antipasti Emerson had put together. Not for the first time, Emerson found herself looking at Darcy with a painter's eye—the line of her jaw, the way her hair curled as it dried. She'd wait until they'd eaten, when Darcy was completely relaxed. She'd ask her then.

Emerson told herself not to be nervous as she made dinner, as they sat on the sofa with bowls of pasta and more wine. Darcy suggested a movie and found an old black and white one on the television. Emerson opened a second bottle of wine. She didn't want Darcy drunk, but comfortable, uninhibited. Then Darcy started kissing her neck.

Thoughts of taking pictures vanished as Darcy pulled Emerson to the bed. She took off Emerson's clothes, then her own. For all that Darcy wanted to relinquish control when they were in Boston, she seemed perfectly at ease running the show now. Emerson went along, happily, touching and tasting in a way that felt both exciting and familiar.

After, as they lay in bed with a sheet thrown over them, Emerson's thoughts returned to her camera. "Would you let me photograph you?"

Darcy raised a brow. "Right now?"

"Now, or later. Whenever. I just…I've been wanting to paint you. And as much as I enjoyed doing sketches on the boat, most of my paintings come from photographs. More of a fixed moment, if that makes sense."

"You want to paint me?"

"Are you really surprised by that?"

Darcy seemed to think about it. "I don't know. Maybe?"

Emerson propped herself on her elbow. "You know I think you're beautiful. It's more than that, though. You evoke something in me. I'd love to try to capture it."

"My hair is a mess and I'm not wearing any makeup."

Emerson ran a finger down Darcy's cheek, along her jaw to her chin. "You are perfect."

Darcy laughed and Emerson feared she was about to say no. But when she stopped, a smile remained. "Okay."

"Okay, yes?"

"Yes."

Emerson got the feeling Darcy's acquiescence was tied, at least in part, to the moment. Not wanting to take a chance on second thoughts, she climbed out of bed. She threw on boxers and a tee, walked to her studio space, and picked up her camera. When she returned, Darcy's mouth offered a smile, but her eyes remained apprehensive. "If you're having second thoughts, it's okay. I don't want you to feel forced into anything."

Darcy shook her head. "No, I want to. I'm just a little nervous. Something about being naked, I think."

"Do you know what I think the sexiest thing about you is?"

Darcy raised a brow. "What?"

"Your confidence."

"Stop."

"I mean it. Don't get me wrong, your body is amazing and your eyes could turn me into a puddle. But you have this thing. It's like you're completely comfortable in your skin. So few women have that. It's sad, really, that it's rare, but you channel it like no one I've ever known."

The hesitation disappeared and, this time, the smile made it all the way to her eyes. Stunning. "Thanks."

"I mean every word."

"What do you want me to do?"

Emerson smiled. "Whatever you want. Show some skin, cover it up. Be coy, be brazen. The only rule is that you be you."

"Okay."

"And I'll show them to you when we're done. You can delete any or all of them."

"And you won't use them in a painting without my permission?"

"Yes, I have a written release that I use with all my subjects. If you don't sign it, then nothing will ever leave this room."

Darcy nodded and took a deep breath. "Okay. I'm ready."

And just like that, Darcy became a model. Emerson snapped furiously while Darcy stared right into the camera, then glanced away. She draped the sheet over herself in a way that tantalized in what it promised more than what it revealed. Emerson took photos of her face, her hands, the curve of her hip. Without coaching, and in the span of about ten minutes, Emerson captured hundreds of images.

Even without looking at them, Emerson knew they'd be amazing. It was the same magnetism she'd felt the first time she saw Darcy in The Flour Pot kitchen, only this was about ten times stronger. When she moved the camera aside for a moment, Darcy looked right in her eyes and Emerson felt a desire stronger than anything she thought possible.

"You are so beautiful."

Darcy rolled to her stomach and rested her chin in her hand. "I'm glad you think so."

"I'd say it's more of a truth universally acknowledged kind of beautiful, but I may be particularly susceptible to it."

Darcy raised an eyebrow. "Did you just Jane Austen me?"

"I might have."

"Officially the nerdiest, yet sweetest, compliment ever."

Emerson shrugged a shoulder. "I'm glad you don't think I'm a total dork."

"Oh, no. You're a dork. I just happen to find it endearing."

"I'll take that."

"So, do I get to see?" Darcy looked at her expectantly.

"The photos?"

"Yes, the photos."

"Absolutely. Let me copy them to my computer so you have more than a two-inch screen to look at." Emerson connected her camera to her laptop and downloaded the images, then carried the computer with her to the bed. She climbed in and positioned herself on her stomach next to Darcy. She slid the computer in front of Darcy and pointed at the arrow keys. "Forward and back. I want to see them too, but this way you can set the pace."

Darcy shot her a flirtatious smile. "I do love setting the pace."

"Not as much as I love it when you do."

Darcy began flipping through the photos, quickly at first, but then she slowed down. Emerson glanced occasionally at the screen, but mostly watched Darcy. Her face reflected a combination of discovery and wonder. "You've…These are incredible."

"You're incredible. I only captured what's there."

Darcy shook her head. She liked to think she had a reasonable amount of confidence when it came to her appearance. Nothing exceptional by any means, but attractive enough, and she enjoyed getting dolled up. This, though, this was something different entirely. The images on Emerson's computer were stunning. Like all the best parts of her without the things she tried to accentuate or hide. Not all of them, of course. In some, her eyes were closed or she'd been caught in motion, blurry and awkward. But the majority made her feel beautiful and, even more surprising, seen. "You're giving me too much credit, but still. I love them. Thank you."

"So, I have your permission to use them?"

Darcy imagined seeing herself on canvas. The idea thrilled and slightly terrified her. Especially the part about that canvas being on display, for sale. But it seemed cowardly to back out now. She contemplated nixing the ones where she'd bared her breasts, but she detested the arbitrary censorship of the female body. "Yes."

"Any of them? All of them?"

Before she could think about it any further, or start picking and choosing, she nodded. "Yes."

Emerson smiled at her. "Thank you. It means a lot that you trust me that much."

Darcy swallowed. Did she trust Emerson? She did, at least when it came to matters of artistic integrity. Tonight, that's all that was on the table. "I'd be honored to be the subject of one of your works."

Emerson got up to set the computer on the table and shed the clothing she'd put on to take pictures, then climbed back into bed with Darcy. "Maybe more than one."

Darcy shook her head. "You're something."

Emerson pulled the sheet over them and moved closer so that their bodies were once again touching. She gave Darcy a quizzical look. "What does that mean?"

Darcy didn't know. She wasn't sure why she'd said it. Instead of making up some explanation, she hooked her leg over Emerson's thigh, moved against her suggestively. "Nothing."

Emerson shrugged. "If you say so."

"I do. Now, how about you turn off the light so I can channel all this confidence you've tapped into?"

"Yes, ma'am." Emerson reached over and switched off the lamp.

Emerson glanced at the clock on her bedside table. The alarm to wake Darcy up for work would be going off in three minutes. The idea that she might be developing an internal alarm clock, and that said clock seemed to be set to seven in the morning, amused her. More, it didn't bother her. It was the little things, she decided, that made a relationship.

She took advantage of being the only one awake and studied Darcy's face. It was such a luxury to spend so many nights together. Emerson wondered when—or if—Darcy's rules regarding Liam might change. Emerson liked the idea of being around in the mornings, chatting with him over cereal or bringing Darcy a cup of coffee in bed. Was it such a leap from what they had now?

Emerson placed a kiss on her arm, her shoulder. Darcy sighed and, without opening her eyes, lifted a hand and ran it through Emerson's hair. "Morning."

"Good morning." Emerson placed a kiss on her lips.

The alarm went off then and Darcy groaned. She rolled over and shut it off before flopping on her back. "I so don't want to get up. Being with you is making me lazy."

"You're not lazy. I've been keeping you up way past your bedtime."

Darcy nodded. "This is true."

"Why don't you hop in the shower? I'll make coffee."

Darcy rolled toward her. She draped an arm over Emerson's shoulder and rested her chin on it. "You're very sweet."

Emerson shrugged. "I try. After last night, it feels like the least I can do."

Darcy climbed out of bed and padded to the bathroom. Emerson hauled herself up and went to the kitchen. She started a pot of coffee, looked at the dishes they'd abandoned the night before, and decided she'd deal with them later. While she waited, she stared out the window and started thinking about which photo she'd use to paint Darcy first. Assuming Darcy hadn't changed her mind. The coffee finished just as the shower cut off. Emerson fixed two cups and returned to bed.

Darcy emerged wearing Emerson's old flannel robe, the one Darcy had made fun of the first time she spent the night. "How is it you manage to make the grandpa robe sexy?"

Darcy smirked and crossed the room. She sat on the edge of the bed and accepted the cup of coffee Emerson handed her. She took a sip before answering. "I guess I'm just that hot."

Emerson nodded knowingly. "That must be it."

"For the record, if my ego is out of control, it's entirely your fault."

"I accept that blame willingly." Emerson enjoyed the teasing. She hoped it meant Darcy still felt good about agreeing to be the subject of a painting, or several. "Now that we're sitting together in the light of day, are you still okay with me using the photos we took last night?"

Darcy smiled. "I would be honored. But out of control egos aside, I also won't be disappointed if you change your mind. My feelings won't be hurt if you decide not to do anything with them."

"Honey, I can assure you that won't be the case." Emerson walked over to her desk and pulled a piece of paper out of a folder. She handed it to Darcy. "It's a pretty basic release."

Darcy skimmed the document. "I don't get royalties? I don't know…"

"If you feel—"

"I was kidding. I meant it. It would be an honor if you decided to use me in a painting." She took the document to the kitchen counter and picked up a pen, printing and signing her name at the bottom.

"I'm the honored one. If I can capture half of what's there, it will be some of my best work."

Darcy shook her head, but smiled. "If you say so."

"I do."

"Now that's settled, I suppose I should get ready for work."

"I suppose." Emerson sat cross-legged on the bed, watching Darcy dress. "What do you want to do tonight?"

Darcy shrugged. "I don't know. I should probably spend some time at my place doing laundry and stuff."

"Come on. It's our last night before Liam comes home. We should make the most of it."

Darcy made a face that Emerson couldn't decipher, but quickly replaced it with a smile. "Sure. What do you have in mind?"

"Other than making passionate love to you until the wee hours of the morning?"

Darcy rolled her eyes. "Be serious."

"I'm completely serious. But that shouldn't be all we do. I'll think of something. Do you trust me?"

"Yep."

Something in Darcy's tone seemed off, just like the face she'd made a moment before. Emerson brushed it off. "Shall I pick you up at your place? Around six?"

"Sounds good." Darcy finished putting her hair up and picked up her purse. "I'll see you later."

Emerson walked to the door to kiss her good-bye. "Oh, hey. Can I go with you to pick Liam up?"

"Nick is meeting me halfway. I only have to go over the bridge."

"I'd still like to go. If you want the company, I mean. If you'd rather have some alone time with Liam, I don't want to be in the way."

"No, no, it's not that at all." Darcy shook her head. What was it? A dozen thoughts and feelings swirled around in her mind. She wanted Emerson with her, and she knew Liam would want to see her, too. She liked having someone in the car with her, but hated feeling dependent on Emerson to provide that company, that comfort. Add to the mix she had no idea where things with Emerson stood, or where they should stand. And while none stood out above the others, the culmination felt like a triggering of her fight or flight response. "Company would be nice."

"Excellent. Have a good day at work."

Darcy made her way down the stairs and onto Commercial Street. It wasn't even nine, but cars and pedestrians jockeyed for position on the narrow thoroughfare, while trucks making deliveries slowed up everyone. Darcy smiled at the jumble. It was definitely the high season.

At the café, she donned her apron and hat, put away her things. Alex was instructing an intern on the proper way to fill éclairs. Since her two interns wouldn't be in for another half hour, she pulled out the day's menu and started planning how she'd assign tasks. Zoe seemed to pick everything up after only one demo, so Darcy decided to put her on stove duty. Stephanie was diligent, but still a little skittish. She could prep vegetables and make the chicken and lobster salads. Darcy turned her attention to salad dressings, mixing up the usual suspects and a batch of her latest creation, a cilantro-lime vinaigrette for a southwest inspired salad.

As her crew arrived, Darcy got them to work, overseeing the béchamel that would be the base of the macaroni and cheese and one of the soups. She offered Stephanie encouragement and made a slight adjustment to the way she held her knife. She was about to slide a tray of scones into the oven when the door swung open. Darcy looked up, expecting to see Alex. Instead, she found Lia standing just on the other side. "I'm not sure where Alex disappeared to."

Lia offered her a warm smile. "She's out front. I was actually looking for you."

"Oh." She dusted off her hands and gave Lia her full attention. "Hi."

"Hi." Lia came the rest of the way into the kitchen. "Liam's coming home tomorrow, right?"

Darcy couldn't repress a smile. "He is."

"I didn't know if Emerson was going with you, but if not, I'm happy to go for the ride."

"That's a sweet offer. Thanks. Emerson did offer to go. I already accepted or I'd totally say yes."

Lia waved her hands. "No, no. You should go with Emerson. I'm sure Liam will be way more excited to see her anyway."

Darcy put her hands on her hips. "Liam adores you."

"He does, but I don't hold a candle to Emerson on that front." Lia flashed a grin. "I don't mind. Emerson is way cool."

Darcy rolled her eyes. "Tell me about it."

Lia narrowed hers. "Is something wrong?"

Darcy sighed. "No. I mean, yes, but no. Or I don't know."

"Do you want to talk about it?"

"I'm okay. Just in a mood, I think. Thanks for the offer."

"It's a standing one. Anytime."

Darcy nodded.

"I think you and Emerson are great together. Whatever I can do to help."

Lia left and Darcy got back to work. In truth, that was the problem. They were good together. Or, at least, good in the various ways they seemed to be together. Emerson was great with Liam.

And, as a girlfriend, she was the best Darcy had in recent memory. More than recent memory, maybe ever.

But that was the problem—it all felt disjointed. It might seem that Darcy's girlfriend plus Liam's best bud should add up to family, but it didn't. Darcy didn't work that way. Even if, right before she fell asleep and her guard was down, she could imagine what being a family would look like. That was fantasy and she lived her life squarely in reality.

The last two weeks didn't help. Spending so much time with Emerson had brought her dangerously close to the edge of falling in love. It wouldn't take much for Liam to get there, if he wasn't already. Liam coming home could make the situation even more complicated if she let it. Darcy sighed. She'd just have to figure out a way to uncomplicate things, for Liam's sake. And hers.

CHAPTER TWENTY-SIX

By the time they got on the road, Darcy was happy to have Emerson's company. She decided it was a nice way to close out the two weeks they'd spent together. A denouement of sorts, a way to ease down from the climax. She glanced over at Emerson, quietly relaxed behind the wheel, and wondered if she felt the same.

Darcy found herself wondering how Emerson felt about a lot of things. But as much as she considered herself a direct person—unafraid of difficult or awkward conversations—she couldn't bring herself to broach the subject with Emerson. She didn't want to waste this last bit of time they had hashing out feelings about what it all meant for their relationship moving forward. Or whether it meant anything at all.

She took Emerson's silence to be an unspoken agreement. That should have made her feel better, but instead it sat heavy in her chest. She tried to shake off the feeling. Moping was not her style.

Although they'd timed the pickup for late afternoon to miss the worst of the traffic fighting its way onto the Cape, the line of cars heading in the opposite direction looked daunting. She was about to say as much when her phone pinged. The text from Nick indicated they were stuck in traffic. Darcy pulled up the maps app on her phone and scowled.

"What is it?" Emerson asked.

"They're not going to make it to the spot we picked in time."

Emerson didn't balk. "What if we meet them a little farther north?"

"But then we'll have to fight our way back through that." Darcy gestured at the vehicles opposite them, slowly inching along.

"We can have a leisurely dinner and hope that most of this clears out by the time we're done."

"You don't mind?"

"Of course not. We'll need to get dinner at some point anyway, and I'm not in a rush to get home for anything."

"I'll find a place and text Nick."

"Excellent. I'll wait for your directions."

That was a relief. Still, Darcy wondered if Emerson's easygoing answer had to do with wanting to spend more time with her or with having virtually no schedule. Not that it mattered. She did a couple of searches, settled on a place, and texted Nick. "Okay, there's a diner in Plymouth."

"Sounds good. Just give me directions."

By the time they arrived, Nick, Julien, and Liam were already there. They exchanged greetings and hugs and Darcy tried to ignore the fact that Liam seemed as excited to see Emerson as he was to see her. They moved Liam's things to Darcy's car. Nick and Julien declined joining them for dinner. Darcy laughed to herself. They'd never say so, but even with as much as they loved Liam, she imagined two weeks pushed their limit on the kid front. They did another round of hugs good-bye before heading into the diner.

The food was surprisingly good and Liam talked nonstop, quiet only when his mouth was full and Darcy reminded him to chew. He told them all about the newest additions to the aquarium, including a giant octopus, as well as going out on the feeding platform to get up close and personal with some barracudas. After that, he launched into his newfound passion for baseball, complete with a demo of the finger positions for different pitches.

Darcy soaked it in. She couldn't speak for Emerson, but the intensity didn't bother her. It was like recharging after being without him for so long. She called a timeout long enough to check the traffic and pay the check and then they were off. In the car, Liam's chatter resumed. There was a new family in Nick's neighborhood and they had a little girl Liam's age, Margie. She had aspirations of being an actress which meant that, in addition to wanting to be a scientist, astronaut, and knight, Liam now wanted to be an actor.

Traffic remained heavy, but at least they were moving. Darcy stole glances at Emerson, who appeared to be enjoying Liam's stream of consciousness conversation. She asked questions and responded often enough that Darcy knew she wasn't zoning out. By the time they hit Orleans, Liam had talked himself out and fallen asleep. Traffic thinned and Emerson took one of her hands from the steering wheel and placed it on Darcy's leg.

Darcy looked up and they briefly made eye contact. There was humor in Emerson's eyes but also something else. Darcy couldn't put her finger on it and it irritated her. When they pulled into the parking lot, Liam didn't stir. "Shall I carry him up?" Emerson asked.

Unlike the day of his birthday, when he'd just started to doze, Darcy knew he was down for the count. "Can you? Do you mind?"

Emerson unbuckled Liam's seat belt and hefted him into her arms. Darcy tried not to notice the way he instinctively wrapped his arms around her neck. Darcy grabbed his bags and they made their way upstairs. Once Liam was settled in his bed, Darcy pulled off his shoes and covered him with a light blanket. "My guess is he won't stir for at least ten hours."

Emerson laughed. "You're probably right."

They left his room and Emerson stole one last look at him, surprised by just how much she'd missed him being around. Not that she had any complaints about the last two weeks. No, she wouldn't trade that for anything. Still, it was nice to have him home.

Emerson and Darcy stood in the kitchen for a moment. For some reason, Emerson felt awkward, unsure of what to do with herself. Not because Liam was home, but because in his absence, the tenor of her relationship with Darcy had changed. Now that he was back, Emerson didn't know whether the rules had changed or if she was supposed to go back to how things were before.

"I'm sure you're beat," she said eventually. "Why don't I head home so you can get some rest?"

Darcy looked relieved. "That's probably a good idea. Thanks again for going with me, and for driving."

"It was my pleasure. I love spending any kind of time with you. I wasn't about to miss the last little bit of our time alone together."

Darcy nodded, but her expression turned into something Emerson couldn't decipher. "Yeah."

"And I missed Liam, too. I'm glad I got most of the stories, so now you don't have to hear them all twice."

That earned her a weak chuckle. "I'm sure there are plenty more."

"No doubt." Feeling like the conversation was getting worse instead of better, Emerson decided to make her exit. "So, I'll see you later this week? You'll text me?"

"Sure."

Emerson knew enough about women to know monosyllabic replies were a bad omen. But for the life of her, she couldn't figure out what she could have done to piss Darcy off. Maybe she was tired. "Okay. Take it easy, then."

With Liam sound asleep in his room, Emerson figured it would be safe to give Darcy a kiss good-bye. Darcy didn't rebuff her, but she didn't encourage her, either. Emerson collected her keys and left.

Darcy remained where she stood for a long while. Emerson's words echoed in her mind. *Wasn't about to miss...time alone together.* She'd had no illusions that the last two weeks were a bit of a fantasy. A vacation from responsibilities and real life. But while she cherished it, Darcy never for a moment wanted it in place of her life. Even if she thought Emerson didn't feel the same, having her say it out loud was jarring.

Now that Liam was home, she'd need to refocus. That meant spending her free time with him, but it also meant scaling things back with Emerson. She could handle that, keep herself from getting too attached. And hopefully prevent Liam from getting any more attached than he already was.

Chapter Twenty-seven

Emerson frowned. It was the second time in as many days Darcy had blown her off. She considered pressing it, asking if Darcy was mad or if Emerson had done something wrong. She shook her head. Darcy was direct. Emerson couldn't imagine her sitting on anything that truly bothered her. She was probably being overly sensitive. The intensity of the last two weeks had brought a lot of emotions to the surface. Emerson wasn't ashamed of them, but she didn't need to fling them at Darcy's feet, either. They were just recalibrating. The dust would settle and they'd be able to pick up where they'd left off before Liam went away.

And it wasn't like Emerson didn't have plenty to do. Her show was less than two weeks away and she needed at least one, if not two, new paintings to include. Although her time with Darcy yielded plenty of inspiration, she'd done virtually no work. Since she had no desire to get a side job, or become a starving artist, she ought to get cracking.

Feeling a new sense of resolve, she put on a pot of coffee instead of wandering down to the café. After some back and forth, she decided to start with an image of Liam and Darcy on the whale watch boat. With both of their faces turned away, Emerson could keep the piece generic. When she finished that, she'd allow herself to start a portrait of Darcy. She had a feeling once she started, it would consume her. Better to have that leading up to her deadline.

She stopped late afternoon for a break. After making a sandwich, she picked up her phone. Nothing from Darcy, but she did have a text from Will. Since they hadn't seen much of each other since Will moved out, Emerson readily accepted her invite to grab a beer. Will confirmed the time and Emerson set the alarm on her phone. Ever since the incident with Liam's show, she didn't take chances. With plans set and her mind just distracted enough from thoughts of Darcy, she got back to work.

When she left to meet Will, Commercial Street was hopping. Couples and families and gaggles of gay men walked and laughed and talked and greeted one another like long-lost friends. The Squealing Pig was bumping, too. The bar was packed and several groups stood outside waiting for tables. She spotted Will walking toward her and offered a wave. "Shall we try somewhere else?"

"What about that new brewery, beer garden place?"

Emerson thought for a moment. "Down by the firehouse?"

"Yeah."

"Sounds good to me." They meandered down the street. Emerson soaked in the sights and sounds, thinking she might try her hand at a street scene. She took out her phone and took a few photos.

"What are you doing?"

"Capturing inspiration."

Will shook her head. "Of course you are."

The bar was busy, but not nearly as packed, so they got a couple of pints and sat at the narrow bar outside facing the street. "How's life?" Emerson asked.

Will nodded slowly. "You know, it's pretty good. My roommates are cool. And we all work different hours, so I have the place to myself more than I expected."

"Nice. And work?"

Will smiled. "Work is great. It sounds dumb, but I really love being on the boat."

"What's dumb about that?"

"Nothing, really. It's just that I'm not doing anything important, you know? I've been hanging out with this grad student who's doing a field experience. A marine biologist. She's doing research and educating people."

Emerson studied her sister. "Is that what you want to do?"

Will laughed. "Not even a little. I'm thrilled to be a friendly face who keeps things running smoothly."

"There's nothing wrong with that."

"I know. I guess I'm just having a moment of guilt for not being more ambitious."

This wasn't the first time they'd had this conversation. When they were younger, Emerson used to try to nudge Will to find her passion. A lot had changed since then. "Ambition is overrated."

"I'll drink to that." They clinked glasses together. "What about you? Are you and Darcy living together yet?"

Emerson rolled her eyes. "Hardly. I haven't seen her in almost a week."

"Did something happen between you two?"

Emerson frowned. "Like a fight?"

"Yeah. Or something like that."

"Liam was with his dad, but now he's home."

"I know that, but it seems weird that you'd go from twenty-four seven to virtually nothing."

"Darcy seems a little distracted maybe, but we didn't have a fight. I figured she needs to settle back in with Liam and stuff, so I'm giving her some space. It's no big deal."

Will did not look convinced. "Does she know that's what you're doing?"

Emerson considered. "We didn't discuss it, if that's what you mean. Dragging her into a whole conversation about the fact that I'm giving her space kind of defeats the purpose."

Will shrugged. "I guess."

"Besides, I have plenty of work to do. I got practically nothing done in the last two weeks and I have a show at the end of the month."

"I hear you. I'm just saying, don't drop off the planet, okay?"

"Okay." Emerson didn't like where this conversation was going. Since when did she take relationship advice from Will? Since their beers were empty, she tipped her head toward the street. "Shall we?"

"Sure. I'm going to grab a slice of pizza for dinner. Want to join me?"

"I'll never say no to pizza." They walked back the way they'd come toward Spiritus. Emerson made the conscious decision to turn the conversation back to Will. "Can I say how much I love that whale watching has become your thing?"

"You may. Despite what I said earlier, I really do love it. It's funny, because if you'd told me six months ago this is what I'd be doing, I'd have laughed in your face."

"And yet here you are. You should let yourself be happy."

"I am." Despite the words, a shadow passed through Will's eyes.

"Are you sure?" Emerson stopped outside the restaurant to let Will answer, but Will opened the door and went in. Emerson followed, wondering if that was the end of the conversation or merely a pause.

They ordered slices and took them outside, sitting on the brick stoop in front of the restaurant. Will took a bite of pizza, chewed it methodically. She sighed. "I think I'm a little bit lonely. Not friends or family or anything. Relationship lonely."

Emerson nodded. "I know what you mean. It'll come."

Will squared her shoulders. "I know. I'm actually not even looking. I think it's good for me to take a break from all that. You know, get myself together."

"I think you're pretty together, but I get it. I'm proud of you for taking care of you."

Will blinked a few times, then swiped a hand across her eyes. "Come on, dude. You're going to make me all sentimental."

"I can't help it. You make me all sentimental." Emerson stood. "But there is work to be done, so we shan't wallow in it."

Will stood as well. "We shan't."

Emerson gave her a hug. "Let's make a habit out of this."

"Getting sentimental?"

Emerson laughed. "Getting together, although I don't mind getting sentimental now and then."

"Agreed. See you soon."

Will headed up a side street toward her apartment near the monument and Emerson continued down Commercial Street toward home. The sun was beginning to set and the air took on a slight chill.

Emerson increased her pace, weaving on and off the sidewalk to avoid collisions. She paused briefly to listen to the woman singing in front of the library and dropped a couple of dollars into her guitar case.

Back at home, Emerson poured herself another cup of coffee. It was only eight o'clock and, now that she wasn't keeping Darcy's hours, her evening was just getting started. She went into her studio area and pulled out the sketches of her day with Darcy on the boat. They captured a playful essence, paired with the joy that comes from being on the water. She had every intention of translating that into a painting, or maybe even a series.

Yet those weren't the images her mind kept going back to. No, it was the photos that called to her. And since Darcy had given her permission to use them, she had no reason not to incorporate one into her show. Emerson flipped through and found herself transfixed by one in particular—sexy without being overtly suggestive, or revealing. It exuded contentment laced with the promise of more. If she could capture half of that in a painting, it would be stunning. The thrill of it pulsed through her. She'd do it large scale, twice the size of her usual pieces. Smiling, she pulled out an oversize canvas she'd been saving—four feet by six—and looked at it. Perfect.

Emerson quashed the desire to set it up and get started. It would be her reward. All she needed to do was finish the one she was working on now. And maybe one more.

Darcy drummed her fingers on the kitchen table. She'd turned down Emerson's last two invitations to get together. She told herself she needed the time to catch up on all the things she should have done while Liam was gone, but that was chicken shit, really. She was avoiding seeing Emerson because she didn't want to navigate new ground rules. But not only had Emerson been asking, Liam had, too. She couldn't put them off indefinitely.

She picked up her phone and sent Emerson a text about spending the afternoon with Liam. It seemed unnecessarily mean to drag him to work without even asking Emerson if she was free. The reply was instantaneous and included a suggestion of dinner after. Darcy sighed. If she was going to do it, she might as well do it.

Liam came out of his room with one of his new books. "Mom, have I shown you this one yet? It's a detailed account of dinosaurs by era."

Darcy smiled. "Not yet."

"It's so cool. We just assume all the dinosaurs lived at the same time and that's totally not true."

"No?" She had a vague idea this was the case, but had never paid serious attention.

"No. Like the brontosaurus and the T-Rex. Movies and cartoons always show them hanging out in the same jungle and stuff, and it never happened. And some dinosaurs were tiny. Like, baby bird tiny."

"Wow. Sounds like you've got next year's science project ready to go."

Liam rolled his eyes. "This is pretty simple stuff, Mom. I'm going to be in the fourth grade. I need to come up with something a little more complex."

"That's a perfectly acceptable plan. Rolling your eyes at me, however, is not."

Liam slumped his shoulders. "Sorry."

"Apology accepted. Now, you know how I told you Grandma is busy tomorrow?"

"Yeah. And Sara is at her aunt's. Does this mean I'm going to work with you?"

Darcy smiled. "No, it means you're spending the afternoon with Emerson."

"Yes!" Liam set his book down and put his fists in the air. "Yes! Yes! Yes!"

Darcy's phone pinged again and she glanced down. "And she says to bring your swimsuit."

"Woo!" Liam kept his arms up and proceeded to run around in circles.

Darcy sighed. She might be recalibrating, but Liam certainly wasn't. What was she going to do about that?

CHAPTER TWENTY-EIGHT

Darcy packed a small bag with Liam's swim trunks, a swim shirt, and some sunscreen. She threw in a beach towel, too, because it felt weird to rely on Emerson to take care of that sort of thing. She resisted sending him with snacks, but she did fill his favorite water bottle and tuck it in with everything else.

They drove into town and Liam gushed his excitement to spend the day with his favorite person. When they pulled up behind the café, Emerson was sitting in one of Alex and Lia's Adirondack chairs. She stood and waved.

Liam hopped out of the car and ran right to her, flinging his arms around her waist. Darcy followed more slowly, grabbing her purse and Liam's bag. "Thanks for doing this."

Emerson grinned back. She seemed to be nearly as excited as Liam. "Thanks for asking me." She slung her arm around Liam's neck and mussed his hair. "We haven't hung out in forever, have we, buddy?"

Liam squirmed, but didn't protest. "Forever."

"If you're going to the beach, be careful. Liam, you know the rules."

"Yes, ma'am."

"We're just staying on the harbor side," Emerson said. "Barely any waves to speak of."

Darcy nodded. "Okay. I'm almost late. Call if you need anything. Otherwise, I'll see you around five."

"Got it." Emerson offered a playful salute and Liam mimicked her.

Darcy shook her head. "Bye, you two."

She headed inside and Emerson looked down at Liam. "Ready to go?"

"Yep." Liam nodded, but then made a face. "Are we really not going to Race Point? Or even Herring Cove?"

"We have plans, my man."

"What kind of plans?"

Emerson shrugged. "I guess you'll just have to wait and see."

Liam pouted a little. "How long do I have to wait?"

"Only as long as it takes you to stop pouting and come with me."

"I'm not—" Liam looked at her and thought better of talking back. "I'm ready."

Emerson led the way to her car, which she'd technically parked illegally, but kept in her line of sight. She opened the back door for Liam to get in and enjoyed watching his eyes get big. "Are those surf boards?"

"Not quite. Paddleboards."

"Awesome!"

"Now you know why we need to be where the water is calm."

He nodded. "This is so cool. Carlos has gone paddleboarding before and he said it was so cool."

"It is."

Liam looked at her with awe. If only Darcy were as easy to impress. "You know how?"

"I do. I don't have a ton of practice, but I've been out a few times."

"This is going to be so fun."

Emerson started the car and made the short drive to a parking lot she'd scoped out earlier that had easy beach access. As she paid the attendant, she realized Liam was still in street clothes. "How do you feel about changing in the car?"

"Sure."

"Okay. I'll get out to give you some privacy and I'll come stand by your window so no one can peek in." By the time she'd rounded the front of the car, he was wiggling out of his clothes. In what felt like less than thirty seconds, she felt the car door bump against her backside. "That was quick."

It was Liam's turn to shrug casually. Emerson popped the hatch and formulated a game plan. "Sunscreen first." Liam made another face, but didn't protest. When Emerson was sure she'd smeared them both in sufficient SPF 50, she put the bottle back in her bag. She picked up one of the life vests she'd rented. "Let's put this on, too, so we don't have to carry it."

"Okay."

Emerson handed it to Liam and watch him slide his arms through and snap the buckles in place. She tightened the straps, making sure it fit snugly and couldn't slide off. "All right, buddy. How does that feel?"

Liam tugged at the vest, then patted his front. "Feels great. Are you going to wear one?"

Emerson didn't usually wear a life vest, but she knew enough that modeling good behavior was way more effective than demanding it. "Absolutely. Safety first."

She donned her own vest, then surveyed their equipment. "If I get both boards, can you carry paddles?"

"Yep." He scooped them up.

She stacked the boards and wrapped her arms around them. She locked her car and they ambled a few hundred feet down the beach, stopping about ten feet from the water's edge. "Let's stop here. We're going to practice in the sand for a little bit."

"Okay."

They plopped down their things and Emerson positioned their boards side by side. She guided Liam on where to plant his feet, how to shift his weight from side to side to maintain balance. Then she demonstrated how to hold the paddle and alternate strokes to move through the water. "What do you think? Ready to give it a try?"

Liam nodded enthusiastically. "Yeah!"

"All right. I'll stay with you at first until you get the hang of it." She handed Liam the paddle and picked up his board, carrying it into the water. She waded in until it was about knee-deep, set the board in the water, and held it in place. "I'll hold it steady and you climb on."

Liam set his paddle on the board, then eased on, ending up on his hands and knees. Even with Emerson holding it, the board rocked under him. "Whoa."

"You're doing great. Just take your time, get steady. If you decide you don't ever want to stand up, that's okay, too."

"No, I can do it."

Emerson couldn't tell if he truly felt brave or if he was pretending for her benefit. "Okay. Just let me know when you're ready."

After about a minute, when everything had stilled, Liam said he was ready. He planted one foot, then the other, bracing one hand on Emerson's shoulder. The next thing she knew, he let go and was standing up completely on his own. "I'm up!"

She smiled at the triumph in his voice and the huge grin on his face. "Okay, I'm going to take one hand off and hand you your paddle. Remember what we practiced. Try to keep your weight evenly balanced. If you feel like you're tipping to one side, lean the other way, but only a little."

"Don't overcompensate."

She'd not used that word, so the fact that he did made Emerson laugh. "Exactly. Don't overcompensate."

She handed him the paddle. "If you fall, it's no big deal. You'll just land in the water. I fell at least a dozen times when I first learned."

"Okay."

"Are you ready for me to let go?"

After only the slightest hesitation, he nodded. "Yes."

She did and he rocked back and forth a little, but didn't tip. "Nice. You've got it."

He dipped his paddle into the water on one side, then the other. From everything she could tell, he was a natural. More so than she'd been at least. Maybe it had to do with him being smaller and having a lower center of gravity. He repeated the motion and, in the still water of the cove, managed to move himself a good ten feet away from her. She climbed onto her board and followed him.

"This is awesome." Liam turned to look at her as he spoke. The abrupt movement threw off his balance. After a few seconds of flailing, he landed in the water with a splash.

Knowing the water was shallow enough that he could still touch the bottom, Emerson didn't immediately jump off her board. Liam bounced up, wiping water from his eyes, but laughing. Emerson took a deep breath. "So, big rule of paddleboarding. No sudden movements."

With impressive dexterity, Liam hauled himself back onto his board. "Now you tell me."

Emerson let herself laugh then. "I think it's a sub-rule of keeping your weight balanced."

She watched him plant his feet and come to a squatting position. He picked up his paddle and stood up slowly. "Right."

"You really are good at this for it being your first time." She would have praised him no matter what, but it was true.

"Thanks. It's a lot of fun."

They paddled along the beach in relative quiet. Emerson liked that, for as chatty as he could be when excited, Liam wasn't one of those kids who talked constantly. She glanced back at where they'd left their things. She didn't want them to get too far away. She'd learned the hard way that fatigue could come on quickly. "How about we circle back?"

"Okay." The fact that he didn't protest told Emerson her instincts were right.

"We can jump off and turn our boards around or we can try to steer a U-turn."

"I can steer."

"Cool. Let me go first, then I can guide you."

Emerson went a little past Liam and started pivoting herself. She was just perpendicular to the shore when she caught Liam out the corner of her eye. Instead of staying put, he'd followed her. Only he was turning wide and heading straight for her. Emerson tried to speed up, but it was too late. She saw the fear in Liam's eyes as his board t-boned hers and they both went flying.

Emerson stood and looked around for Liam. His head was above water, but he didn't stand. Instead, he clutched at his arm and started screaming. Panic rose in her chest as she sloshed over to him. "Liam, it's okay. I'm right here."

The screaming stopped, but in its place came tears. Fat, genuine, in pain kind of tears. Emerson resisted the urge to scoop him out of the water. "It's okay. You're okay. Tell me what hurts."

"My…arm…" He choked out the words and Emerson thought her heart might break.

"Can you let me see it?" He moved the uninjured arm out of the way. "Can you point to where it hurts?" He used his good hand to point at his wrist. "Can I touch it? I promise I'll be gentle." He sniffed and nodded.

Emerson ran her fingers along his wrist and forearm. He flinched, but didn't cry out. Nothing felt out of place, so that was good. Still, it could be fractured. She needed to get him checked out. Which meant she'd also need to tell Darcy. She swallowed the new wave of panic. One thing at a time; focus on Liam for now. "Everything's going to be all right. First, we're going to get you out of the water, okay?"

Liam nodded. She contemplated trying to get her car closer, but didn't want to leave him alone. She walked him to dry sand. "I'm going to go get our boards and stuff, okay?"

"Oh…kay." He continued to cry, but with less intensity.

Emerson sloshed back into the water and dragged their stuff in. She made a split-second decision to impose on Will's day off instead of taking the time to lug it down the beach. "Do you think you can make it to the car?"

"What…a…bout…the…boards?"

The fact that he was even thinking about them was a good sign. "I'm going to ask my sister to get them. Don't you worry about it."

It seemed to take ages to walk back to where they'd started. In truth, it probably wasn't more than a hundred yards. Emerson grabbed their bags and guided Liam to the car. "I'm going to leave your vest on so we don't jostle anything. How are you holding up?"

"It really hurts," he managed, although he was breathing normally and got the whole sentence out at once.

"You're being super brave. I'm going to call your mom and ask her to meet us at the doctor, okay?"

Emerson helped him into the backseat and buckled his seat belt. He blinked at her; the tears had stopped, but some still clung to his eyelashes. "Do you think we're going to be in trouble?"

"No, buddy. You are most definitely not in trouble." She wished she could say the same about herself.

Emerson climbed into the driver's seat and tried to stay calm, which proved to be no easy feat. It might be nothing but a bump or he could have a broken arm. Not knowing, combined with knowing she needed to tell Darcy, made her sick to her stomach. Before starting the car, she picked up her phone to call Darcy. As it rang, she closed her eyes and took a deep breath.

Chapter Twenty-nine

Darcy hung up the phone. For a moment, she stood in the kitchen, frozen to one spot, unsure what to do next. Before she could sort herself out, Alex came into the kitchen. She stopped just short of running into Darcy.

"What's wrong?"

"Liam got hurt."

"Just now? Where? How serious?"

The barrage of questions yanked Darcy back to her senses. "He was with Emerson. They were paddleboarding. I need to go."

"Of course. Go. I'll take care of whatever needs attention here."

"Thanks. Emerson said he may have fractured something."

"Okay. Text me when you have more information and let me know if you need anything."

Darcy nodded, her body still refusing to spring into action.

Alex placed a hand on her shoulder. "He's going to be fine."

For some reason, that permeated the fog. "Yes. I'm sure of it. It's not like he's in an ambulance or anything."

"Exactly. And Liam's a tough cookie."

Darcy nodded again. Alex was right. But still. She'd feel a lot better when she could see for herself. "Thank you. I'm so sorry to take off in the middle of lunch."

"It's not the middle. We're almost done. And this is way more important. I'll let Lia know and we'll both be sending good vibes."

Darcy stashed her apron and grabbed her bag. It took no more than five minutes for her to make it to the clinic. She parked and went in, frantically searching for Liam. She found him sitting in a chair next to Emerson, talking animatedly about something. As she made her way over to them, Liam glanced up and caught her eye. "Mom!"

Darcy knelt in front of him, trying not to be too obvious about looking him up and down. "Are you okay? How did this happen? What did you hurt?"

"Mom, it was so cool. We were paddleboarding and I was doing really good. But then I ran into Emerson and fell off."

"You were what?" Darcy shifted her focus for a second to Emerson, who looked like she might throw up.

"Emerson taught me how to paddleboard. She said I was a natural. Only I didn't know how to stop and I ran my board into hers and we both fell off."

Darcy closed her eyes for a second, willing herself to be calm. Liam was okay. Actually, he seemed more than okay. She needed to focus on that, make sure he didn't think she was blaming him for what happened. Emerson was another matter entirely, but she'd deal with that later. "It sounds like you were super brave."

"I cried, but only a little. It really hurt."

"It's okay to cry when it hurts."

Before Darcy could ask any more questions, the nurse called them back. Emerson stood, but then froze. "I can wait out here."

As much as Darcy wanted to scream at her to go away entirely, that would only upset Liam. And since Emerson had been there when it happened, she might be able to answer some of the doctor's questions. "No, you can probably relate the details better than Liam can. Let's all go back together."

They were ushered into an exam room and she helped Liam onto the table. She was about to ask Emerson for the story when the doctor came in. Seeing a familiar face eased a little of her anxiety.

"So, what do we have here?"

Liam retold his version of the story. Emerson didn't have much to add. She hadn't been able to tell if Liam hit one of the boards on his way into the water. Between that and the fact that it started to swell, she hadn't wanted to take any chances. The doctor did a cursory look at Liam's arm, deciding they'd do an x-ray to be on the safe side. Liam insisted he could go on his own, so Darcy and Emerson were left alone in the exam room.

Before Darcy could open her mouth, Emerson launched in. "I'm so sorry. I'm pretty sure I'm overreacting, but I'd much rather that than have it be something serious."

To her credit, Emerson looked about as traumatized as Darcy felt. Still. It didn't change the facts of the situation. "What the fuck were you doing paddleboarding?"

"I..." Emerson trailed off. Clearly, she wasn't expecting that question.

"Don't you think you should have run that by me beforehand?"

Emerson's look of confusion turned defensive. "I didn't think it was a dangerous activity. We were wearing life vests and were never more than twenty feet out."

"And yet my son may have broken his arm." The thought still made her shudder.

"Which he could have also done falling down some stairs."

Darcy fisted her hands and tried not to yell. "But he didn't. Are you really going to stand there and tell me this was a good idea?"

"Well, I don't think it was a bad one. Liam had a good time and we were careful."

Darcy shook her head. Unbelievable. "And you don't think you should have asked me ahead of time?"

"Would you have said no?"

"That's not the point."

Emerson swept her hand in front of her. "It kind of is. If you wouldn't have stopped us, we wouldn't even be having this conversation."

"But we'd still be here."

Emerson understood that Darcy was upset, but the why didn't make any sense. Part of her wanted to say as much. The much larger part still felt immensely guilty about the fact that they were there at all and Liam might be seriously hurt. Before she could have an internal debate with herself, Liam and the doctor returned. Liam was sporting a bright blue sling.

"It's not broken. I don't need a cast." Liam sounded almost disappointed by this fact.

Both Darcy and Emerson looked at the doctor for confirmation. "Only a mild sprain. Put ice on it for twenty minutes every couple of hours for the next day or two so the swelling stays down. And the sling is more to help him remember not to use it than anything else."

Emerson couldn't remember the last time she felt so relieved. And if the look on Darcy's face counted for anything, she wasn't the only one. "That's good news," Darcy said. "Thank you so much."

"Ibuprofen is better than acetaminophen because it helps with inflammation as well as pain, but either is okay. If it's not substantially better in a week, come back and we'll take another look."

They filed out to the reception area where Darcy took care of the paperwork and payment. Emerson offered to cover the copay, since the visit to the doctor probably wasn't necessary in the first place, but Darcy waved her away. They walked out of the clinic and, for a fleeting moment, Emerson felt like they were a family that had just weathered a storm together. One glance at Darcy dispelled that notion. To Emerson, it seemed like she might, at any moment, bite Emerson's head off.

"Look, I'm—"

"How would you like pizza for being such a trooper?"

Emerson didn't know if Darcy didn't hear her or if she cut her off intentionally. At the mention of pizza, Liam spun around. "Yes!"

"Why don't you take him home and I'll pick it up and bring it over?"

"I want pepperoni," Liam said. Meanwhile, Darcy looked like smoke might come out of her ears at any moment.

Emerson gave Darcy a pleading look. "Please, let me. It's the least I can do."

"Fine." She glared at Emerson for a moment, then returned her attention to Liam. "You're with me, big fella."

Emerson watched them get into Darcy's car and pull away.

❖

On the drive home, Darcy listened to Liam chatter on as though nothing had happened. Well, not as though nothing happened. All he wanted to talk about was getting an x-ray and being in a sling. Discussing his injury was topped only by his exploits on the paddleboard. He talked about how good Emerson said he was, how much fun it had been. When he asked how long it would be before he could try it again, Darcy barely contained her temper. "Let's focus on getting your arm better, okay?"

"Okay. Emerson said a sprain can heal in a couple of weeks, but that I'll have to be careful with it because the tendons and muscles are weak after."

"Yes, we need to make sure it's completely better and then we can talk about building your strength back up."

"Emerson says I can do physical therapy. She says she knows a few exercises that can help."

Darcy gripped the steering wheel. "Let's not worry about what Emerson says, okay? We'll take you back to the doctor for that."

"But Emerson went to school to be a doctor, so she knows a lot."

"But she also didn't finish, which means she doesn't know everything." Instead of answering, Liam turned to look out the window. Darcy knew it was the nastiness in her tone more than what she said. "I'm sorry."

Liam looked at her. "Are you mad at me?"

Darcy reached back and patted his leg. "No, honey, I'm not mad at you."

"Are you mad at Emerson?"

Darcy kept her gaze on the road. "Maybe a little."

"You shouldn't be, Mom. It's my fault I fell."

"It was your first time. Of course it isn't your fault."

"Yeah, but Emerson told me to wait while she turned around and I didn't listen. I wanted to do what she was doing."

The tangle of emotions fighting it out in Darcy's mind took another turn. Not that she had any intention of blaming Liam for his injury, but if Emerson was giving him instructions that he didn't follow...It didn't matter. Emerson shouldn't have taken him out in the first place. Especially without her permission. Or even her knowledge. "I'm not mad. I promise."

Liam's shoulders slumped. "You seem mad."

Darcy plastered on a fake smile. Her kid was astute, a fact that made her proud. It was a pain in the ass sometimes, but she was proud. "I'm just glad you're okay." She took a deep breath and added, "And glad we're about to have pizza."

The smile plus the mention of pizza did the trick. Liam once again looked out the window, but without the shadow of worry on his face. When they got home, Liam unbuckled his seat belt and hopped out of the car. She said a silent prayer of thanks it was the left arm he hurt.

They made their way upstairs and Darcy realized he was still in his swimsuit. "What do you say we change clothes before Emerson gets here?"

He agreed and they went to his room. Darcy slid the sling over his head and helped him out of his swim clothes and into a clean T-shirt and shorts. She'd just put the sling back in place when there was a knock on the door. "I'll get it," Liam said as he ran from the room.

"Careful," Darcy called after him. "No running."

By the time Darcy followed, he'd let Emerson in. She stood in the living room holding two pizza boxes with an uneasy look on her face. "Hi."

"Hi." Darcy took the boxes and set them on the table. "You didn't have to get two."

Emerson shrugged. "I figured it never hurts to have leftovers."

"Cold pizza is so good," Liam said.

Darcy pulled out some paper plates left from Liam's birthday and set them next to the pizza. "Liam, what do you want to drink?"

"Coke?" He looked at her hopefully.

Since there was some of that left from the party, too, she decided to indulge him. "Emerson?"

"Uh, same, please. Can I help?"

"Nope." Darcy poured drinks and they sat down to eat. Liam, confident that he wasn't in trouble for his exploits, relayed them again in minute detail. Darcy made sure to keep her reactions positive and light, although she did manage an occasional glare at Emerson.

In truth, it sounded like they had a lot of fun. And that Emerson took all the appropriate safety precautions. Plus, there was the fact that Liam wasn't seriously injured. Darcy would have taken him to the doctor, even if it hadn't been necessary. But that wasn't the point. The point was that Emerson took Liam on an activity without telling her. Whether or not the oversight was intentional, it was a huge overstep of her role. And that was unacceptable.

When they finished eating, Darcy told Liam he could watch whatever he wanted on TV. She let Emerson queue up some old episodes of *Bill Nye* while she prepared an ice pack. She went to the living room to situate him, but Emerson already had him on the sofa with his arm propped on a stack of pillows.

"In addition to ice, keeping an injury elevated helps prevent swelling," Emerson said to Liam. "Do you know why?"

Liam shook his head.

"Gravity."

Liam narrowed his eyes, trying to decide if she was teasing him. But then he nodded, as though he'd worked through the logic of it in his head and it made sense. "Cool."

Darcy tucked the ice into his sling, then turned to Emerson. "I'll walk you out."

Emerson glanced at her, but didn't comment on the less than subtle hint. Then she looked at Liam. "You did great today. I'm really sorry you got hurt."

Liam shrugged and offered her a lopsided grin. "I had fun, too. Next time I won't try to turn around."

"Take it easy, buddy." Emerson offered him a wave.

"Bye, Emerson." He lifted his uninjured hand.

Darcy followed Emerson to the door. "Liam, I'll be right back."

"Okay, Mom." He was already engrossed in his show.

Outside, before Darcy could say anything, Emerson turned to face her. "I really am sorry. I hope you know I'd never have taken him if I thought he might get hurt."

"Maybe you should have asked me first."

Emerson frowned. "I'm sorry I didn't. Would you have said no?"

"I don't know. That's not the point."

"Then what is the point?" Emerson looked genuinely confused.

"The point is he isn't your son. You don't get to make decisions for or about him." Darcy had never had to draw that line with anyone before. It didn't feel good.

"I've never tried to step on your parental toes."

"The fact that you're even referring to it as stepping on my toes means you don't get it."

Emerson took a step back. "Darcy, I'm not being flip. You have to know that I care about Liam. I care about him outside the context of us."

"I know you care about him. But you're his friend, not his step-parent."

"Okay, we're friends that forgot to ask Mom's permission before doing something a little crazy." Emerson cracked a smile. "Does that mean we're grounded?"

"Don't patronize me."

Emerson's eyes got big and she lifted her hands defensively. "I'm not patronizing you."

"Look, we're not getting anywhere. I think you should go."

"Darcy." Emerson's tone was exasperated, a fact that irritated Darcy even more.

"Don't 'Darcy' me. You crossed a line, Emerson. I'm not okay with it, and I'm not going to be." She knew she was overreacting, but she couldn't help herself.

Emerson lifted her chin. "Well, I'm not the only one. You've made me feel about this big." She lifted her thumb and finger, spaced less than an inch apart. "I've done everything I could to be there for you, and for Liam. And you're treating me like a stranger."

"That's not true."

Emerson shook her head. "You're right. It's worse. You're acting like I'm some irresponsible babysitter. Who I guess also happens to be your fuck buddy."

Darcy's mouth opened, but no sound came out. She watched Emerson walk to her car and, without another word, get into it and drive off. Darcy stood in the parking lot staring at the spot Emerson vacated. Another car pulled in and one of her neighbors got out and offered a friendly greeting. That snapped her back to reality. Darcy returned the hello, then climbed the stairs back to her apartment. Liam remained on the sofa with his arm propped on a pillow. "How's that ice holding up?"

"It's good." His tone was chipper and he smiled at her before returning his attention to the television.

Darcy pressed her fingers to her forehead, willing away the headache that raged behind her eyes. She shook her head at the stupidity of doing that and went to the bathroom for some ibuprofen. She swallowed three before checking her watch. Liam wasn't due for another hour or so, which was good since that was right around his bedtime. She returned to the living room and checked on him. Again, he seemed fine.

She went to the kitchen to clean up, unsure whether his blasé attitude made her feel better or worse. That was dumb. Of course it made her feel better. It confirmed that he hadn't been seriously hurt. That's what mattered most. Still. It didn't lessen how mad she was at Emerson, the paddleboarding now overshadowed by how defensive she'd gotten outside. Like Darcy didn't have a right to be upset.

She crammed paper plates into the trash, put the leftover pizza in a container and into the fridge. She wiped down the table and the counters, then stood there with her arms folded. How the hell had the conversation gone from her being upset about Liam to Emerson picking apart their relationship? She shook her head. It just proved that Emerson didn't get it. And that Darcy was a fool for letting herself think otherwise.

CHAPTER THIRTY

Emerson glanced at the window, surprised to find it light out. She blinked a few times and rolled her shoulders. She took a step back and looked at the painting. It put a lump in her throat. Darcy looked back at her, her expression holding the same teasing promise as the night Emerson photographed her. The effect on Emerson was the same as that night—a mixture of desire and awe. Like Darcy herself, the painting managed to be both classic and fresh, modest in what it revealed but pulsing with sexual energy. For the first time in a long time—maybe ever—Emerson captured the object of her own desire. Her artistic appreciation paled next to the ache in her chest, the longing to have Darcy there with her, in the flesh.

Emerson tried to shake off the torrent of emotions coursing through her. She'd just finished the most stunning painting of her career. She should be thrilled. When she couldn't seem to muster that, she turned away. Maybe a shower and some sleep would help. Even with her night owl tendencies and bursts of energy while working, she was getting too old to pull all-nighters.

She walked to the bathroom, stripping off clothes as she went and realizing she was drenched with sweat. An angry rumble came from her stomach. Emerson shook her head. She was a mess.

After showering and putting on fresh clothes, she bypassed the coffeepot for a banana and some peanut butter right out of the jar. She checked her phone, but there were no texts or missed calls from

Darcy. It had been three days since Liam had been hurt and not a peep from her. Well, except a terse reply to Emerson's text checking on Liam.

The silent treatment was probably preferable to another fight. Even knowing that, Emerson had to stop herself from calling her. Just to hear her voice.

She was in no condition to fight or make up. Maybe after some sleep. Things would work themselves out. They had to. Darcy was mad and Emerson was, too. Or, at least, she had been. They needed some space. She was enough of an adult to give it to them. She wouldn't be one of those obnoxious and pushy women, making demands and forcing Darcy to push back.

But telling herself that didn't make her miss Darcy any less. Or Liam, for that matter. They'd started out as buddies, but her feelings for him had grown into so much more. Maybe not full on parental, but Emerson felt protective of him—she wanted to be his friend, but also his champion. One of the people who would help him grow into a young man.

Clearly, lack of sleep was making her soppy. Emerson shook her head as she walked around her apartment, pulling the blackout shades down. She returned to the painting one last time, switching off her work lights. Then she crawled into bed, pulling the covers over her head. It didn't take long for the fatigue of her body to overcome the swirling of her mind and Emerson gladly gave herself over to sleep.

She woke with a start, only to realize through the fog in her brain that her phone was ringing. She reached for it, only it wasn't on her nightstand. The sound seemed to be coming from somewhere in her bed. By the time she riffled through the sheet and duvet and located it, the call had gone to voice mail. She saw with disappointment that it was Will calling, not Darcy.

Emerson chided herself. She was never disappointed to hear from Will. She waited a moment for the voice mail to register, but it didn't. She swiped her finger across the screen and called her back.

"Hey." Will's voice registered surprise.

"You didn't leave a message."

"I didn't have anything important to say. I was just checking in."

Emerson rubbed a hand over her face. She'd talked to Will after the paddleboarding debacle, but not since. "Checking in because you miss me or because you're worried about me?"

"Can't it be both?"

Emerson sighed. "Yeah."

"So, how are you?"

Instead of saying "fine," Emerson thought for a moment. "Out of sorts, exhausted from work, but okay. You?"

"Better than you, I think. Are you still avoiding Darcy?"

Emerson sighed again, but this time out of exasperation. "I'm not avoiding her. She's avoiding me."

"God, I don't know which of you is more stubborn."

"She is."

"Easy there, glass house."

Emerson scowled. "I thought you called to check on me, not harass me."

"I did. Sorry. I'm off today. Want to grab a late lunch?"

Emerson pulled the phone back to check the time. Just after two. "Sure. When? Where?"

"Burger Queen. Three o'clock."

"Great. I'll see you there."

Emerson sat up and looked around. Bright light outlined her shades. Everything was just as she'd left it, including the painting of Darcy. Emerson shook her head. She'd slept for six hours, not gone away for a month, even if she felt detached and disoriented. She stretched her neck and tried to shake off the rest of the haze. She crawled out of bed, contemplated another shower, but decided to just get dressed instead. It's not like she was trying to impress anyone.

She walked out of her building twenty minutes later. Even with her sunglasses on, the brightness of the sunshine made her wince. Between her weird sleep schedule and the fact that she hadn't been out in a few days, she felt like a bit of a vampire. She laughed as she walked, grateful that Will had called and pulled her out of her cocoon.

They ordered burgers and milkshakes and squeezed into an opening at one of the picnic tables. Emerson took a huge bite of her burger and sighed, realizing she hadn't had a real meal in days. Will pointed a fry at her. "You don't look so good."

Despite the insult, Emerson smiled. "Thanks. I'm okay, really. I get like this before a show. It's always a scramble to finish one more piece, you know? Add that wow factor."

"I hear you. I remember the panic you were in the entire month before your first show."

Emerson smiled at the memory. "I don't panic anymore. Mostly. But I do tend to work in a frenzy. I think I might be getting too old for that."

"I know what you mean. How about Darcy? No change?"

Emerson rolled her eyes. "Giant. Fucking. Mess."

"You need to talk to her." Will's eyes held concern, but Emerson detected a hint of bossy older sister as well.

"I thought I made it clear. She's avoiding me."

"So, you've tried calling her?"

"No." Emerson had thought about it plenty, but didn't know what she would say.

"Texted?"

Again, she couldn't decide whether she was supposed to apologize or demand that Darcy did. "I reached out to check on Liam and she replied with like two words."

Will nodded. "And then what?"

"Nothing."

Will sucked on her straw, a look of complete exasperation on her face. "What do you mean nothing?"

"She didn't elaborate, apologize, or anything. She basically told me I don't matter. I'm not going to grovel for crumbs." Even as she said the words, Emerson knew she would if it came to it.

"Asking to talk isn't groveling. And I know you're saying it's the show, but you're miserable and work has nothing to do with it."

Emerson glared. She hated it when Will was right. "Okay, fine." She picked up her phone and texted Darcy. "I asked her if we could talk."

Will nodded. "Good."

"You think I should grovel, don't you?"

Will lifted her hands. "Not at all. As the poster child for sticking it out in shitty relationships, I've learned my lesson."

Emerson frowned. "I'm sorry. I'm sure my problems seem ridiculous compared to what you've been through."

Will reached over and grabbed her hand. "It's not a competition. And the reason I'm nagging you is that your relationship with Darcy has seemed like the exact opposite of shitty."

"Yeah." It was the best relationship she'd ever had, especially after Darcy took away some of the rules and the boxes. That's what made their last fight so bad. It felt like all the boundaries and walls were back. Or, worse, that they'd never really left.

"You're in love with her, aren't you?"

Emerson sighed. "Yeah."

Will nodded. "In that case, a little groveling might be okay."

Darcy looked at her phone. Seeing Emerson's name filled her with equal parts elation and dread. The text didn't reveal much, just a simple request to talk. It made her feel childish that she'd not reached out first, but she couldn't change that now. What mattered was being able to apologize for overreacting.

Darcy went in search of Alex and found her rearranging things in the pastry case. "Hey, would it be okay if I snuck out half an hour early today?"

Alex looked up, a muffin suspended midair in a pair of tongs. "Of course. Is everything okay?"

"Yeah." She almost left it at that, but then added, "Emerson wants to talk and I'd rather do it in neutral territory."

Alex nodded. "Neutral territory is good. That's how Lia and I hashed through our first fight."

Darcy cringed. Did being compared to Lia and Alex make her feel better or worse? "Well, I don't know how much hashing we'll do, but whatever it is, I don't want Liam around for it."

"Take all the time you need. And you're welcome to use our place if you'd like."

"Thanks. I may borrow your chairs out back if that's okay."

"Any time. Are you…" Alex trailed off and Darcy wondered if she was wishing Lia were around. "Do you need anything?"

The fact that she offered meant so much to Darcy. "I'm good, but thanks."

Darcy returned to the kitchen and replied to Emerson, asking to meet at the café. Emerson confirmed immediately. Darcy nodded at no one in particular. That was a good sign. Probably. She gave instructions to the kitchen staff, then spent a few minutes touching up her makeup and trying to get rid of her hat hair. When eating crow, it never hurt to look good.

She walked out the back door five minutes before their scheduled meeting time, but Emerson was already waiting. "Hi."

"Hi." Emerson offered her a half smile that said, if not apology, at least not more fighting.

"Look, I—" Darcy said, but Emerson spoke at the same time. Darcy didn't catch what she said.

"You first." Emerson waved her hand in deference.

"No, you go ahead. You asked to talk." That might help her gauge how much groveling would be called for.

"I'm sorry I took Liam paddleboarding without your permission. And I'm really sorry he got hurt. You have to know I wouldn't have if I'd even thought for a minute it might be dangerous."

"Yeah, but you didn't think." The words were out of Darcy's mouth before she could contain herself. "I'm sorry, that's not what I meant."

Emerson raised a brow.

"I mean, it is what I meant, but that's not what I wanted to say."

Emerson waited silently. She was prepared to hear Darcy out, or perhaps give her enough rope to hang herself.

Darcy plowed on. "I was upset that you did it without telling me, but I would have said yes. You went in shallow water, you wore life vests, you did all the things I would have insisted on. I don't blame you for Liam falling."

Emerson sighed, relief visible not only on her face, but in her whole body. "Thank you."

"And I'm sorry I flipped out. It was definitely a moment of maternal panic." Emerson smiled and Darcy wondered if it might be as easy as that.

"So, that just leaves the fact that you are shutting me out." Emerson's tone wasn't angry, but the words stung.

"I'm not."

"You are."

She was. She knew she was. But owning it meant admitting how much she'd let Emerson into her life in the first place. Darcy wasn't ready for Emerson to see how much her heart—and Liam's— were in Emerson's hands. "I'm recalibrating. I'm just trying to get things back to the way they were."

"You mean when we were just sleeping together? When Liam and I were just friends?"

"You say that like it's a bad thing."

Emerson took a breath and tried to slow her pulse. Was it a bad thing? That's what she'd wanted going in. Darcy had been the one obsessed with labels and rules and boundaries. Emerson went with the flow. But somewhere along the way, it all started to matter. Really matter. She'd said it more crassly than she would have liked, but she'd meant what she said about feeling like Liam's friend and Darcy's fuck buddy. "It might not be bad, but it's not what I want."

Darcy folded her arms and locked eyes with Emerson. "What exactly do you want?"

"I don't know, exactly, but I know I don't want to be compartmentalized, allowed into little parts of your life as you see fit."

Darcy shook her head. "Don't you get it? The reason you don't know is exactly the reason I have to keep things compartmentalized."

"Would you feel better if I made you a million promises? That doesn't guarantee anything either, you know."

"I do know. But it doesn't mean I won't do whatever it takes to spare Liam unnecessary heartbreak."

It was such a narrow, literalist way of looking at things. Emerson shook her head. "Is that what you think you're doing?"

Darcy lifted her chin. "I know I can't do it perfectly, but I'm still going to try."

"And you think that's what I am, a heartbreak waiting to happen."

Darcy didn't respond.

Emerson's chest ached, but she didn't know what would bring Darcy around. She contemplated flinging herself at Darcy's feet, but had a feeling that would make things even worse. "Look, I have a lot of work to do to get ready for my show next week. Why don't we take a breather until then? I want to be part of your life, and Liam's. I don't know what it will take to convince you of that, or if we can come to some sort of compromise." She took a breath, then added, "But I'm not ready to throw in the towel."

Darcy nodded, her face impassive. "Okay."

"Tell Liam I'm super busy with work." Emerson hated even saying that, because no matter how busy she was, she'd make time for him. "I mean, I'm not too busy for him, but it's okay if you say it. For a little while at least."

"I will." Darcy looked away, then down at her watch. "I need to go."

"Okay." Emerson wanted to ask Darcy if she'd see her at her show, but she was afraid of what the answer might be. "Take care."

Emerson thought about giving Darcy a hug, or maybe a kiss on the cheek, but before she could decide, Darcy turned and walked back into the café. She stood there a long moment, trying to decide if the conversation had started to mend things or end them all together. Loitering wouldn't give her any answers. And since she did have a lot of work to do, she headed home.

CHAPTER THIRTY-ONE

Emerson kept her promise and didn't reach out to Darcy in the days leading up to her show. She had plenty to keep her busy—finishing another small painting, transporting everything, deciding the layout of her work in the space—but that didn't stop her from thinking about Darcy. Liam, too. She fell asleep thinking about them and woke up thinking about them. And just when her mind seemed to be consumed by something else entirely, they'd pop up, unbidden. It didn't help that the painting of Darcy, nearly life-size, was a constant presence.

The morning of the show, the gallery was closed and she was able to do a final walk-through. Although she'd signed the contract six months prior, before she'd met Darcy or even considered doing a large-scale piece as a focal point, the space was perfectly suited to it. The large square room had a single dividing wall in the center. She'd initially considered four smaller paintings on a single theme, but now she couldn't imagine anything but the painting of Darcy anchoring the space and commanding attention from every angle.

She wondered if Darcy would come. They hadn't discussed it, nor had they discussed that Darcy would be featured in it. Had things not taken a turn, she would have invited Darcy to her studio, given her a private viewing before anyone else saw it. But those plans, and so many others, had changed.

She did her best to stay focused. Will took the day off to help and, by some unspoken agreement, kept her attention where it needed to be. They chatted with Peter, the gallery manager, walking around and making sure everything was set. Emerson had decided to arrange things by theme, so she had a wall of landscapes, another with paintings of women, and one with men. She used the back of the focal wall to display three animal paintings she'd done—the turtle from her time with Liam, the tail of a whale from a photo she took on the whale watch, and a bird she found nesting near the beach. She liked that the works inspired by her time with Liam were the flip side of Darcy.

Satisfied she was ready, she went home to change. Will followed. She'd even brought her change of clothes so Emerson wouldn't have the chance to mope or fret or do any of the other things a moody artist with relationship problems might be prone to do.

She put on the charcoal pants and vest she'd bought herself when she booked the show, gray shirt, and a purple tie. She indulged in a little extra time on her hair, using just enough wax to give it the intentionally disheveled look. By the time she laced up her boots, Will was ready and waiting. "You look great."

Emerson took a deep breath, blew it out in a huff. "Thanks."

"Ready?"

"As I'll ever be."

They walked the short distance back to the gallery and found Alex and Lia already there, arranging snacks and setting out the case of wine Emerson had bought. "This isn't your first Gallery Night, is it?" Lia asked.

Emerson shook her head. "No, but it's my first time having a Gallery Night opening with a whole show to myself."

Lia beamed. "So exciting. I know it might be cheesy to say, but we're so proud of you."

Alex nodded and Will slung her arm around Emerson's shoulders. "We all are."

Despite telling herself a hundred times she was cool, Emerson found herself choked up. Partly because she'd never get to have her parents at a show and, even now, the desire to make them proud stuck with her. But if she was being honest with herself, part of it was Darcy. She'd really hoped to share this night with Darcy. She'd taken for granted that Darcy would be there and now that she wasn't, something about the celebration felt hollow. Emerson shook her head. Now was not the time to wallow. She cleared her throat. "Your support means the world to me."

Not long after, people began to arrive. Emerson recognized a few former clients, some friends. Most were strangers—a few collectors, maybe, and tourists wandering the East End for Gallery Night. Emerson worked the room, chatting and trying to be a good host. Even with that effort, she remained distracted. Every movement near the door got her attention; each time it wasn't Darcy, her heart sank.

She lasted almost two hours. Long enough to see the people who'd come specifically for her, to thank them for their support. She did okay finding the right balance of soaking in and deflecting their praise. By all accounts, her opening was a success. But all she could think about was Darcy. That fact, and all its implications, hit her as she shook hands with a couple who'd just purchased the man in the yellow Speedo.

She loved her. Like, make babies and live happily ever after loved her. She needed to tell her. Now.

She went in search of Will, who was chatting with Lia and Alex. "I need to get out of here."

Lia put a hand on her arm and Alex asked, "Are you okay?"

"I need to talk to Darcy."

Will frowned. "Is she not coming?"

"I don't know. She hasn't shown up yet."

"Do you want me to call her?" Alex asked.

"No, I don't want to make it weird. I just need to see her."

Will nodded. "Okay. What do you need from us? What can we do?"

Emerson shook her head. "Nothing. I just wanted to let you know."

"We can stick around in case Darcy shows up," Lia offered.

"You don't have to do that."

Alex waved a hand. "No big deal. Things are starting to wind down. We're going to pick up the food in little bit anyway."

"And I'll help," Will said.

"You guys are the best. You know that, right?"

Lia smiled. "We do. Now, go. Good luck."

Emerson jogged from the gallery to where her car was parked. She didn't want to be cheesy-movie desperate, but she felt it. Deciding you want to spend the rest of your life with someone created a sense of urgency. And she did. She wanted it more than anything. She got on the road, reminding herself repeatedly not to speed.

"What's wrong, Mom?"

Darcy stopped pacing and stared at Liam. "Nothing, honey."

He raised an eyebrow and gave her a look that said he didn't believe her. "Clearly, that's not true."

Darcy laughed. She couldn't scold him for talking back when he was completely right. "You know how sometimes there's something you want to do and don't want to do at the same time?"

He considered a moment. "Like a karate tournament."

"Yes, exactly. You want to go, but you're kind of nervous and part of you just wants to stay home."

Liam nodded. "So, there's something you want to do and not do? What is it?"

She shouldn't be telling Liam all this, especially given how tenuous things were with Emerson. Anything that got him more invested had the potential to come back and bite her in the ass, tenfold. "Emerson has a show of her paintings tonight. I want to go, but since we haven't seen her much lately, I'm nervous." Darcy took a deep breath. It was a truthful, if simplified, answer.

Liam looked at her like she'd grown a second head. "Mom. Emerson's paintings are a big deal. We have to go."

"I'm not sure she wants to see me."

He angled his head. "Did you have a fight?"

"Sort of."

"Well, then you should apologize."

"It's more complicated than that."

Liam shook his head, clearly unconvinced. "What do you say when I don't want to go to karate?"

"That you'll have fun once you're there."

"And that I'll be proud of myself. Don't you want to be proud of yourself?"

Darcy looked at him. So much innocence and wisdom rolled into one package, it made her heart hurt. "You're right."

Liam folded his arms and smiled smugly. "I know."

Okay, so they'd still have to work on humble. Still, he was right. "All right. I'm going to go."

"Yes!" Liam jumped up from the sofa. He'd stopped wearing the sling the day before and his wrist seemed to be completely healed.

"I'm going to see if Sara can come stay with you for a little while."

Liam stopped jumping up and down and planted his fists on his sides defiantly. "Why can't I go with you?"

"Because I need to have a grownup talk with Emerson."

"But she's my friend, too."

"I know, but you don't need to make up with her. I do."

"You should have moral support."

"Liam."

Whether he didn't want to get in trouble or sensed what a big deal it was, he didn't argue further. "Okay, Mom."

"Thank you."

"You better make up with her."

Darcy laughed again as she picked up her phone to call Sara. Even with no idea what the situation was, he managed to hit the nail right on the head. "I'm going to try."

An hour later, Darcy walked into the gallery and stopped dead in her tracks. The painting hung in the center of the largest wall, more than twice as big as any of the others. The size alone would have caught her attention, as would the vibrant colors of Emerson's signature palette. But neither of those things held a candle to the painting's subject matter. In the middle of a public gallery—complete with track lighting artfully creating a spotlight—Darcy was faced with a life-size portrait of herself.

The painting wasn't a photographic likeness. It had the stylized vintage feel that seemed to be the hallmark of Emerson's work. Yet, anyone who knew her would see the resemblance. Emerson had a way of capturing her essence even without the specificity of precise detail. And Darcy remembered posing for it. Or, rather, posing for the photo that inspired it.

Darcy shook her head. It was stunning. More than beautiful, it was intimate. It captured something Darcy didn't know she possessed—a heady mix of playfulness and joy, tinged with something that felt at once sexual and innocent. She felt both enthralled and exposed. Someone called her name and Darcy turned, trying to rein in the jumble of thoughts and emotions crowding her mind. She was relieved to find Lia and Alex standing only a few feet away.

"I didn't think you would be here," Lia said.

Darcy hadn't said anything to either of them about the show, but given how things with Emerson were, the assertion shouldn't surprise her. Still, the show was a big deal. It's not like she and Emerson had such a dramatic falling out that she wouldn't want to show her support. Of course, it had been enough of a falling out that she had no idea she'd be the centerpiece of it. "I…"

"Are you looking for Emerson?"

Was she? Clearly, she was. She wouldn't have come otherwise. "Yes. I didn't…she isn't…"

Alex placed a hand on her arm. "Are you okay?"

Darcy nodded. "She's not expecting me. We haven't spoken. She's been working. I didn't realize—" She turned to face the painting again.

"Ah, okay." Alex's hand moved from her arm to under her elbow. "Do you want to sit down for a minute? Or get some fresh air?"

Darcy tore her eyes away from the painting to look at Alex. "Sorry. I was caught off guard is all. I'm fine."

"Yes, but you look like you might pass out," Lia said.

"And you're shaking." Alex looked worried.

The last thing Darcy wanted was to seem fragile. She mustered a smile. "Just surprised. I'm fine, I swear."

"It's beautiful." Alex glanced at the painting. "Did you not know Emerson was working on it?"

That was a loaded question. "Not exactly. She took some photos. I told her she could use them, I just..." Darcy trailed off again. Apparently, she'd lost the ability to form coherent sentences.

"Didn't expect such a prominent display?" Lia's tone was sympathetic.

Darcy laughed then, glad that she could have this reaction with her friends instead of with Emerson. "Something like that."

"There's just one thing," Alex said.

What could be more noteworthy than her own face looking down at her? "What's that?"

"Emerson isn't here."

That didn't make sense. Darcy yanked her gaze from the painting and turned to her. "Wait. What?"

Lia put a hand on her arm. "She left to go find you."

That couldn't be right. This show was the biggest thing to happen to Emerson—her career—all year. There's no way she'd leave. "She wouldn't do that. Besides, I'm here."

Alex shook her head. "I'm guessing you passed one another on the road. She was heading to your place."

Suddenly, Darcy did feel the need to sit down. Instead of indulging it, she tried to absorb this new information. And what it meant. And what the hell she was supposed to do about it. "I should go back there. Unless she gets there and realizes I'm here and comes back. I should—"

Lia interrupted her jumbled attempt at a plan. "You go. We'll call her and let her know you're on your way."

"Okay." Darcy didn't like the idea of leaving. She hadn't even seen all the paintings. But if Emerson left her show to see her, the least she could do was go to where Emerson was.

She looked down at herself, then around, like she might be forgetting something. Alex put a hand on her shoulder. "You're fine. Go."

She nodded. "Yes. Going."

Lia grinned. "Good luck."

She had no idea what she wanted to say to Emerson, much less what Emerson had to say to her. "Thanks. I think I'm going to need it."

Chapter Thirty-two

Darcy's car wasn't in its usual spot, but lights shone in the window of her apartment. Emerson took the stairs two at a time and knocked on the door. When no one answered, she pressed her ear to it. She couldn't make out anything specific, but heard the TV. Knowing Darcy wouldn't leave the house with it on, she tried again. Still no answer. Would Darcy ignore her?

She turned to leave and had gone down the first couple of stairs when the door opened. She recognized Sara, Liam's regular babysitter, standing on the other side. "You're Emerson, right?"

Emerson smiled. Sara would be trained not to open the door for strangers. She was probably debating whether or not Emerson qualified. "I am. Hi, Sara. I was looking for Darcy, but I'm guessing if you're here, she isn't."

"She went out. I've been trying to reach her, but she's not answering her phone."

Darcy always answered her phone, at least when Liam wasn't with her. And Emerson guessed Sara didn't call her randomly. "Is something wrong?"

Sara hesitated, glanced back into the apartment. "Liam's sick."

"Sick how? What's wrong?" Emerson was in the doorway in a flash. She looked around, but saw no sign of Liam. "Where is he?"

"He's in the bathroom. He's throwing up."

Without asking for permission, Emerson headed straight for it. She found Liam sitting next to the toilet, looking green and a little woozy. "Hey, buddy."

He half-smiled. "Em—" A stream of vomit interrupted his greeting.

Most of it landed in the toilet. Unfortunately, it came in tandem with a burst of diarrhea. The sound came first, followed in quick succession by the smell and visual evidence all over Liam's khaki shorts.

"Oh, God."

Emerson turned to find Sara in the doorway, a look of horror on her face. She returned her attention to Liam. Whether it was Sara's comment or his own realization, the scales tipped toward chaos and he began to cry. Without thinking it through, Emerson took charge. "It's okay, buddy. You're going to be fine. I'll take care of you. I promise." She looked at Sara. "Can you get me a couple of trash bags and a roll of paper towels? Then fresh underwear and a set of pajamas from Liam's room."

"Got it." Sara seemed grateful for something to do that didn't involve coming back into the bathroom.

"Okay. We're going to get you out of these clothes. Do you think you can stand up?" Liam sniffed and nodded. Emerson started removing his clothes. "If you need to be sick again, aim for the toilet as best you can." Another nod.

Emerson managed to get him naked and sitting on the toilet before the next round of diarrhea hit. She grabbed the trash can and handed it to him. As was so often the case with kids and stomach bugs, he spent the next half hour like that. Sara returned with the things Emerson requested, then disappeared. When Liam seemed to be done, at least for the time being, Emerson helped him into the shower. After promising not to leave him, she filled one bag with dirty laundry and another with trash. The mess wasn't the worst she'd seen by a long shot. Med school had helped her build quite a tolerance.

"I finally got through to Ms. Belo. I told her Liam was sick. She's on her way."

Even if Emerson felt like she had things under control, that was for the best. Sick kids always wanted mom more than anything else. She wondered if Sara had mentioned her presence, but she didn't ask. She wasn't entirely sure she'd be welcome. She'd worry about that possibility later. "Great. I'll finish cleaning up in here. Could you see if there's any ginger ale in the kitchen?"

"Sure." Sara started to walk away, but turned back. "Thanks. I'm glad you were here."

Emerson nodded. "Me, too."

Sara headed to the kitchen. Emerson found a can of disinfectant spray under the sink. She gave the toilet a spray and a quick wipe down. Not perfect, but an improvement. The water stopped and a tiny voice came from behind the curtain. "I'm done."

Emerson helped Liam dry off and put on his pajamas. He looked worn out, but his color was better. "How are you feeling?"

His sigh spoke volumes. "Better, I guess."

Emerson opened her arms and wrapped him in a hug. He lingered there. "Let's hope the worst is done. How do you feel about getting into bed?"

He stepped back and looked down. Emerson feared he was about to puke again. Instead, he looked up at her with a mixture of embarrassment and longing. "Will you stay with me?"

Emerson fought to keep the emotion from her voice. Tears pricked her eyes. She blinked them back. "Not going anywhere."

They met Sara in the hall. She'd found ginger ale and had poured Liam a glass. Emerson thanked her and took it. She encouraged Sara to hang out in the living room and wait for Darcy while she walked Liam to his room. Emerson got him situated in his bed, then sat next to him. Without a word, he curled up against her and put his head in her lap. Emerson rubbed his back gently, hoping he was, in fact, through the worst of it.

She heard the front door and the sound of voices. A moment later, Darcy was in the doorway and then kneeling next to the bed. "Liam, honey, are you okay? I'm so sorry I wasn't here. And the stupid traffic on Route 6 was a nightmare."

Liam sat up and offered her a weak smile. "I'm okay, Mom. I was really sick, but Emerson was here."

Darcy made eye contact with Emerson, but for the life of her, Emerson couldn't read Darcy's thoughts. "It looks like she took excellent care of you, too."

"It was so gross. I was pooping and puking at the same time."

Darcy closed her eyes. "That sounds awful."

"He was such a trooper about it," Emerson said.

"Is that so?" Darcy put her arm on his leg.

Liam looked at Emerson, then his mother. "I guess so."

"How are you feeling now?"

"Okay. Better. I'm glad you're back."

Emerson smiled. No substitute for mom. "How about I take Sara home so you can stay with him?"

Liam grabbed her hand. "Will you come back?"

"Emerson is supposed to be at her art show, tonight. I think she probably should be there."

Liam's face was crestfallen. "Oh, yeah."

"I'd like to come back, if that's okay with your mom."

Darcy narrowed her eyes. "You don't—"

"I want to. If it's okay with you."

Darcy looked to Liam, then back at Emerson. She needed to stop pushing Emerson away. She nodded. "Of course. If that's what you want."

"It is. I won't be long."

When Emerson left, Darcy turned her attention back to Liam. He sat on the bed, looking far more interested in her conversation than his stomach. When Sara got through to her, she mentioned that Emerson had shown up and was with Liam. On what felt like the infinitely long drive home, she wrestled with that bit of information. She'd fought it for so long, but Darcy knew in her heart Emerson would take care of him, probably as well as she could herself. "Are you really feeling better?"

He nodded affably. "I really am. My stomach hurts a little, but not like I'm going to puke again."

She sat on the edge of the bed and ruffled his hair. "That's good."

"I felt fine and then boom. It was like an explosion. Both ends, Mom."

"Liam."

"I'm serious. It was the grossest thing ever. I pooped my pants. Like, seriously pooped them."

Sara hadn't mentioned that part. Darcy added that to the list of details of the evening. She needed to track down said pants for washing ASAP. She also had to acknowledge just how much Emerson had taken on in her absence. "Sounds rough."

"I was kind of scared, but Emerson was cool. I'm glad she was here."

"I'm sure Sara was glad, too."

"She was freaking out."

Sara was a great babysitter, but a sick kid would be enough to frazzle even an adult. Hell, it frazzled her. "I really am sorry I wasn't here."

He shrugged. "It's okay. Emerson was the next best thing."

The meaning of his words sank in. She'd accepted that she'd allowed Liam to get close to Emerson, and that he'd fallen hard for her. Only now did she realize how deep that feeling was. Sure, Emerson was fun and smart and cool to hang out with. More importantly, Liam felt safe with her. Knowing that made it easier to think about her own feelings, and where they might lead.

"Hey, Mom?"

"What, honey?"

"What was Emerson doing here?"

In the frenzy of the moment, she'd forgotten that's what she'd been trying to sort out. On such an important night, it made no sense for Emerson to leave her show to stop by for a visit. "You know what? I don't know."

Liam made the face he did anytime he tried to solve a puzzle or sort out a problem. "Didn't she have her art thing? Isn't that where you went?"

"It is."

"That doesn't make sense, then. Didn't you tell her you were coming?"

"I didn't." She hadn't told her she wasn't, either.

"If she thought you weren't coming, maybe she came looking for you."

"Maybe." Darcy let that sink in. Along with the fact that Emerson asked to come back after dropping off Sara. The show was probably over by this point, but still. That's where Emerson should want to be.

Liam nodded. "We'll have to ask her when she comes back."

"I think you should focus on getting some rest. Even if you feel better, you're officially sick." Liam sighed, but didn't protest. That told Darcy all she needed to know about how worn out he was. "Do you want me to stay with you until you fall asleep?"

"I'm okay. Thanks, Mom."

"You holler if you need me."

"I will."

She bent down and kissed his forehead, relieved that he showed no signs of fever. "Good night, honey."

"Night."

Darcy shut off his light and closed his door, leaving it cracked just a little. She went to the kitchen and looked around, not entirely sure what to do with herself. She leaned against the counter and tried to wrap her head around the last few hours—being the focal point of Emerson's show, the fact that Emerson left to find her. And then there was the image of Emerson in Liam's bed, with Liam curled against her. It managed to be both parental and sexy. Darcy pressed her fingers to her forehead. It's how she imagined she'd feel about her wife, if she ever had one.

Before she could dissect that revelation, there was a soft knock at the door. Darcy opened it for Emerson and was greeted with a shy smile. "Thanks."

Darcy shook her head. "I should be thanking you."

"It was nothing."

"Don't say that. You saved the day. Even if you don't think so, Liam does." Darcy stepped back so Emerson could enter.

"I kept my cool. In the moment, I'm sure it felt like a lot more."

Darcy chuckled. "Don't underestimate the power of keeping one's cool."

"Fair enough."

"Can I get you something to drink?"

Emerson smiled. "I'm good."

She started toward the sofa, but stopped; she was too nervous to sit. Darcy decided not to beat around the bush. "Why weren't you at your show?"

"Do you really want to know?"

"That's why I'm asking."

"It didn't feel right."

"What do you mean? Was something wrong with how everything was set up?" From the little she'd seen, it was flawless.

"No, not that. Everything looked great. It just...It felt like something was missing. Someone, maybe."

Great. She'd managed to put a damper on one of Emerson's most important nights. "Look, I don't want to presume anything, but if it was me, I'm sorry if I in any way ruined your—"

"I love you, Darcy."

Darcy blinked a few times and tried to decide if her mind was playing tricks on her. "What?"

"I love you. I'm in love with you. Liam, too, for that matter. And no big moment in my life feels right if you're not part of it."

"I..." The words were there, but she couldn't get them out.

As if sensing hesitation, Emerson shook her head. "You don't have to say anything. In fact, please don't say anything if you aren't sure."

Darcy forced herself to look into Emerson's eyes. She did love her, and she was absolutely sure. Darcy had no idea when or how that had happened, but to deny it would be a lie. She took a deep breath. Now was not the time to be a coward. "I love you, too."

"Darcy, please don't—"

"Let me finish."

"Sorry."

Darcy smiled at Emerson's sheepish expression. "I didn't want to love you. Really, I didn't want to love anyone. Too messy, too much work. And then I met you—night owl, artist, up for anything you. Nothing about you screamed 'looking to settle down.'"

Emerson nodded slowly. Darcy wondered whether she would agree with that assessment. "And then?"

"And then casual dates turned into more. You kept coming around. You kept showing up for me, and for Liam."

Emerson smiled ruefully. "Not every time."

Darcy shook her head. "I was unnecessarily hard on you. I thought that would make it easier, keep good boundaries. But no matter how hard I pushed you away, you never gave up or walked away. Tonight reminded me just how much that's true."

"Really, handling a sick kid is what did the trick?"

"That. And you left your show. Oh, and there's the matter of that painting."

Emerson looked alarmed. "You don't like it?"

"I don't like it. I love it." Seeing Emerson with Liam may have made the mom in her fall in love. The painting did it for her as a woman. "It's like you've captured all the best parts of me and none of the bad."

"I painted what I see. Which isn't to say I have some unrealistic, idealized vision of you."

Not idealized. If anything, Emerson saw all of her. Darcy hadn't realized how much she wanted that, or even that it was possible. "Emerson?"

"Yeah?"

"I love you."

Emerson's smile spread slowly and went all the way to her eyes. "I love you, too."

Darcy hadn't given it much thought, but she imagined if she ever did say those words to a woman, it would be in some romantic setting. The beach, maybe, or even in bed. But here they were, standing in the middle of her living room, with Liam sleeping in the next room. Not romantic, perhaps, but for them, perfect.

Darcy closed the space between them and slipped her arms around Emerson. She took a moment to absorb the feel of Emerson against her. It had only been a couple of weeks since they'd last been together, but Darcy realized it felt like an eternity. She leaned in and brushed her lips against Emerson's. One of Emerson's hands went to her hip, the other into her hair. Emerson took the kiss deeper, her tongue inviting Darcy into a slow exploration of one another.

When Emerson finally pulled away, she offered Darcy a soft smile. "I'm sure you're exhausted. I should go."

Darcy looked at her hands, then into Emerson's eyes. "Or you could stay."

"Stay?"

Darcy chuckled. "Not for a sexual escapade or anything."

Emerson ran a hand through her hair. "Of course not. I just... Liam's here."

Darcy laughed again. Emerson would have to get used to the idea of sex with Liam in the house. They both would. But tonight wasn't the time to hash that out. "I know. And he asked if you'd come back. Even though he fell asleep before you did, I'm sure he'd love to see you in the morning."

"I'd love to stay."

"Are you sure everything is okay at the gallery?"

"Absolutely. They run it. Sometimes, the artist isn't even there."

That made her feel better. "Okay."

Emerson nodded, but didn't move. It meant a lot that she was waiting for Darcy to take the lead. Instead of saying anything, Darcy took her hand and led them down the hall. Emerson stood awkwardly for a moment. "Do you have a non-girly shirt I could borrow?"

Darcy pulled out a plain gray tee. "Will this do?"

"Perfect. Thanks." Emerson undressed, leaving her boxers on and swapping her undershirt for the one Darcy handed her. She got into bed.

Darcy climbed into bed as well. She shut off the light and realized that Emerson was lying rod straight, leaving a six-inch space between them. She turned onto her side. "I didn't mean...we don't have to not touch at all."

Emerson shifted and rolled toward her. "I'm totally following your lead here."

Darcy smiled into the darkness. "Liam usually sleeps pretty soundly, but given how he spent his evening, I don't know."

"Darcy?"

"Yeah?" She wanted Emerson to stay, but she didn't want it to be weird.

Emerson put a hand on her side. "I just want to be close to you."

And with that, the tension melted away. Darcy moved closer and Emerson rolled onto her back. Darcy curled into the crook of her arm and slept better than she had in weeks.

CHAPTER THIRTY-THREE

Emerson woke feeling more rested and more at peace than she could remember in a long time. Ever, maybe. When Darcy stirred against her, she kissed the top of her head. "Morning."

Darcy lifted her head and returned the kiss, but on her lips. "Morning."

"I'm taking it Liam slept through the night. That's a good sign."

Darcy nodded. "Agreed. I don't know if he's up or not. Sometimes he watches television on Saturday mornings, but just as often he reads a book."

"One of the million things I love about him. Why don't we get up either way?" Emerson didn't want to press her luck. The idea of Liam finding them in bed together seemed weird, at least until they had a chance to talk to him about being together.

Darcy climbed out of bed. "I'll make coffee."

"Should I get dressed?" Emerson looked down at the boxers and T-shirt she wore. She didn't want to take anything for granted.

"You're fine. I wouldn't have asked you to stay over if I wasn't ready for Liam to know."

The matter-of-fact way Darcy said it made Emerson smile. "Okay."

They walked down the hall. Darcy peeked into Liam's room, then gently closed the door. "Still conked out."

Darcy put coffee on and they stood in the kitchen. Emerson drummed her fingers on the counter. "I think I should talk to Liam."

"About what?"

"Us. What it means for him."

"What are you going to say?"

"I don't know exactly. I mean, if you have it all set in your head, I don't want to step on your toes, but...I feel like I owe it to him."

"Owe it to him?"

"Yeah. Since he and I are friends, I don't want him to get the wrong idea."

"Like I'm stealing you?"

Emerson chuckled. "Not that, exactly, but sort of."

Darcy took a deep breath and nodded. "No, I think you're right. I don't usually tell him about who I'm dating, so it's not like I'm keeping a secret. But he might feel like you are."

Emerson wouldn't have put it in those words, but Darcy was exactly right. "Yes."

"I think you should. And I'm glad you thought of it."

"Thanks."

When the coffee was done, Emerson poured cups and Darcy led them to the living room, which was a little farther away from Liam's room. They sat on the sofa facing one another, legs entwined. Emerson realized she wanted to wake up every day exactly like this. Which wasn't realistic, given that Darcy had work and Liam had school. But still. They'd have occasional Saturday mornings and Darcy's days off. And on the mornings they needed to bustle around, they'd do that. Emerson wanted it all, the whole package. She looked at Darcy. "If I sold my place, it would give us enough for a down payment on a house."

Darcy looked at her, wide-eyed. "What?"

"I don't mean tomorrow. Sorry, I was thinking out loud."

Darcy still looked alarmed. "You want to move in together?"

"Um…" Emerson refused to backtrack. "Not right away. I get that it's complicated, especially with Liam, but eventually. Yeah."

Darcy nodded slowly. Emerson couldn't decide if she was mulling it over or forming an exit strategy. Eventually, she sighed. "Not in Provincetown."

Relief washed over Emerson and she smiled. "It doesn't have to be in Provincetown."

"You don't want to give up your place there. It's your studio. And it's in the middle of town. It's perfect."

It was perfect, a dream come true in a lot of ways. A dream that kept her afloat during the darkest time in her life, when nothing made sense and nothing felt certain. But that dream had changed. "Buying it was about living the life I wanted instead of the life I was supposed to want."

"And you're trying to tell me you'd let it go, just like that?"

"I'd be letting it go for something better, a different version of that life. A version that includes you. And Liam." Saying the words aloud only reinforced Emerson's certainty that she was ready for the next phase of her life.

Darcy let the idea of a life with Emerson sink in. If a small part of her brain screamed that it was too soon, too risky, her heart knew it was exactly what she wanted. And even if it was messy or hard sometimes, she knew in her heart it's what Liam wanted, too. "Yes."

"Yes, that's what you want, too?"

Darcy smiled. "Yes, I want that, too."

Emerson's face grew serious. "I can't promise it will be perfect, but I'm in it for the long haul. I need you to believe that."

Before Darcy could respond, Liam's door opened and he emerged, hair standing on end and wiping his eyes. She squeezed Emerson's hand. "I do," she whispered before turning her attention to Liam. "Hi, honey. Are you feeling better?"

"Yeah. I slept like—" His gaze landed on Emerson and he narrowed his eyes. "Did Emerson spend the night?" His tone held a mixture of excitement and suspicion.

Emerson shot Darcy a sideways glance. Darcy locked eyes with her before turning to Liam. "She did."

Liam looked at Emerson, then Darcy, then Emerson again. "Cool."

Emerson gave her a look that said, "Was that it?" and Darcy shrugged. "Are you hungry?"

"Starved. Can we have pancakes?"

Emerson jumped in. "I think maybe we should go easy on your tummy. How about toast?"

He sighed, clearly unimpressed. "Okay."

"And a ginger ale?" Darcy added.

That helped. Liam smiled. "Yeah."

Darcy stood. "You hang out with Emerson while I make it. Emerson, do you want some toast?"

Emerson smiled at her. "I'd love some. I haven't eaten since lunch yesterday."

"You got it." Darcy got up and walked to the kitchen. Because the spaces sort of flowed into each other, she could keep both an eye and an ear on the conversation.

"Hey, Liam. Can I talk to you for a minute?"

"Sure." He joined Emerson on the sofa, sat cross-legged and put his hands in his lap. Darcy chuckled. Even in dinosaur pajamas, he could be such a grownup.

Emerson mirrored his pose. Her expression was so serious, Darcy wondered if she was more nervous to talk to Liam than her. She couldn't see, perhaps, that Liam was—had been for a while—completely in love with her. Not more so than herself, but without the burden of doubts and insecurities and all the boring adult things that get in the way. "I was hoping we could talk about something."

"Okay." The apprehension in his voice seemed to make Emerson even more uneasy. Darcy could have interjected, explaining that serious talks usually meant Liam was in trouble. She didn't, wanting to give both of them the chance to work it out. Wanting, really, to see how Emerson would handle the conversation.

"We're buddies, right?"

"Yeah." Some confidence returned to his voice.

"What about your mom? Are you buddies with her, too?"

Liam furrowed his brow, wondering probably if it was a trick question. "She's…my mom."

"So, family."

"Yeah." Liam nodded. "Family."

"What if I said I wanted to be more like your family instead of your buddy?"

Liam curled his lip. "Like another mom?"

The look on Emerson's face was priceless. Clearly, not the response she was expecting. Darcy remained quiet. She wanted to hear Emerson's answer, too. "Not exactly. You have a special relationship with your mom. I could never duplicate that and I wouldn't want to try. But I'd like to be more than your friend."

"More how?"

"I'd like to be around more, maybe even live with you guys. Kind of how Julien is with your dad."

"Awesome!" Darcy could see that Liam was jumping ahead, imagining day after day of adventure and excitement.

"But it wouldn't be all fun times. I still have to work. I'd be enforcing the rules, too."

It was fascinating to watch Liam process what Emerson was proposing. His excitement tempered, but was not lost. Darcy wouldn't have framed the possibilities that way, but she respected Emerson for not going for the easy sell.

"But you'd be around all the time?"

"That's the plan. I want to count on you and I want you to feel like you can count on me."

At the mention of being counted on, Liam sat up straighter. "I'd like that."

Darcy's heart, already full, pressed even more insistently against her ribs.

"I can't promise that it will always be easy, or that you won't get sick of me sometimes."

Liam nodded. So serious. "I won't get sick of you."

Emerson smiled. "I'm sure you will. I'll probably get sick of you, too."

Liam's face fell and Darcy took a step toward him, ready to intervene.

"But," Emerson continued, "that's part of life. We have bad days and disagreements. What I can promise is that I won't give up on you or your mom. I'll stick around so we can work it out."

Liam stole a quick glance at Darcy before looking squarely at Emerson. "I won't give up on you, either."

"Even if I get on your nerves?"

Liam hung his head and squirmed a little. He clearly didn't want to acknowledge that Emerson might get on his nerves. "Even if we get on each other's nerves."

"Good. I can get—"

"Wait." After interrupting, Liam looked back and forth between Emerson and Darcy. "Does this mean you guys love each other? Like kissing and stuff?"

Emerson let out a small cough and even Darcy couldn't suppress a smile. Darcy had no intention of answering, but Emerson shot her a pleading look. She relented. "We do."

Liam wrinkled his nose in the way most little boys did regarding matters of romance. When the initial shock of the revelation passed, however, he nodded. "I guess that's cool."

Darcy crossed the room to join them. "I think this calls for a pact." She stuck out her hand.

"Yeah." Liam put his hand out, on top of Darcy's.

They both looked to Emerson, who clearly had no idea what was happening. But she added her hand to the pile. "I'm in."

Darcy thought about the words she'd use to seal the deal. "Good times and hard times. We're in it together. Family."

Liam's nodded matter-of-factly. "Family."

Darcy looked at Emerson, who used her free hand to wipe away a tear. "Family."

About the Author

Aurora Rey grew up in a small town in south Louisiana, daydreaming about New England. She keeps a special place in her heart for the South, especially the food and the ways women are raised to be strong, even if they're taught not to show it. After a brief dalliance with biochemistry, she completed both a B.A. and an M.A. in English.

When she's not writing or at her day job in higher education, she loves to cook and putter around the house. She's slightly addicted to Pinterest, has big plans for the garden, and would love to get some goats.

She lives in Ithaca, New York, with her partner, two dogs, and whatever wild animals have taken up residence in the pond.

Books Available from Bold Strokes Books

A Date to Die by Anne Laughlin. Someone is killing people close to Detective Kay Adler, who must look to her own troubled past for a suspect. There she finds more than one person seeking revenge against her. (978-1-63555-023-8)

Captured Soul by Laydin Michaels. Can Kadence Munroe save the woman she loves from a twisted killer, or will she lose her to a collector of souls? (978-1-62639-915-0)

Dawn's New Day by TJ Thomas. Can Dawn Oliver and Cam Cooper, two women who have loved and lost, open their hearts to love again? (978-1-63555-072-6)

Definite Possibility by Maggie Cummings. Sam Miller is just out for good times, but Lucy Weston makes her realize happily ever after is a definite possibility. (978-1-62639-909-9)

Eyes Like Those by Melissa Brayden. Isabel Chase and Taylor Andrews struggle between love and ambition from the writers' room on one of Hollywood's hottest TV shows. (978-1-63555-012-2)

Heart's Orders by Jaycie Morrison. Helen Tucker and Tee Owens escape hardscrabble lives to careers in the Women's Army Corps, but more than their hearts are at risk as friendship blossoms into love. (978-1-63555-073-3)

Hiding Out by Kay Bigelow. Treat Dandridge is unaware that her life is in danger from the murderer who is hunting the woman she's falling in love with, Mickey Heiden. (978-1-62639-983-9)

Omnipotence Enough by Sophia Kell Hagin. Can the tiny tool that abducted war veteran Jamie Gwynmorgan accidentally acquires help her escape an unknown enemy to reclaim her stolen life and the woman she deeply loves? (978-1-63555-037-5)

Summer's Cove by Aurora Rey. Emerson Lange moved to Provincetown to live in the moment, but when she meets Darcy Belo and her son Liam, her quest for summer romance becomes a family affair. (978-1-62639-971-6)

The Road to Wings by Julie Tizard. Lieutenant Casey Tompkins, air force student pilot, has to fly with the toughest instructor, Captain Kathryn "Hard Ass" Hardesty, fly a supersonic jet, and deal with a growing forbidden attraction. (978-1-62639-988-4)

Beauty and the Boss by Ali Vali. Ellis Renois is at the top of the fashion world, but she never expects her summer assistant Charlotte Hamner to tear her heart and her business apart like sharp scissors through cheap material. (978-1-62639-919-8)

Fury's Choice by Brey Willows. When gods walk amongst humans, can two women find a balance between love and faith? (978-1-62639-869-6)

Lessons in Desire by MJ Williamz. Can a summer love stand a four-month hiatus and still burn hot? (978-1-63555-019-1)

Lightning Chasers by Cass Sellars. For Sydney and Parker, being a couple was never what they had planned. Now they have to fight corruption, murder, and enemies hiding in plain sight just to hold on to each other. Lightning Series, Book Two. (978-1-62639-965-5)

Summer Fling by Jean Copeland. Still jaded from a breakup years earlier, Kate struggles to trust falling in love again when a summer fling with sexy young singer Jordan rocks her off her feet. (978-1-62639-981-5)

Take Me There by Julie Cannon. Adrienne and Sloan know it would be career suicide to mix business with pleasure, however tempting it is. But what's the harm? They're both consenting adults. Who would know? (978-1-62639-917-4)

The Girl Who Wasn't Dead by Samantha Boyette. A year ago, someone tried to kill Jenny Lewis. Tonight she's ready to find out who it was. (978-1-62639-950-1)

Unchained Memories by Dena Blake. Can a woman give herself completely when she's left a piece of herself behind? (978-1-62639-993-8)

Walking Through Shadows by Sheri Lewis Wohl. All Molly wanted to do was go backpacking...in her own century (978-1-62639-968-6)

A Lamentation of Swans by Valerie Bronwen. Ariel Montgomery returns to Sea Oats to try to save her broken marriage but soon finds herself also fighting to save her own life and catch a murderer. (978-1-62639-828-3)

Freedom to Love by Ronica Black. What happens when the woman who spent her lifetime worrying about caring for her family, finally finds the freedom to love without borders? (978-1-63555-001-6)

House of Fate by Barbara Ann Wright. Two women must throw off the lives they've known as a guardian and an assassin and save two rival houses before their secrets tear the galaxy apart. (978-1-62639-780-4)

Planning for Love by Erin Dutton. Could true love be the one thing that wedding coordinator Faith McKenna didn't plan for? (978-1-62639-954-9)

Sidebar by Carsen Taite. Judge Camille Avery and her clerk, attorney West Fallon, agree on little except their mutual attraction, but can their relationship and their careers survive a headline-grabbing case? (978-1-62639-752-1)

Sweet Boy and Wild One by T. L. Hayes. When Rachel Cole meets soulful singer Bobby Layton at an open mic, she is immediately in thrall. What she soon discovers will rock her world in ways she never imagined. (978-1-62639-963-1)

To Be Determined by Mardi Alexander and Laurie Eichler. Charlie Dickerson escapes her life in the US to rescue Australian wildlife with Pip Atkins, but can they save each other? (978-1-62639-946-4)

True Colors by Yolanda Wallace. Blogger Robby Rawlins plans to use First Daughter Taylor Crenshaw to get ahead, but she never planned on falling in love with her in the process. (978-1-62639-927-3)

Unexpected by Jenny Frame. When Dale McGuire falls for Rebecca Harper, the mother of the son she never knew she had, will Rebecca's troubled past stop them from making the family they both truly crave? (978-1-62639-942-6)

Canvas for Love by Charlotte Greene. When ghosts from Amelia's past threaten to undermine their relationship, Chloé must navigate the greatest romance of her life without losing sight of who she is. (978-1-62639-944-0)

Heart Stop by Radclyffe. Two women, one with a damaged body, the other a damaged spirit, challenge each other to dare to live again. (978-1-62639-899-3)

Repercussions by Jessica L. Webb. Someone planted information in Edie Black's brain and now they want it back, but with the protection of shy former soldier Skye Kenny, Edie has a chance at life and love. (978-1-62639-925-9)

Spark by Catherine Friend. Jamie's life is turned upside down when her consciousness travels back to 1560 and lands in the body of one of Queen Elizabeth I's ladies-in-waiting…or has she totally lost her grip on reality? (978-1-62639-930-3)

Taking Sides by Kathleen Knowles. When passion and politics collide, can love survive? (978-1-62639-876-4)

Thorns of the Past by Gun Brooke. Former cop Darcy Flynn's heart broke when her career on the force ended in disgrace, but perhaps saving Sabrina Hawk's life will mend it in more ways than one. (978-1-62639-857-3)

You Make Me Tremble by Karis Walsh. Seismologist Casey Radnor comes to the San Juan Islands to study an earthquake but finds her heart shaken by passion when she meets animal rescuer Iris Mallery. (978-1-62639-901-3)

Complications by MJ Williamz. Two women battle for the heart of one. (978-1-62639-769-9)

Crossing the Wide Forever by Missouri Vaun. As Cody Walsh and Lillie Ellis face the perils of the untamed West, they discover that love's uncharted frontier isn't for the weak in spirit or the faint of heart. (978-1-62639-851-1)

Fake It Till You Make It by M. Ullrich. Lies will lead to trouble, but can they lead to love? (978-1-62639-923-5)

Girls Next Door by Sandy Lowe and Stacia Seaman eds. Best-selling romance authors tell it from the heart—sexy, romantic stories of falling for the girls next door. (978-1-62639-916-7)

Pursuit by Jackie D. The pursuit of the most dangerous terrorist in America will crack the lines of friendship and love, and not everyone will make it out under the weight of duty and service. (978-1-62639-903-7)

Shameless by Brit Ryder. Confident Emery Pearson knows exactly what she's looking for in a no-strings-attached hookup, but can a spontaneous interlude open her heart to more? (978-1-63555-006-1)

The Practitioner by Ronica Black. Sometimes love comes calling whether you're ready for it or not. (978-1-62639-948-8)

Unlikely Match by Fiona Riley. When an ambitious PR exec and her super-rich coding geek-girl client fall in love, they learn that giving something up may be the only way to have everything. (978-1-62639-891-7)

Where Love Leads by Erin McKenzie. A high school counselor and the mom of her new student bond in support of the troubled girl, never expecting deeper feelings to emerge, testing the boundaries of their relationship. (978-1-62639-991-4)